William Richard Wood Stephens

A Memoir of Richard Durnford, D.D. - Sometime Bishop of Chichester

With Selections from his Works and Correspondence

William Richard Wood Stephens

A Memoir of Richard Durnford, D.D. - Sometime Bishop of Chichester
With Selections from his Works and Correspondence

ISBN/EAN: 9783337280949

Printed in Europe, USA, Canada, Australia, Japan

Cover: Foto ©Raphael Reischuk / pixelio.de

More available books at **www.hansebooks.com**

A MEMOIR

OF

RICHARD DURNFORD, D.D.

SOMETIME BISHOP OF CHICHESTER

WITH SELECTIONS FROM HIS CORRESPONDENCE

EDITED BY

W. R. W. STEPHENS, B.D.. F.S.A.

DEAN OF WINCHESTER

WITH PORTRAITS AND ILLUSTRATIONS

LONDON
JOHN MURRAY, ALBEMARLE STREET
1899

PREFACE BY THE EDITOR

As my name alone appears as Editor on the title-page of this Memoir, I wish to state at the outset that the first two chapters have been written by the late Bishop's sons, Mr. Richard and Mr. Walter Durnford. In connexion with these two chapters I have only exercised an Editor's privilege of offering a few suggestions and revising the proof-sheets. My own acquaintance with the Bishop began with his episcopate, and I thought that the earlier portions of his life could be more satisfactorily dealt with by two members of his family whose ability was unquestionable, and who could draw partly on their own recollections, as well as upon old family records and traditions.

For the remaining chapters, covering the period of the episcopate, I am solely responsible.

The materials for the work throughout have been far from copious. Owing to the Bishop having outlived most of his contemporaries and many of his juniors, it was difficult to recover much of his correspondence, or to collect many personal reminiscences relating to the earlier periods of his life. Nor did the invitation to lend letters or furnish other information relating to his episcopate produce a very plentiful supply; but fortunately the Bishop was in the habit of making copies of his correspondence on all questions of much importance, and it is upon these that I have largely depended for the purpose of the present work. My aim in the selection of letters has been to give specimens illustrative of the sagacity, sound judgment, spirit of comprehensiveness, and fairness towards all parties in the Church which rendered the Bishop's administration so eminently happy and successful.

Many of the letters and extracts from his visitation and ordination charges deal with questions which have recently been subjects of much vexatious controversy; and they may be read, I venture to think, with much profit by the disputants, and partisans of opposing views. They prove, at any rate, how constantly he was engaged in restraining excesses and correcting defects in ritual and teaching in the Church, a duty which bishops have been, of late, so freely accused, in some quarters, of neglecting. That his episcopate, although full of active work, was not marked by exciting incidents is perhaps the highest praise that could be bestowed upon it; for there were at times abundant materials for serious discord and strife in the diocese, which were only composed or kept in check by the wise counsel and firm action of the spiritual ruler.

Readers of the following pages will be interested to see how this wise administration was carried on with unfaltering firmness and unabated energy into extreme old age, long past the ordinary limits of human life. I trust, also, that the Memoir, however imperfect, may be found an instructive study of a rarely gifted mind, singularly rich in variety of interests and stores of knowledge; a personality delightful to contemplate from its wonderful completeness, and the even balance of all the elements composing it—physical, moral, and intellectual.

I have been much indebted throughout the work to Miss DURNFORD, the Bishop's daughter, for information, and for valuable assistance in collecting and sifting the materials, and correcting the proof-sheets. I am also indebted for help to my dear friends the Venerable F. J. MOUNT, Archdeacon of Chichester, and the Rev. Prebendary COWLEY POWLES, who were for many years my colleagues as examining chaplains to the Bishop; also to the Rev. A. M. DEANE, Canon Residentiary of Chichester; the Rev. J. WAKEFORD, formerly Diocesan Missioner in Sussex, now Vicar of St. Margaret's, Anfield, Liverpool ; and Sir R. G. RAPER, the Bishop's acting registrar and secretary.

And, lastly, I must acknowledge very special obligations to the President of Magdalen College, Oxford, T. HERBERT WARREN, Esq., D.C.L., for his kindness and trouble in obtaining some information concerning the Bishop's life as an undergraduate, and for his own very interesting reminiscences of him In his latter years.

W. R. W. STEPHENS.

THE DEANERY, WINCHESTER :
September 1, 1899.

Erratum.

Page 316, line 17, *for* because of *read* license at.

CONTENTS

CHAPTER V

CHAPTER VI

CHAPTER VII

ILLUSTRATIONS

A MEMOIR

OF

RICHARD DURNFORD, D.D.

CHAPTER I

Early Life—Eton and Oxford

THE subject of the following memoir was born at Sandleford, near Newbury, on November 3, 1802, being the eldest child of the Rev. Richard Durnford and Louisa, daughter of John Mount of Wasing Place, in the county of Berks, and Christian his wife, whose maiden name was Hyett. It is not very clear how the Rev. Richard Durnford came to be settled at Sandleford, but it is probable that it was through his sister Ann living at Speen, of which parish the Rev. E. Houlditch, whom she married in 1801, was then vicar.

The house has not been clearly identified, but it is believed to be that now known as Sandleford Lodge, which stands on the banks of the Emborne, a tributary of the Kennet.

The Rev. Richard Durnford was the first of his

family to become a member of one of the learned professions. His ancestors for several generations had carried on the business of pinmakers in Camberwell, their office being in Gracechurch Street, and the pins known as 'Durnford's London pins' had a practical monopoly in the market. In this business Richard Durnford, great-grandfather of the Rev. Richard Durnford, acquired what was for those days a considerable fortune, and the family owned property at Dulwich, and subsequently at Woodmansterne, in Surrey, where the father of the Rev. R. Durnford lived.

In 1789 Mr. Durnford, after an education at Winchester College and Pembroke College, Oxford, was ordained by the Bishop of Winchester, and became curate of Betchworth, a parish in the neighbourhood of Woodmansterne. On the death of his father in 1793 he appears to have sold the Woodmansterne property, and, abandoning for a time the exercise of his clerical profession, to have started for a prolonged absence on the Continent with a view to improving himself in the French and Italian languages, and otherwise enlarging his experiences. That such an undertaking was in those days no light matter may easily be imagined ; and we gather from one of the letters written during his absence to his friend Mr. Charles Baratty, that the traveller was kept waiting for several weeks at Portsmouth before the admiral in charge of the convoy was able to give the signal for sailing. He eventually arrived safely at Leghorn, and spent the ensuing eighteen months in visiting various Italian cities which were soon to be occupied by the armies of the French Republic, including Rome, Naples, Florence, Pisa, and Siena. During the whole of his stay in the country he devoted himself assiduously to the study of the Italian language and to observing the manners and customs of the people, his account of the society of that date, especially in Tuscany, being sufficiently startling.

His impressions and experiences were chronicled in a series of letters to Mr. Baratty, all of which were preserved and subsequently restored to his family. While at Siena, in anticipation of spending the winter at Rome, where he thought a uniform would be useful to him for official and other entertainments, he wrote to Mr. Baratty requesting him to send him out the uniform of a captain of militia, adding that it did not much matter what militia it was, but as Surrey was his county he supposed it had better be that of the Surrey militia. It is presumed that the uniform duly arrived, but we are not informed of the success of his appearance in the character of a member of the church militant. In 1795 he turned his steps homewards, but on the way stayed some time at Lausanne for the purpose of improving his knowledge of French.

On his return to England he settled at Sandleford, without, however, undertaking any clerical duty. The house was the property of the Dean and Canons of Windsor, and was let on a beneficial lease to the person from whom it was rented by Mr.

Durnford. Some negotiations took place with a view to his purchasing the freehold, but failing in his object, for reasons which cannot be ascertained, in the year succeeding his marriage (1801) he was under the necessity of finding another home ; and finally decided to rent the rectory house at Chilbolton, five miles from Andover, from the Rev. Mr. Hopkins, a minor canon of Winchester, who was at that time acting as *locum tenens* to the rector, the Rev. Dr. Pett, Canon of Christ Church and Rector of Newington, Oxford. Dr. Pett must have been a pluralist of the old school, and was content to live at Oxford or Newington and to leave the charge of the parish of Chilbolton to a *locum tenens* or curate.

After several years' occupation of the rectory house, Mr. Durnford undertook the spiritual charge of the parish, Mr. Hopkins having probably resigned. The remuneration allowed by Dr. Pett for these duties was not colossal, and for some years, over and above the occupation of the rectory house and certain land adjoining, all that Mr. Durnford received from his rector was the magnificent sum of 40*l.* and a small allowance for charities and educational purposes. There might, therefore, be some difficulty in appreciating the reasons for which he decided to settle at Chilbolton when presumably it would have been easy to find a parish where his services would have been more adequately remunerated, and other advantages would have been afforded. The reason is probably to be found in a partiality for the neighbourhood, with which Mr.

Durnford must have been familiar in his Winchester school days, affording him, as it did, opportunities for the sports to which he was keenly addicted—namely, shooting, fishing, and coursing.   At that date the greater part of the surrounding country was unenclosed, and manorial rights were proportionately neglected.   The ownership of copyhold property in Chilbolton carried with it the right to fish in the river Test with rod or shoe net, within the bounds of the manor, and there was little reason at that time to apprehend that these rights would become the subject of a *cause célèbre*,[1] as has recently been the case.   Among others who visited Chilbolton Rectory for the purpose of the fishing was Dr. Gabell, the Headmaster of Winchester, whom the Bishop remembered as taking part in the sport clad in knee breeches and silk stockings.

The results of the days and evenings spent on the banks of the Test were duly recorded in a series of fishing journals which are still preserved in the family, and which contain information as to each day's sport, the fly used, of which specimens are attached, and the number of fish taken.   On one day in the Mayfly season of 1827, Mr. Durnford and his friend Mr. Penrose captured 70 lb. weight of fish.   But it must not be supposed that in consequence of his partiality for sport the parochial duties undertaken by Mr. Durnford were neglected.   The following is the Bishop's own account of his father's

---

[1] See case of Tilbury *v.* Silva, reported *Law Reports*, Ch. Div. Vol. 45 (1890).

labours contained in a short memorial written by him after his mother's death in 1864 :

'The village of Chilbolton was miserably poor, being a long straggling street of thatched cottages intermixed with a few small farmhouses, all held under the chapter of Winchester on leases for lives. Owing to the wretched condition of these dwellings and the dampness and unwholesomeness of the place, for many years ague was so common in Chilbolton that scarce a family escaped.

'The chief occupier of land was a man of bad moral character and a great oppressor of his work-people. Dear bread, hard and scanty work, and, above all, the baneful operation of the Poor Law combined to reduce the condition of the labourer to the lowest ebb. The poor had many masters, but no friends except the curate and his wife.

'My father, who abhorred extortion and oppression, stood up manfully to defend the poor against farmers and overseers, and he did much, according to his ability, to relieve their distress and to teach them to help themselves. With a charity and wisdom not usual at that day, he gave up a portion of the glebe for the use of the poor, saying it was unjust that the tillers of the land should have no share of it, and he made and maintained regulations for the proper cultivation of these allotments. At his own sole expense he set up a National School long before such schools were generally introduced, and for many years he entirely supported it. He also laid in, yearly, a large store of faggots, and sold them to the poor in winter at reduced prices, a great boon in a country where fuel was always scant and dear.'

The following description of his mother from the same source may be worthy of insertion :

'She was at the time of her marriage, and indeed long after, of remarkable grace and beauty, so that she was the delight of all who approached her, for she had a native charm of manner springing from inward goodness of heart, and such was her simplicity of mind that she never seemed conscious that she was fairer than other women. No admiration could make her vain. Her humility, which was a remarkable part of her character, her entire freedom from self-conceit, made her always willing to learn, and besides my father's conversation and direction she had the great blessing of two friends of rare talents and excellence, Arabella, daughter of Richard Barwell, Esq., and Harriet Dorothea, the eldest daughter of James Croft, Esq., of Greenham, Berks.

. . . . . .

'My mother had not commanding abilities, nor was she very quick in understanding nor ready in repartee, but she had what is infinitely more valuable, excellent common sense, sound and correct judgment, and, what is often found in pure minds, quick discernment of character. Her conversation, being entirely free from all affectation, was easy and agreeable, and her lively sympathy with the interests and circumstances of her friends, as well as her natural calmness of mind, made her always a ready and attentive listener. So I may say few persons were ever more generally popular and acceptable, though she never laid herself out to please.

. . . . . .

'It was my mother's province to feed and tend

the sick, to clothe the naked, and comfort the suffering. Day by day she used to visit the poor at their houses, and she knew them all as if they were part of her own family. She provided daily good soup for the most destitute, wine, medicine, and other necessaries for the weak and sick. Such works of mercy are, thank God, common now, but they were not common then, and she was in this respect, like my father, in advance of the times. The same may be said of the Penny Club which she established at Chilbolton, having seen the plan of such clubs recommended by Mrs. Trimmer, in order to teach the poor to lay by something for the purchase of clothing. She also never failed to attend the Sunday School of the parish, and, indeed, continued to do so long after her daughters were well able to take her place. There was a quiet patience and perseverance in all she undertook which was very unlike the fussy, bustling, noisy philanthropy of more pretentious lives. She never forgot that her first duties were to her husband and her family, as though remembering our Lord's wise counsel : " These ought ye to have done and not to leave the other undone." '

In this atmosphere and among these surroundings, the childhood of the future Bishop was passed. In due course other children were born : Louisa (1807), who died unmarried in 1884 ; Edmund (1809), for many years Rector of Monxton, a King's College living near Andover ; Francis Edward (1816), Lower Master and afterwards Fellow of Eton College; Laura Vittoria, born 1814 on the day of Wellington's great victory, died unmarried 1885, and Paulina, who died at Chilbolton in her childhood.

Their life might now be regarded as monotonous, the only variations consisting in occasional visits to friends and relations, such as the Mounts at Wasing, the Lomax's at Netley in Surrey, the Rev. Henry Barlow at Burgh in Suffolk, who married Mrs. Durnford's sister, and an occasional trip to Winchester, Salisbury, or some quiet watering place on the Hampshire coast. But the children were attached to their home, and even in their old age recalled its features with interest. As to its intrinsic merits, it may seem a dull country to casual observers, especially to such as derive their impressions from travelling by railway between Whitchurch and Salisbury ; but on a closer acquaintance it must be admitted that there is a peculiar charm in its green valleys and transparent chalk streams, and especially in the valley of the Upper Test—the ' Silver Whit ' of Kingsley—which, owing to its several branches becoming here united, is seen at its best at Chilbolton. Separated only by the river from Chilbolton was the village of Wherwell with its curious old Priory house, under which a branch of the river flows, and its beautifully timbered grounds, then occupied by the owner, Colonel Iremonger, between whose family and the Durnfords a strong and lasting friendship grew up. Further to the north-east lay Harewood Forest, commonly known as Wherwell Wood, containing in its recesses many plants and flowers peculiar to the chalk, and flanked on its outskirts by patriarchal yew trees. To the south in the direction of Winchester, eight miles distant, lay a rolling open country, practically unenclosed and commanding extensive views in the direction of Salisbury and Stockbridge, the two great Roman camps of Quarley and Danebury Hill being the most conspicuous objects.

It was here, no doubt, that the boy acquired that habit of observing natural objects which he cultivated through life, and which made it instinctive with him to investigate the flora and fauna of whatever locality he visited.   Thus a favourite relaxation at Middleton was an expedition to the Greenfield Moors, and a search for the cloudberry or andromeda ; at other times an afternoon was spent in visiting the home of the osmunda at Hopwood Clough, or of the moonwort on Tandle Hill.   In later days during his visits to Switzerland and the Italian lakes he delighted in the beauty and variety of the Alpine flora ; and some of his happiest moments in Sussex were spent in the gardens of Mr. Sclater, of Newick Park, and the Rev. W. Boardman, of Glen Andred, where many of these plants have been successfully acclimatised.   At other times he noted the arrival of the summer migrants and rejoiced in recognising the first note of the chiff-chaff.   He never aspired to a scientific knowledge of botany or ornithology, but appreciated the society of those who had made these subjects their special study.   There also he was initiated in that love of fishing which he retained to comparative old age, and which he gratified year after year during his summer holiday, especially during the time when his mother was resident at

Clatford and the waters of the Anton were available.   In fact, it is not too much to say that the two factors controlling the date of his holiday and return to work were the appearance of the Mayfly and the date of the Middleton Wakes, when the great Sunday School festival of the year was held.

The Bishop was much interested in the closing years of his life by the following reference to Chilbolton in a letter dated October 21, 1731 :

Chilbolton.

' You that are in the midst of the Beau Monde will not be entertained with what I can relate from hence, which only consists of the pleasures of the field ; where last Monday we were particularly well pleased, for by invitation we had Dr. Burton, the master of Winchester School, with his ten young noblemen's sons who live with him, for whom he has 200*l.* a year for each, and is as a private governour to them ; and they also have the advantage of a publick school at the same time, which surely must be a fine way of educating them.

' These, with other young gentlemen of the school, met us in the field a-hunting.   They and their attendants and ours made about 40 people, and after very good sport all came home to dine here. Indeed, I have never seen a finer sight than these boys and their master together—Lord Deerhurst and his brothers Coventrys, Lord Ossulston, Lord Brook, Master Duncomb, and Sir Robert Burdett, Master Greville, Master Wallop (Lord Lymington's son), Lord Drumlanrig the Duke of Queensberry's son, who is under his peculiar care, though not in the house because he would not exceed the fix'd number.'

The above passage was copied out by the Bishop in his own hand after he had reached the age of ninety.[2]

À propos of Wherwell, he used to mention in connection with the extreme severity of the winter of 1812–1813 and the horrors of the French retreat from Moscow, that in that season the various streams of the Test between Chilbolton and Wherwell were frozen so hard that it was possible to walk from one place to the other on the ice without resort to the bridges.

The boy's early education was undertaken by his parents, and at the age of eight it was decided to send him to a small preparatory school at Epsom, kept by the Rev. E. C. James. His cousin, Edward Houlditch, was at the same school. On what grounds this school was chosen cannot be stated. Mr. James may have been known to his father in the Woodmansterne days, or he may have been recommended by Mr. Lomax[3] of Netley, which was in the neighbourhood of Epsom. It may be interesting here to note that the Duchesse de

[2] From *Political and Social Letters of a Lady of the Eighteenth Century*, edited by Miss E. F. D. Osborn, 1890. The letter here quoted (p. 45) was from Mrs. Osborn to her brother Robert Byng, M.P. for Plymouth.

[3] Mrs. Lomax's maiden name was Frances Pate. She and her sister Mary, afterwards married to the Baron de Rolle, were the daughters of Mrs. Hyett, mother of the wife of John Mount, by her second marriage with Mr. Pate. They were therefore aunts of the half-blood to Louisa Mount, afterwards Louisa Durnford. Miss Lomax, daughter of the above,

Gontaut, Gouvernante des Enfants de France, in her Memoirs published in 1892 refers to the Lomax family. The Duchesse and her husband were both *émigrés*. They were married in London in 1794, and for a time lived in a small house at Epsom. The Duchesse writes as follows: ' Les personnes de notre voisinage se firent aussi présenter à nous, et parmi eux, une respectable famille, M. et Madame Lomax et sa sœur, furent, pendant notre séjour à Epsom, remplis d'attentions et de prévenances. Quinze ans plus tard la sœur de Madame Lomax épousa notre vieil ami le Baron de Rolle ' (described before as ' Officier Suisse, aide-de-camp du Comte d'Artois ').

An early letter from the young Richard to his mother, written from Mr. James's Academy, is endorsed ' by favour of the Baroness de Rolle,' and on the above passage being pointed out to the Bishop after the appearance of the memoir, he said: ' Oh, I remember Madame de Gontaut perfectly.'

The life at James's school appears to have been a hard one, perhaps not worse than at other preparatory schools of the same date, but the master had the character of a miser, and one of the peculiarities

married the Hon. Peter Scarlett, C.B., sometime British Minister at Florence. The event was celebrated in the following *jeu d'esprit* :

' To deck the lovely Mina's cheek
In red and white was Cupid's freak,
But Hymen chid the varlet ;
And led her to the altar, where
In his own chains he bound the fair,
And Mina then was Scarlett.'

of the establishment was that the sheets in which the boys slept were made of the towels of former pupils sewn together.   Once a term, whatever their state of health, the boys were drenched with Epsom salts instead of breakfast; a curious parallel to the brimstone and treacle administered by Mrs. Squeers. James was a good teacher, and the forward and intelligent boys fared better than the more backward, who were made the victims of what James called his system of peripatetics, which consisted in making a boy walk before him while he examined him *viva voce*, and if the boy answered wrong, corrected him by the application of his stick.   One of the Bishop's reminiscences of the school was being taken by some older boys to make a raid upon a neighbouring garden when they were surprised by the gardener *in flagrante delicto*.   He being the smallest was unable to escape, and was brought by the gardener before his master while the family was sitting at dessert.   This gentleman seems to have recognised that the small victim was there under compulsion, and made him sit down with the rest of the party and drink a glass of wine.   Every year the boys were taken by their master to the Downs to see the race for the Derby.   The late Mr. Dowdeswell, Q.C., one of the official Referees of the High Court, who spent the latter part of his life in Sussex, was educated at the same school; and he used to say that the example of Richard Durnford was held up to the boys of his time for imitation.   In 1893 the Bishop, while paying a visit to the Bishop of Winchester at Farnham Castle, identified the old posting house at Farnham where formerly he used to take the coach for Epsom, after driving there from Chilbolton under the charge of his father's old coachman, Eli. The latter on these occasions used to inquire, before seeing him off, ' Now, Mr. Richard, have you had a good dinner, for that be the main thing ? '

After three years' grinding at James's school, his father seems to have decided that he should stand for a scholarship at Winchester, and in order that he might be adequately prepared in Latin versification, a proficiency in which was considered at Winchester no less than at Eton a necessary accomplishment, withdrew him from Epsom and kept him for some time under his own instruction. In this matter he took the opinion and advice of his old friend the Rev. Dr. Goddard, late Headmaster of Winchester, who was, according to the ' Dictionary of National Biography,' at various times Prebendary of St. Paul's Cathedral, Canon of Salisbury, Rector of Bapton (*sic*), Sussex, and Vicar (*in commendam*) of Wherwell.

The following letters from Dr. Goddard on the subject of his preparation are of some interest :

Letter 1

Not dated, but probably December 1813.

My dear Sir,—We thank you kindly for your congratulations, and have a very sincere pleasure in hearing a good account of you and Mrs. Durnford.

.   .   .   .   .   .

The part of your letter most material to you is

that respecting your boy. If I were to advise I should say, Why look out for a person at a heavy expense to do that which you can do at home much better yourself? . But you are out of the habit of making verses, &c. What then? It is easily resumed ; for instance, get an Ovid or a Florilegium. Take a few easy verses and *figure* the English of them thus :

Parvula progenies Veris Zephyrique, Cicada,
Quam te Phœbus amat, quam favet alma Ceres !

6   1   2   3   5   4
O Grasshopper | little | offspring | of the spring | and | the Zephyr.

1   3   4   2   5   7   8   6
How | Phœbus | loves | thee. | How | courteous | Ceres | favours thee!

Then make Ricardo turn them as well as he can, or let him make four every day ; by degrees he will be able to turn a fable of Phaedrus or a Psalm. You can easily get Johnson's psalms. After this let him ransack his brains and make a Vulgus. I take it for granted he can scan and prove ; if not, he will learn this in a week.

Now for your prose tasks : give him an easy subject ; make him write his thoughts, first in English, then put them into Latin.

If you are not afraid to undertake the task of teaching your boy (and I am sure you will be more likely to do it effectually) for a few months, I will write to you again, for he should learn to make his themes by a plan—viz. he should *explain* the subject ; he should give a reason why it is true or false, or proper, &c. He should illustrate by examples ; he should apply them. He should draw his conclusion. All this may be done sufficiently with practice *every day.* But there are books to help.

Reflect seriously on what I say and let me know your determination. I know not where Wells is to be found ; he is a good man, but if he has other pupils he may not pay so much attention as may be necessary.

The boy should also be worked constantly at Greek Trees and Syntax in Ellis and in Huntingford's exercises. Write to me at the 'Alfred,' Albemarle Street. I am rather hurried to-day.

Mrs. G. joins in kind wishes to Mrs. Durnford with   Yours truly,

W. S. Goddard.

Letter 2

Not dated, but probably January 1814.

My dear Sir,—We were much puzzled at receiving a basket on Monday at breakfast time by the Brighton stage (for it was so marked), when on examination it proved to have been sent by you. Mrs. G. desires me to thank you very kindly for the pheasants, and I am sure you will be glad to hear that they come just at the time we could have wished, for we have a pretty large party to dine with us on Thursday next.

I have looked over Ricardo's verses, which I assure you are done infinitely better than I could have conceived possible, and I think you ought to be satisfied ; as to writing with facility, which you seem to wish, this can only arise from practice, and having had a little experience I can point out an evil which sometimes arises in great schools from writing exercises too hastily, or doing any of the business with too much ease. Boys of this description are frequently employed to write or work for others as well as for themselves, and they almost invariably· get into a slovenly and careless habit which goes through life with them. But I should recommend you to pay attention at present rather to Elegiac verse than to Hexameter only or to Metre ; occasionally these may be useful, but long and short will be most wanted. And try to make him write themes constantly and with some method, as, for instance : (1) to explain more at large the meaning of the theme ; (2) the reasons on which it is founded ; (3) the end to which it may be directed, the good or bad consequences, &c., to be deduced from it ; (4) by what comparisons and examples it may be proved or illustrated ; (5) the conclusions to be drawn from it ; and, lastly, a summing-up and pointing out of the application to the theme.

I fear I have expressed myself rather loosely, but you will understand me to mean that a prose task should not be (as in our time it used to be) merely a string of sentences thrown or huddled together, but formed on something of a plan and arranged methodically. By degrees this artificial method will not appear (as it must at first) unless when it is examined ; but the art of method and arrangement will have been learned, and this I believe constitutes the great merit of composition. Ellis should never be out of his hands. He may read half a dozen sentences in different rules every day ; it will not take five minutes, and the benefits will be prodigiously great ; and the Greek exercises, too, will be of the greatest use.

.   .   .   .   .   .

I thought to have sent Dick's verses to-day in Mrs. Sawbridge's basket, but I have been hindered and cannot look them over ; besides, you must recollect I am out of practice.   I will send them the latter part of the week.   You are going, I find, to spend a few days at Doles,[4] therefore I address you there.

.   .   .   .   .   .

With our best regards to Mrs. D., and Mr. and Mrs. Sawbridge,

I am, truly yours (in haste),
W. S. GODDARD.

Letter 3

February 27, 1814.

My dear Sir,—I have been so much engaged of late in various ways that I really had almost forgotten my friend Ricardo (not very kind, methinks) ; but as soon as I recollected myself I set to work and finished my criticisms, which are too minute perhaps —however, the more accurate a boy can be made, and the earlier he can be made so, the better.   On the whole you have good reason to be satisfied—all is going on right.   The worst faults are a few false quantities and grammatical inaccuracies, common to all boys.   Mr. Pedder has a book of English 'Themes,' which, if it would not be the means of teaching him when to shirk his tasks, might be useful in giving him the plan or method of arranging his materials ; but you may borrow or buy it and keep it from Dick, only writing down what you think proper, or correcting his plans by it.   I forget the author, but he showed it to me, and I think you may find it useful. I strongly recommend the constant exercise of

---

[4] Doles House, between Andover and Newbury, then occupied by Mr. Sawbridge.

translating backwards and forwards from good Latin authors, Cicero and Cæsar.

Take sentences, first short, then longer ; let him turn them into as good and elegant English as he can ; then do you correct it and make him transcribe a fair copy, with large letters and proper stops, &c. After a week or ten days bid him turn it into Latin ; observe the grammatical faults, and when free from these make him compare his Latin with the original. This will gradually give him the idiom, and if pursued constantly, cannot fail of giving him a facility in writing. I would also every day make him read a few sentences in Ellis for the sake of keeping up an exact knowledge of the rules of Syntax, for boys soon forget what they have learned. The Greek exercises, too, should be translated a few every day ; three or four will do, and the declensions and tenses carefully examined into (*sic*),[5] for these are the parts of education most essential at first, and if a boy does not go to a public school with a tolerable acquaintance with them, he seldom, I believe, is found to acquire them afterwards, and consequently grows up super-ficial. This is the reason why I used to be so very attentive to what many persons would despise, but if the foundation be well laid the building will be firm, and not otherwise.

Mrs. G. thanks you for the hare. She is, I think, rather better, but has been thrown back by a dreadful cold, which has reduced her to a skeleton. She is indeed a poor creature, and it is a great drawback on my comfort ; but, however, there must be something. If our friend P—— be of a discon-

---

[5] It is interesting to find this solecism, now so common, perpetuated by an ex-headmaster.

tented turn of mind, nothing will ever make him happy. I know several men with large preferments who are just as anxious for further promotion as ever they were. I would not change conditions with them, for though I have been disappointed, I often think it may have been for the best. I have much to be thankful for, and I endeavour never to suffer this reflection to escape me for a moment, and I am sure it has made me ten times happier than great preferment would be able to without it. . . .

Mrs. G. joins in kind regards to Mrs. D. Remember me to Dick, and tell him never to let me see a false quantity or tense again, such as *ausisset*, which frightened me.

Yours truly,
W. S. G.

Letter 4

No date.

My dear Sir,—I am perfectly aware of the difficulties of composition to juvenile authors, for according to the maxim of Lucretius, *E nihilo nihil fit*, many persons hold that it is absurd to make boys attempt to write before they have obtained a certain store of knowledge ; however, experience is the most certain guide. At all events, make him write constantly ; you may try several ways.

Make him read several times one of Addison's moral papers. Afterwards give him a subject of the same kind, and bid him recollect what he has read. Then, or before, make him read a chapter in the ' Selecta e profanis,' which will furnish him abundantly with examples. This will give you a little trouble in the arrangement ; but, depend on it, by accustoming him constantly to making tasks he will enter the school with advantages few boys have. I advise you not to omit the Greek exercises and Trees, and in translating ' Ellis ' be careful to have the corresponding rules of ' Lilly ' carefully and accurately repeated. With best regards to Mrs. Durnford,

> Believe me, truly yours,
>
> W. S. GODDARD.

The studies pursued under Dr. Goddard's advice were diversified by the extraordinary experience of an expedition to the Naval Review held at Portsmouth on June 25, 1814, in honour of the allied sovereigns then visiting this country on the occasion of the Peace. Here the boy was present with his parents, and saw the Emperor Alexander of Russia, Frederick William III. King of Prussia, the Prince Royal of Prussia and his brother, Prince William (the late Emperor of Germany), Prince Blücher, and other distinguished persons. He was much impressed by the magnificent appearance of the Emperor Alexander, but his recollection of the King of Prussia was of a dull, phlegmatic-looking man.[6] At that age he could hardly realise the bitter

---

[6] This impression corresponds remarkably with that of Capt. Robert Blakeney, who, in a work recently published, *A Boy in the Peninsula*, describing the review of the allied troops during the occupation of Paris succeeding Waterloo, says : ' The King of Prussia wore his hat fore and aft. In saluting he bent his right hand perpendicularly upwards, the palm turned towards his face, his fingers stiff and their tips brought suddenly against the point of his hat. Sullenness was portrayed on his countenance. His figure was tall, but I saw nothing lofty about him save his station, which, had it not been hereditary, would never have been his. He was what we call in a horse " wall-eyed." Nothing

trials to which that monarch had been subjected ; the catastrophe of Jena, the flight to Königsberg and Memel, the crowning humiliations of Tilsit, and the loss of his incomparable queen, Louise, from a broken heart caused by the misfortunes of her country. At a later date he was familiarised with the details of these events through his marriage with the grand-daughter of Sir Charles Brown, the chief physician and confidential friend of that unfortunate Princess.

The following description of the review is contained in the 'Annual Register' of 1814 :

'The grandest and most appropriate spectacle in this country presented to the royal visitants was a naval review at Portsmouth, which took place this day (June 25). The illustrious personages had arrived at the town in the evening of the 22nd, where were already the Prince Regent and the Dukes of York and Clarence. The two following days were employed by the party in surveys of the harbour, examinations of the *Impregnable* man-of-war, and visits to all parts of the vast naval establishments and stupendous machinery of that port, intermixed with banqueting and festivity. On the concluding day a fleet consisting of 13 sail of the line and about as many frigates formed a line in front of the Isle of Wight, and, having received with a general salute the royal visitors on board the *Royal Sovereign* yatcht (*sic*), stood out to sea and

indicated the determined warrior, polished courtier, or profound statesman ; and during the whole time in which I presumed to regard him I do not recollect that a single thought of the Great Frederick flashed on my mind.

performed some of the manœuvres of an engagement. They returned to their anchorage in the evening, when the Emperor and King, the Regent, &c., accompanied by an immense number of pleasure vessels of all descriptions, came to land, and the day terminated with a great entertainment given by the Regent at the Government House. The whole was calculated to impress the illustrious strangers with the most lively ideas of the national power and greatness.'

In this connection it may be mentioned that during the Easter holidays of the following year he rushed into the schoolroom at Chilbolton with the news of Napoleon's escape from Elba, to the consternation of the French governess, Mdlle. Gayère, a royalist *émigrée*. She nearly had a fit.

The attempt to capture a Winchester foundation scholarship was not successful, for reasons which are explained by Dr. Fearon, the present headmaster of Winchester. Dr. Fearon writes as follows:

' The only Durnford on the rolls for election between 1804 and 1815 is one who stood eleventh in 1814. Only ten got in that year; he was the first left out. The mode of election was as follows: Two founders' kin voted for by the whole body were put first; then the six electors nominated in turn as follows: the Warden of New College, the Warden of Winchester, the Sub-Warden of Winchester, two Posers from New College, the Headmaster. Durnford must have been the second nominee of the Senior Poser. The examination was a pure farce; each boy brought up any passage of

Latin poetry he liked; he was asked to construe and say by heart the first two lines. He was then asked, "Can you sing?" to which the answer was, "All people that on earth do dwell." The whole thing took perhaps half an hour; then the electors nominated. This was abolished in 1854.'

After the failure at Winchester, Mr. Durnford was advised, apparently by Dr. Pett, to send up his son for a King's Scholarship at Eton, where at election (1814) he was successful. There was no honour attaching to this, for King's Scholarships were in low repute and the competition was far from keen, the number of scholars falling frequently below the 70 prescribed by the statutes. This state of things was not remedied till the succession of Provost Hodgson, who at once applied himself to the improvement of the position of the collegers, and a correction of the various abuses which had existed under Dr. Goodall, his predecessor.

Durnford became the pupil of the Rev. Charles Yonge, of whom he always spoke with regard and attachment. His tutor was unquestionably a good scholar, and besides being an accurate teacher of Latin and Greek—at that time the principal staple of an Eton education—he appears to have had the power of creating in his pupils an interest in other subjects and extending their ambitions beyond the narrow limits recognised by the traditions of the school and the practice of the authorities. The house in which he lived is that now occupied by H. Broadbent, Esq., the upper story, however, being an addition of recent years. Durnford was placed in the Remove. Among his contemporaries were Wood, afterwards the first Lord Halifax; Winthrop Mackworth Praed, poet and M.P.; Hon. S. Best, afterwards the rector of Abbotts Ann, Andover, one of the pioneers of elementary education and a life-long friend; W. J. Trower, afterwards Bishop of Gibraltar; W. G. Cookesley, for many years assistant master at Eton and editor of Pindar; W. H. Tucker, from 1845 to 1892 Rector of Dunton Waylett, Essex (a King's College living); Wellesley ma., afterwards the first Earl Cowley, ambassador at Paris; Richard Hurrell Froude, brother of the historian; Stanley, afterwards the first Lord Stanley of Alderley, and Wilson mi., afterwards John Wilson-Patten, M.P. for North Lancashire, created Lord Winmarleigh, between whom and the Bishop the friendship originating at Eton and continued at Magdalen remained unimpaired up to the death of the former in 1892.

Of these the Rev. W. H. Tucker alone survives. It is astonishing that in 1892 he should have produced a work[7] on Eton full of interesting recollections, and containing probably the best analysis of Keate and his system that has ever appeared.

Not many particulars respecting Durnford's early life at Eton can be supplied. The description of the school experiences of the young Rashleighs in ' The Rashleigh Letter Bag' (No. 8 of the ' Etonian') may

[7] *Eton of Old, or Eighty Years Since*, 1892. By an Old Colleger.   N.B.—The incognito is believed to be no longer preserved.

be taken to be to some extent an autobiography.
Being a strong and healthy boy, he probably suffered less than others from the hardships of College,
the insufficient and badly served food provided for
the juniors in hall, and the system of fagging, which
in those days extended to cricket.   He had a vivid
recollection of keeping watch on cold winter evenings to signal the approach of Dr. Keate, when he
paid his daily evening visit to college.   Among
the senior boys was Richard Okes, afterwards lower
master of Eton and Provost of King's College,
Cambridge, whose kindness was gratefully remembered.   He gave the boy the benefit of his criticisms
and of that taste in scholarship for which he was so
conspicuous; and in this intercourse he appears to
have been impressed by the promise of his junior.
In a letter to the Bishop of quite recent date he
recalled a line with which at the time he seems to
have been particularly struck, contained in a copy of
verses on the Garden of Eden :

Et fera legitimum quæque fatetur herum.

‘ Often,’ said he, ‘ has this line rung in my ears.’

In due course Richard Durnford was ‘ sent up for
good,’ and the welcome intelligence was communicated
to his parents in a letter sealed with the coin which
at that time was part of the reward.   The honour
was frequently repeated ; and he became distinguished for a facility in original Latin verse equal to
anything achieved by his contemporaries.   Many of
these exercises still survive, and are the admiration
of all.   Two specimens are included in the ‘ Musæ

Etonenses,' edited by Dr. Okes (1869), the subjects being, οὔρεσιν οἰκῆσαι, and

Semperque recentes
Convectare juvat prædas, et vivere rapto.

both in Latin Hexameters.

He was not particularly distinguished in athletic exercises, but seems to have devoted himself to football in the winter and boating and swimming in the summer, and also to have indulged to some extent in his favourite occupation of fishing. He remembered the sudden termination of a game of football caused by the news of the death of the Princess Charlotte on November 6, 1817. He never cared much for cricket, though he understood the points of the game and always enjoyed the spectacle of a good match. Possibly the apprenticeship of cricket fagging gave him a dislike for its scientific pursuit, and his taste for desultory and miscellaneous reading disinclined him for that vigorous application and constant practice which is the only road to excellence in the game. At that time it was quite possible for a boy of his temperament after reaching a certain position in the school to take his own line and to amuse himself as he thought best without interference from his contemporaries.

He seems at an early date to have secured the good opinion of Dr. Keate, and when he came under the personal notice of that distinguished scholar his ability and promise were at once recognised. This partiality is illustrated by the following anecdote which appears in Tucker's ' Eton of Old ' referred to above.

'Keate, like most persons in authority, had his favourites.   To his credit, they were mostly—not to say always—clever fellows.   A clever fellow under him always stood a good chance of blossoming into a favourite.   Amongst them was Dornton (name fictitious).

'He was fairly up in the Fifth without ever having come under the rod.   Why should he ?   It was of course known in College ; and after a time began to be talked of at night in bedstead assemblies among certain of his contemporaries of the envious sort.

'At the head of these was a youthful orator, Bond, who had often been under the forks himself—generally known by the name of " Guinea Bond," whether from a *lucus non* I will not venture to intimate.   I am not in knowledge of how many *séances* took place in the discussion of remedial plans ; but one at length was matured.   Nor do I know by what arts Dornton was inveigled by Bond to accompany him, between dinner and chapel if I remember aright, to Sheepsbridge on a quest for eels ; lines prepared if not set before.

' Now, there was at that time, as there is at this, the bubbling, rippling drip of a waterfall, fed by Queen's Spring and Chalvey.   Below it were some planks, and in the hollow below them a strong suspicion of eels.

' It is dangerous to look into motives ; but it may safely be said that Dornton went in for eels and Bond for time.   And the end proved it.

' Whether Bond's talk cheated the time, or whether

they continually felt the quivers of eel or lamprey, I cannot presume to suggest. All I know is that, what with the eels and the musical flow of the water-fall, time slipped away until it became too late for chapel; and both were down in Keate's black memorandum book as an introduction to the library without books.[8]

'"Bond, why were you not in chapel?"

'"Please, Sir, I was down in the playing fields, and did not hear the bell."

'"Down in the playing fields, and didn't hear the bell." Evidently disbelieving him.

'"Well, Dornton, and where were you that you didn't hear the bell?"

'"I was down at Sheep's Bridge, sir, sniggling for eels."

'"Well, well; I dare say you were there on a good motive. Bond, you will stay after twelve to-morrow."

'And so Bond was soundly flogged, and Dornton passed unscathed into the un-Library shades of Oxford life.

'I should be sorry to chronicle Bond's thoughts, often expressed in words; but no doubt they were natural too. The phrase "good motive" lived amongst us long after the occasion and cause of it had lost mention.'[9]

---

[8] I.e. the place of execution.

[9] On the appearance of the work from which the above passage is extracted, it was generally believed that Dornton was a thin disguise for Durnford; but before including the anecdote in these pages it seemed desirable to communicate with the venerable author, who immediately replied in an autograph letter confirming the identity of Dornton with Durnford.

In October 1820 the first number of 'the Etonian' magazine appeared. At that time Durnford was nineteenth in the sixth form, which then consisted of twenty-six boys. The editors were Winthrop Mackworth Praed and Walter Blunt, the latter a country neighbour and friend. It is generally supposed that the authors were all Eton boys; but a reference to the list at the end of Vol. II. shows that some of the most frequent contributors were then members of the universities— e.g. Henry Nelson Coleridge, of King's College, Cambridge; John Moultrie, of Trinity College, Cambridge; Henry Neech, of Merton College, Oxford; and William Sydney Walker, of Trinity College, Cambridge. But Praed, who was in the sixth form, four places above Durnford, was the life and soul of the enterprise and author of the most brilliant contents of the magazine.

Among Durnford's contributions were 'A Visit to Eton' (No. 1), 'The Miseries of the Christmas Holidays' (No. 2), 'On Signs' (No. 3), 'A Peep into Rawsdon Court' (No. 3), 'Golightly's Letter of Condolence' (No. 4), 'A Party at the Pelican' (No. 6), and 'The Rashleigh Letter Bag' (No. 8 and following numbers). The characteristics of these articles consist in an assumption of old world wisdom and superiority, and a cynical disapproval of the levities of youth, hardly perhaps in accordance with the taste and spirit of modern times, but amusing enough in contrast to the ambitious productions of some of his *confrères*. The author had always an intense admiration for the style of Addison, and several of these articles are obvious imitations of the 'Spectator.' The 'Visit to Eton' is amusing from an esoteric point of view as embodying the satisfaction felt by the author that his destiny had associated him with the foundation of King Henry VI. rather than with its more ancient but less emancipated model of Winchester.[1]

But whatever may be the merits or defects of these compositions, the light in which Durnford was regarded by his contemporaries is illustrated by the short poem by the late Bishop Trower on 'Genius' in No. 1. The verses are as follows :

> 'What is Genius ? 'tis a flame
> Kindling all the human frame ;
> 'Tis the ray that lights the eye
> Soft in love, in battle high ;
> 'Tis the lightening of the mind
> Unsubdued and undefined ;
> 'Tis the flood that pours along
> The full clear melody of song ;
> 'Tis the sacred boon of Heaven
> To its choicest favourites given ;
> They who feel can paint it well,
> What is Genius . . . . tell.'

A note to the above is as follows :

'It is proper to state that these lines have appeared surreptitiously a few weeks back in the

[1] *Cf.* the following passage : 'There are some associations connected with the sight of a school, particularly a large one, which always bring me back to the time of my boyhood . . . . I must confess that my situation at that time, both in point of happiness and liberty, was very different from that of an Etonian. The walls were my boundaries ; and merely to pass them without any consequent misdemeanours was reckoned among the heaviest of

" Morning Chronicle," in which the blank in the last line was filled up with the name of Lord " Byron." We deem it right to mention this because the name which originally occupied the space was that of a schoolfellow whom we are happy to reckon among the number of our contributors.'— P.C.[2]

It was confidently stated by Lord Winmarleigh and other contemporaries that the name was Durnford.

During Durnford's school life at Eton promotion was entirely by seniority, and school places were not determined, as now, by periodical examinations. Thus a boy moved up in the order in which he was originally placed, subject only to the changes owing to vacancies, with the result that the senior in the year in college, though possibly inferior to his juniors intellectually, was entitled to election to King's. In 1819 it became evident that in the ordinary course of events Durnford would not

those crimes to which the wisdom of the legislative founder had allotted punishment. This place of my education I always considered as a better sort of prison, and left it with all the joy that a prisoner would feel on obtaining his Habeas Corpus, except on stated occasions, when, preceded by our master, we walked in due order and regularity up a high green hill, at a short distance off, famous for its having been formerly the station of a Roman camp. Well do I recollect how often I unwillingly encountered the cold frosty air of a winter morning on this bleak and desolate spot; how often, under a sweltering summer sun, I laboured and toiled up the entrenchments with which the caution of our ancient enemies had fortified the natural steepness. However, such an excursion as this was some relief, and I generally contemplated with increased horror on my return the grim bars, the narrow courts, and the closing gates of —— school,' &c.

[2] Peregrine Courtenay.

succeed to King's, and we find his father writing to Dr. Pett as follows :

Chilbolton : August 9, 1819.

My dear Sir,—I shall make no apology for addressing you, being fully confident of the disposition you will have to serve me. You know the state of my family. My eldest son has been for some time at Eton, and from the character given of him by his masters, as well as from the manner in which he has distinguished himself in the school, I have reason to entertain a flattering opinion of his talents, and I thank God his disposition and conduct are everything that a parent could wish. When he entered the college we had hopes of his succeeding to King's, but this is unfortunately not likely to happen ; and it is of great consequence to me as well as to *his* future welfare to place him in the university, where his education may be completed advantageously. It has occurred to me that possibly it may be in your power to assist us. If you can procure for him a Studentship at Christ Church, it would both be of the greatest benefit in a pecuniary point of view and in furnishing also the best means of improvement ; and I trust I may venture to add he will never disgrace your patronage. He is now nearly seventeen, and will quit Eton in about two years. . . . .

I am, my dear Sir,
Sincerely yours,
RICHARD DURNFORD.

Dr. Pett's reply, however, was not favourable, and he intimated that his interest was engaged in other quarters. At the same time he suggested that inquiries should be made as to other foundations where natives of Hampshire had a preference, Magdalen and Corpus being mentioned.

It will be remembered that the subject of the correspondence was a native of Berkshire, not of Hampshire as supposed by Dr. Pett; and in the result of inquiries instituted by his father with the assistance of Mr. Baratty, it was ascertained that there were at Magdalen demyships restricted to natives of Berks.

Mr. Durnford's anticipations as to the succession to King's were realised. The scholars elected in 1821–2 were W. G. Cookesley, W. H. Tucker, Samuel Best, and James Flamank, and at election 1822 Durnford was superannuated. Meanwhile his father had caused him to be matriculated at Pembroke College, Oxford; but in July 1822 he was elected to a demyship at Magdalen, where he went into residence in the following October.

The editor is indebted to Mr. T. Herbert Warren, the present President of Magdalen, for the following information respecting Mr. Durnford's life at Magdalen and the position and constitution of that society during his residence at Oxford.

'Bishop Durnford's connection with Oxford began by his matriculating at Pembroke College while still a boy at Eton, at the age of seventeen, on March 24, 1820.

'It was the custom in those days for boys who intended to go to Oxford to matriculate, while still at school, at some college, scholarships often not being available until later in their career.

' Pembroke was the family college. His father was at Pembroke in the years 1784–8, and had a recollection, which he was fond of reviving, of being asked in as an undergraduate by the Master, Dr. Adams, to a party at the lodgings, to meet the great ornament of Pembroke, Dr. Johnson. He saw Johnson, the centre of an admiring throng, but as a youngster was naturally enough not introduced to him. After a short interval a fussy little man came rushing in, crying, " Has he said anything? Has he said anything?" This, it is hardly necessary to explain, was Bozzy.'

Two years later the famous Dr. Keate, who was afterwards to be Bishop Durnford's father-in-law, sent him up to Magdalen with the following letter commendatory addressed to President Routh :

Eton : July 18, 1822.

Sir,—The father of Mr. Richard Durnford, who is proceeding to Oxford to stand for a demyship at your college, has requested me to supply his son with testimonials of conduct, &c. I have expressed my doubts whether anything of the kind is required by your electors, but I should be very sorry if the young man should be unsuccessful from want of any necessary forms, and therefore I proceed to state that he has been under me for near seven years, and during the whole time has merited my entire approbation. Indeed I cannot help saying that I consider him as an ornament to the school, both for his conduct and his attainments.

I have the honour to be, Sir, with great respect,
Your very obedient humble servant,

J. KEATE.

Demy, it is perhaps hardly necessary to explain, is the name given at Magdalen to a scholar on the foundation. The name would seem to have sprung up as a sort of cant term or piece of college slang in the first years of the college, possibly from the *dimidia portio* allotted by statute to these junior members of the foundation.

By custom, though not originally, the demyships had become confined to particular counties or dioceses. Bishop Durnford came in on what was called a Berkshire demyship.

The examination and mode of admission of Demies would appear in those days to have been a somewhat uncertain affair, nomination by the officers of the college playing an important part ; but it was understood that the President, who took the first nomination, made it a rule never to pass over any young man of eminent merit, and it speaks well for both parties that Durnford was the only Demy of the year, and therefore, no doubt, came in on the President's nomination.

The Latin letter in which, according to custom, the young foundationer acknowledged his election is a very happy specimen of its class, going far both in spirit and Latinity to justify the election. And, what is more, its expressions were more faithfully put into practice than is sometimes the case with such complimentary effusions.

' Tales tibi, vir admodum Reverende, gratias pro tot tantisque tuis in me beneficiis debeo, quales ne perfectissimum quidem ingenium digne posset exsolvere. Liceat mihi sperare te pro solitâ tuâ clementiâ voluntatem meam potius quam verba spectaturum esse et sinceram gratissimi animi oblationem accepturum. Hoc saltem possum polliceri te neminem unquam aut tibi devinctiorem, aut legum observantiorem habiturum esse quam tui studiosissimum RICARDUM DURNFORD.'

When young Durnford entered Magdalen the foundation consisted of the President, 40 Fellows, 30 Demies, 4 chaplains, and 8 clerks, with an organist, choristers, schoolmaster, and usher. Of the Fellows, however, many were non-resident, and the same was the case with the Demies, only nine of whom were undergraduates. There were also the 'gentlemen commoners,' of whom there were from a dozen to twenty in residence. These were, as their name implies, men often of family, and always of fortune. According to popular report they paid double tuition fees on condition of being excused tuition, and they certainly were then, as in Gibbon's time, allowed a great deal of liberty and even license, and treated with a very light and easy hand by authority.

'The Demies or Scholars on the foundation were,' says a contemporary whom we shall quote later on, 'much more strictly looked after.'

'When I was at Oxford,' said Lord Brabourne, then Mr. Knatchbull-Hugessen, 'I belonged to a class of men who ought never to have existed, the gentlemen commoners of Magdalen.'

It is only fair to say that gentlemen commoners

were not confined to Magdalen, and that if at Magdalen the faults of the system were on a glorified scale, not a few of the gentlemen commoners were men who afterwards became distinguished, and honourably so. Thus of Bishop Durnford's contemporaries, some eighteen or nineteen in number, not less than five became Members of Parliament and members of more or less note, and one became a man of science of world-wide fame.

A Scotchman of some ability and descriptive power, Mr. John Hamilton Gray, afterwards Vicar of Bolsover and Scarscliffe, who was one of them, just two years senior to the Bishop, has left an account of their society as it was in his time and some slight sketches of many of his contemporaries.[3]

Gray entered Magdalen originally in 1818. After residing about fourteen months he went abroad for some time, studying at Göttingen, but returned into residence in 1822.

Among those he mentions more particularly are John Forbes, eldest son of Sir Charles Forbes of Newe and Edinglassie; John Marshall,[4] 'a clever, amusing, brazen-faced Irishman, the possessor of an independent though not large fortune, a great reader, drinker, tennis player, talker and boaster, who was given to history and politics and expressed his intention of going into Parliament;' William Henry

[3] Autobiography of the Rev. John Hamilton Gray of Cartyne. Printed for private circulation, 1868.

[4] John Marshall, eldest son of Ralph, of Deerhurst, Kerry, Ireland, Armiger; matric. Magdalen, Feb. 3, 1821, aged 17.

Gore Langton, afterwards M.P. for Bristol; Harry Goring, afterwards Sir Harry Goring, also later a Member of Parliament; Henry Mitford, grandson and heir of the historian of Greece; Mr. Delmè Radcliffe, son of the friend of the Prince Regent; Montague, afterwards Sir Montague Cholmeley; and two better-known names, Lord Oxmantown, who together with his brother, the Hon. John Parsons, was placed in the first class in mathematics and physics in Durnford's first term, and who afterwards, as Lord Rosse, achieved high repute as a man both of affairs and of science, and in particular gained world-wide fame as an astronomer and the creator of the celebrated colossal telescope; and John Wilson, afterwards Colonel Wilson-Patten, M.P. for Lancashire, Chairman of Committees, Chancellor of the Duchy of Lancaster, Chief Secretary for Ireland, and finally, the first, and alas, the last, Baron Winmarleigh.

All these appear in the calendar for 1822–23; with some of them Durnford was more or less intimate. With Wilson-Patten, who was his exact contemporary, and had been with him at Eton, and was to be his neighbour for many years in Lancashire, he had much, as we shall shortly see, in common.

Another gentleman commoner, Robert Henry Daubeny, who survived till 1892, is mentioned in that year by the Bishop as an old friend.

Among the Demies may be noted R. Meadows-

White, afterwards Professor of Anglo-Saxon, and the well known editor of the ' Ormulum ; ' F. C. Massingberd, for many years a famous Chancellor of the diocese of Lincoln, and Henry Linton, whose name as a devoted and valuable Evangelical clergyman has within the last few years been re-called to Oxford memory ; and, nearer to Durnford's own time, Richard Sewell, one of the well-known family of brothers and sisters, children of Mr. Thomas Sewell of Newport, in the Isle of Wight, still represented in Oxford by the venerable War-den of New College.   Richard Sewell, whatever defects of character he showed in after life, inherited a full portion of the literary gift of his family.   He won the Newdigate Prize with a poem of unusual promise, and afterwards became the author of several legal works of acknowledged merit.   A little junior to Durnford were : Francis Knyvett Leighton, afterwards Fellow and Warden of All Souls and Canon of Westminster, and Frederic Bulley, destined to succeed Dr. Routh as Head of Durnford's own college ; Edwin Martin Atkins, the heroic Squire of Tom Hughes' ' Scouring of the White Horse,' and William Palmer, elder brother of the late Lord Selborne, amply commemorated by him in his autobiography recently published.

Leighton, Bulley, and Palmer were all excellent scholars.   Borrett, a Demy a year or two junior, was one of the first to win Dean Ireland's recently instituted scholarship, and, considering the small

number of undergraduate Demies, there is no reason
to think that the average standard either of their
ability or their attainment was otherwise than distinctly high.

Such were the Bishop's own contemporaries.
To go to the senior members of the College. *A
Jove principium.* When Bishop Durnford entered
the College, the President was Dr. Routh, then in
the sixty-seventh year of his life, the fifty-first of
his connection with the College, the twenty-first of
his reign as President. Of this remarkable person
so much has been written, that it is needless here to
say more than that he was a man of real piety and
goodness of heart, and profoundly and originally
versed in both sacred and secular scholarship. He
had published in 1784 an edition of Plato's ' Euthy-
demus ' and ' Gorgias,' still favourably known, and
in 1814–18, the four volumes of his ' Reliquiae
Sacrae.' He was also strong in history, particularly
in family and personal history, and was still to give
the world his edition of Bishop Burnet.

Though even in 1818 apparently regarded and
regarding himself as an old man, and though certainly old-fashioned—for, born in the middle of the
eighteenth century, he carried its habits and ideas
into the middle of the nineteenth—Routh was both
respected and liked by his young men.

' I well remember,' writes Bishop Durnford, ' the
old Patrist, his venerable face and figure ; ' and again,
' little did I think in the days of the ancient Routh
that I should ever be a guest in that house which I

used to visit with such awe, but never without pleasure.'   In another letter he speaks of the *mitis sapientia* of the old President.

And though in a sense living much retired, he had a considerable acquaintance in the great world, and on one occasion, in the advice he gave to Dr. Seabury as to the consecration of the American bishops, may be said directly to have affected the course of history.

But perhaps the most remarkable thing about him when Durnford came under his charge was that he had only just married a lady of nine and twenty, and that he had still thirty-two years to live, and thirty-two years to reign over Magdalen.

I once asked Bishop Durnford who were the Fellows of his time, and what they were like.   He began the list. 'There was Dr. S——,' he said, 'who edited " Apollonius Rhodius," and Dr. J——, who did nothing ; there was old Dr. Ellerton ; there were old Grantham and young Grantham '—and then with a smile he stopped the recital.

Gray tells much the same tale. ' About the time that I became a member of Magdalen College, there was a knot of ancient Fellows nearly coeval with the President, who had grown up from youth to age amid its venerable groves and cloisters ; ' and he goes on to apply to them the well-known words of Gibbon about the chapel, the coffee-house, and the common room.

' I remember,' he says, ' these old men, Drs. J——, S——, T——, L——, and C——.   They had done little to illustrate their college or to benefit mankind.   They lived and gossiped, joked and feasted, and drank long and deep potations of excellent old port.'

The only Fellow who appears as tutor in the Calendar for 1822–23, is Dr. Ellerton, now chiefly remembered as the founder of the University prizes for a Theological Essay and for Hebrew, associated with his name, but long a conspicuous and important person in College.   His lectures figure as a regular *pièce de résistance* in Gray's account of the College, but in Durnford's time more important persons were the Rev. William Mills, afterwards Professor of Moral Philosophy, a man of a high order both of attainment and ability, and an excellent teacher, and the Rev. George Booth, an excellent and elegant classical scholar, like Durnford himself an Etonian.

Among the other Fellows was R. Waldo Sibthorp, a member of an old Lincolnshire family, who afterwards became famous as having, to use Mr. Gladstone's forcible language, 'thrice cleared the chasm which separates the Roman from the Anglican Communion.'

But those best known to general fame are Dr. Daubeny, who having begun as a distinguished Latin scholar was already in those days Professor of Chemistry and a Fellow of the Royal Society, and somewhat later added to the Chair of Chemistry that of Botany, a man of real note, both for his own achievement, and still more as pioneer in the cause of physical science, alike in Oxford and in England; and Mr. Ichabod Charles Wright, who along with Daubeny commenced the study of medicine, but finally became a banker, an authority on currency, and the well-known translator of Dante.

In this little, but not unremarkable society, the Bishop passed his Oxford career. His time must have been pretty fully occupied. That he read hard his record in the schools is sufficient evidence. For the rest, his generation would seem to have spent its time generally as all undergraduates at Oxford and Cambridge have done from the early years of the century, and probably *mutatis mutandis* from a much earlier period. Tennyson has told us what it was at Cambridge half a dozen years later :

> They boated and they cricketed ; they talked
> At wine, in clubs, of art, of politics ;
> They lost their weeks ; they vext the souls of deans ;
> They rode ; they betted ; made a hundred friends
> And caught the blossom of the flying terms.

Durnford used to play cricket. The leader in college in this sport was a certain Henry Jenkins, a Sussex Demy, headmaster of the college school, afterwards Rector of Stanway in Essex, a good scholar and antiquary, and a very successful school-master, the founder of what was called the 'Magdalen Cricket Club,' whose ground on Cowley Marsh still bears its name—for many years with the exception of the Bullingdon Club, the only cricket club in the university. The Bishop well remembered making the winning hit in a match for Jenkins against the last-named club on the Bullingdon Ground. In those days it was usual to ride up to the ground and tie up the horses while the game was being played, and another of Bishop Durnford's recollections was seeing Wilberforce of Oriel, afterwards the famous Bishop, galloping round the field. 'Even in those days,' he used to say, ' I noted that he was a very indifferent rider and that there was a good deal of what is technically called "daylight" between him and the saddle, and when I heard of his death the recollection came back to me.'

Hunting was a favourite pursuit of the gentlemen commoners. ' Our college turned out,' says Gray, ' fourteen red coats four days a week, out of twenty men.' Marshall and I, who did not hunt, made a league to talk down hunting in the common room.' In those days every gentleman could ride. Whether the Bishop hunted or not, he doubtless rode ; but he and Marshall, who was his friend as well as the friend of Gray, had other interests in common.

They belonged to the ' Union,' and were indeed among its founders and first members.

As is pretty well known, the name under which this now historic school of public speaking and life has grown famous, was not its original title, or rather the ' Oxford Union ' is not, strictly speaking, the original society. As first started the club called itself the United Debating Society. Of this society in its first year (1823) and again in 1825, Durnford was one of the presidents. Among the others were his contemporary of Eton and Magdalen and lifelong friend already mentioned, Wilson-Patten, the Hon. T. A. Powys, afterwards Lord Lilford, and Viscount Ingestre, afterwards Lord Shrewsbury. In 1826 the society adopted the extreme but ingenious device of dissolving itself to get rid of certain objectionable members, and then reconstituting itself immediately as the Union Debating Society.

To the earlier society probably belongs, for there is no trace of it in the minutes of the Union, a good story associated with Durnford's name. When the society was sitting, the proctors who were at that time not sufficiently acquainted with its proceedings, or perhaps in these earlier and less orderly days had reason to think poorly of it, presented themselves at the doors, and sent in word to the president that the society must break up its proceedings and disperse. To this it was at once moved in due form and carried, that the following answer be sent, 'That the House will consider the message.' The proctors, well pleased with the wit and constitutional instinct of the young men, and recognising the situation, drew off and have ever since recognised the liberties of the ' Union.'

It is often said that Bishop Durnford was the originator of the reply, but as he told me it originated not with himself, but with another member of Magdalen, a ' witty Irishman of the name of John Marshall '—that is, of course, the gentleman commoner already mentioned above.

Coming to the Union Society, the first page of the first minute-book records that the society met on December 5, 1825, with Mr. Dodgson, Ch. Ch., as president.[5]   Among gentlemen elected members of the committee at this first meeting are Mr. Durnford, Magdalen, and Mr. Wilberforce, Oriel.

Mr. Durnford was secretary in the spring of 1826, and the first minutes appear to be in his handwriting.   In the summer term of 1826 he appears as president himself, but is absent a good deal, probably owing to his being in the schools in that term.

The society further has in its possession a book with a list of subscriptions dating from 1825 or thereabouts, also possibly begun in Durnford's own hand, in which his name appears as a subscriber.

He appears, too, occasionally as taking part in the debates.   On February 2, 1826, the following motion was proposed by Mr. Wortley, of Christ Church :

That the present system of Mechanics' Institutions for the scientific education of the labouring classes is not likely to prove beneficial to the country.

Among those who supported Mr. Wortley was Mr. Durnford of Magdalen.

On February 23 of the same year the motion was :

That the act for Septennial Parliaments in the reign of George the First was consistent with sound policy and constitutional justice.

[5] Afterwards Master in the Court of Common Pleas.

Against the motion, Mr. Durnford, Magdalen, and Mr. Wilberforce, Oriel.

Durnford 'went up' for his final examination in the summer term of 1826. Dr. Heurtley, Canon of Christ Church, who took his own first class in the next year, remembered and has recorded in his reminiscences, published in Mr. Henry Daniel's 'Shadows of Old Oxford,'[6] that the schools were crowded with voluntary listeners to hear Durnford's *vivâ-voce* examination. Among his compeers in the first class in classics were a Mr. Hatton of St. Edmund Hall, a man of extraordinary memory and information, afterwards nicknamed 'Procopius,' because he offered that very unusual author for examination; Mr. Francis Newman of Worcester, brother of the Cardinal, a very distinguished scholar though an eccentric man, author of 'Phases of Faith;' and Mr. D. C. Wrangham of Brasenose, afterwards Serjeant-at-Law, Q.C., and M.P. for Sudbury. Newman and Wrangham took Double Firsts. Newman survived the Bishop by a year or two. In the second class in the same list appeared Mr. Francis Faber of University, afterwards, along with the Bishop, Fellow of Magdalen.

Amid this eminent company then, the Bishop shone out. His *vivâ voce* is said to have been chiefly conducted by Archbishop Longley, who was then Censor of Christ Church and was certainly one of the examiners.

---

[6] *Our Memories :* 'Shadows of Old Oxford,' Daniel, Oxford.

Thus creditably ended Durnford's undergraduate career.   He had not long to wait for a Fellowship, for he was elected Probationer Fellow the next year and became full Fellow in due course in 1828.   He held his Fellowship till 1836, when his appointment as Rector of Middleton caused him after the customary period of grace to vacate it, and his connection with the foundation of Magdalen ceased until it was renewed *honoris causâ*, much to the satisfaction of the college and himself, more than fifty years later, in the autumn of 1888.

Durnford was apparently a 'dry' rather than a 'wet bob,' but like a good Etonian he thoroughly sympathised with boating.   When in after years he was asked to subscribe to provide his college with a barge, he not only sent a pleasant letter and a good subscription himself, but suggested some other old members of the college to whom application might be made, among them Lord Winmarleigh, who sent £10, and said : 'I look back with pleasure to the time I spent at Magdalen, especially to my having been under the late Dr. Routh, and to my having been associated with several distinguished contemporaries, three of whom, Lord Rosse, his brother, Mr. Parsons, and the present Bishop of Chichester, obtained first-class honours.'

His taste for natural history showed itself in his recollections of the college.   In his day Magdalen Hall was all in ruins.   It had been largely destroyed by fire in 1820 and not rebuilt.   He remembered that two ravens and a kite built in the little turret of the Grammar Hall, but 'unfortunately a farmer, a tenant of the college, was allowed to shoot them.' In those easy days, apparently, the few undergraduates in residence were allowed free access to the 'Grove.' On one occasion the Bishop found there under a tree a little dead leveret, doubtless brought there by one of these lamented birds of prey.

There was a sort of shrubbery with earth piled up against the front of the Founder's Tower, and in the corner towards the Lodgings. The same day that the Bishop was elected Demy the college passed an order for the rebuilding of the north and east side of the cloisters, and this was in process when the Bishop was in residence.

He thought highly of Winchester as a home of scholarship, and in particular said to me, 'There has always been a succession of masters at Winchester who have given the boys a taste for the classics as literature, like Joe Wharton.'

At the time of his return to Eton as a private tutor Mr. Gladstone was a boy there. I asked him whether he had had anything to do with Mr. Gladstone. 'Not directly,' was the answer, 'but when he was going up to Oxford he asked my advice as to his classical reading, and I remember amongst other things I said, "Above all, don't neglect Homer."'

I talked to him once about modern poetry. He liked Tennyson's early poems very much when they came out and afterwards, and *In Memoriam.* 'I never cared much,' he said, 'for those Welsh pieces of his,' meaning the Idylls.   He enjoyed Tennyson's fidelity to nature. This led him to speak of Sir Walter Scott.   Mr. Morritt, of Rokeby, whom he knew, told him how Sir Walter had questioned him very minutely about the flowers in which Rokeby is very rich, saying that as he was going to write a poem on Rokeby he must have them correct.

Once when they were both breakfasting with me, the Bishop of Winchester said to him, ' You know everything.'   ' Oh, no,' he said laughing, ' there are a great many things I don't know, and if I know some things, you must recollect that I have been rather a long time in the world.'   He was then in his eighty-sixth year.   And unlike many old men of remarkable memory he seemed to retain the power of being interested in and retaining new knowledge.

But what struck me even more was, not only the range and capacity of his memory but its accuracy. He seemed to take great pains to observe accurately and to inform himself exactly, and then remembered the result with absolute fidelity.

Sitting in the senior common room after dinner, and talking of his recollections of its members in his day some sixty-five years before, he happened to mention Mr. Berners, ' a member of a good Suffolk family, who used to come up and stay and frequent the room a good deal, and discourse on classical subjects.'   I said we still had a snuff-box which Mr. Berners had given to the room.   ' Oh, yes,' he said, 'I remember it.   I haven't seen it since I went down.   I should much like to see it again.'   The snuff-box was brought.   He looked at the inscription ; 'In usum Cam. Com. Soc. S. M. Magd. Oxon. d.d. Car. Berners, MDCCCXV.   Nulla dies unquam memori vos eximet.'

'But,' he said, 'I think I remember his arms were somewhere on the box.'   'If you'll turn it round you'll find them,' I said, and there indeed they were.

At this moment, if the Bishop had said he remembered Addison or Cardinal Wolsey or the Founder himself, I should hardly have thought it strange.

Indeed, I amused myself in conversation or letters by asking him if he recollected this or that event of the earliest years of the century, of which it seemed hardly possible an eye-witness could still be living.

The first important event he remembered he told me was the Jubilee of George III.   He was a boy at school at Epsom and saw the light of the illuminations in the sky, and asked what it was. That was in 1810.   In 1830 he saw Charles X. as king of France, a fine dignified-looking man.

His memories of Oxford belonged to the same period.   'When I was up at College,' he said, 'Newman was a strong Evangelical.   He crept about knowing no one.   Pusey had just come back from Germany, and was supposed to be deeply tainted with German neologism.'   No wonder the Bishop, an old-fashioned thorough Churchman, regarded the Oxford movement as by no means so much of a discovery or new departure, as many have since deemed it.

In 1829 he, with another distinguished Magdalen divine, Henry Phillpotts, afterwards Bishop of Exeter, was one of the small minority who voted for Peel as member for Oxford University when the majority went against him. He thought the time and manner which Peel chose were inopportune, but that the measure on which he was turned out, Catholic emancipation, was just, needful, and must come.

The winter of 1889-90 was very severe. The Thames and Cherwell were frozen hard, above and below Oxford. I skated one day with some friends from Oxford to Nuneham, getting off at Sandford for a space. I happened in writing to tell the Bishop this. He wrote back :—

' I envy you skating on such clear and deep waters. I do not remember 1824, but I do remember 1813-14, the Moscow frost, which was bitter indeed, and lasted long ; a memorable epoch.'

As the name of J. W. Marshall occurs several times in the President's contribution it may be of interest to add the following particulars respecting him. He was the son of Col. Marshall, an Irishman, who served in the Spanish army during the War of Independence, and is mentioned by Southey as one of the victims of the memorable siege of Gerona in 1809. The son inherited a con-

siderable property in Kerry, to the improvement of
which he applied himself with great zeal, thereby
earning the gratitude and affection of his tenants at a
time when the feeling against all landlords if supporters of the English Government was most bitter.
Here he entertained Durnford during one of the
long vacations while they were at Oxford, and the
latter derived his personal impressions of Ireland
entirely from this visit, as he never again entered
the country.   The correspondence between the two
friends continued till Marshall's early death in 1837.
He fell a victim to consumption, which had already
carried off all his brothers and sisters ; and during
his last illness, while lying a hopeless invalid at
Torquay with his mind entirely devoted to his
approaching end, he was visited by Durnford, who
recorded with great minuteness the substance of their
conversation on Marshall's religious convictions,
and also on his intentions respecting the succession
to his property, which he had determined to leave
to a distant relative not yet arrived at manhood.
Among his letters to Durnford are several references
to the life at Magdalen.   The following was written
in April 1827, after Durnford's election to a Fellowship :

'I am delighted at ——'s secession and your
consequent elevation.   Your mind is doubtless ere
this filled with the full dignity of Donship, though
that countenance of yours, with the exception of the
[*word illegible*] is little indicative of the High Table.
I am not surprised at the account you give of the

Magdalen gentlemen commoners.   I should only be surprised if, constituted as the College is, they were other than they are.   That common room is a most pernicious thing.'

The next letter is dated May, 1829, and was written after Durnford had decided on taking Holy Orders and had abandoned his previous intention of adopting the Bar as his profession :

'Confess that your change of profession had its origin in idleness. . . . You know as well as I do that you require some present stimulus to exertion which the profession of the Law would have afforded you, but that of the Church will not.   I am confident if you had applied you would have succeeded at the Bar, having great elocution and quickness of repartee. I fancy I see you some years hence such a being as old Chapman—to whom, by the way, I think you have a considerable likeness—perambulating the cloisters with a bare sufficiency of ideas to keep the centre of the *pavé* and find the way to the Hall.'

While reading for his degree Durnford became a private pupil of James Garbett, Fellow of Brasenose, and first-class in Lit. Hum. in 1822.   Garbett was a fine scholar and was elected Professor of Poetry in 1842 after a contest with Isaac Williams, which stirred the University to its depths, being a trial of strength between the Evangelical and Tractarian parties.   Subsequently he became a Prebendary and Archdeacon of Chichester, which office he held during the first nine years of Bishop Durnford's episcopate.   During this time he never fully realised that the former relations of tutor and pupil had been reversed, and his advice was tendered in a manner rather suggestive of their permanence.

Among the friends outside his own college with whom Mr. Durnford principally associated were J. G. Cole, of Exeter, Sir S. R. Glynne, of Christ Church, C. Palairet, of Queen's, and T. W. Carr, of Brasenose, to whom reference has been already made. He was with Mr. Durnford in college at Eton, though somewhat senior, and gained the Ellerton Theological Essay Prize in 1826. He was subsequently ordained and held several curacies in the diocese of Norwich, from which he corresponded with his friend in a spirit of affection and intimacy showing the strength of their attachment. The following letter, written by him in April, 1827, is interesting :

'I have been at J. B. Sumner's since I saw you, and had a delightful time. He, indeed, is a charming Christian and true pastor. Never was there a person more judiciously zealous. I preached before him, and he since has written, I think, inviting correspondence. We spoke much of you. He said all he wished to hear of you was that you had a lively interest in "the one thing needful." I told him I was afraid you used at Oxford to abuse Evangelicals, but I hoped you would soon be more forbearing.'

Another letter from Carr, of the same year, describes Mr. Durnford as follows :

'There is a certain *bonhomie* about your manner

of saying things, even in condemnation, which always saves you from resentment. Just the reverse with me, who, G. Vernon used to say, showed so much of " the lurking devil in my sneer," that I am sure to make enemies. I get on much better with ladies than men. I sometimes flatter myself that I have found the key to their vanities, but however that may be, they are the only persons I am ever a favourite with, whilst you are always in all men's praises and in ladies' also.'

Some further reference to Carr will be made in connection with Mr. Durnford's return to Eton as a private tutor. He died in 1840. Of the other friends, J. G. Cole became a Fellow of Exeter, where, in April, 1827, he is reported by a common friend to be 'endeavouring to improve the vulgar taste of the High Table by introducing sundry French *ragoûts* and *fricassées*.' He subsequently inherited property at Marazion, Cornwall, from his uncle, Sir Christopher Cole, K.C.B., and owned a house in Charles Street, Berkeley Square, where Mr. Durnford afterwards frequently stayed with him. Of Sir S. Glynne, whose name is so well known in connection with his brother-in-law, Mr. Gladstone, it is unnecessary to speak. Charles Palairet devoted himself to clerical work in Newfoundland. In all these cases the friendship which originated at school or college was maintained through life.

CHAPTER II

Private Tutorship—Travels on the Continent—Extracts from Journal —Presented to Rectory of Middleton—Description of the Parish— His Influence with the People—Description of the Church—Parish Work—Schools—Visiting—His Marriage—Relations with the First Bishop of Manchester—Made Archdeacon of Manchester—Interest in Municipal Affairs—His Garden—His Friendships—Bishopric of Chichester accepted.

IN 1826 Mr. Durnford was offered and accepted the position of 'private tutor' at Eton to Edward Harbord, the eldest son of Lord Suffield, and the next five years were spent either at Eton or at Gunton Park, Lord Suffield's country seat. He had ultimately two of Lord Suffield's sons under his tuition. It was then far more common than it is now for boys of good family to have, in addition to their regular tutor at Eton, a private tutor who supervised their work and gave the individual attention which could not be given in any other way owing to the small number of masters ; and Mr. Durnford found among the private tutors of that day one at least whose society was thoroughly congenial, and with whom he formed a close and lasting friendship—George Augustus Selwyn, who became the first Bishop of New Zealand, and afterwards Bishop of Lichfield. In a letter from his friend Carr, of Brasenose College, written in 1826, his correspondent says : 'I have no objection to your quarrelling with the Keate, Carter, and Bethel girls if you like'—an amusing permission, as one of the 'Keate girls' was afterwards to be his devoted and beloved wife.   In the same letter Carr gives a pungent estimate of the principal characters in Eton society at that time, but it is too personal for extraction, and only the conclusion of the letter can be quoted.   'As for hot water, do not fear that, *experto crede* there is a certain *bonhomie* in your manner of saying things even in condemnation which secures you from resentment.'   Into hot water Mr. Durnford certainly did not fall.   His relations with his employers were always of the most friendly character ; in Lady Suffield, a woman of many gifts and graces, he found a kind and valued friend, and Lord Suffield showed his appreciation of the young private tutor's character and abilities by appointing him, when a vacancy occurred, to the large and important living of Middleton.   Nor was the life at Eton by any means uncongenial.   There was a sufficiency of necessary occupation, there was an abundance of amusement—for the river, to a man fond of boating and bathing, was a constant delight—there was a pleasant society of cultivated people, and, best of all, there was ample time and opportunity, which Mr. Durnford wisely used, for improving the knowledge of foreign languages which he already possessed.   With the family of Dr. Keate, then headmaster, he was soon on terms of intimacy, and among other friendships begun at this time and continued in later life were those with Edward Coleridge, afterwards his brother-in-law, Edward Craven Hawtrey, who became Headmaster and Provost of Eton, the two Selwyns, George Augustus and his elder brother William, subsequently Canon of Ely and Lady Margaret Professor of Divinity, and James Hope, afterwards Hope-Scott.

In 1827 an offer was made to Mr. Durnford of an assistant mastership at Eton, although such appointments were then looked upon as almost perquisites of the Fellows of King's College, Cambridge. The correspondent already quoted writes in a strain of intense dismay on hearing the news of the offer :

'I never could have supposed that the authorities would have seen anything in you that could have led them to suppose you would become one of them. That your talents would have made you a most valuable prize I do not indeed suppose them so blind as to doubt, but surely they must have seen that you had too enlightened a spirit to descend to a position of such drudgery and delving. . . . I hope you will never give up to a school talents and dispositions which were meant to be the delight of a much more extended sphere.'

What were Mr. Durnford's reasons for declining the offer it is impossible to say, though it may be predicated with some certainty that he did not agree with his correspondent in the pessimistic view taken of the profession of a schoolmaster ; but it is probable that he chose wisely, and that his undoubted talents were more usefully employed as parish priest and Bishop than they could have been in the career which he declined. He was ordained Deacon on his Fellowship by the Bishop of Oxford in 1830 and Priest in 1831. In 1832 his occupation as private tutor ceased, and between that date and the close of 1834 he spent a considerable amount of time on the Continent. The longest of these tours, longer than was common then, or indeed is now for a young man who had recently taken Holy Orders, extended from March 1834 to January 1835. During this period he spent some considerable time in Paris, then made his way through France to Savoy, and so by Genoa to Rome, Naples, and Sicily. Thence travelling northwards he crossed over into Germany, and in October 1834 was in Vienna; but the winter months were again spent in Rome, and he reached Paris on his way back to England in January 1835.

Several volumes of journals kept during these tours exist, but they are minute accounts of proceedings from day to day, written evidently to refresh his own memory, but not of sufficient general interest to warrant extensive extracts in a memoir such as this. Some few extracts are, perhaps, admissible, partly as showing his receptive, observant mind, already stored with literary thoughts and fancies, and open to every new impression; partly from the interest which naturally attaches to a life which, beginning in the first decade of the century, closed when the century was nearing its end.

1829.[1]   *Weimar.*—'As we were walking out of the town a gentleman joined us and talked of Goethe, who is still living there.   He said he drove out every day in his coach, looking *sehr majestätisch.*'

1829.   *Köthen (under Dr. Hahnemann, the founder of homœopathy).*—'To-day a fête was given to celebrate the fiftieth anniversary of Hahnemann's practice.   Homœopathic doctors flocked from all parts, and I made a point of dining with them. There were, I should say, about thirty, myself and two other patients not included.   There was great enthusiasm.'

1830.   *Paris.*—'In the evening we heard "Hernani," a new tragedy by Victor Hugo, a young poet of considerable merit who is attempting to introduce the English style of poetry and drama.   All the men ranted, but Mdlle. Mars acted divinely.'

1834.   *Siena (it is characteristic that he goes and spends three days in the hills with one Signor Cospi to see the life of the country folk, and returns).*— 'Having spent three days very pleasantly, learnt and forgotten the names of unnumbered plants, and seen more of Italian life in three days than a fashionable traveller does in as many years.'

1834.   *Vaucluse.*—'Indeed a *vallis clausa* : at the very end, under a precipitous wall of rock, issues forth a most abundant limpid stream ; the river is considerable, as large as the Test at Whitchurch.   The sky is so cloudless and the river so bright, that the legion of fly-fishers, armed with long bamboos, had very little chance.'

---

[1] This tour must have been made during his pupils' holidays.

1834. *Nice.*—'Sweet narcissus abundant, on the hills several sorts of sage, the *Genista spinosa*, and many spurges. In the Bois d'Estrelles the hills covered with a tall white heath, with flowers of the same shape as the little pink one which grows in Wherwell Wood.'

1834. *Genoa (this entry depicts a curious state of society).*—' The Genoese detest the Sardinian yoke but cannot shake it off, so they vent their discontent in a thousand ingenious ways. The women will not dance with any of the officers, or invite them to their houses ; they dress in tri-coloured garb, and entertain their friends with tri-coloured jellies, &c.'

1834. *Rome.*—'One of my letters of introduction was to Monsignore Acton. He received me in a vast apartment covered with green baize, underneath which was a quantity of straw, so that we stole along as if in an enchanted land. The Monsignore young, but in violet stockings and full priestly garb. His manner, though civil, put me in mind of Scott's "Oliver le Dain."''

1834. *Rome.*—'I went to the Severns' house in the evening. They asked me how I came, and when I said up the steps of the Piazza di Spagna, were frightened, and told me not to do it again, as assassinations were frequent there.'

The Sicilian tour, 1834, shows a mind stored with memories of Theocritus. Near Salerno they catch a large cicada, 'but unfortunately no shepherd has made us an ἀκριδοθήρα of asphodel.'[2] Near Agrigentum 'the valleys remind us of Theo-

---

[2] A locust trap, Theoc. *Id.* i. 52.

critus, ὄχναι μὲν παρ' ποσσί, παρὰ πλευρῇσι δὲ μᾶλα.[3] The shepherd still plays on his pipe, sometimes not unpleasantly; and his jerkin is still ταμίσοιο πότοσδον.'[4]

1834. *Florence.*—' The only redeeming acquaintance I made [of the English colony] was Sir Stephen Glynne. He has a great passion for old church architecture, has seen all the best ecclesiastical buildings in his own country, and many in Germany and France. A wonderfully tenacious memory enables him to combine and compare all these different structures, so that it is interesting to visit churches in his company.'

Thus was renewed the friendship, afterwards so intimate, which ended only with Sir Stephen's death, and through which the Bishop became acquainted with Sir Stephen's brother-in-law, Mr. Gladstone, or rather improved the acquaintance which he had formed with the latter while he was still a boy at Eton.

In the journal for 1834 there is an entry of all the seas, lakes, and rivers in which he had bathed on his travels, an entry doubtless inserted in accordance with the rules of the ' Psychrolute Society,' to which he and his friend G. A. Selwyn belonged; rules which enjoined, among other things, a bathe, where possible, on every day of the year.[5]

---

[3] 'Pears at our feet, and apples by our sides ' (were shed), *Id.* vii. 144.

[4] 'Smelling of rennet,' *Id.* vii. 16.

[5] A former neighbour of the Editor's in Sussex, the Rev. Dr. Dyne, who died a short time since at the age of ninety, told him that being on a visit to Eton as a young man he was permitted to join this society during his stay. He was

Read as a whole, the journals show very clearly that wonderful power of assimilating and retaining information on every conceivable subject which in later and even in latest life made the Bishop so instructive and delightful a companion. Nothing escapes his observation ; the flowers and shrubs, either wild or introduced, the method of cultivation and managing stock, the grafting of trees, the particular kind of wheat necessary to make the best macaroni, the quickset hedges of a tree, which (strange to say) he does not know, between Bologna and Venice—all are noted down, and, more remarkable still, all were remembered. Half a century afterwards his memory of the places he had seen as a young man was as fresh as ever, and put to shame the halting reminiscences of younger travellers. Not less remarkable is the readiness, most unusual in an Englishman, with which he associates with the natives of the various countries which he visits. He talks to old officers who had served under the great Napoleon, whom he casually meets at a Paris restaurant, to German doctors engaged in a medical congress, Italian priests and Italian peasants—all, be it remembered, in their own languages—with the same ease and the same delight with which he talked to Hampshire rustics or

taken by a friend to the bathing-place and introduced to G. A. Selwyn, the Captain, who was undressed and about to take a header. Selwyn took him by the hand, and admitted him with the following formula in dog Latin : 'Admitto te in hanc societatem ad melodiam dimidiæ coronæ' (' I admit thee into this society to the tune of half-a-crown ').

Lancashire mechanics.   He had no doubt been un-usually well grounded in the three great continental languages while he was quite a young man, or indeed while he was a boy, and his studies were shared and encouraged by the elder of his two sisters, a person of remarkable mental endowments. His foreign tours made him what he continued to be to his latest years, a fluent speaker in all three languages ; German and Italian he spoke with extraordinary purity, and it was no small part of the pleasure which his annual visit to Cadenabbia towards the close of his life gave him to find himself among an Italian-speaking people.   As regards literature, that of Germany and Italy was more to his taste than that of France, though he read with keen interest French books when they came in his way, as Victor Hugo's 'Les Misérables' and Prosper Mérimée's 'Letters to Panizzi.'   But the old favourites remained his favourites to the end of his life.   Goethe's 'Hermann and Dorothea' was the constant companion of his travels, though he could have repeated much of the poem had no copy been available.   'I Promessi Sposi' and the poems of Leopardi were never displaced from his affections, and the old edition of Dante in crabbed print which his family can remember as long as they can remember anything, was even in his later years often studied as a solace and refreshment when the rest of the household had retired for the night.   In the midst of the mass of necessary correspondence which so often reduces the modern Bishop to despair, and which Bishop Durnford conducted with but little aid from a secretary, he would still find time to answer in choice Italian, with all the necessary turns of phrase, the letters received from time to time from friends in Italy.

Such prolonged and leisurely travel as the subject of this memoir enjoyed between 1829 and 1835 might seem at first sight not the best preparation for the pastoral work in which his whole life was to be spent, but it is possible that after all it was so, and it is certain that in the midst of laborious occupations and heavy responsibilities for a period of half a century the lessons learnt during those years of travel, and the memories of places and things then seen, were a constant source of pleasure and refreshment.

On July 1, 1835, Mr. Durnford was inducted to the living of Middleton,[6] then in the diocese of Chester, on the presentation of Lord Suffield, owner of Middleton Hall and patron of the benefice as the representative in the female line of the family of Assheton, who since the middle of the fifteenth century had been the lords of the place. The presentation had actually been made in 1833 on the death of the then Rector, Mr. Archer ; but as there were reasons which made it difficult for Mr. Durnford at once to take charge of his cure, the living was held, by an arrangement common enough then, though it would perhaps seem indecorous now,

[6] The writer of this chapter wishes to acknowledge his obligations to the Rev. George Jackson, formeriy Curate of Middleton.

during two years, by the Rev. Charles Way, until the presentee was able to enter upon his duties as Rector. Judged by ordinary tests and common experience, the appointment of a man who had little or no parochial training to a large and important living with which he was totally unconnected by family ties or previous knowledge might well have seemed a hazardous venture. From a life of ease and culture, whether spent in the quiet Hampshire home, or in the cloisters of Magdalen, or among congenial companions at Eton, or in leisurely travel in foreign countries, Mr. Durnford was suddenly transplanted into a great Lancashire parish, a place just growing into a considerable manufacturing centre, where he would be not merely the Rector, but the most important person of the community, not merely the organiser of church work, but the leader in all public matters. After spending all his youth and early years in the South, he was suddenly to be brought into contact, often in difficult and delicate relations, with the people of the North—a people generous indeed and warm-hearted, but wedded to their own views, independent often to the verge of rudeness, and not too willing to accept guidance or counsel from strangers.

Certainly there was ample opportunity for church work in Middleton if we take into account what had been done or left undone by Mr. Durnford's predecessors. Of the four Rectors who preceded him, one, Dr. Ashton, at the beginning of the century, was a type of the well-born pluralist of those days.

A member of the important Assheton family, he was Warden of the College of Manchester as well as Rector of Middleton, and, according to common report, would day by day perform his statutable residence in Manchester by driving solemnly in his coach to Barnes Green, which was just within the parish of Manchester; there he would turn round and solemnly drive back again—he had kept his residence!

He was succeeded by Mr. Walker, who, appointed at the age of seventy, held the living for seventeen years without apparently making the smallest mark; and after him came an Irishman, Mr. Haughton, of whom it was recorded that such was the power of his voice that he would shout from the rectory gate to his sexton on the top of the Church Hill: 'Any funerals to-day, Ben?' and that 'Ben Saxan,' even from the bottom of a grave, would hear and answer. Yet it must be laid to his credit that he started, or at all events fostered, at Middleton the system of Sunday School teaching which later became so great a feature in the church life of the place, and so important an agency in influencing young men and women at a critical period of their lives. Lastly, the living was held for four years by Mr. Archer, whose monument stands in the chancel of the church with the pathetic inscription : 'For fifty years Curate of this parish, afterwards Rector.' He died at the age of eighty-six, and on his demise Mr. Durnford was presented, though, as we have seen, he did not immediately undertake the charge of the parish. It was time, indeed, that somebody should come to this important living who would spend not only his money, but the best years of his life and the best powers of his mind, in 'repairing the waste places.'

The town of Middleton, as its name indicates, was half way between Manchester and Rochdale on the great high road leading over Blackstone Edge to the manufacturing districts of Yorkshire. The parish—though perhaps not to be compared in extent, and certainly not in the greatness of its endowments, to the neighbouring parishes of Rochdale, Bury, or Prestwich, which in those days were almost like small bishoprics—yet stretched its arms wide, and embraced no less than six 'townships,' as they were called, some, as Great Lever and Ashworth, cut off by the intervening towns of Bolton-le-Moors and Heywood; others, as Thornham and Rhodes, nearer at hand, but as yet unprovided with church or schools or parsonage houses. So for a radius of several miles of country, becoming every day more thickly populated, all looked to Middleton Church for the ministrations of religion—a church situated on the very edge of that vast parish. The town of Middleton, like so many of the smaller towns of that country, was about the time of Mr. Durnford's appointment in a state of transition, growing from a peaceful centre of a rural population into one of the busy grimy manufacturing towns of South Lancashire. The change had not come, but it was surely coming, and the signs of change were not to be mistaken. The old house of the Asshetons, which had passed into the ownership of the Harbords, still stood with its little park, its gardens and warren, but the large park and demesne had been broken up for building, and about 1845 the Hall itself was pulled down and all traces of the ancient family of Assheton disappeared. The great factories which are now to be seen on every side—and which, even as far back as the present writer can recollect, made the air dark and heavy with smoke—were beginning to appear and usurp the places of the picturesque cottages and timbered houses, some of which even now are to be seen in strange and incongruous company.

As in the town itself, so was it in the country. Although in every direction coal-pits were beginning to rear their chimneys and disfigure the country with their heaps of slag, yet in the parish there was still a great extent of land under cultivation, and close up to the mouth of the pits were cottages as primitive as any to be seen in the untrodden solitudes of Cumberland ; and farmers, as shrewd in wit and racy in tongue as any to be found in the Yorkshire Dales, still grew their crops and waged an unequal war against the wet and cold of that un-genial climate. The natural features of the country, although year by year becoming more altered and defaced by smoke and building, were pleasant enough—undulating ground, on which the beech, the sycamore, and the mountain ash grew well ; deep ‘ cloughs,’ each with its stream flowing at the bottom on the way to the Irk—streams which soon were to become black and foul with the pollution and refuse of mills and coal-pits, but which in the early thirties must have been clear and pure—while along their banks, even in the writer's recollection, rare ferns and plants still grew, eagerly sought out and in some cases, it is to be feared, destroyed by enthusiastic local botanists. Two considerable houses of the country gentry still remained—one on the Rochdale side even now comparatively unspoiled—Hopwood Hall, a good specimen of a Jacobean house of the smaller kind, with paved courtyard and low panelled rooms. There at the time of which we are speaking lived Mr. Robert Gregg Hopwood, a typical Lancashire squire, hospitable and shrewd, still keeping harriers and 'Foumart'[7] hounds, clinging to the old ways and old customs, so that at his table the toast was still proposed of the 'pious and immortal memory of William III.' Between him and the new Rector a warm friendship grew up, a friendship continued in a more intimate form with his younger son, the Rev. Frank Hopwood, afterwards Rector of Winwick ; but on the death of the old squire the intimacy between Hall and Rectory ceased as a consequence of the famous ' Hopwood Will ' case, which divided Lancashire society into two parties in the early fifties. On the Manchester side, among groves of rapidly dwindling trees, stood Alkrington Hall, a fine old Georgian house where lived the last of the ancient family of Lever, but in

---

[7] Polecat.

state greatly diminished since the time when Sir
Assheton Lever had ruled there in much magnificence
and gathered together the collection which bears his
name. Scattered through the country and now
turned into farmhouses were old black-and-white
houses, like those which may be seen in so many
parts of Cheshire, such as Langley Hall, the
residence of Cardinal Langley, who built the south
porch of the church, Chadderton Hall and Tonge
Hall, which told of properties long since dispersed
and families of gentle blood extinct or departed.
Everywhere throughout the district the signs were
plain and becoming plainer that the day of the squire
and the peasant was over, and their place was to
be taken by the manufacturer and the mechanic.
Very different from those among whom the new
Rector had passed his boyhood and his youth
were the people among whom his lot was now cast.
Instead of the slow-speaking, slow-moving Hampshire yokel, wedded to the soil on which he was
born and little inclined to new ideas, he found a
people quick-witted and sharp-tongued, with a great
idea of their own importance, full of what he afterwards called in no unkindly spirit ' the true Lancashire conceit,' eager to get on, receptive of new ideas,
however crudely and inadequately presented to them.
Moreover, the times were troubled times. The Tory
Government, it might almost be called the Tory
tyranny, from 1815 to the time of the Reform Bill had
left its mark on the population in deep discontent and
ultra-Radical views. Some of his flock had bled for their

principles at Peterloo and known the inside of a gaol. The wave of Chartism which swept over the country took firm hold of South Lancashire ; and the sight was seen, which English people do not love, of soldiers called out to put down local disturbances at the time of the so-called Plug Drawing Riots. As early as 1833 the Middleton Radicals had invaded the parish church and occupied some of the appropriated sittings, insisting on the principle, which the Rector long afterwards carried to its fullest conclusions, that they were in a parish church and that the parish church is free to all. Not a few of the people of Middleton might have sat for ' Owd Sammy Cradock ' in Mrs. Hodgson Burnett's admirable story, and most of them before long would have been willing to make what Sammy called his ' pollygy : ' ' I was allus one as set more store by th' state than th' church, an parsons were na' i' my line an happen I ha' been a bit hard on yo' an ha' said things as carried weight agen yo' wi' them as valleyed my opinion o' things i' general. And I ha' made up my moind as I would na moind telling yo' as I were going to wi'draw ma oppysition sin' it seemed as if I'd made a bit o' mistake : theer now ! ' ' Thrutch [8] him up,' shouted some noisy malcontents at a stormy vestry meeting during the first years of Mr. Durnford's incumbency before the people got to know the Rector as well as they afterwards did. ' Thrutch away, gentlemen,' replied the young Rector, jumping on to an oak chest which stood in the

---

[8] Lancashire for ' crowd ' or ' hustle.'

corner of the room, 'and now let us get to business.'

An interesting illustration of the hold which the
Rector had gained over his parishioners even in the
early years of his life in Lancashire was supplied by
Bishop Abraham some fifty years later. Writing
to the 'Guardian' in October 1895, shortly after
Bishop Durnford's death, he says :

'In the appreciative notices of Richard Durnford's career and character that have appeared in
the public press, I have seen no trace of what was
really the most (in those days) unique feature of his
pastoral work at Middleton fifty years ago. So far
back as that, he had mastered the fundamental points
of the disputes and strikes in the cotton manufacturing districts of Lancashire. I can well remember
paying him a visit about the year 1843, just after
the Stalybridge rioters had marched down to
Middleton and urged the Middleton operatives to
join the strike. I learnt from some of these men
how the Rector had stood at midnight between the
two parties and had argued the question for several
hours in their own dialect, which he spoke like a
native. He was a real ἄναξ ἀνδρῶν, fearless and
cool, sure of his facts and data, but kindly and able,
as willing, to sympathise with the hard trials men
had to bear in those days before the trade unions
were legalised. When the question had been fairly
threshed out, the Middleton men resolved not to
join the Stalybridge party, and marched home,
cheering the Rector ; and subsequently (as I often
heard them) acknowledging that it was all owing to
" Mester " Durnford that they were all at work, and

not starving like many others. There are probably now to be found not a few clergymen who have studied and understand these labour questions to some extent; but then Richard Durnford stood out almost alone, as one who had carefully formed his opinions and 'had the courage of them.'

The principal industry of Middleton, until Mr. Gladstone's treaty with France in 1860 practically destroyed it, was silk-weaving. The silks woven were of the best and costliest kind, and the weaving was done for the most part by hand, in rooms behind the houses. There the cumbrous looms were erected, and all day long whole families— fathers, mothers, and grown-up children—worked at their trade in a fashion and with implements not very unlike those which Homer knew when he spoke of Circe 'going backwards and forwards at the loom.' The ceaseless clack of the shuttles in the cottages was then one of the most characteristic sounds in the district. Gradually, as the Lyons silks were introduced without duty, the industry died out, new mills arose, cotton manufactures largely took the place of silk, or the cheaper kinds of silk were woven by steam power, until 'hand-loom weaving' became a thing of the past. It is obvious that such a change must have affected greatly the habits of the people, and though it was inevitable, its effect on the family life is certainly to be lamented.

The church of St. Leonard at Middleton, stand-ing on a lofty knoll and overlooking the town, was a building of no small beauty and archæological interest. The building, as it now exists, shows clearly the work of three different periods. Fragments of the earliest church exist in the western arch of Norman work, dating from about the year 1120, an arch which in the later times was rebuilt in the pointed style, but which still contains the Norman mouldings put in almost at haphazard, and of which the pillars have suffered no violence. The tower, never apparently finished, and crowned since 1709 with a quaint four-gabled wooden structure, and the fine south porch, belong to the church erected about 1400 by Thomas Cardinal Langley, Bishop of Durham from 1406 to 1437, and Chancellor to Henry IV. He himself a Middleton boy, remodelled the ancient church and founded a chantry for the instruction of the youth of Middleton. The clerestory, the roof, and the greater part of the walls were rebuilt in a style of somewhat debased perpendicular in 1524 as a thank-offering for the victory of Flodden Field, in which the Lancashire lads had played a prominent part. In that famous fight of September 8, 1513, Richard Assheton—whose grandfather had, by marriage with Margaret Barton, become the lord of Middleton—led the Middleton archers, and was for his valour knighted upon the field of battle. On the south side of the chancel still exist the fragments of an interesting contemporary window designed to commemorate the part taken by the Middleton lads in an event which deeply stirred the people of the north of England.

Middleton Church.

Richard Assheton and Anne his wife, with Henry Taylyer, chaplain, kneel in the church, while behind them kneel the archers, before going forth to the war, each with a sheaf of arrows at his back and a long bow on his shoulder, with his name clearly inscribed above the bow. Across the whole width of the church stretched a fine but sadly mutilated oaken rood screen, with stalls for the clergy, the lower panels ornamented with coarse but very vigorous carvings, representing the coats of the various families who were allied by marriage to the Asshetons. This screen has now been most carefully and successfully restored as a memorial to Bishop Durnford. When he came to Middleton in 1835, the church exhibited all those signs of gradual defacement and degradation now appreciated only by the fanatics of anti-restoration. The western arch had been bricked up, and the organ and choir occupied a large gallery at the west end ; the walls had been covered with plaster ; large and unsightly galleries, in which the pews were private property, blocked the arches ; the sittings in the church were appropriated from end to end. The chancel was cumbered with two huge pews—one for the Rector, the other for the Levers, of Alkrington ; the traditional 'three-decker' filled a large space in the nave.

It may be convenient here to notice the various steps taken by the Rector at different times to restore the church to something of its original character. The first changes were made in 1846, a time

when church restoration was but ill understood;
and it is fortunate that the great changes were
deferred for more than twenty years. In 1846 it
became necessary to rebuild the eastern wall, and
the opportunity was taken to clear away the pews
which obstructed the chancel, bring back the ancient
singing benches, to re-arrange the level of the
sacrarium, and to replace the three-decker by pulpit
and reading desk of carved oak. At the same time
the east window of debased Tudor perpendicular
was removed, a measure which probably the Rector
would not have adopted had the work been done
later, when true principles of church restoration had
won their way.

The final restoration was begun in 1868, but in the
meantime a great change was made in 1863. More
and more the Rector had begun to feel that, except
in certain special cases, the evils of ' appropriation '
in churches, and especially in parish churches, were
great and serious. What his views on this subject
were at the close of his Lancashire ministry may
be seen from a speech—probably the last speech
made by him in Lancashire—delivered in the
spring of 1870 in the Manchester Town Hall,
at the annual meeting of the Manchester Church
Building Society :

' It is a simple mockery to set down a church in
a vast population, and then to say this church is
portioned out to 500 people, they shall pay for their
sittings, and none other shall enter, whatever be
their desire, whatever their longing for spiritual

food, they shall not find it.   I am no fanatic in the matter of free churches.   I do not say that the opening of all churches would be a panacea for all the evils that are growing ; but when we look at the multitudes which swarm in the towns and villages, if we mean to attract the people to the Church of England, if we mean to induce them to join in the worship and to feel they have a share in it, we must open the church doors wide, and proclaim " this is free to all because it is the Church of Christ." '

The means which the Rector took to carry out his views in his own church (being ably seconded by his churchwarden, Mr. H. Wheeler), are thus described in a letter written in April 1863 to the Rev. George Hales, a former curate and intimate friend :

' Last Sunday I effected a *coup d'état.*   During the week all the pew doors were taken off, and it was announced that henceforth no seats would be taken, but that the body of the church was free and would remain free.'

The change worked smoothly, the worshippers who came regularly were not disturbed in their accustomed seats, weekly collections took the place of pew rents, and people soon forgot that such a system had ever existed.

The galleries still remained, and the pews in the galleries were private property ; moreover, it might be urged that to remove them would curtail too seriously the space available for worshippers.   But it was felt that the galleries rendered useless almost

as many sittings in the aisles as they themselves
provided, and in 1866 or 1867 an energetic curate,
the Rev. Bruce Ward, got up a petition signed
by 1,000 parishioners for the removal of the
galleries ; the owners, whose private property they
were, with great liberality relinquished their rights,
and the work of thorough restoration at last became
possible.   The galleries disappeared, the pews in
nave and aisles were cleared away, the tower-arch
was opened, the roof repaired and decorated, the
organ re-erected in the Rector's chapel, and the
whole floor of the church covered with good oak
benches, in which every seat was free and unappropriated.   The work was completed in 1869,
and so, one year before he left the parish in which
he had ministered so long, the Rector had the
satisfaction of seeing the church restored to something like its ancient beauty and dignity.   Long
before this time the singers had been brought down
from the west gallery to the singing benches in the
chancel, then a surpliced choir had been established,
much to the satisfaction of the people, naturally
musical and gifted with singularly sweet voices, and
the Sunday services had been made fully choral.
To those who are accustomed to the great multiplication of services common at the present day the
services in Middleton Church would probably seem
inadequate ; certainly, those who approve of what is
now known as a high ritual would think that they
fell far short of the proper standard, for the Rector's
views then, as in the later years of his life, were in

the main those of the early so-called Tractarians,
who did not lay great stress on ritual, and while in
matters of doctrine he sympathised with Keble
and others of that school, he ever regarded with
apprehension and dislike the practices of the extreme section of the High Church party.   But
having regard to the standard of forty years ago,
the services in Middleton Church were frequent ;
the festivals of the Church were observed, and there
was service on Fridays and Wednesdays, with an
address on Wednesdays at evensong.   No heartier
or better congregational services could be heard in
Lancashire than were heard in Middleton Church on
Sundays, and from youth to manhood, from manhood
to old age, the people were instructed to listen to
the teaching of the Church, and to accept no less and
no more than the Book of Common Prayer as their
guide.

But while the parish church demanded and
obtained a large share of the Rector's attention,
there was much to be done in other parts of the
parish, and he set himself with characteristic energy
to provide for the wants of some of the outlying
parts of his scattered charge. The township of
Thornham, lying off the Rochdale Road and some
miles distant from the mother-church, was the first
to engage his attention. A school-chapel was
erected, and the place was worked for some time
from Middleton by the Rev. Julius Shadwell, afterwards the Rector's brother-in-law, a man at that
time of unusual physical and athletic powers, who

acquired a wonderful hold on the people of the district, and whose name is even now, after an interval of forty years, mentioned with admiring veneration. Later there arose beside the chapel a sufficient parsonage, built by the Rector on land purchased by him, and the place had a resident clergyman and good day and Sunday schools; while as years went on and the population of the upper part of the district increased, a second school-chapel was erected at Gravelhole. Then Rhodes had to be provided for, a place lying some two miles distant on the Manchester side. There a considerable population was being attracted by the calico-printing works started by the Burtons, which have since grown to very large dimensions under the ownership and management of the family of Schwabe. First a curate was provided for Rhodes, church and schools followed, and in due time Rhodes became an independent district chapelry with a perpetual curate residing in a vicarage of his own. Lastly, the fast growing suburb of Parkfield, which lay between the parish church and Rhodes, demanded the Rector's attention, and here he did not rest till he had seen church, parsonage, and schools erected, and had set working the full machinery of the Church in the district chapelry of Holy Trinity, Parkfield. How these works, and works such as these, engaged Mr. Durnford's thoughts may be seen from extracts of letters written to the correspondent mentioned above —the Rev. G. Hales.

1861.—'The whole of the Church Hill is now

enclosed as a cemetery for Middleton and Thornham, not without many difficulties and much correspondence. Of course the Dissenters will have their part, and I am glad of it; it is an odious thing to force unwilling services on anyone, and still more to be paid for it.'

1861.—' We have worked hard for a church to be built at Parkfield. Towards this edifice we have raised about 1,600*l.*; the pinch is always to get the odd money—about 400*l.* Of all places this is the last where money can be got, especially now, for our silk trade is gone, Gladstonised into annihilation. The place is growing in this direction, and when I have done this business, if I am allowed to finish it, I shall rest on my oars and seek to perfect what is begun, say at Rhodes and Thornham.'

1862.—' On October 11, please God, the Bishop consecrates our new church. True, it is not paid for, but the deficiency will not be serious. Schools and parsonage will be wanted, but again the incumbent must take his share in getting up these. The next thing is to erect Rhodes into a district. So it goes on.'

In all this church work, as indeed in everything started for the advantage of the parish, much help was given by Mr. Thomas Ashton, a Manchester merchant residing at Parkfield House, and almost the only resident in Middleton of means and inclination to further such schemes. Not only did he give material and liberal assistance, but his strong common-sense and knowledge of the likes and dislikes of the Lancashire people enabled the Rector to combat many difficulties and to carry to completion many plans which without his active and cordial co-operation would have been difficult of accomplishment.   Side by side with the extension of Church work went also the progress of education in the parish of Middleton.   Sixty years ago there was but one regular educational institution for Middleton and a wide district round—the Grammar School founded by Dean Nowell, and left by him to the fostering care of Brasenose College, Oxford, which had proved but a stepmother as time went on.   The master had a very meagre, almost nominal, stipend, and was obliged to eke out his pittance by taking into his house some boarders whom he taught himself, and by acting as curate, or taking occasional duty if, as was generally the case, he was in Holy Orders.   Under him was the real master, who could probably teach reading, writing, and arithmetic fairly well, and to him perforce resorted those who wished for elementary education.   But the time was past when such an education sufficed for the wants of the population ; in the north, at all events, the need of better teaching for boys and girls alike was beginning to be recognised, and the quick-witted people had begun to see that if the children were to succeed in the race of life they must at all events get a good start.   It took the Rector some few years to accomplish, but in 1842 school buildings were erected, spacious and convenient for the time— indeed, with some necessary alterations they are found adequate at the present day—a trained master with proper staff of assistants was appointed, and the school was placed under Government inspection. Fortunately the master who for many years was at the head of the school, Mr. G. H. Wheeler, now clerk to the Rochdale School Board, was a man of real capacity, and under him it flourished greatly. It has now been at work for over fifty years ; two generations of Middleton children at least have been trained there. Men are now living—Mayors, County Councillors, rich mill-owners, substantial tradesmen—who say with pride and satisfaction that they got their education in Middleton Church School ; and in a district where Nonconformists are many and Radicals not a few, there has never, we believe, been any serious attempt to establish a School Board. In the education of the boys and girls the Rector took the deepest interest, an interest not merely sentimental or theoretical, but practical ; he knew exactly what work was being done, and every morning without exception, when he was at home, he would be at the school to open the proceedings with prayers, and afterwards to take the religious instruction of the elder scholars. In a letter to the present writer Mr. Wheeler thus speaks of the Rector's interest in the work of the National School :

‘ The Rector evidently looked upon teaching in the parish school as both a pleasure and a duty. When at home it was his wont to go to the opening of the school, when he would read the prayers himself and take the first class, boys and girls. The

Scripture lesson over, he would often give out a short piece of dictation, which the scholars parsed, and the master's attention was afterwards drawn to the merits and defects of particular children's work.'

One of his former curates writes on the same subject:

' He gave me charge of a school, which he begged me to open every morning at nine and teach till ten. This I did and still do, and regard that start in life as one of the greatest blessings that ever helped me as a clergyman. He said, I remember, " By so doing you will learn punctuality ; you will feel that you have begun the day well, and be inclined to continue your labour in some other way ; " and this I found correct.'

The following letter from one of the Bishop's old scholars, addressed to him on his ninety-first birthday, will be read with interest in this connection :

At Euston Station, London, N.W. : Nov. 13, 1893.

My Lord Bishop,—As one of your old National School boys at Middleton, in the days of your Rectorship there, I am writing a line or two to congratulate your lordship upon having attained your ninety-first birthday.

I have lively recollections of your frequent visits to the schools for the morning Scripture lesson, and can look back with pleasure for that instruction, and generally for the instruction imparted under the then master, Mr. Wheeler.

After leaving school I joined the service of the Lancashire and Yorkshire Railway Company for about three years, then took up a position under the North-Western Company, in whose service I am to-day as a District Traffic Manager, having charge of the West Cumberland Division of the line.

I trust your lordship is well, and that God may bless you with a continued measure of health and strength is the humble prayer of your

Most Obedient Servant,
A. ENTWHISTLE.

To the Right Rev. the Lord Bishop of Chichester.

In the buildings of the National School were held also the Sunday School classes, often numbering as many as 600 scholars, of ages varying from five and six to twenty and thirty. Such classes were not new at Middleton, but under Mr. Durnford the system became immensely developed. He held most strongly that in no other way could the boys and girls be kept so readily and so certainly in touch with the Church ; he enlisted in the work men and women of various degrees, but all animated by the same desire to do good in their generation ; scholars in their turn became teachers ; many who had passed the week in mills and weaving-sheds did not grudge their Sunday leisure to teach and to help, and to them all honour is due, but, as a very competent witness testifies : ' Some of their self-denial, faithfulness, and perseverance may be attributed to the example of the Rector and Mrs. Durnford, morning and afternoon the most regular and painstaking of teachers '—' not to their exhortation or solicitation, but just the example.'

And here some mention must be made of one who assuredly exercised a great and potent, though most unobtrusive, influence on the work of the Church in Middleton. After five years the Rector married in 1840 Emma, daughter of the Rev. John Keate, D.D., Canon of Windsor and Rector of Hartley Wespall in Hampshire, some time head-master of Eton School, a woman whom the con-current testimony of those who were brought into contact with her, no less than the memories of her children, show to have been endowed with many gifts and singular graces of character. Carefully educated herself by her mother and aunt—the latter a woman of remarkable attainments—she educated her children with no less care, as she was well able to do, for she had been thoroughly instructed in French and German, and had some acquaintance with Italian literature, while her taste in English, formed on good models, was true and discrimi-nating. To say that in all parish matters she was her husband's right hand, that she was, as he himself expressed it, 'his prudent and liberal almoner,' that she entered into and furthered all schemes for the welfare of the people, is only faintly to describe the part which she played in the parochial life of Middleton. It may, perhaps, be permitted to quote two appreciations of her work there. The first is from a paper written immediately after her death, in 1884, by her husband, written, as he says, 'that my children, perhaps my children's children, may read hereafter with interest this poor account of one who was a bright example in her life, and is now assuredly among the saints of God.'

'In 1840,' says the Bishop, 'she was transplanted from the quiet village of Hartley into a very different country, and became the wife of the Rector of a populous Lancashire parish. No change could have been greater. She plunged at once into a busy manufacturing population of manners and habits she had never known. One of the first trials, and not a small one, was to be introduced as teacher into a Sunday School of many hundred children; yet hardly children, for not a few of the young women were of marriageable age, and all possessed of a spirit of independence unknown in the rural districts of Hampshire. In this sphere she soon gained the affections of a rude but singularly warm-hearted people. Her gentle sympathy, pleasant manners, and large charity so won upon them, that without any effort, any seeking of popularity, she was the most popular woman in Middleton. Her husband had reason to know her value, for she never lost a friend and never made an enemy. Simple and true, courageous and outspoken when necessary, always acting on religious principles, always listening to the conscience informed by God's Word and guided by His Holy Spirit, she held her even course respected and beloved by the whole community.'

The second is by a former curate of Middleton, and is in remarkable accord with the passage just quoted, though its source is independent and the time of its writing separated by many years.

'Under a sky, never so blue as in southern parts,

and before long always thick with smoke and grime except on Sundays, amid a people of free and easy manners and of speech which to a southerner must have sounded harsh and uncouth, bringing herself into close contact with them in their houses as well as with their children in the schools, simple in dress, gentle in speech, quiet and winning in manner, she lived among them for thirty years meek and gentle, persevering and patient, peaceable and therefore a peacemaker. Not at all the up-to-date Rectoress, but just a lady and a Christian woman, she was a felt and acknowledged blessing to the women of Middleton and their daughters.'

It is easy to see what must have been the effect of such a helpmate on the daily relations between the Rector and people. For daily relations there were. No parson probably ever was more thoroughly persuaded of the absolute necessity of regular visiting among his poorer neighbours. Without undervaluing the importance of church services or school instruction, he was firmly persuaded that the first duty of the *Pastor in Parochia* was to know his people, and if they were to be known they must be known at home. So he was unwearied in house-to-house visitation ; in the damp 'cellars' and grimy backyards of the town no less than in the scattered cottages which still stood among fields in the more distant portions of his parish, his presence was a familiar one and always welcome. ' Eh, Mester Dunford, A'm fain to see ye' was the familiar greeting. He knew the circumstances and wants of his parishioners, their troubles and anxieties about their children, the best way of helping them and their families, and thus there grew up between the Rector and his people a bond of no ordinary character, so that after nearly thirty years his memory is still green among them, and parents and grandparents still speak to their children of ' T'owd Rector ' as of a personality never to be forgotten. No doubt this was greatly owing to the wonderful power which he possessed, noticeable in his younger days, but which grew with his growth and endured far into his old age, of acquiring and assimilating knowledge of every imaginable kind. He could talk to the farmer about his crops and his beasts and to the mechanic about his looms or his dyes with equal readiness, and, what is more wonderful, with a knowledge which was rarely at fault. Many of his parishioners were skilled horticulturists, raising beautiful flowers even in that cold and wet climate, and in them the Rector found congenial spirits, and was ever ready to criticise or admire their auriculas or dahlias or carnations. ' He'll ax yo five hundred questions in a minute,' said one of his flock, and indeed it was scarcely a hyperbolical way of expressing the Rector's determination to find out all about that which interested him, and it was difficult to say what did not interest him. Trained from boyhood in the habit of observing bird and beast, insect and plant, he kept always adding to his stores of knowledge, and though no man ever affected omniscience less, few knew so much about so many things.

When he was well over eighty years of age, and

was staying at Gordon Castle with the Duke of Richmond, some of the visitors, ardent fishermen themselves, were astonished to find that the ' old Bishop ' knew as much as they did about the Stockbridge water, memories of his youth treasured and never effaced ; and the annual holidays in Hampshire or Wales or the English Lakes were always fruitful in fresh experiences and added knowledge— new plants observed, new scenery enjoyed, new traits of character in country folk gathered and stored up in that capacious memory. Aber in Carnarvonshire, then a tiny village in a country little known, was one of the favourite places for a brief holiday from parish work—the Rector, the Rev. Thomas Norris Williams, a cultivated and charming Welsh gentleman, became a close friend, and the children of both families rambled over the hillsides of a country which, beautiful in itself, seemed a Paradise after the smoke and dirt of Lancashire.

Outside the parish, in the larger field of the diocese and county, Mr. Durnford's influence was widely extended and fully recognised. During the early years of his incumbency the diocese of Chester included Manchester and the surrounding district, but in 1848 the Diocese of Manchester was formed, the collegiate church became the cathedral, and the Warden and Fellows of the college formed the capitular body. The first Bishop of the newly formed diocese was James Prince Lee, a man who, as headmaster of King Edward's School, Birmingham, had gained a great and deserved reputation.

Not only had he trained many brilliant scholars—of whom, perhaps, the most eminent were the famous trio, Lightfoot, Benson, and Westcott—but his scholars had for him an admiration which is rarely excited except by men of real genius. ‘For about ten years,’ says one of his most distinguished pupils, ‘boys came to him and left him in even flow : their intercourse with him was hourly, their loyalty absolute. Their love of him was always at its height ; they were bound together by it then and ever since ; it was the perfectness of affection for him which made so many of them seek his own profession.’[9] But with great merits, for a Bishop, and especially for the Bishop of a new see including many vast manufacturing towns, he had great defects. No one could look at the man's face without seeing that he was a man of power, no one who saw him could doubt that he was obstinate. He had a rooted suspicion of new methods, he had a great dislike to anything approaching to what is now called Ritualism, he was always masterful, he was often harsh, and the consequence was that he was frequently in conflict with some of the most important of the clergy, to whom he showed himself at times both overbearing and unreasonable. In such a light he rarely showed himself to the Rector of Middleton. Probably one bond of union was that of scholarship, of a kind rare among the country clergy. However that may be, the Bishop admitted Mr. Durnford to

---

[9] Σαλπίσει, a sermon preached in Manchester Cathedral, by E. W. Benson, D.D.

his confidence and intimacy (a thing which he did to few), and though there were times and occasions when the Rector's opinions and sympathies, which he never disguised, diverged widely from the Bishop's, yet the friendship between the two men remained unaltered down to the time of Bishop Lee's death in 1869. Before the new diocese had been long established, Mr. Durnford was made Rural Dean and honorary Canon, and in 1867, on the death of Archdeacon Master, the Bishop appointed him Archdeacon of Manchester, while in 1868 he prevailed on him to accept a Residentiary Canonry, an office which he had previously declined, but which now, owing to circumstances which need not here be detailed, he felt bound to accept. A member of the cathedral body says: 'I well remember that he gave an impetus to us all by his character, ability, and effective preaching.' He also sat as one of the Proctors for the clergy in the Convocation of York, which, under the rule of Archbishop Thomson, had acquired a liberty of discussion refused by his predecessors. As Rector of Middleton, he was called upon to take his part in the management of many important institutions in Lancashire and Cheshire, besides the usual diocesan societies. Thus he was a governor of Rossall School, in the growth and prosperity of which he took the deepest interest. He was associated in the management of the Warrington Training College and Clergy Daughters' School with his lifelong friend the Rev. George Heron. No sketch of Bishop Durnford's life would be complete in which George Heron's name did not find a place. The two men had been contemporaries at Oxford, and on Mr. Durnford's appointment to Middleton he was brought into intimate contact with Heron, who was a nephew of Mr. Hopwood, the squire, or at all events the principal landowner, of the parish. From that time till the death of Heron, which happened only one year before that of the Bishop, no year probably passed without visits interchanged between Moore Hall and Middleton, or in later years the palace at Chichester. Without being a great scholar or profound divine, Heron was a man of uncommon shrewdness, of a mind naturally capable and carefully cultivated, and a memory which never seemed at fault. Deeply interested in Church questions, he spent his ample means in the exercise of a judicious munificence, and grudged neither time nor trouble when he felt that his services would be useful. Advancing years, though they crippled him sadly while they left the Bishop's bodily powers wonderfully unimpaired, brought no change and made no difference in the friendship of the two men, and when both were in extreme old age perhaps the greatest pleasure remaining to them was the occasional meeting, when they would talk over old scenes and recall old friends with the zest and interest of boys. Truly, they were pleasant in their lives, and in their deaths they were scarcely divided.

With another Oxford friend he was in the same way brought into contact, Colonel Wilson-Patten,

afterwards Lord Winmarleigh, who up to the close
of his long and useful life retained his affection for
the Magdalen undergraduate of sixty years before,
and delighted in the renewal of ancient ties, while
a friend of more recent standing was Bishop Jacobson of Chester, with whom during the later years
of the Lancashire life Mr. Durnford was brought
into close relations in connection with the Chester
Training College.

But it must not be supposed that Church work,
either in the parish or in the diocese, absorbed the
whole of Mr. Durnford's energies.　In a parish like
Middleton, where there were few resident gentry and
no resident squire, the Rector perforce took a leading
place, and was the guiding and controlling spirit in
matters relating to the well-being of the town and
district.　On the Bench of Magistrates he never
would consent to serve, thinking it better that the
clergy should not be concerned with the administration of justice ; but he was for years on the Board of
Guardians, an office involving much disagreeable
work in a Union which was both populous and large
in extent, and among a people to whom the new
Poor Law was so distasteful that the workhouse
was always called in popular phrase the ' Bastile,'
with some strange reference to the French prison,
though the word had long ceased to have any
meaning to those who used it.　A still more
important piece of secular work first engaged his
attention in 1861, and till the close of his connection
with Middleton took up no small part of his time.

From a mere village ruled by the ' Hall,' Middleton had developed into a large manufacturing town, factories had everywhere sprung up, and, though trade had suffered a temporary eclipse in the terrible years of the American Civil War, there were clear indications of that prosperity which was afterwards to advance 'by leaps and bounds.' Under these circumstances it was obviously necessary that the town should organise itself for local self-government, and that a proper authority should control such questions as roads, gas, drainage, and the like. Writing in 1861 to the Rev. George Hales, the Rector says :

'The busy heads of Middleton have framed a local Act, and last week I was in London to advise with lawyers and consult with M.P.s and generally forward the matter. To-morrow I have again to go up to appear before the committee. There is no great or formidable opposition, but there is also no leading person to manage our business, hence the necessity of my coming forward rather out of my proper line. We might rub on without the Act, but as the movement is started it is best to direct it.'

The Act was in due course passed, and until his appointment to the see of Chichester Mr. Durnford was the Chairman of the New Commissioners. His reasons for accepting the position were fully explained in his last speech at Middleton.

'I feel that during my long residence here I may have given what some people may have thought too much time and too much labour to the material interests of the place—I mean as Chairman of the Improvement Committee, or as Chairman of the Local Authority and other kindred offices. Certainly I did take a considerable amount of interest in business not directly connected with my high office, but not, on the other hand, opposed to it, because I believe that to advance the material interests of the people is as much the clergyman's duty as it is to watch over their spiritual welfare. I am sure that cleanliness is next to godliness, and am satisfied that without proper drainage, proper paving, water and light, cleanliness is a matter of impossibility. I know from sad experience what ravages fever used to commit in this district, and how even slight disorders were increased and engendered by the neglected drainage. All this as a clergyman I know, having to visit sick people, and many dying from typhus fever, family after family. Tracing the cause, I know perfectly well that it arose from the entire want of all the appliances for the promotion of health. That being the case, I think it was impossible as a Christian man that I should fold my arms or put my hands into my pockets, not to bring out money, but to keep them there. I say it was impossible to sit by and not give a helping hand to the material improvement of the place.

'That is my defence, and I hope I did not neglect what I freely confess are the higher duties to which I was more particularly bound, in common with all the clergy, in watching over the spiritual instruction and interests of the people. Now in these matters I have been greatly associated with all classes of men in this place, with the working men as with the middle classes, because the Local Board of Surveyors consisted of a mixture of both these classes. I may say that in the Bill which was prepared I did provide that the working man should be represented as well as his richer neighbour, because I thought that the working man had a fair claim to such representation, and it was expressly provided for in the drawing up of the Bill. I have a belief in the integrity and in the ability of the working population of Lancashire, of Manchester, and of Middleton ; inasmuch as the industry of the latter place is of a very high and refined character—the silk industry—it tends to elevate their minds above the mere mechanical nature of the employments that prevail in this district generally. Now that you have well-drained streets, well-paved streets, well-lighted streets, you will not think that I stepped beyond my duties in endeavouring, in conjunction with many others, to promote these appliances which were so necessary to the health of the population.'

Twenty years afterwards, on one of his visits to his old Lancashire home, an address was presented to the Bishop of Chichester by the Mayor and Corporation of the newly incorporated borough of Middleton in recognition of the great advantages which had accrued to the town from the Bishop's connection with it as Chairman of the Commissioners.

Among these multifarious occupations, both ecclesiastical and secular, to which must be added the education of his two sons until they went to a public school, it might be supposed that Mr. Durnford had

not much time for social enjoyments, and indeed of
society in the ordinary sense of the word there was
but little at Middleton.   But he was a man who did
not allow himself to be crushed or unduly absorbed
by his work ; his mind was so active, his intellect so
fresh, that he was incapable of being dull, and he
had interests and amusements simple enough, but
sufficient to prevent the disease of overwork telling
on him, as it does on so many who allow themselves
little or no recreation.   Chief among those interests
was gardening.   A love of flowers and an extraordinary practical knowledge of botany had been
one of the many advantages which had come from
his country life as a boy, and the present writer
remembers how, under the stress of a great and
recent sorrow, the Bishop, then over eighty years of
age, told him how great a consolation and resource
the love of a garden had been to him through his
whole life.   The Rectory at Middleton, an old house
spoilt by mean alterations, was surrounded by a
large garden containing some fine beech trees, now
rapidly succumbing to the influence of smoke and
noxious vapours.   Here the Rector exercised his
favourite pursuit, and his two trusty gardeners, John
Lawson and James Fitton, under his never-ceasing
supervision grew with some success such flowers
and fruits as the sandy soil and the wet and unkindly
climate of South Lancashire allowed.   In the annual
Horticultural Show, and, later, in the Agricultural
Show then held in the Rectory Field, he always
took the greatest interest.   Only second to his love

for gardening was his love of archæology and his interest in all things which were curious from their age or associations. He had an eye, naturally good and carefully trained by reading and observation, for everything that was best in art, for old furniture and the like. During the early days of his Lancashire incumbency he had many opportunities which he wisely used of collecting among the cottages and farmhouses of the neighbourhood specimens of old oak furniture such as now scarcely come into the market, and the 'oak room' in the Rectory was completely furnished with fine old oak which he had picked up in different places. In this pursuit he found a most congenial helpmeet and guide in Mr. George Shaw of Saddleworth, an accomplished antiquarian and indefatigable collector, whose house at Upper Mill—where the Durnford family, young and old, were always welcome—was a perfect museum of Lancashire curiosities, while the owner was himself a storehouse of Lancashire and Yorkshire legend and history, told often with great effect in the vernacular. And though it is true that in Middleton itself there was little society, yet in the neighbourhood and the county there was no lack of cultivated and congenial friends. With Edward Hornby, Rector of the large and important parish of Bury, a scholar, and a man of taste and refinement, Mr. Durnford was brought into contact in much county and diocesan business, and the friendship between them ceased only with Mr. Hornby's death long after his friend had become Bishop. There were pleasant and friendly relations with many of the residents in Manchester and the vicinity, among whom may be mentioned Robert and Murray Gladstone, leading Manchester merchants, Thomas Dudley Ryder, son of the Bishop of Bristol and Registrar of the Diocese of Manchester, and Miss Eleanor Atherton, a very rich and benevolent maiden lady who lived in an old-fashioned house in the heart of Manchester and used her large means judiciously in the promotion of Church work in the diocese. She was full of recollections dating back to a time long past, and would tell how as a child she was carried into Westminster Hall to see the impeachment of Warren Hastings. Another friend in whose society Mr. Durnford took great pleasure was Mr. William Langton, manager of the Manchester and Salford Bank, who in 1860 came with his family to live at Litchford Hall, about two miles from Middleton. Mr. Langton was a man of remarkable ability and the most cultivated tastes. Gifted with considerable skill as an artist, he was a lover and acute critic of art of every kind, but his devotion to Italian literature was even a greater bond between him and the Rector of Middleton; and years after the removal of the latter to Sussex, Mr. Langton, who had become totally blind, would amuse himself by writing Italian sonnets to be submitted to the critical judgment of the Bishop of Chichester. Perhaps the most intimate and valued friends in early Lancashire days were the Hornbys of Winwick. The Rev. James Hornby, whose sister was wife of the Earl of Derby, had been presented by him to the great living of Winwick, then worth 7,000*l.* a year, though during Mr. Hornby's incumbency it was reduced to 3,000*l.* by the endowment of various *townships.* Mrs. Hornby was an Irish lady of unusual attainments, and the son Robert, during all the later years of his life a confirmed invalid, had been from Oxford days one of Mr. Durnford's closest friends and most constant correspondents. No visits were more enjoyed by the busy Rector of Middleton and his wife than those paid from time to time to Winwick, or to Wansfell, the charming house on Windermere which was built by Mr. Hornby during his life and was the home of his widow after his death.

In December 1869 James Prince Lee, Bishop of Manchester, died. It was thought by many and hoped by almost all that the vacant bishopric would be offered to the Rector of Middleton, since he was then by far the most conspicuous of the Lancashire clergy and had the experience of thirty-five years' active work in the diocese. The idea was entertained by Mr. Gladstone, then Prime Minister, but he decided that under the peculiar circumstances it would be right that a younger man should be appointed to so laborious an office, and the bishopric was offered to and accepted by James Fraser, Rector of Ufton, who in his episcopate, by his unceasing labours, his single-hearted devotion, his exquisite simplicity of character, won the affection of all classes and conspicuously justified Mr. Gladstone's appointment. But though the parting between the Rector and his Lancashire flock was postponed, it was not long delayed.

In the early spring of 1870 the see of Chichester became vacant by the death of Bishop Gilbert, and was offered to Mr. Durnford by Mr. Gladstone in the following terms :

'There is now a vacancy on the Episcopal Bench in the southern province, which offers a charge of far less anxiety and toil' (than the see of Manchester), 'though no Bishop who does his duty can have an easy place. With the sanction of the Queen I have to propose to you that you should be nominated to the Dean and Chapter of Chichester as the successor to Bishop Gilbert. Your character, attainments, and capacity are too well known to render it needful for me to dwell on the reasons which have led me to believe you would add weight to the Bench and in every way further the highest interests of the Church. But agreeable to me as it is on personal grounds to convey this proposal, I could not have enjoyed that pleasure but for the belief that I should best discharge my very solemn duty to the Church of England by asking the Queen's permission to make it.—Believe me, with great regard, very faithfully yours, W. E. GLADSTONE.'

No man could have a higher view than Mr. Durnford of the responsibilities pertaining to a Bishop's office, and be under less illusion as to the hard and trying work which that office necessarily involves ; but no work could well be harder than that of the great Lancashire parish in which he had laboured for thirty-five years, nor was he a man to shrink from responsibility.   So the Prime Minister's offer was accepted, and the Rector of Middleton became the Bishop-elect of Chichester.   Some few doubts were naturally enough expressed in the news-papers whether sixty-eight was not too advanced an age for a man to undertake the duties of a Bishop, but from those who knew him best, and especially from those who were to be his colleagues on the Epis-copal Bench, the congratulations were general and hearty.   The Bishop of Winchester (Wilberforce), an old and loyal friend, wrote in the most affec-tionate style :

' I am so very glad you did not go to Manchester. 1. You are my Bishop now, and won't we welcome you and make the most of you in Sussex !   2. You have the nicest diocese in England.   3. You are a Hampshire man, and that is next to dear Sussex. I am quite delighted.   I do not know anyone in whom I have a more perfect confidence that, please God, I shall always agree with him.'

The Bishop of Chester (Jacobson) wrote :

' Fraser will come to his work *prope mancus*, with-out you.   However, you have my heartiest wishes for God's blessing going with you, although I am sure that in the stormy days which are surely coming I shall sorely miss you.'

Dr. Fraser himself, on the eve of his consecra-tion, wrote in a strain which shows how he shared

Bishop Jacobson's feelings with regard to his own loss :

'If I were actuated by selfish motives I should unfeignedly regret, but for the sake of the Church and nation I truly rejoice at your preferment to Chichester. But oh! how I shall miss you as a counsellor and a guide, on whom I had hoped thoroughly to depend. Trembling as my heart was before, it seems more than ever ready now to sink within me. But I know you will always let me have the advantage of your experience and knowledge when I need it. I wish you would find time, before your avocations become too pressing, to set down in a list for me the names of the *best* clergy and laity in the diocese, good men, irrespective of their opinions, on whom you think I may rely.'

Such expressions of confidence and pleasure were no doubt cheering, but nothing could make the wrench other than a painful one which was to separate the people from their pastor, who for thirty-five years had 'fed them with a faithful and true heart.' During that period—a large slice out of the life of any man—which he had spent among the people of Middleton, he had won their confidence and affection in no ordinary degree ; they had come to trust him and lean upon him, and his life had been so bound up with theirs that his removal from them seemed almost impossible.

The feeling cannot, perhaps, be better expressed than in the words of one who was then curate of Middleton :

'In 1870 came the parting. For five-and-thirty

years he had lived among them as one of them, and they had all come to think that there, too, he would end his days.   Middleton liked him and he liked it. I do not suppose that it was with unmixed feelings that he received from Mr. Gladstone the offer of the Bishopric of Chichester, and certainly it was with very mixed feelings that we at Middleton heard the news : " T' Rector's going to be made a Bishop." That was a feather in our cap as well as his ; but " T' Rector's going "—that soon took down our pride, and made us feel that we wished he was not going ; we should miss him sore.'

So the long chapter of the Lancashire incumbency came to an end.   It is fitting that in this memoir it should be closed in his own words, the last public utterance to a Lancashire audience while he was still a Lancashire Rector :

' I have found an amount of love which I never expected, and, I am sure, never deserved ; I can only attribute it to this, that I have loved you too, and I believe that there is a power in Christian love which no power in heaven or earth can equal : that it is which unlocks the hearts of men and binds them fast to one another.   That chain never can be broken.   The further we go the longer it is and the stronger it is ; and that is one of the solaces I feel in parting from this place and people, for I love both.   I love the rugged place, the rugged climate, and love the people as rugged as their land. . . . And now let me thank you once more—wishing you every blessing here and hereafter. Let me pray that you will never forget me ; I can never forget you.   Whether we meet again, that stands not with us, but with Him who orders all things wisely for the best. To the blessing of Jesus Christ our Saviour I commend you and all that are dear to you, all that I know and that know me. May they be happy, happy in mutual love and happy in their attachment to their minister ; happy in the services of the Church, and faithful in all their professions. So may they adorn the doctrine of their Saviour in all things.'

CHAPTER III

The First Seven Years of Bishop Durnford's Episcopate, 1870-1877—
Nature of the Diocese—Special Difficulties of the Time—Speech in
Convocation on Confession—Church Congress at Brighton—Bishop
Otter's College—The Theological College—The Diocesan Associa-
tion—Dr. Hannah made Vicar of Brighton—Elementary Education
—First Diocesan Conference—Bishop's Fund—Correspondence.

BISHOP GILBERT died at the age of eighty-four;
and, as he had been infirm for several years, the
diocese anxiously hoped for a vigorous successor.
Churchmen, therefore, heard with feelings of disappointment, and almost of dismay, that the new
Bishop was sixty-eight years of age; and when he
appeared in the diocese, his spare frame, and his
voice, clear and musical indeed, but not robust, did
not encourage a confident expectation of prolonged
activity and strength. Many were the predictions
that he would inevitably break down in the course
of two or three years beneath the strain of novel
and harassing work, or else that very few of the
new activities in administration which the condition
of the diocese and the spirit of the age demanded
would be attempted.

Never were gloomy forebodings of failure more
completely falsified. The Bishop soon showed that,
alike in bodily strength, and in clearness, vigour,

and alertness of intellect, he was not to be surpassed by any of his younger brethren on the Bench, and equalled by few ; while the freshness and energy which would have been looked for in a much younger man were happily combined with the discretion and prudence that naturally accompany old age, together with that sympathetic appreciation of the difficulties and trials of the parochial clergy which only a long experience of life as a parish priest can secure.

'I come among you,' he said in his primary charge, 'with an earnest desire to be to all, according to my dearest and highest title, a Father in God. My experience, not of short duration nor of limited extent, has been in that very field of pastoral work which the Great Shepherd has called you to cultivate. I know the labours, the trials, the difficulties, the disappointments, and, I may add, the comforts which wait upon the work of a parochial clergyman. Therefore, among many disadvantages, I have this qualification for my office—that I can truly sympathise with you all ; and·I would fain give to all, according to my poor ability, counsel, help, support, encouragement.'

It has been commonly said that the diocese of Chichester is easy of administration ; but the statement requires qualification. The diocese, which is almost exactly co-extensive with the county of Sussex, is nearly eighty miles in length, and the ancient city of Chichester, where the Bishop's dwelling is situated, stands at one extremity of it. In ancient days the roads of Sussex were pro-

verbially bad, carriages were often overturned or
stuck fast in the mire, and even in the present
century a clergyman instituted to a Down parish
in September was recommended by the Bishop to
settle in without delay before the autumn rains
rendered the roads impassable.

Those days are long past, but even now the high
backbone of hills which runs through the whole
length of the county from east to west forms a
hindrance to rapid communication between the
northern and southern divisions, while the railway
service is one of the slowest and most unpunctual
in England. Some of the villages in the seclusion
of the hills are not easy of access, and the Bishop
found that many country parishes were of inconvenient size and shape, being either very long and
narrow or very wide and rambling. Much had to
be done to provide satisfactorily for their spiritual
needs, either by the formation of new ecclesiastical
districts, or by the erection of new churches or
mission chapels, with a corresponding increase in
the staff of clergy. And these provisions were
equally required in the less remote parts of the
diocese, where a rapid increase of the population
was taking place, not only in the towns on the
seacoast, but in many districts inland, to which
residents were attracted by the beauty of the country,
or by direct communication between London and
Brighton.

The census of 1881 showed that during the
preceding decade the population of Sussex had

increased in a larger proportion than that of any county south of the Trent, with the exceptions of Surrey, Essex, and Middlesex.

Moreover, the first seven years of Bishop Durnford's episcopate were an anxious and critical period in the life of the Church of England. They were years of much controversy and strife about matters of doctrine, ceremonial, and discipline. And there were few places in which the stress of these controversies was more severely felt than in some of the towns with which the seacoast of Sussex is thickly fringed: Brighton, Eastbourne, St. Leonard's, Hastings, Worthing. These fashionable resorts were filled with large mixed populations representing all varieties of opinion in the Church : churches and chapels were erected by ardent partisans of opposing schools, in which the characteristic teaching and practice of each were carried to the furthest extreme, and the dividing lines between religious parties were thus sharply accentuated.

In 1872 the Athanasian Creed had been the subject of warm debate at public meetings as well as in Convocation. While some clamoured for its disuse in the public services of the Church, others, like Dr. Pusey and Canon Liddon, declared that if it were removed from its present position they would resign their office as ministers in the Church ; others, again, asked for a new translation, or for a rubric explanatory of the so-called damnatory clauses.

In May 1873 60,000 persons memorialised the two Archbishops in favour of 'the entire suppression of ceremonies and practices adjudged to be illegal.' On the other hand, in the same month of the same year, 483 clergy petitioned the Convocation of Canterbury, through the Archbishop, that ' in view of the widespread and increasing use of Sacramental Confession, the House would consider the advisability of providing for the education, selection, and licensing of duly qualified confessors, in accordance with the provisions of canon law.'

The judgment on appeal in the Purchas case by the Judicial Committee of the Privy Council in March 1870 had caused much discontent and even indignation among the great majority of High Churchmen, including men of the most moderate type, and the passing of the Public Worship Regulation Act in 1874 was yet more bitterly resented.

It was, in short, a time when the relations between Church and State were severely strained, and when the two parties which have always existed in the Church since the sixteenth century—the one consisting of those who think that reformation was carried too far, and the other of those who think that it was not carried far enough—were in active opposition. To act with strict fairness and wise consideration towards these two extremes, restraining the vagaries and excesses of those who coquet with Rome, and correcting the defects and negligences of those who fall short of the plain requirements of the Book of Common Prayer, has long been one of the chief difficulties of the episcopal office ; and but for the wisdom, patience, and tact with which as a body the Bishops have acted in the face of this difficulty, the Church of England must ere now have been shattered to pieces.

In his primary charge, delivered in 1871, Bishop Durnford laid down the plain principles on which he purposed to deal with some of the critical questions of the day, and from those principles he never afterwards deviated.

The most pressing of these questions was as to the attitude to be taken in reference to the recent judgment of the Privy Council in the case of Mr. Purchas, of St. James's Chapel, Brighton. The judges had declared, not only the eucharistic vestments and the use of wafer-bread, but the eastward position of the celebrant at Holy Communion and the mixed chalice, to be alike illegal. The two latter had so long been customary points of ritual amongst a large number of very moderate High Churchmen that the pronouncement against them had excited the strongest dissatisfaction and resentment. A memorial had been presented to the Archbishop of Canterbury, signed by 4,700 clergy, amongst whom was the Dean of Chichester, Dr. Hook, praying that the Bishops generally would abstain from a rigorous enforcement of the recent decision in regard to the position of the celebrant in Holy Communion. Had they attempted to enforce it there can be no question that a very serious disruption would have been the consequence. Many of the clergy who could not convince themselves that the Judicial Committee, as then constituted, possessed legitimate authority in things sacred, would have felt bound to refuse obedience, whilst some would have submitted, but with reluctance and distress. Many men who wished to take Holy Orders deferred offering themselves as candidates, others who were already in the diaconate refrained from proceeding to the priesthood, until they saw what attitude the Bishops would assume towards the obnoxious judgment.

The reply of Archbishop Tait to the memorialists encouraged them to hope that the Bishops would, as far as possible, adopt a wise policy of forbearance, recognising the conscientious objections entertained by many to the constitution of the court, the ambiguity of some of the rubrics, and the complexity of some of the questions on which the court had ventured to give a positive decision. Bishop Durnford, in his primary charge, expressed his views in language which exhibited a calm and independent judgment, and a charitable and tolerant spirit, which reassured the minds of his clergy. He insisted earnestly on the principle of large comprehensiveness in which the real strength and safety of the Church of England lies, but at the same time indicated very plainly the limits beyond which his sympathy and forbearance could not be stretched.

'Under the law,' he said, 'thus laid down, I may be called upon to act as Ordinary; and for this reason, if for no other, it would be unbecoming in me to question the soundness of a decision pronounced, as it would appear with singular unanimity, by grave and learned judges. . . . The observations which I think it my duty to make refer chiefly to the principles involved in the judgment, and the consequences which may arise from it.'

After remarking that the defendant was not represented by counsel, and that the court therefore lost the advantage of hearing arguments in his favour, he proceeds :

'Great difficulties confessedly presented themselves. If some of the questions proposed were clear, others were encumbered by doubts ; and a decision could be reached only by long processes of reasoning, and comparison of documents and authorities of very diverse nature and value. But the court found itself constrained to determine positively every point involved in the voluminous indictment. The effect is to close questions which have long remained open, and to compel a uniformity which practically has never existed.

'This, I say, is the effect of the decision if it could be enforced. But to suppose such general coercion possible is to ignore the liberal spirit of the time and the deep conviction of many devout and enlightened Churchmen.

'Decrees of councils, it is agreed, must be confirmed by the assent of the Church testified by general reception. So the decrees of courts ecclesiastical will scarcely carry the moral authority which we desire they should possess unless they commend themselves to the general approbation of the Church.'

After observing that those who signed the recent memorial to the Archbishop represented various schools of thought, and that many of them were, like himself, not personally affected by the decision touching the position of the minister during the Consecration Prayer at Holy Communion, he proceeds :

'Yet they join in this remarkable representation to the Bishop because, in their opinion, the liberty of the Church is by this judgment unduly narrowed. . . . They well know that general toleration is essential to our common safety as an established body, and more agreeable to the freedom of the Gospel. . . . They might urge that from the days of the Reformation our Church was designed to comprehend and not to exclude, and that with this view its formularies are so framed as to give a reasonable latitude in things indifferent. An eminent and philosophic statesman compared our Church to a ship at her moorings, which, safely anchored so that she cannot drift away, yet may safely swing within certain limits.

'I heartily wish that the whole Church could have accepted with willing minds the last decree of the Court of Final Appeal, even though it may, as is alleged, disagree with preceding judgments. But it is evident that it does offend many consciences. And when law contends with conscience the issue can only be disastrous. You may have martyrs, but not converts.

'The opposition is all the more serious because it proceeds from men who are dutiful members of our Reformed Church, attached from their hearts to its doctrine and discipline, and therefore most anxious to yield obedience to their rulers, whether in Church or State.

'Were it otherwise, their claim to consideration would be greatly weakened. I have no sympathy with that disloyalty which delights to spy out, to proclaim, and to aggravate with almost open contempt the weak points of our Church, which magnifies other communions at the expense of our own, which in word, gesture, dress, and ceremonies delights to go as near to Rome as it may. People of these tendencies ought to remember that the corruption of the Middle Ages made a reformation of religion to be a necessity and a blessing. . . .'

In view of the attacks which were being made upon Christianity as a whole, and upon the Church of England as the chief embodiment of that truth, it was lamentable, he said, that the strength of her position should be impaired by differences and disaffection among its sworn defenders. 'Syracusae nostrae capiuntur, et nos in pulvere pingimus.'[1] 'While we need above all things union, courage, devotedness, and charity, which is the bond of all, Churchmen are biting and devouring one another, and exaggerating points of difference, instead of searching out and dwelling upon points of substantial agreement.'

Especially did he deprecate that the Sacrament of Holy Communion, 'which ought to be the very cement of our union with Christ our Head, and in Him to one another,' should be made the 'instrument of torture to tender consciences. We might have learned a better lesson from the days of persecution.'

'There is small wisdom,' he continued, 'and less charity in applying logic to a subject beyond

---

[1] I have not succeeded in tracing this quotation to its source.

its reach.   We owe to this abuse of logic the dogma of the immaculate conception and of papal infallibility.   Let us beware of submitting to its merciless grasp matters even more sacred. . . .   The Lord's Supper is confessedly a mystery, and so it must remain.   No definition of our reason can avail.   The words of our Lord Himself at the Institution, and in the discourse in the Sixth Chapter of St. John, illustrated by St. Paul, these are the foundation of our liturgies ; these are the treasure of believing men.   In these the hearts of the faithful rejoice ; they ask no more, and will be satisfied with no less.

' Therefore in this most sacred mystery, which so deeply moves the very springs of heart and conscience, I earnestly deprecate not only what a holy martyr called " the heady setting forth of extremities," but also the chilling deductions of human reason.   It would be no small blessing if all parties could adopt the words attributed to one of our wisest and greatest sovereigns :

> Christ was the Word that spake it ;
> He took the bread and brake it ;
> And what that Word doth make it,
> That I believe and take it.'

When the Bishop delivered his second Visitation Charge in October 1875 the excitement caused by the Public Worship Regulation Act of 1874 was at its height.   The circumstances under which the Act was passed and the form which it finally assumed were alike unfortunate.   That the ecclesiastical courts needed reform had been long generally admitted.   A Bill for amending them, introduced by Lord Shaftesbury and supported by Bishop

Wilberforce, had passed the second reading in the House of Lords in three successive sessions; and although it had been crowded out of the House of Commons, Mr. Gladstone, in the debate of January 1872, had declared that the subject was one on which legislation was urgently needed. Convocation also had requested legislation 'for facilitating, expediting, and cheapening procedure in enforcing clergy discipline.' The intention of the Act of 1874 was to provide a more effective and less costly instrument than the existing court for dealing with teaching or ritual alleged to be contrary to the laws of the Church of England.

The Bill, however, in its final shape was a totally different thing from the measure originally proposed by the two Archbishops, Tait and Thomson, which had provided for the formation of a Council or Board of Assessors in every diocese under the presidency of the Bishop, to consist of eight elected members, three clerics, and five laymen, together with the Chancellor, the Dean, and an Archdeacon, who were to sit *ex officio*. The council were to hear complaints as to ritual irregularities, and to advise the Bishop whether it was desirable to take further proceedings. An admonition or order, issued by the Bishop at the advice of the council, was to have the force of law, but an appeal lay to the Archbishop, whose decision was to be final. This measure received the approbation of nearly all the Bishops, including Bishop Durnford.

It would take too long to describe the curious

chain of incidents by which the measure was trans-
formed into the shape which it finally assumed.
It was unfortunately pressed through Parliament
in a time of excitement and panic, and without
reference to Convocation, while Mr. Disraeli's
foolish announcement to the House of Commons that the intention of the Act was to 'put
down Ritualism' aggravated the irritation of the
clergy.   The Bishops generally voted for it in the
end, less because it met with their approbation than
because they feared that, if they did not, one less
favourable to the Church would be carried.   Archbishop Tait, by patient and strenuous exertion, in the
face of much opposition, succeeded in securing the
right of the Bishop to determine in every case whether
proceedings should, or should not, be taken under
the Act.   But for this check upon its operation a
very serious disruption in the Church would have
been, humanly speaking, inevitable, although at the
time no one seems to have foreseen the profound
resentment which the Act would provoke.

The remarks of Bishop Durnford, in his second
Visitation Charge, upon this obnoxious measure,
animated as they were by a spirit of Christian toleration and love, had a significance which reached
beyond the particular subject to which they referred,
and may be borne in mind with profit amidst the
trials that beset the Church at the present day, and
from which indeed it is never wholly free.

He looked forward to a reform being made in
the Final Court of Appeal, but urged the duty of

obedience meanwhile to the existing courts as well as to the Bishops.

'We are told that Churchmen cannot obey the courts, as they are now constituted, because they are contrary to the law of Christ, inasmuch as He hath said, " Render unto Cæsar the things that be Cæsar's, and unto God the things that be God's." But in this care for the honour of God it is not clear that the rights of Cæsar are remembered, which also are from God. Neither are we informed with equal plainness what court would be sufficient. The Bishops cannot be trusted because they are creatures of the State, and have betrayed, according to their wont, the interests of the Church. Convocation cannot be trusted because it is not a true representation of the clergy. Would a diocesan synod, supposing it to possess authority, command greater confidence ? What, then, are we to fall back upon ? What is left but the rule of self-will, the absolute dictation of arbitrary, irresponsible, private judgment ? . . . The truth must be spoken in charity, but not without sorrow. No pains have been spared to cast mistrust and odium upon recent church legislation. Reproaches and imputations are showered upon the Bishops as the sole authors of it. It is denounced as a new engine of partial tyranny. But the judge, I repeat, can only administer the law. He cannot invent new means of repression. His decisions are open to the revision of a superior court which is itself to be greatly improved in its constitution. Nor is the Bishop superseded, for discretion is left in his hands for the restraint of frivolous or vexatious suits, for the protection of such as may have erred in ignorance, for the reconciliation of disputes. You will, I am sure, be of opinion that the intention of the legislature would be best fulfilled, and the welfare of the Church promoted, by the exercise of the discretion reposed in them without fear and without partiality. With God's help, to the best of my poor ability, I wish to exercise it ; and I pray myself and I entreat your prayers that I may have a right judgment in all things. But without your confidence and your co-operation no pacification is possible. The high hand of power can never crush excited passions nor reach the source and spring of contention. There must be a gentler and holier influence breathed into the Church by the Spirit of Peace, from the Prince of Peace whom we serve and whose Gospel we preach.

'Much depends upon the temper in which moral, and still more religious, questions are approached. If my voice could hope to be heard above the din and strife of louder and more confident voices, I would entreat you all not to be swayed by the violent utterances of your contemporaries, but give yourselves to the Word of God and to prayer. And you will also do well to study what sober and deep-read men of the widest and exactest learning wrote on the relation of Church and State in days when the same principles were in debate ; when, as now, the advocates of Rome on the one hand and of Geneva on the other perplexed the minds of men and darkened their counsels.

'Much would be gained if this controversy could be removed from excited platforms and ephemeral writings scarcely less inflammatory into the cooler atmosphere of religious reflection, when men commune with their own hearts and are still. Then there is room for judgment without passion, and without prejudice. . . . For myself, I can only say that I have endeavoured to hold a fair and equal balance without fear or favour, and to acknowledge zeal, piety, and devotedness wherever I seemed to have found them.

'I never was and I never will be the slave of a party, whether political or religious. . . . We have a common end—the salvation of souls through the Gospel of Jesus Christ: a common interest, the glory of God and the advancement of His kingdom upon earth; a common faith founded on God's infallible Word as the Church has ever interpreted and received it. These are mighty bonds. And surely, my dear brethren, that Holy Sacrament of which we have partaken shall exercise an influence far beyond our present meeting. It shall knit us to Christ and in Him to one another. Only through mutual love constraining us can that increase of grace and blessing for which we long, and labour, and pray, be with us and abide.'

Now as always he earnestly deprecated attaching undue importance or significance one way or the other to the vesture or position of the officiating clergy at Holy Communion.

'The advocates as well as the opponents of the eastward position and eucharistic vestments must allow,' he said, 'that the validity of the Sacrament is in no wise affected by these accessories. The significance attached to them is arbitrary. The highest doctrine that our Church allows as to the sacrificial aspect of the Lord's Supper, and as to the presence of Christ in that Holy Sacrament has been preached (and is still preached) by men who wore no. distinctive dress and were content to consecrate the elements looking southward. . . . Neither party can deny that the position and habit of the officiating minister are within the category of things indifferent, and that being such they come within the control of the Church, "which hath power to decree rites and ceremonies." Article 20.

'This power was exercised by the Reformers, who, as the prefatory directions in the Prayer Book show, had groaned under the burden of ceremonies, and saw and knew how many had been abused to error and superstition. There were then, as in after times, some who complained that too many of the old ceremonies had been taken away, others that too many had been retained. But the Church stood firm, and we have reason to be thankful for the wisdom, a wisdom from above, which guided her counsels. . . . It may be said that the spirit of compromise is visible in the structure and contents of the Prayer Book. So long as no doctrine of the faith is compromised, I know not that the Church is forbidden to use means of conciliation, to embrace and comprehend rather than to repel and exclude ; to consult human feelings and to be, in a pious sense, all things to all men. . . . If it be said that our Prayer Book is insufficient, that it needs to be supplemented by " Catholic usage," as some teach— which means not the usage of primitive times to which our Reformers appealed, and which they desired to recall, but the usage of the times immediately preceding the Reformation, when all manner of superstitions had crept in and were set forth in teaching and practice ; or, as others in an opposite direction urge, that certain parts of our service should be cut out or left optional, because they are infected with medieval error ; I see in such demands the elements of disaffection and disloyalty. . . . Where shall minister or people find security but in a dutiful adherence to the directions of the Prayer Book, and is it not a form of presumption to suppose that either by curtailment or addition private judgment can improve upon them ? It would be well if the meaning of our rubrics and services were more studied and more taught. Such an admonition cannot be needless when in many congregations kneeling is unknown, when the responses are scarcely heard, when the alms of the people are not asked or duly presented at the holy table, when the sacramental elements are not placed upon it at the proper time, when the days which our Church appointed to be observed, and for which special Collects, Epistles, and Gospels are provided, are passed over, when that prayer which best sums up all our petitions, the prayer for the Church Militant, is never heard. There are, my brethren, defects which need correction as well as excesses, and neither can be corrected unless we do abide by the rules which we of the clergy have sworn to obey, and to which the whole laity as faithful members of the Church are bound.'

If it were asked, How can we obey rules which are ambiguous ? he replied : ' This objection was foreseen, and a remedy provided in the prefatory matter to the Prayer Book concerning the services of the Church, where it was ordered ' that to appease all diversity (if any arise), and for the resolution of all doubts concerning the manner how to understand, do, and execute the things contained in this book, the parties that so doubt or diversely take anything shall alway resort to the Bishop of the diocese, who by his direction shall take order for the quieting and appeasing of the same : so that the same order be not contrary to anything contained in this book ; and if the Bishop of the diocese be in doubt, then he may send for the resolution thereof to the Archbishop.' If this wise provision had been by mutual consent put in force, the Church would have been spared many trials in which the legal mind has laboured to reconcile Rubrics, Canons, Statutes, and Advertisements with very partial success.'

He ended by saying that when judgment was delivered in an undefended suit, as in the Purchas case, it could hardly be considered as conclusive ; but when judgment had been given after arguments had been heard and carefully considered on both sides, cheerful obedience should be rendered to the law then declared. For it was obviously intolerable that each clergyman, or any confederation of clergy and laity, should constitute themselves the interpreters of law ecclesiastical, and should refuse to acknowledge the jurisdiction of courts lawfully constituted.

The practical wisdom and discernment of the Bishop were exhibited in a speech of remarkable force and boldness, which he made in Convocation in 1873, on the subject of confession.

A petition to the Upper House, signed by 483

clergy, asking, among many other things, 'for the education, selection, and licensing of duly qualified confessors, in accordance with the provisions of canon law,' [2] led to a long debate, which ended in the appointment of a committee to 'consider and report on the teaching of the Church of England on the subject of confession.'

The Bishop expressed his dissatisfaction with this decision.

'Into what,' he said, 'were the committee to inquire? Into the facts? They were notorious. Into the teaching of the Church of England on the subject? It was well known, being contained in a very few pages of the Prayer Book.

'It would be more philosophical to consider whence this system of confession came, and how it had extended. It was very well stated by Whately in the "Difficulties of Romanism" that there was a real reason for all the excesses of Romanism, and that all Rome ever did was to carry good things to an unwarranted excess. People's minds,' he said, 'are at the present time awakening as to the state of their souls. They feel the weight, the burden, and the misery of sin, and they look everywhere for a remedy. Now that was provided in a great measure by Wesley in the system which he first introduced, and which his followers have continued. There is in Wesleyanism a confession of sins habitually made, but it is made in the presence of many instead of in the presence of one, and therefore it very often degenerates into an ostentatious proclamation of piety and faith which is very

[2] See above, page 115.

injurious to those who make it. The Church of England is coming round to acknowledge the necessity of confession in some shape, and this is more generally felt than it ever was in former times. This we are to trace, not to the teaching of this man or of that man, but to an admitted want in the souls of men. It is to this that we are to trace the prevalence of confession in our day, and it should be our desire to direct and guide it. It cannot be our duty, and it certainly is not our wisdom, to repress it. If we try to repress it we shall be only laughed at for our pains ; we shall be accused of exerting an authority which does not belong to our office, and merely sitting in our chairs to put a damper on all true and vital piety.

'Repression, then, I think is perfectly impossible ; but the guidance of the practice may be possible, and I entirely admit what has been said as to the inadequacy of those persons who set up as confessors. Of all the duties that can fall on a minister, that is beyond measure the most delicate and difficult. . . . I think those young persons with no experience who set themselves up as confessors, and are too much followed by silly women—I will not pursue the quotation—who have a right to exercise their choice, but who cruelly abuse the right, are placed for the most part in a very dangerous position. But we cannot restrain the right ; if we attempted to restrain it we should miserably fail. . . . What, then, can we do? I think that in our confirmations we may teach those who are confirmed that while confession in certain cases is a most excellent remedy provided by the Church, "direction" is as great an evil. . . . Another opportunity is afforded in preparing candidates for ordination, when we might show them the true grounds on which the Church of England justifies and approves of confession. Another opportunity is afforded in our addresses and sermons—and in our charges (if they are read), which enable us to declare our minds on this most important subject. But any measure of general repression, I do believe, would not be acceptable to the Church of England generally viewed. I feel that it would utterly fail; and, moreover, I think that it would deserve to fail. For I believe that there is a great and confessed necessity for some such dealing with the hearts and consciences of devout people, and it is those which of all others we must respect and desire to respect, and those which of all others we should be loth in the smallest degree to wound.'

This speech elicited the following letters from Canon Liddon and the present Bishop of Lincoln, who was at that time the Principal of Cuddesdon Theological College.

On the other hand, the letter to Mr. Wagner, of Brighton, from the Bishop, defines the limits within which he considered confession desirable or permissible in the Church of England.

From Canon Liddon to the Bishop

Christ Church, Oxford : May 15, 1873.

My dear Lord,—Your lordship, I trust, will not deem me impertinent if, on the strength of having once met you at Mr. Gladstone's, I venture to thank you respectfully and most sincerely for your recent speech in the Upper House of Convocation on the subject of confession.

It was the only speech in the whole debate which showed a serious appreciation of the real difficulties of the question : I do not mean that other Bishops did not feel these difficulties, but at any rate they did not say so.

The Bishops can no more stop confession than they can stop the Thames.   It rests, not on 'a diseased state of mind,' but on a profound moral basis ; and it is practised, as by the late Mr. Keble, by men who care little for anything but living as close as they can to our Lord.   Those who have made proof of it for some twenty years or more can say whether it does or does not lead to the evils which are ascribed to it by speakers who do not assure us that they speak from personal experience, and who are not generally supposed to do so.

I regretted the petition exceedingly.   I am thankful for the Prayer Book as it is ; and when Infidelity is trying to mutilate or silence our creeds, any change in the formularies is peculiarly unadvisable.   And I sincerely deprecate compulsory confession, although, speaking from experience, I know that confession need not be in any degree compulsory in order to be habitual.   But I could wish, for the sake of many people of whom I cannot but think, that such a debate, if inevitable, had been more generally marked by tenderness and consideration for bewildered consciences.   Your Lordship's speech, at any rate, deserves and has my sincere gratitude for its courage and its true charity.

I am, my dear Lord,

  With much respect,

    Your faithful Servant,

      H. P. LIDDON.

From the Rev. Edward King (now Bishop of Lincoln)

Cuddesdon : May 17, 1873.

My Lord,—I hope that your lordship will not think it an act of too great presumption if I write one word to thank you for your speech in Convocation on the subject of confession.

No doubt there are difficulties connected with it, and some persons will require checking, but surely the thing itself is good, and only wants careful use. No one, I think, could consider the question in relation to the whole *army and navy*, without seriously reflecting how far we have done our duty towards them as priests. It is sad that the over-zeal of a few good women and a few young men should prevent the matter being fully considered ; in the main I am sure your lordship's position is the right one, viz. that the subject relates to a right awakening of the religious life, and that what it demands is not suppression, but the consideration and guidance of the rulers of the Church.

With apologies for thus troubling you,

I have the honour to be, my Lord,

Your faithful Servant,

EDWARD KING.

To the Rev. A. D. Wagner, Chancellor of Chichester Cathedral and Vicar of St. Paul's, Brighton

Lollards' Tower, Lambeth : July 18, 1873.

My dear Mr. Chancellor,—The memorial with your letter of explanation did not reach me until Convocation had been prorogued. But had I had the opportunity I should scarce have ventured to be the mouthpiece of the memorialists in conveying to the Archbishop of Canterbury and to the other Bishops a protest against language employed by them. This could hardly have been done without offence—and perhaps it was this consideration which withheld the signatures of your fellow presbyters.

The memorial, I am glad to find, is addressed to me alone, but I do not wish you or any of the clergy of my diocese to be ignorant of my views as to confession and absolution.

The term used in the now famous 'Petition' is 'sacramental confession.' This term is so far ambiguous that it may mean 'confession' previous to the sacrament of the Lord's Supper, or it may mean that confession is a sacrament as the Romanists hold it to be. In the latter sense the Bishops for the most part seem to have understood it, and to that their words referred.

The question is, not whether the Church of England sanctions confession and absolution, but whether she so encourages confession that it should be pressed upon all, even the very young, as being the one means of obtaining forgiveness of sin committed after baptism—that is, really of all sin whatever. Now I believe that in special cases confession has been greatly blessed. I believe that absolution has the warrant of our Lord himself, and when spoken *clave non errante* does convey pardon and comfort to wounded spirits.

But I also believe that such pardon may be obtained by confession to God in secret, as the Psalmist obtained it. 'I said I will confess my sins unto the Lord, and so Thou forgavest the wickedness of my sin.'

Therefore I cannot but think that it is not agreeable to the teaching of our Church, or to the testimony of God's Word, that Christians should be taught to look upon confession as binding upon all —*jure divino*—and as necessary for all in order to the forgiveness of their sins.

This, in my opinion, would be to adopt Roman doctrine and Roman practice rather than Anglican, and I have grave misgivings as to the result. Scandals there were in other days; possibly they may be repeated in our own. Scandals there are abroad, let us beware of them at home.

Great caution in my judgment is necessary, not denying confession and consequent absolution to those who need and desire it (I do not, indeed, see how it can be denied), yet not offering it as daily food instead of occasional medicine.

Believe me,
Sincerely yours.

The question of confession did not excite public attention until four years after this date, when Lord Redesdale on June 14, 1877, called the attention of the House of Lords to a book bearing the title of 'The Priest in Absolution, Part II.,' which purported to be a manual of instruction and reference for the use of the clergy in discharging their duties as confessors.

Some of the directions in this book were justly considered as objectionable in the highest degree, and it was reprobated by several members of the

Society of the Holy Cross, by which, unknown to them, it was originally printed. The Archbishop of Canterbury brought the subject before Convocation on July 3, when, after a long debate, the Bishops unanimously expressed their strong condemnation of any doctrine or practice of confession which could be thought to render such a book necessary or expedient.

The two following letters from the Bishop of Chichester were written shortly after these events. The first is in reply to a clergyman who, not being a member of the Society of the Holy Cross and ignorant of the book in question, had been long accustomed to hear confessions, and who cited many instances in his own experience to prove the great blessings which had resulted from the practice. He had been pained by some of the remarks of the Bishops in Convocation, which were uttered, he thought, in ignorance of the urgent need that there was for the due and proper use of confession as a means of combating sin and elevating the standard of Christian life.

On Confession

The Palace, Chichester : July 12, 1877.

Dear Mr. ——,—I have read your letter with much interest, knowing that you write on a subject familiar to you, and, so far from blaming you for expressing your feeling, I am obliged to you for your unsought testimony.

I have never denied, nay I have always admitted, the value of confession when the conscience is burdened and cannot find peace. Further I admit what no priest of the Church of England can gain-say, the importance of absolution in such cases—*clave non errante.*

But all the instances you produce are exactly such as I should have supposed to require confes-sion—instances in which no minister of Christ could have refused to listen to it, and to afford such help by instruction, comfort, and absolution, as he is entitled by his office to give.

The question is whether such confession is to be continually repeated, pressed upon all as a duty, erected into a sacrament. We who put forth the declaration to which I suppose you object think that such practices and such teaching are not agreeable to the mind of our Church—that a yoke which our fathers were not able to bear is now riveting on our children.

As to the book which has caused such alarm and disgust, I suppose it is no worse, we hope better, than many Romish manuals. But we cannot but suspect the system which uses such instruments and finds them necessary.

I certainly acquit the members of the Society of the Holy Cross of any personal impurity ; but the book is not, so far as I know it, a pure book, and it exactly runs with the Romish requirements that the *species peccatorum* should be extracted *singillatim.*

Some may feel differently ; but if my wife pro-posed to confess, and I knew the confessor used this book, I should certainly forbid her—and show him the door.

I believe that this constant preaching of and urging on the young and old repeated confession is making even necessary confession more difficult, just as Rome has in many other cases made impossible to us what is harmless and might be edifying. I do not think, either, that what is needed in a penitentiary is the measure for women in general or for men.

This is my opinion plainly expressed, and I want you to know it because I hold you to be among the wisest and most moderate of your party, and have much personal respect for your character.

Sincerely yours.

A few months later he received the following

Memorial on Confession.

At a large and influential meeting[3] it was resolved : ' That while we recognise humble and heartfelt confession of sins to Almighty God as an essential part of Christian worship ; and while thankful for the privilege of consulting our ministers concerning what may at any time perplex our minds and disquiet our consciences ; we desire to express our deep conviction that sacramental auricular confession and judicial absolution are opposed to the Word of God, the practice of the Primitive Church, and to the formularies of the Church of England ; and that they are destructive of domestic peace, social virtue, and the best interests of morality ; and that a copy of this resolution be signed by the chairman on behalf of the meeting, and respectfully forwarded by him to the Bishop of the diocese and the Primate.'   Douglas Fox, Chairman.

[3] In the Dome, Brighton, December 11, 1877.

Answer to Memorial on Confession

7, Prince's Square, December 14, 1877.

My dear Sir,—I have this day received the memorial agreed to by the meeting held under the Dome, December 11, and signed by yourself as chairman.

I am glad to observe that while condemning the practice of systematic and regular confession, the resolution admits the lawfulness and the benefit of such special confession as under certain circumstances our Church, in common with all Protestant communities, permits and even recommends. It is the approach to the Romish practice of habitual and compulsory confession which I understand the meeting to condemn, and in my opinion with good reason.

Believe me, very truly yours.

The Church Congress was held in Brighton in 1874, when the excitement caused by the Public Worship Regulation Act was at its height. It was only by the exercise of great firmness combined with courtesy and tact that the Bishop was able to prevent some of those violent and vehement utterances which bring discredit on the speakers and inflame party feeling, which a well-restrained conference tends to moderate.

' I do not ask,' he said in his inaugural address, ' that any man should give up or compromise his convictions, if he has arrived at them after thought and from experience. Let him cling to them, let him uphold them, let him with all the force and eloquence that he can command endeavour to draw others to his side ; but let him bear in mind that strong language is not argument. In those assemblies of philosophers who treat, it might be supposed, of subjects far above human passions and prejudices, and who from their pinnacle look down with complacent pity upon the quarrels of religionists, explosions of partisanship have been heard from which I trust this present Congress will be preserved—preserved by a sense of its own dignity, of its high calling, of the solemn matters to be treated, of the need of patience and moderation to deal with them, for the advancement of truth, the good of our common Church, and the honour of our Lord and Saviour.'

It was true, he remarked, that a congress decided nothing, for no vote was taken. It had no commission. It was but the humble unofficial handmaid of the Church. But its functions were none the less useful because it disclaimed all coercive authority. It prepared the public mind for measures which hereafter might prove salutary or necessary. Just as the aeronaut sent up his first balloon to ascertain the prevailing currents in the sky, the Church Congress explored the drift of popular opinion for the guidance of higher councils—popular opinion, not as reflected in leading articles, anonymous letters, or one-sided meetings, but as displayed after both parties, if parties there must be, had been heard, and their respective pleadings duly weighed in a pure, free, and enlightened assembly.

The correspondence appended to this chapter will prove how consistently the Bishop endeavoured to act upon the principles indicated in the two charges to which reference has been made in the preceding pages. The diocese, indeed, soon discovered that he possessed in a high degree all the qualities most needful for the critical and anxious times in which his lot was cast—strict impartiality, much patience, sympathy, and forbearance, combined with constant vigilance, and courage to speak and act decisively when the occasion required it. He had ever in his mind and was wont frequently to quote the beautiful admonition in the service for the consecration of Bishops : 'Be so merciful that you be not remiss : so minister discipline that you forget not mercy.' It was no doubt mainly owing to the firm but conciliatory attitude of the Bishop that his diocese was spared the calamity of a prosecution for doctrine or ritual.

Turning now to the actual administration of the diocese, a great hindrance to Bishop Durnford at the outset of his work was his position as junior Bishop for more than three years in the House of Lords, which involved the duty of attending the House every day during the session to read prayers. He grudged very much the time thus lost from the important business of making acquaintance with every part of his diocese. 'If this goes on much longer,' he exclaimed one day to Lord Chelmsford, 'I shall be tempted to follow the example of the modern labourer and strike work.' 'No, no,' was the reply ; 'remember a Bishop *must be no striker.'* On another occasion he was just too late for prayers, which had consequently to be read by the Lord Chancellor. The Bishop of course apologised, pleading in defence that he was 'but a moment behind time.' 'Ah, Bishop,' replied the same ready punster, 'but we *made a minute* of that.'

Owing to his parliamentary duties the Bishop had to do much of his diocesan work in the late summer and autumn months, but he made the most of his time, and in his Primary Visitation in March 1871 he could announce to the clergy that he had held confirmations in seventy places in the course of the past summer, and 'had surveyed in its length and breadth the pleasant land in which their lines had fallen.' The entries in his diary for August of the same year show that he was busily occupied in re-arranging the rural deaneries, providing for the religious inspection of elementary schools, and making plans for the resuscitation of Bishop Otter's Memorial College at Chichester.

This institution had been originally established as a training college for schoolmasters, but owing to various causes it had not been successful, and the buildings had for several years been standing empty. A proposal was now made to convert it into a college for training the daughters of professional men to become mistresses in elementary schools. One of the principal originators and promoters of the project was Miss Hubbard, the daughter of W. E. Hubbard, Esq., of Leonardslea, Horsham. It was warmly supported from the first by the Bishop, the Duke of Richmond, and other leading persons in the diocese, and the college thus revived was re-opened in February 1873.

Another institution in Chichester was animated into fresh life in the first year of the Bishop's episcopate. The college founded in 1838 for the training of candidates for Holy Orders was the earliest experiment of the kind in the Church of England. The first principal had been Charles Marriott, Fellow of Oriel College, Oxford, a leader of the Tractarian School, distinguished alike for learning, ability, and Christian holiness. But from various causes neither under him nor his successors, although all of them were able men, had the college attained a very high degree of prosperity.

At the time of Bishop Durnford's appointment to the see the office of principal was held by Dr. Swainson, a Canon Residentiary of the cathedral, who had also been recently made Norrisian Professor of Divinity at Cambridge. His duties as Professor involved frequent absences from Chichester, the work of the college devolved almost entirely upon the vice-principal, and the numbers of the students had shrunk to a very low average. Dr. Swainson resigned the principalship in 1870, and in the same year one of the Residentiary Canonries became vacant through the death of Mr. Hutchinson. Bishop Durnford filled up the stall and the office by conferring both upon the Rev. Arthur Rawson Ashwell. Mr. Ashwell had been the first head of the Training College for Schoolmasters established at Culham by Bishop Wilberforce, and at the time of his prefer-

ment to Chichester he was Principal of a like institution at Durham. He was a pronounced High Churchman, with strong, clear-cut opinions which he could
express either as a writer, a preacher, or a lecturer
in remarkably terse and incisive language. His
talents and reputation soon attracted a large number
of students to the college, who looked up to him as
an able teacher and director with respect and
admiration, coupled with some degree of awe, for he
could say and do severe things. He certainly gave
a fresh impulse to church life in Chichester and the
diocese, while as editor, first of the 'Literary Churchman' and afterwards of the 'Church Quarterly,' as
a writer of articles in these and other periodicals,
and as a public speaker and preacher, he had his
share of influence on the Church at large. As time
went on he became increasingly absorbed in literary
work, culminating in the life of Bishop Wilberforce.
This difficult biographical task, in addition to the
strain of all his other labours, broke down his
health, and he only lived to complete the first
volume of the work ; dying in 1879.

Another institution into which the Bishop
speedily infused new life was the Diocesan Association, which, like the Theological College, had
been founded during the episcopate of Bishop Otter
in 1837. Its objects were threefold :

(i.) To assist in providing additional churches
and increased or improved church accommodation.

(ii.) To assist in providing further endowment

for poor benefices, and in maintaining therein such additional clerical help as might be required.

(iii.) To promote education in the diocese on the principles of the Church of England.

The constitution of the society was excellent, and nothing was wanting but more general and cordial support to make it a potent instrument in effecting the work for which it was designed. When Bishop Durnford began his episcopate, out of ninety-two magistrates in the Archdeaconry of Chichester only thirty were members of the Association, and out of 111 magistrates in the Archdeaconry of Lewes only twenty-nine. The total number of members was 310, of whom 147 were clergymen. 'I must therefore suppose,' said the Bishop in his primary Visitation Charge, 'that the diocese in general is ignorant that the Association exists.'

It was certainly not allowed to remain in ignorance, for on every possible occasion and in every possible way, at public meetings, by sermons, by visitation charges, by pastoral letters, by his personal influence with individuals, the Bishop made the Association known far and wide and enforced the obligation of supporting it. In short, finding a machine ready to his hand in working order, he devoted his best energies to supplying it with fresh motive force.

By far the most important piece of patronage in the Bishop's gift fell into his hands in the first year of his episcopate by the death of the Rev. H. M. Wagner, who had been for forty-seven years Vicar of Brighton.

The once insignificant fishing village of Bright-helmstone had grown during this century, with a rapidity only surpassed by London and some of the manufacturing centres in northern England, into a great town with nearly 100,000 inhabitants. Mr. Wagner, who was a man of great zeal and ability, had laboured energetically to provide for the spiritual needs of this vast and ever-increasing multitude ; but there was still only one huge un-divided parish, containing seventeen consecrated churches and four licensed chapels. Six of the churches had been erected under Acts of Parliament, and were subject to proprietary rights, with the pro-vision that at the end of forty years the patronage should be vested in the Vicar of Brighton. Con-ventional districts were assigned to most of these churches and chapels, but, not being legally defined, they were liable to be varied or cancelled at the direction of the Vicar. With the exception of the old parish church, St. Nicholas, all the churches were more or less occupied by rented pews, on which the incomes of the clergy mainly depended.

After the acceptance of the Bishopric of Chiches-ter by Dr. Durnford, Mr. Gladstone had offered the Rectory of Middleton to Dr. Hannah, who had recently resigned the wardenship of Glenalmond College. He paid a visit to the Rectory at Middle-ton before the Durnfords had quitted it, and decided not to accept the living, fearing that the cold, damp climate would be unsuitable to the delicate health of his only daughter. 'Short as his stay was,' wrote

Bishop Durnford, 'it gave me the opportunity of observing his rare gifts, his varied and accurate learning, and his genial temper. So when the Vicarage of Brighton became vacant my thoughts turned to Dr. Hannah as a person eminently fitted to fill a post of great importance and of no less difficulty.'

The offer was accepted (Dr. Hannah's daughter had died on June 20, 1870), and the appointment proved in all respects a very happy one. Dr. Hannah had the comprehensive mind and the wide sympathies necessary for success in the administration of a parish which had been the scene of warm party conflicts, where opposing schools of thought had been represented by men of such ability and influence as Henry Venn Elliott and Frederic Robertson, where there were still such strong leaders of the High Church and Evangelical parties as the Rev. Arthur Wagner (son of the late Vicar) and the Rev. James Vaughan, and where the ferment of excitement produced by the judgment in the Purchas case was at its height. He had also the clear head and capacity for business, the resolution and the tact which were necessary for accomplishing the difficult task of reorganising the ecclesiastical arrangements of the town, and for dealing with the anxious problems created by the Elementary Education Act which had just been passed. The Bishop made him Archdeacon of Lewes in 1876, and has recorded his obligations to him in that capacity. 'His help in the diocese as a wise, discreet counsellor, a trusty coadjutor, a capable administrator, and, above all, a sure and true friend, was invaluable.   He was at once the eye and the right hand of his diocesan.'

' In Brighton,' said his intimate friend, the Rev. F. A. Stapley, ' he brought about a peaceful revolution in the condition of the Church.   He found the town one unwieldy parish ; he left it well ordered, with many centres of parochial life.'   In the last public meeting which he attended before his death in 1888, he stated that when he came to Brighton there was only one titular Vicar, whereas now there were thirteen, and that out of twenty-five churches and chapels, fifteen were entirely free and unappropriated, ' according to the law of England and the lines laid down by St. James.'

In all this work the Bishop cordially supported him, more especially in insisting that the sittings in the churches should be free and unappropriated. There was no subject upon which the Bishop felt more strongly or spoke his mind more freely than this.   He recurs to it again and again in his charges, condemning with severity and indignation any violation of the principle of freedom and equality in God's House as illegal, unjust, unchristian, and impolitic, because it supplied the enemies of the Church with a powerful weapon of attack, and alienated the poor from her ministrations, to their own great loss and damage.

Another matter which he felt to be absolutely necessary, if the Church was to have its proper influence upon the spiritual life and moral character of the people, was that the clergy should give regular religious instruction to the children in the elementary schools, and to the pupil-teachers. There was an ever increasing rivalry and competition between board schools called into being by the Education Act of 1870 and the voluntary schools in connexion with the Church. The importance, therefore, of direct pastoral superintendence in those schools to which the clergy still had free access could not be over-estimated.

'Our duty is to our country, to our Church, and to our God' (so he spoke in his primary charge in 1871); 'all considerations of patriotism and wisdom and true religion urge us to make the most of a great opportunity. The religious instruction of the young, as well as of the adults, is solemnly entrusted to us. Such a work can never be done by deputy. No teacher, however accomplished or well-principled, can fill the place of the parish priest who has, as we all believe, a commission from Christ Himself to feed the whole flock. He comes among the children of his parish, not with the rod, but in the spirit of meekness. He learns to know each by name, by sight, by character. He wins their love not for the present time only, but for their whole lives. And by his care for the children he wins also the affection and confidence of the parents. There is no such ready introduction into the families of the middle and working classes, and no way so sure to their hearts, as through real concern for and interest in their children. Why, then, should not every pastor, whether in town or country, daily visit his own school ?   Why should he not every morning, when not specially hindered, open it with prayer and hymn, and give personally, now to one class, now to another, that teaching which none can give with equal authority and power ? . . . If the clergy are but little known in their schools and less felt, then they justly incur the taunt which I have heard, that while loud in asserting their right to direct the education of the young they make but scanty use of their privilege. . . . My reverend brethren, you will, I trust, suffer the word of exhortation and accept it as it is given, not in the spirit of reproof or suspicion, but of advice founded upon practical experience.' [4]

He recurs to the subject in his third Visitation Charge delivered in 1878.   After mentioning that the average number of children in the diocese at that time attending Church of England schools was 30,412, that the whole number presented to the Inspector in Religious Knowledge in 1878 was 33,747, that ten only were withdrawn wholly from inspection and 143 partially—so ill-founded was the assertion that the teaching of the Church was unacceptable to the mass of the people—he proceeded to urge again the importance of sparing no pains to maintain the schools of the Church in their integrity.

'For there the pastor holds his proper place : the whole tone and feeling of the school may be formed by his influence.   But to this end frequent and personal intercourse with the children is required.   There can be no more fruitful, and in my judgment no more delightful, duty.   The Church

---

[4] See above, pp. 87, 88.

and the country look to us to fulfil it.   Would it not be a grievous thing if it could be said of the clergy: " These were men clamorous for their right to teach the young of the flock.   That right is reserved to them, but how do they use it ?   They are content to delegate to the paid teachers what they have contended for as their special and inalienable duty." '

And he insisted on the duty of instructing the pupil-teachers as not less imperative.

' They have a peculiar claim. . . . Think of the future destination of these youths and maidens ; think of their temptations at that critical time of their lives when their hearts and minds are most impressible ; when the choice must be made whom they will serve.   Think how much they need fatherly help and guidance, and then surely you will feel that they are not only objects of anxiety but of sympathy.   " They are the Lord's vessels, ordained to honour : let us keep them clean.   They are the lambs and sheep of the flock : let us lead them forth into wholesome pasture.   They are the seedplot of heaven : let us water them that God may give the increase." ' [5]

He observed that many pupil-teachers on their admission into training colleges were found to be very deficient in religious knowledge, the most precious of all learning ; whereas those who had received regular religious instruction from the clergy-man of the parish always took a high place in the examinations conducted by the diocesan inspector.

[5] Quoted from Bishop Jewel.

In the same charge he dwelt with thankfulness on the many encouraging signs of increased efficiency in the Church, not only in his own diocese, but throughout England: a higher standard of clerical work, more frequent services, more devout congregations, better music, better preaching and more careful observance of rubrics, an increasing number of institutions, associations, and agencies for charitable or religious purposes of all kinds, heartily supported by the laity, finding their natural centre in the parish church and their natural leader in the parish priest.

But amidst so much that was hopeful and satisfactory, there was one cause for disquietude and anxiety in a species of ceremonial and teaching (happily confined to a small minority of clergy) which could not possibly be reconciled with the principles of the Reformed Church of England, and the results of which were manifest in secessions to the Church of Rome. In one parish alone in Brighton five of the clergy had passed over in little more than twelve months.

Nor had the secessions been confined to the clergy; some members of the flock had followed their pastors in the path of error.

'This fact,' said the Bishop, 'ought to open the eyes of all who encourage and accustom their people to a form of divine service which the ignorant can hardly distinguish from that of Rome, who recommend the use of manuals, hymns, and devotional books in which Romish doctrine is thinly veiled, and of a ceremonial which our Church for good reasons rejected, and which for three centuries and more it has never known.'

He did not wonder at the alarm, mistrust, and suspicion that were excited, although he considered that these feelings were more widely spread than the state of things justified. Extreme Ritualists were but few even in the places most suspected. Like all minorities, they were zealous, active, self-sacrificing; but they failed to influence largely the mind of England, which had never forgotten, and would never forget, the black days of the Marian persecution—least of all in that diocese. 'The fires of Lewes,' he said, 'are not yet extinguished in the memory of the people.'

These utterances were all the more forcible and weighty because in the very same charge he showed plainly enough that he wished to extend rather than to narrow the existing limits of permissible ritual.

He had been one of the Episcopal Assessors on the Judicial Committee of the Privy Council which had given judgment on the appeal from the Court of Lord Penzance in the case of the Rev. Mr. Ridsdale; the first case that had been tried in the new court established by the Public Worship Regulation Act.[6]   The Court of Appeal, in a very long

[6] The lay members of the Judicial Committee who heard this appeal were the Lord Chancellor (Cairns), Lord Selborne, Sir J. W. Colville, the Lord Chief Baron, Sir R. Phillimore, Lord Justice James, Sir M. Smith, Sir R. P. Collier, Sir B. Brett, and Sir R. Amphlett. The Episcopal Assessors were the Archbishop of Canterbury (Dr. Tait), the Bishop of Chichester, the Bishop of St. Asaph, the Bishop of Ely, and the Bishop of St. David's.

and elaborate judgment read by the Lord Chancellor (May 12, 1877), had pronounced against the legality of the eucharistic vestments and the crucifix, but sanctioned the eastward position provided due care was taken that the 'manual acts' were so performed as to be visible to the congregation. The Bishop did not profess to be entirely satisfied with the judgment. The ingenious method of reconciling the rubric, which seemed fairly to justify the use of certain ornaments, with custom which had abandoned the use, by 'reading into the rubric' certain words in the Advertisements of 1564, was, he observed, a subtle line of argument which *might* be the true solution of a difficult problem, but was not so clear as to command general acceptance.

It was the duty indeed of loyal Churchmen to yield obedience to decisions such as this, even though they might not be prepared to accept the arguments upon which the decisions were founded, or might entertain objections to the court, which had pronounced them. Some final tribunal there must be, and it could hardly be shown that the existing Court of Final Appeal was not well qualified to interpret the sense of documents, to which province its duties were restricted. If any were dissatisfied with the constitution of the court, they were free to do their utmost to procure its abolition or amendment, but meanwhile they were not at liberty to set at nought its authority or to erect their private opinion in opposition to its decrees. In the present state of feeling, however, he deprecated recourse to litigation, which had rather exasperated difficulties than composed them.

' Some openly proclaim their defiance of the law and maintain the condemned vestments and usages as if they were matters of faith. Others, a greater number, and in my opinion better worthy of consideration, think in their hearts that the " ornaments " have been unjustly proscribed. The refined and subtle line of argument by which the Ridsdale judgment is supported is either not understood by them or not approved. The recalcitrant clergy and laity seem to them to have the letter of the rubric in their favour, and beyond the letter they are not careful to inquire. So they give a sort of passive countenance to opinions and practices which are not their own ; and by their attitude swell the ranks of partisans with whom they have little real sympathy.'[7]

He entirely concurred with the remarks of the Rev. W. Walsham How (the late Bishop of Wakefield) in a very able pamphlet on the ' Revision of the Rubrics ' : ' It seems tolerably obvious that in a matter touching the earnest convictions of many, and strongly arousing the feelings of more, absolute clearness of law should be a prerequisite of stringent

---

[7] The Chief Baron (FitzRoy Kelly) dissented from the decision against the legality of the eucharistic vestments, and expressed great regret that his request to be permitted to append his dissent to the judgment was rejected. The question of the vestments had been submitted to him and eight other counsel in 1866, including Mr. Bovill (afterwards Lord Chief Justice of the Common Pleas), Lord Coleridge, Mr. (afterwards Lord Justice) James, Sir James Hannen, Sir Robert Phillimore, and Dr. Deane, who had all pronounced in favour of their legality.

enforcement.' The Bishop himself was in favour of what has been called the 'Cope Compromise'; he wished that the new rubric might have been adopted which had been passed in the Lower House of the Convocation of Canterbury by four to five in July 1877 as a substitute for the Ornaments Rubric.

This proposed rubric authorised the wearing (with the Bishop's consent) of a cope in addition to the surplice and stole in the celebration of Holy Communion. This vestment, the Bishop remarked, was prescribed by the twenty-fourth canon to be used in cathedral and collegiate churches. Why should not the same liberty be extended to churches generally, subject to the sanction of the Bishop in each case? Meanwhile there had been an earnest hope that a decision of the Final Court of Appeal would set these disputed questions at rest once and for ever—'a hope,' observed the Bishop, 'that has been cruelly disappointed.'

The first diocesan conference was held in Chichester in October 1877. Twenty years ago such conferences were still novelties, and were regarded as being in an experimental stage. The Bishop felt his way very cautiously before he determined to make a venture. A memorial largely signed by the clergy, including Dean Hook, had been presented to him in 1871 praying that a diocesan synod might be convened, which should contain a representation of the laity. The Bishop, however, thought it would be only prudent to test the working of mixed assemblies of clergy and laity on a small scale before committing himself to a conference of representatives from the whole diocese.

Accordingly it was resolved in January 1872, at a meeting of Rural Deans over which he presided, that one conference at least of clergy and laity should be held annually in each rural deanery. The lay element was to consist of the churchwardens, being communicants, and of other lay communicants nominated by the incumbent, the whole number of such lay members not to exceed three for each parish or church. The Rural Dean was ex-officio chairman of the conference. This tentative measure worked well, and from these ruri-decanal conferences arose the demand for a larger assembly to be representative, by election, of the whole diocese. The Bishop still proceeded with cautious deliberation. He consulted the Great Chapter of the cathedral, and at length, after they had pronounced unanimously in favour of the conference, a carefully selected committee of clergy and laity was appointed, which framed the constitution of the body and drew up standing orders.

Even these preliminary steps, however, were not taken without opposition. The Archdeacon of Chichester, Mr. Garbett, declined to attend the meeting of the Great Chapter, and printed a letter to the Bishop in which he indulged in some very acid criticism of the proposed conference, representing it as not only uncalled for, but charged with all kinds of frightful dangers to the peace and welfare of the Church. Bishop Gilbert, he said, had been subjected to the strongest party pressure on the question and had been disposed to give way, but after consultation with the Archdeacon and some leading laymen, who were all opposed to the measure, he had been wise enough to reconsider his purpose and heroic enough to say 'No.' 'So the tempter fled.' This singular production called forth a doughty defender in the person of Dean Burgon, who penned a reply to the Archdeacon characterised after his manner by remarkable vigour and plainness of speech.

' I insist,' he said, ' that the promulgation of your pamphlet is nothing but an act of deliberate misrepresentation, gravely reprehensible in anyone, but in an Archdeacon simply monstrous. Trained, thank God ! in the Oxford diocese, where faithfulness to our chief was a part of our religion, I find it difficult to express how much your conduct offends and disgusts me. . . . I am astonished that one of the Bishop's Archdeacons, not content with thus reproaching him with the crime of being green and vigorous in his age, should insinuate that for him to entertain a notion of holding a diocesan conference is a temptation of Satan.'

Even the Bishop's right to summon and preside at a meeting of the Great Chapter did not pass unchallenged by some members of the residentiary body, who maintained that the Canons thus irregularly convened did not constitute a Chapter at all, but were merely a concourse of clerical atoms.[8] But however the meeting might be designated, the result

---

[8] The Bishop's right was vindicated (I trust I may say successfully) in a printed letter addressed to him by the present writer, entitled *Cathedral Chapters considered as Diocesan Councils.* June 1877.

was the same. The opinion of the body had been obtained, and, fortified by that opinion, the Bishop could act. But he always firmly insisted upon his right to summon the Great Chapter for consultation on diocesan affairs. In his charge in 1878, he said: 'Whenever in my judgment it is desirable that the Great Chapter should assist me with their advice, I shall cause them to be summoned in such manner as law and custom may require, nothing doubting that they will, as loyal clergy, yield ready obedience.'

The first resolution carried at the primary Diocesan Conference was 'that a committee be appointed to inquire into the wants of the diocese and to report upon them, and as to the mode in which such wants may in their opinion be best supplied.' Old supporters of the Diocesan Association were inclined to be a little jealous of this move, as an interference by the newly created Conference with the proper work of the elder institution ; but the Bishop did much to allay these feelings by some timely remarks in his charge delivered in the following year.

'Jealousies,' he said, 'and misunderstandings have no place among Churchmen confederated for noble, beneficent, and godly ends. I am persuaded that a way will be found by which the two bodies, still preserving their independent existence and functions, may co-operate with unity of mind and action for the common good.'

In this confident hope he was not disappointed. Not long afterwards a joint committee was formed of members elected from the Conference and from the Association to administer a fund called the Bishop of Chichester's fund, the objects of which were defined to be ' the provision or license of churches, chapels of ease, mission chapels, districts, parsonages, and permanent endowments.'

Six years later, in his Visitation Charge of 1884, the Bishop announced that the fund, which had then come to an end, had aided materially in building fourteen new churches and enlarging five, in erecting six mission chapels and twenty-two parsonages, and in increasing endowments in twelve cases.

The total amount raised had been 14,646*l.* 13*s.* 3*d.* The balance of the fund, amounting to 14*l.* 2*s.* 4*d.*, was paid over to the Diocesan Association, and a resolution was passed at the Diocesan Conference held in Lewes in 1883 recommending that the Conference and Association should be brought into closer relation, with a view to their co-operation in relieving the spiritual needs of the diocese, which were still pressing. The practical result of this resolution was that all members of the standing committee of the Conference were made members of the general committee of the Association ; and this accession of strength to the executive was followed by an appeal for new and increased subscriptions to the Association, with very satisfactory results. In 1892 the fund was resuscitated, as a kind of thanksgiving on the occasion of the Bishop completing his ninetieth year, and the first appeal produced a response in promises to the amount of 11,840*l.*

CORRESPONDENCE 1872—1877

Increase of the Home Episcopate

Chichester: March 8, 1872.

My dear Sir,—I delayed my answer to Lord Lyttleton's inquiry respecting the increase of the Home Episcopate, because I hoped that the subject would have been brought before the Bishops collectively, when I should have had the opportunity of hearing the opinion of the bench, and especially of those who have had experience of large dioceses, which is not my case. It appears to me that so far as the subdivision of overgrown dioceses has been tried, it has been eminently successful. It is not conceivable that the vast results obtained in the dioceses of Ripon and Manchester could have been obtained unless one had been separated from York and the other from Chester. The appointment of suffragan Bishops and the employment of *emeriti* colonial Bishops must be looked upon as palliatives rather than cures of a confessed evil. No doubt in this way overworked Bishops are relieved, but perhaps hardly to the extent which is supposed. Much must still be referred to the chief pastor; all business of great importance must be submitted to him; nor are the dioceses content to be handed over to Bishops, however able, whom they can hardly consider as equal in authority to their ancient Ordinary.

Both in the northern province and in the southern there would appear to be ample room and demand for permanent subdivision.

The diocese of Chester might well be relieved of that part of Lancashire which is attached to it. The population of Durham is enormous and increasing.

In the southern province there are cases which I need not point out, no less strong, whether as regards population or extent.

For these reasons I should gladly welcome a moderate extension of the Home Episcopate by the means of the subdivision of the larger and more populous dioceses.

Believe me, my dear Sir, faithfully yours,

R. CICESTR.

It is very probable that the subject will be formally considered and reported on in the convocation of the two provinces, but if not, it would be wise and proper that it should be submitted for their consideration and deliberate opinion.

Answer to Purchas Memorial

Chichester : April 1, 1872.

Dear Sir,—I beg leave to acknowledge the receipt of the memorial forwarded by you, and signed by the members of St. James's, Brighton, and by others who do not appear to be connected with that chapel, or with the ministrations of the Rev. John Purchas.

You must be aware that the Court of Final Appeal, with whom the whole matter now rests, can compel obedience to its decrees, or at least enforce penalties for disobedience. I have no power to shelter the Rev. Mr. Purchas, nor to sanction the continuance of a ritual which, as it would appear, the memorialists prefer, but which has been pronounced illegal.

It is a subject of great regret to me that matters have been pushed to an extremity which they never would have reached had my counsel been timely listened to.

It is on every account too late for me to interfere.

Believe me, your faithful Servant and Friend.

To Colonel Wilson Patten, afterwards Lord Winmarleigh. On celebration of the fiftieth year of the Oxford Union

October 25, 1873.

.   .   .   .

You may like to know how the great night went off. The Corn Exchange, a very high and spacious room, was completely filled. A high table for elders and dignitaries in Church and State, the others in rows of tables below. Opposite, a ladies' gallery all open at the end, and along the gangways, so far as I saw, undergraduates and others admitted by ticket. Of our time few, very few, only Lord Stanhope and I—at least I recognised no more. The best speaker was Manning, incomparably clever and artful. 2. Attorney-General Hardy was best received, then Lord Salisbury, Liddon, Manning, Archbishop Cantuar. But they were good-natured to all; only Lord Chancellor (Selborne) let drop some words about Gladstone, which provoked noise and contest.

Hardy was not half so good as usual. Lord Salisbury dull, wonderful to say, Cardwell commonplace, Goschen ditto, Mowbray good, Archbishop

Cantuar. (Tait) solemn, but rather effective. Of course such men could not boggle nor speak ill. Lord Stanhope reminded me really of what he was years ago, rather prosy and lispy, but sensible and full. The dinner—to which, as well as the wine, Ward Hunt did full justice—lasted till past nine, the speeches till one A.M. and after. I had to return thanks for the Ex-Presidents, which *you* should and would have done, to a tired room, little caring for 'fifty years ago,' *nostræ incunabula gentis.*

.   .   .   .

Sincerely yours.

Letter from Mr. Stokes

26 Stamford Road, Prestonville : December 24, 1873.

My Lord Bishop,—Forgive one who is fond of the Church for writing a few words which may be unpalatable tho' true.

I have lived in or near Brighton for near twenty years and have observed the late Vicar Wagner making dissenters by hundreds and also radicals by his determined dislike and driving away of young Low Church Ministers. Now this Vicar with your help will make dissenters and radicals by hundreds of the rich people by your nonsense about free Churches. The School Board Election people voted against the Vicar because you won't let this new Church near me be opened without being all free. Poor people won't go a bit the more because the seats is free if they don't preach the plain Gosple. If you go on keepen Churches shut up, all the people will be dissenters and radicals and next Election the Vicar won't get in at all, mind that from your well wisher

RICHARD STOKES.

Answer to Mr. Stokes

The Palace, Chichester : December 26, 1873.

Dear Sir,—You write like an honest man, and therefore deserve an answer.

I do not believe that what you say of the late Vicar can be substantiated. To my certain knowledge he put into churches young men of the very sort which you say he drove away. However, my business is rather to defend the present Vicar.

What interest can he have in promoting the free admission into churches but the interest of all alike ? Ought not a church, if it calls itself a parish church, to be open to all ? What right has any man or body of men to say a certain number of persons shall have seats appropriated to them, and the rest shall have no claim to a seat ?

And if the persons so favoured belong to the middle and upper classes only, the case is worse, because these classes can very well afford to build churches and pay their ministers : the poor cannot.

If a working man were to come to the wardens of one of these churches, and ask that seats in a good part of the church should be appropriated to himself and his family, would his request be granted ?

You will say such a request is never made. Perhaps not—but the reason is evident, because the poorer classes do not believe that such a request would be granted.

As to the church in Prestonville to which you allude, you are entirely misinformed.

I think every church ought to have a district in which the minister can work ; and if his district is more than conventional—that is, if it aims at being a parish, small or great—then the church, like all parish churches, should be free.

The building is not opened for Church of England services yet, not because I stand in the way, but because the parties cannot come to terms about the purchase.

I beg you to understand that I take your letter in good part, though I think you are mistaken, and am

Faithfully yours.

Answer to a Gentleman who objected to the Incum-bent presenting the Alms kneeling at the Altar

Chichester: January 11, 1874.

Dear Sir,—If you go to spy out another's liberty in a censorious spirit, no doubt you will find something you disapprove. But there is a more excellent way, surely; to 'think no evil,' to culti-vate a spirit of 'moderation'—that is, of fairness and charity.

Mr. Beckles, to whom I communicated the contents of your letter, entirely denies that he bowed on presenting the alms. The rubric orders that he should present them humbly, and the posture of kneeling is the posture of humility. To whom can he kneel but to God, and who can con-demn anyone for kneeling before God? It would be well, in my opinion, if there were more kneeling in our churches and less sitting.

Again, if, after having presented the offerings of the congregation thus humbly, he were to go to the north side of the Lord's table only to dismiss the congregation with the usual benediction, surely that change of place would only be construed to mean that one part of the chancel is more holy than another, and might very well be called an act of superstition.

For the sake of convenience he goes forward and says the solemn words of dismissal.

To the Bishop of Lincoln, Dr. Wordsworth, in reference to an Episcopal Allocution proposed by him

Chichester: January 24, 1874.

My dear Bishop,—The Church owes you thanks, and I tender you my own, for your labour in drawing up the 'Allocution' which you kindly forwarded to me, and which I herewith return.

No doubt the so-called Ritualists are the chief offenders. Their demonstrations, *oculis subjecta*, rouse the antipathies of that large body of Englishmen who agree chiefly in hating the Pope and Papists. And some of them, I fear, do mean even more than these outward things signify. They do hold, and would implant in the minds of their disciples, distinctive Roman principles and doctrines. There is, however, a minus as well as a plus. There are many who are disloyal to our Church in the direction of Geneva or modern Dissent, and that in outward things—e.g. omitting the presentation of alms on the Lord's table, placing the elements on it before the service, omitting prayer for the 'Church Militant,' not giving the elements severally into the hands of communicants, and so forth.

Is this irregularity, which does also offend many, because the laity take more interest in church ritual and have better sources of information and consult them, is this error in defect to be unnoticed altogether ?   I fear if this be so we shall address in vain those whom we most wish to have on our side, the really thoughtful and loyal.

Might it not be possible to say that in our view the duties of minister and people are defined by the rubrics and order of the Church, as interpreted by legal decisions ? and the only ground of safety is to be found in honest, loyal adherence to this order, admitting that such adherence may involve here and there some sacrifice of private judgment.

It seems to me that this is lacking to make your paper authoritative and persuasive.   For we do wish to persuade.

Then you hint only darkly at the way in which we are to be assisted in the administration of our new powers.   It would roll away a great stone of offence if something more clear could be said as to the Bishop in disputed cases being assisted by an impartial court, partly laymen, partly clergy.

I see the difficulty of plainer speaking, that we are ourselves in the dark ; and I see, too, the enormous difficulty of satisfying our body.

It is with the greatest hesitation, not without earnest thought and prayer, that I have ventured to submit these remarks to you—so much in all ways my superior.   And trusting to your great charity, I am

Your affectionate Brother.

Answer to a Gentleman who recommended a Synod

Chichester : June 16, 1874.

My dear Sir,—Now let me ask, supposing a diocesan synod were called (of course, of clergy only)—e.g. in this diocese—what questions would you submit to it ?

Not that of the position of the celebrant, which is not clearly made out, though in my opinion, which I give with great submission, the primitive position was a westward one ; not vestments, though these probably offend more than anything, owing to the splendour of them. What is left ? I speak, of course, of your side of the question. Many things, indeed, might be referred on the other side, but these are things chiefly enjoined—such as the proper oblation of the elements, the surplice in preaching, use of the prayer for the Church Militant, the offertory, and so on. But no synod could heal strife when the great objects of strife were withdrawn from its discussion. And, looking at the constituent members of a synod, could you be very sanguine of impartiality ?

There is the promise of inestimable value that the Holy Spirit will guide hearts open to His influence, but are there not hearts that will be closed ?

Then there is Convocation—a more hopeful body perhaps—as representative. Would you accept the opinion of Convocation pronounced, not treating of the business under the broad Seal, but giving its voice after discussion ?

For my part, ' I long for peace, but when I speak to them thereof they make them ready for battle.'

No doubt there are more Anglo-Catholics than their opponents suppose, but I think they are few relatively to the multitudes who suspect and even hate whatever has the stamp of Catholicity.

Very truly yours.

Answer to a Gentleman who complained of the Ritualism in some Brighton Churches

The Palace, Chichester : October 3, 1874.

My dear Sir,—I have to thank you for your letter and the information it contains respecting Mr. Wagner and his early and present opinions. Also about certain practices in St. Mary Magdalen's and St. Paul's. What church bears the name of St. Mary Magdalen I do not know ; of St. Paul's I only know that the chancel is so dark that lights are unfortunately necessary. St. Michael's is, so far as I am aware, not under Mr. Wagner's influence.

There are certain persons—I will not suppose you to be one—who will not acknowledge good because they see something about it which in their opinion is suspicious.

A vast church is built at one man's charges in a district where a church was sorely needed. This church is free and unappropriated, and thousands are ready to take advantage of the opportunities of worship and prayer hitherto denied them. Am I to hinder such a work as this, or to discourage by cherishing doubts and insinuating dangers? I cannot act in this manner as chief pastor of the Church in this diocese.

But so far from committing myself to superstitious doings, I did clearly say that if anything superstitious were attempted I should be ready, God being my helper, to check it.   On this point I spoke, as I feel, strongly.   And I am not blind to the tendencies in word and deed which betray themselves in the ritualistic portion of our Church.

I see their studied approximation to Roman phrases, and I fear to Roman doctrine, with great alarm and equal dislike.

On the other side, I see a studious depreciation of the divine character and origin of the Church, a denial of any special sacramental grace, of any priestly office, an approximation to the language of Presbyterians and Dissenters, and this said to be the Reformation truth.   I cannot accept this any more than the Romanising view.   And I pray that we may be led on both sides to a sounder and fairer judgment.

Faithfully yours.

From a Lady, on the word ' Altar '

Brighton, 8 York Road : October 30, 1874.

My Lord Bishop,—In common with several others who indistinctly heard your remarks at the Church Congress, on the question whether the Communion Table in our Protestant Church is rightly called an 'altar,' may I be pardoned in troubling your lordship to give me your opinion on this matter ?

As an attached member of the Church of England, I feel that this is a point of great importance, and that I trust will be a sufficient plea for troubling your lordship, who is the spiritual head of this diocese.

Am I justified in considering that the enclosed letter, which I cut from the ' Standard,' conveys a correct idea on this subject ?

Waiting a favour of your lordship's reply,
I have the honour to be
Your faithful Servant.

Answer to the Foregoing

Chichester : November 4, 1874.

Dear Madam,—It would be very inconvenient if every member of the Church in this diocese should request me to give my judgment upon letters which eminent divines may publish in the newspapers. I will, however, briefly answer your question, as I am bound to believe it is put with an honest purpose.

So far as I am acquainted with the facts, Dr. Howson's statement as to the Prayer Book is correct.

The terms ' altar ' and ' sacrifice ' were so grossly abused by the Church of Rome that the reformers were justified in banishing the former from our service books, and in restricting the second to its true and Scriptural meaning.

The Settlement of 1662 simply retained the existing phraseology, as it retained the doctrine of the Holy Sacrament.

So far I agree with Dean Howson. But I hold him to be mistaken in his view of Heb. xiii. 10. Our Hooker says that, in the interpretation of Holy Scripture, the sense furthest from the letter is commonly the worst.

Now the literal sense leads to the conclusion

that the 'altar,' of which Christians alone have a right to 'eat,' can be no other than the table of the Lord spoken of in the Epistle to the Corinthians, and of which Christians were (1 Cor. x. 21) to 'be partakers.'

I commend this text to your earnest consideration (Heb. xiii. 10). I further refer you to one of the latest commentators on the Epistle to the Hebrews, Mr. McCaul, who wrote, however, before the question was so hotly disputed.

Thus both terms 'table' and 'altar' are, in my mind, Scriptural. Both refer to the Sacrament of the Lord's Supper ; both may be safely used.

Up to very recent times the 'Companion to the Altar' was bound up with the Book of Common Prayer for private use. Books lettered 'Altar Services' not of modern date lie, as I can testify, on many Communion tables. In quieter and less suspicious times no one scrupled to use the word 'altar' in a Christian sense.

I will, however, add in confirmation a passage from the writings of one who will not be suspected of Romanising tendencies, the Rev. John Wesley:

'To men it is a sacred Table, where God's minister is ordered to represent from God his Master the Passion of His dear Son, as still fresh and powerful for their eternal salvation. And to God it is an Altar whereon men mystically represent to Him the same sacrifice, as still pleading and sueing for mercy. And because it is to the High Priest Himself, the true Anointed of the Lord, both His Table, and the Altar for the Communication of His Body and Blood to men, and for the representation of both to God, it cannot be doubted but that the one is most profitable to the penitent sinner, and the other most acceptable to His Gracious Father.'

It would require far more leisure than I can command to state all the collateral reasons which lead me to this judgment on the question you have proposed to me.

Commending it to your impartial consideration as one who loves the Lord Jesus in sincerity,

I am faithfully yours.

*Answer to an Inquiry about a Church at
Prestonville*

Dale Park, Arundel : Nov. 19, 1874.

Dear Sir,—Your letter of November 9 has remained unanswered, because I have been moving about continually and too much engaged to give proper attention to your inquiries.

The principle adopted by the Vicar and myself in Brighton is this—that no church should be constituted a *parish* church unless all its sittings are free. If a church should be consecrated and a district attached to it, it then becomes a parish church with parochial rights. I am not inclined to follow a different rule in Hove.

Neither can I license buildings for the service of the Church of England unless a conventional district is assigned to them by those who have authority so to assign—viz. the Vicars of parishes.

This rule is necessary in order to prevent the erection of proprietary chapels, built with speculating views.

Further, supposing such conventional district to be assigned, I could not license the chapel unless one-half of the seats are free, as under the Blandford Act.

Before consecration, as I said, all seats must be freed.   It is needless for me to discuss with you the constitution of the Trust that you suggest.

As at present proposed it would not meet my approval, and must be mate rially modifiedin order to secure my consent.

I regret as much as is possible that the building should be not used ; but it was secured without my knowledge, and I really cannot hold myself responsible for the present condition of things.

Believe me faithfully yours.

To a Clergyman who had written to say that one of his Churchwardens wished to marry his deceased wife's sister, and to ask the Bishop whether he could so far give a moral sanction to the marriage as to authorise him to admit the parties to Holy Communion

The Lollards' Tower, Lambeth : June 30, 1875.

My dear Sir,—By the law of the land it is not allowed to a man to marry his deceased wife's sister.   By the law of the Church, as set forth in the table of prohibited degrees, such marriages are forbidden.

The children of such marriages are in the eye of the law illegitimate.

No one would endure that a woman should marry two brothers in succession.   Neither may a man marry two sisters.   By matrimony the wife's relations become the husband's relations.   Affinity, no less than consanguinity, is recognised as a bar to marriage.   So it has ever been since the Reformation ; the Roman Church allows such marriage, as they do the marriage of uncle and niece, by dispensation.

That is, they make void God's word.

I am sorry that respectable people should go counter to law and Scripture—as I understand Scripture, and as our Church understands it. But it is quite clear that such marriages are null and void, and we, as clergymen of the Church, cannot go counter to its law and mind.

Very truly yours.

To the Right Hon. W. E. Gladstone

The Palace, Chichester : July 26, 1875.

My dear Mr. Gladstone,—I have to thank you for a copy of your Essay, which, however, was already familiar to me, for I had read and reread it in its original form. Moderation has, I fear, departed—*ultima cœlestium*—from the English clerical mind, else the arguments you adduce for the essential indifference of the 'position'[9] might prevail, as they ought to prevail. In the Bishops' pastoral address it was asserted, and cannot be disproved, that the use having varied and the Church having never ruled that any doctrinal significance was involved, no such significance ought to be attached arbitrarily to one way of standing at the altar or the other. But I do not think either party accepted this peacemaking conclusion ; rather, we were condemned because we did not declare one or the other to be alone permissible. If fear can exorcise the evil spirit, it will do what reason has failed to effect,

---

[9] I.e. of the celebrant at Holy Communion.

N

and there is, as your startling title proclaims,[1] good reason for fear.

I have small hopes from any judicial decision, because one of the parties concerned has no confidence in the courts. What court they would obey they have never told us; only the courts that exist, they reject.

For this reason, seeing the evils of litigation—which rather inflames wounds than heals them, and while it exasperates, settles nothing—I was desirous that Convocation should run the risk (for I confess it to be a risk) of framing some clear and intelligible rubrics as to vestments and position, not with a view of abridging reasonable liberty, but of defining its limits; and unless there is among English churchmen sufficient ἐπιείκεια to allow a fair space within which, to use a metaphor of your own, the Church ship may swing, though still firmly held to its moorings, I cannot see how disruption in one form or another can be avoided.

How often have I missed our great friend of Winchester, whose counsels in these days would have been invaluable, and how I shall miss him in what I fear is coming on—when we shall have to exercise that ' discretion ' which has not yet been taken from us.

If you are still in London, and likely to be there this week, it would be a great satisfaction if I could have half-an-hour's conversation with you; Thursday or Friday would suit me best.

Not knowing your address, I take my chance of the House of Commons, and with renewed thanks and much respect, believe me,

Most truly yours.

---

[1] *Is the Church of England worth Preserving?*

*From the Right Hon. W. E. Gladstone, thanking
   the Bishop for his sermon after the death of Dean
   Hook*

Hawarden : November 18, 1875.

My dear Bishop of Chichester,—Many thanks for your sermon. I cannot say more of it, or less, than that in reading it I find the noble Dean stand alive before me.

Are you disposed to try your hand at translating Tennyson's ' Epitaph on Franklin ' — with perfect freedom of tongue and metre? It is, I believe, for the Abbey. Lyttelton, Selborne, and Roffensis have had it in hand.

I was much pleased to see you looking brilliantly well on Thursday.

Ever sincerely yours.

Your letter came to-day.

The Bishop sent two translations : one in Latin and one in Italian :

Not here ! the white North has thy bones; and thou—
 Heroic sailor-soul !—
Art passing on thy happier voyage now
 Toward no earthly Pole.

  Non hic quiescis. Arcticæ nives habent
   Herois ossa, at spiritus
  Feliciore cælitem cursu petit
   Terrestris haud memor polum.

  Non quà; ma sotto l' arctico
   Cielo in gelata fossa
  Del capitan Britannico
   Giacen le stanche ossa
  Mentre che l' alma eroica
   Con più felice volo
  Tranquilla verso naviga
   Ad non terrestre polo.

From an Old Friend

Balcombe : November 23, 1875.

My dear Bishop,—*Somebody* has kindly sent me your sermon on the Dean ; and, as I cannot thank the unknown, I must thank the author.

I need hardly say that I was much pleased with it. I venture to say that it has the rare merit of discriminating praise. Nothing could be more stale and unprofitable than the funeral sermons of other days—stuffed with forcemeat of general eulogy. One grew sick of *fortemque Gyam fortemque Cloanthum.* It used to remind me of a sermon on a saint's day at the end of a volume for every Sunday in the year, and to which was appended a candid note : ' With some slight addition to meet a peculiar case, this sermon will do for any saint's day !'

Do you think your sermon would do for *any Dean ?*

I think also you have hit the mark in describing the Dean's character as *thoroughly English.* I remember when ' Hear the Church ' burst on the world like a comet, perplexing many good men ' with fear of change,' and when we were told that Rome was at our gates ; people little thought that if the invader *had* come the Dean would have been among the first to do battle with him.

The first time I met his name (alas ! more than forty years ago) was in Forster's ' Life of Bishop Jebb.' He was then a parish priest at Coventry, while the Bishop was at Leamington, rallying from an attack of paralysis, which shattered his frame but left his fine intellect unimpaired. And this reminds me that it was in this book that I thought I discovered the germ of what has since grown up as the ' High Church,' and there also I first read of the *Quod semper, quod ubique,* &c., which have since become household words, and which the good Bishop quotes mainly to demolish the claim of Rome to the appropriation of the test.   But you must excuse the garrulity of old age.   It is long since I heard anything of you except in the county paper, but I trust all has gone well in the meantime with you and yours.   We escaped the damaging floods because we had no river but the shallow and sluggish Ouse. The absence of water is often made a reproach to the scenery of Sussex, but here comes in Paley's favourite theory of compensation.

Believe me
Affectionately yours,
J. G. ROBINSON.

From the Rev. J. Ingle on Exeter Churches

Mount Radford House, Exeter : May 22, 1876.

My Lord,—There is in Exeter a very strong feeling that in the Union of Benefices Bill there ought to be provision made for—

(1) Requiring the consent of parishioners to the demolition of churches.

(2) Securing that sites not necessary for public improvements, sanitary or other, should not be needlessly and indiscriminately sold for any secular purposes without limit or restriction, but should be fenced off as open spaces and so preserved.

It has been publicly stated that your lordship

approves of the Bill; as, indeed, most of those by whom I am commissioned do in a general way so far as regards the union of benefices. But I am directed to ask your lordship whether you would be willing to allow the provisions just named to be incorporated in the Bill.

I have the honour to be

Your Lordship's obedient and humble Servant,

JOHN INGLE,

Rector of St. Olave, Exeter.

Answer to the above

Chichester: May 25, 1876.

My dear Sir,—The city of Chichester contains three churches of sufficient size, and with an adequate population attached to each. But it also contains six other churches, of small dimensions, with small parishes and still smaller endowments.

If the Bishop of Exeter's Bill could facilitate the union of some of the small parishes, a great public advantage would be secured, and for this reason I am so far favourable to it that I consented that Chichester should have a place in the schedule.

With respect to the conditions which you and those who act with you wish to introduce into the Bill, the second has my hearty concurrence. Indeed, I might be disposed to go further in preventing any needless demolition of churches or appropriation and sale of the sites of churches and churchyards than you do. In Chichester certainly no demolition and no sale would be contemplated so far as I am concerned.

With regard to your first condition, if the consent of the parishioners were required only for 'demolition,' and not for any measure short of 'demolition,' I should be inclined to accept that also. I have little doubt that the Select Committee will be as jealous of the rights of parishioners as of the rights of patrons. But it is obvious that if such consents are in all cases required, the Act founded on such a principle will be much hampered [?] [2] in its operation.

Believe me
Truly yours.

To the Rev. A. Wagner, Chancellor of Chichester Cathedral

Chichester : July 6, 1876.

Dear Mr. Chancellor,—When you expressed to me your intention of building a chapel in the new parish of St. Paul's, you said that it was to serve as a chapel of ease to the church of St. Paul's, so that persons who could not be accommodated in the church might find accommodation in the chapel. Chapels of course, like their mother-churches, may and ought to be consecrated, when consecration is possible. I should have supposed that upon your own principles as a Churchman you would have attached as much value to consecration as I do myself, and would not have been content with a license in preference to consecration. But in your letter of June 17 you omit altogether the offer of consecration then made to you. If your new buildings had been encumbered with debt, or had there been legal difficulties in the way of consecration, I should not have refused to license it upon your giving a proper undertaking that when such

---

[2] The word is very illegible in the MS.

hindrances were removed it should be consecrated. But you did not allege any reasons for the delay of consecration, nor did you offer any guarantee that the chapel would be permanently secured to the Church of England.

I need not remind you that the chapel when consecrated would be under the control of yourself and your successors, Rectors of St. Paul's. You would lose no right nor surrender any privilege consistent with honest allegiance to the Church of which you are an ordained priest. You charge me with partiality in refusing to you in this case the license which I have granted to others in similar cases. But the cases you bring forward are not similar. Some of the buildings to which I have granted licenses are so-called school-chapels, of which St. Luke's, Albion Hill, is one. Another, St. Luke's on Cliftonville, is licensed until it can be consecrated, there being legal difficulties in the way, which it is hoped may be removed. Temporary buildings, such as Dr. Winslow's, and iron churches cannot, as you know, be consecrated on account of their construction. There is a plain distinction between all these buildings and the chapel of ease which you require me to license, and I am not without some hope that you may perceive a certain unfairness in your statement and inference.

I must also correct your version of our conversation. The first mention of the Act[3] was made by *you*. I was ignorant of the existence of such an Act. You said that you could hold religious services in your chapel of ease without the Bishop's

---

[3] The reference to the Act is here given, but the numerals are so illegible that I have not been able to identify it.

license, and the Act would exempt you from penalties.   I replied that if the law allowed you such liberty, I did not desire to abridge it.   What I then said I now repeat.   But I give no opinion as to the Act itself, nor do I consider it my duty to advise you when your conscience ought to be your adviser.

.   .   .   .   .   .

Having now read the Act, I am of opinion that it does not enable a clergyman to officiate in unlicensed or unconsecrated buildings within his parish, and that it does not exempt any in Holy Orders from their liability to ecclesiastical censure or penalty, if by so officiating they break the law ecclesiastical. It is not in my power, if it were my desire, to relieve you from obedience to the law of the Church in this matter.   Let me say in conclusion that it was not necessary to remind me of the large sums you have for so many years devoted to church building and the maintenance of churches in Brighton, to say nothing of your personal labours.   I have never shown myself insensible to these sacrifices on your part, nor can you say with truth that I have ever thwarted your plans for the good of your fellow-townsmen.   But when, without valid reason, you reject the offer of consecration for your chapel, it is reasonable that I should be alarmed.

Believe me
Very truly yours.

From the Archbishop of Canterbury
Addington Park, Croydon : August 23, 1876.

My dear Lord,—Some time early in October it will be the duty of the Judicial Committee of the Privy Council with the three Prelates on the Council to consider and recommend to her Majesty the mode in which the clerical assessors are to be appointed in accordance with the provisions of the New Judicature Act. I am instructed by the Lord Chancellor to consult with my brethren in order that the Judicial Committee may have the benefit of understanding their feelings on the subject. I shall, therefore, be obliged by your writing to me, if anything occurs to you which you wish mentioned to the committee.

Believe me to be
Your faithful Brother and Servant,
A. C. CANTUAR.

The Lord Bishop of Chichester.

Answer to the Archbishop

My dear Lord Archbishop,—In obedience to your Grace's invitation, I beg leave respectfully to submit to you my views on the subject proposed in your letter of August 23.

It being the special duty of the clerical assessors to give advice to the Judical Committee upon questions touching the doctrines and laws of the Church, it is of the greatest moment that they should be men of large and accurate theological knowledge, and well learned in the history and usages of the Church generally and of the Church of England in particular.

It is no less important that such assessors should command the confidence of the Church.

They ought, therefore, to be men of proved impartiality and moderation.

I cannot doubt that a competent number of assessors fulfilling these conditions may be found among the present Bishops of the Church of England.

With regard to the selection of assessors, I would suggest that it should be made by the whole body of English Bishops (excluding Suffragans) and secretly, so far as practicable, each Bishop naming those who in his judgment are the best qualified.

Further, it is material that the ecclesiastical assessors, when called upon to advise, should, like the judges in the Highest Court of Appeal, give their opinions openly.

I should suggest adding that they should not be fewer in number than (four or five?). It will be important to move the institution out of the groove of the former *triad.*

If the number still stood at three there would be a temptation to acquiesce in the old monopoly of Canterbury, York, and London.[4]

Letter from Mr. Vassall on Authority

Balliol College, Oxford : Thursday, March 18, 1877.

My Lord,—In your letter to Chancellor Wagner, which appeared in yesterday's 'Guardian,' occurs the following passage : ' I see no disposition on the part of those with whom you sympathise to defer to spiritual authority—on the contrary, they stand stiffly on their rights'—and you proceed to most justly animadvert on the inconsistency of such a course. I trust that your lordship will kindly excuse the great liberty I feel that I am taking in writing to you on the subject of the above state-

---

[4] These last two paragraphs are in another hand, on the opposite page, and may be the suggestion of some friend, episcopal or other, whom the Bishop had consulted on the matter.

ment, but as a High Churchman who has for some years earnestly desired to become a thoroughly loyal priest of God's Church in England, I have now for some time felt that one can only do so honestly if one is prepared to abandon one's 'rights' and to defer most entirely to 'spiritual authority.' It is for this reason that I, in common with many others, have so intensely sympathised with Mr. Tooth and his congregation, because they have seemed to draw such a clear distinction between the 'spiritual authority' of the Bishop and the entirely civil and Erastian authority of the ex-Divorce Court Judge. If your lordship will have the goodness to read the enclosed extract, which I have ventured to mark, from a letter from Mr. Tooth to his Bishop, I almost hope that you will at least in his case modify the statement which has drawn this from me.

Again apologising for my presumption in troubling your lordship, a course which can only be justified by the exceptional difficulties in which we candidates for Holy Orders are placed at the present time—difficulties which must needs be intensified if we are misunderstood by our Fathers in God—

I remain

Your Lordship's most obedient Servant,

OLIVER R. VASSALL.

Answer to Mr. Vassall

April 2, 1877.

Dear Sir,—I mark this letter 'Private' because it is written to satisfy certain difficulties which present themselves to your mind. I should not have answered your inquiry, which perhaps more properly might have been addressed to your own tutor or the head of your college or your Bishop, if I had not some hope of giving you a reasonable degree of satisfaction. You seem to fear that submission to the spiritual authority of the Bishop which you promise to yield at your ordination may conflict with certain 'rights' (not defined by you) which belong to you as a member of the Catholic Church. I apprehend that you are a member of the Catholic Church, because you are a member of that branch of it which is called the Church of England. Only by your baptism received from a priest of that branch are you a member of Christ's Church. Now the Church of England is governed by diocesan Bishops, as is every other branch of the Catholic Church, and even as a layman you acknowledge their spiritual authority. At their ordination all, whether priests or deacons, engage to obey the Ordinary. Now here is a clear duty.

Here is a promise made solemnly in accordance with Scripture as well as the requirements of the Church. It may fairly be presumed that the Bishops will not exercise their authority in an arbitrary manner. But even should that impossible contingency happen, or rather should you think that it happens in your case, it would be safe to obey, although perhaps obedience would be hard and unwelcome. It would be a sacrifice, but a sacrifice made to duty. I wish you had not imported Mr. Tooth's name or doings into this question ; but as you have done so, I must consider what you advance, though I certainly disclaim all personal feeling in this matter.

I find, then, that Mr. Tooth did not submit himself unreservedly to the judgment of the Bishop. In a letter dated March 22, 1876, he writes (a copy is before me) : ' I have gone to the very limits of canonical obedience. I have placed myself unreservedly in your hands, only according to the law and primitive use of the Christian Church.' He places himself in the Bishop's hands, but not 'unreservedly'; on the contrary, he lays down conditions to be fulfilled. Where is the ' law ' of the primitive Church to be found ?

I suppose by 'use' is meant the 'ritual,' which varied in almost every diocese and in all ages. You must see that such conditions altogether nullify all this offer of unreserved submission, which seems so plausible, and which has had its effect on your mind. No judge would accept them or act upon them, and thus Mr. Tooth is left free to claim primitive law and primitive use as favouring all his practices. I think one who so writes does ' stand on his rights,' though I had not Mr. Tooth in my mind at all when I penned those words. Whether they are substantial or imaginary rights any fair mind can judge. But I hope you will not be misled by the concluding part of the printed letter, which I return herewith. Certain doctrines are specified which I suppose faithful members of the Church of England generally hold—' We do believe,' &c.—and which may be preached and taught now as ever, no man forbidding them. But then it is added : ' Vestments, incense, lights, and *many other things* form a part of the Order for right Celebration of the Mysteries of- the Faith. So that these extra ceremonies are as necessary as the doctrines " I trust I may never yield." ' Now this position is quite contrary to the views which sound theologians entertain—viz. that external ceremonies are things indifferent (if not commanded in Holy Scripture), and that the Church and every branch of it 'has power to decree rites and ceremonies'; and of course to alter such as have been found inexpedient and abolish such as have been abused. 'The principle' is laid down in Holy Scripture, when Hezekiah broke to pieces the brazen serpent, and at the Reformation it was carried into execution.

Things innocent in themselves may be perverted to purposes of superstition, and in the mediæval Church were so perverted; hence the necessity for their abolition. Mr. Tooth's argument is that because some ceremonies were retained, all ought to be retained which were in use in the mediæval Church. This is to deny us that liberty which the 20th Article claims.

Faithfully yours.

From Dr. Pusey

Ascot Hermitage : September 2, 1877.

My dear Lord,—You will not, I know, think me meddling if I write to your lordship about one whom I have known since his boyhood, now near forty years, who is in great sorrow and depression, A. Wagner.

The cause of this depression is the non-opening of a church, upon which 12,000*l.* has been expended, and which is much wanted. The last new church, St. Bartholomew's, which holds (your lordship of course knows) 2,000 people, was so thronged on Sunday week that some who went from the little sisterhood of St. Mary's, Hove, could not get in. St. Paul's is equally crowded. St. Bartholomew's has a great hold on those whom it is so difficult to get hold of for the Church, the men of the lower class. On Ascension Day forty of the men signed a petition to the head curate for Holy Communion at 4.30 A.M., because they had to go to their work at 6. There were ninety-six communicants at that service. The Guilds, which are so useful in keeping young women in the right way, contain 300. The new church would be equally full, and your lordship must, I am sure, feel grieved that 1,000 people are kept from the public worship of God who would worship Him if the church were opened.

And yet, my dear lord, we have a case against putting our churches in the power of the Parliament.

Fellowships were founded some three years ago at Hertford College for the Church of England : it was ruled in the Queen's Bench that Non-Conformists (and of these in Oxford more would be Atheists than would belong to any ' religious denomination ') must be admitted to competition and be eligible.

At Keble College the Council (which yet had such men on it as Lord Carnarvon, Lord Beauchamp, Gathorne-Hardy) was obliged to decline to have the chapel consecrated for fear it should fall into the hands of the State.

Your lordship knows better than I what difficulty there was in staving off the Burials Bill. Yet I suppose there is hardly a person in your lordship's house or out of it who is not morally certain that that Bill was but an instalment. It is a shorter step from the churchyard into the church than it is from outside of the churchyard inside. As things are going it is, I suppose, morally certain that the Dissenters will ask for, and will have, permission to use our consecrated churches at any hours that they should not be used by the clergy of the Church of England. Even this restriction would be regarded as a large concession to us. For what the Non-Conformists desire is ' religious equality,' and this would not be equality. They claim for themselves all their own buildings, because they are not the property of the State, and an equal right in ours, because they are, they say, its property. Whoever, then, has a church consecrated gives over one building more which may, like the child in Solomon's judgment, be divided, half to the Church, half to any unbelievers.

Your lordship may not know that John Keble (whom all so respect and love) as things grew worse became decided against consecrating new churches. He wrote this to me, on occasion of one of the decisions of the Judicial Committee, which made the belief in the inspiration of Holy Scripture and the eternity of punishment open questions. I wrote to him about the non-continuance of endowments ; he replied that he, too, thought so, and included, to my surprise, non-consecration of churches among endowments.

I have marvelled how, with the continued increase of alienation of the State, people go on building churches, or how, amid all this discouragement, the young enter Holy Orders. This, of course, I keep to myself, and speak cheerfully amid a continual heartache. But the only hope, under God, is in gaining the hearts and prayers of the poor, and it is in the hope that 1,000 more hearts may be gained, and those who will work for the Church may not be discouraged, that I now write to your lordship.

Answer to Dr. Pusey

September 8, 1877.

My dear Dr. Pusey,—Any representation of yours will always command my respectful attention, and in this instance I readily admit your right to interfere in the behalf of your old friend Mr. Wagner.

I am sure that you do not depreciate or despise the consecration of churches, nor could you designate the rite of consecration as a 'farce' (the word used by Mr. Wagner in a letter addressed to me on this subject). On the contrary you would, on the principles you have always upheld, desire that a building designed for the worship of God should be set apart and dedicated to Him with all possible solemnity, so that the sanction of religion shall be superadded to the force of human law.

Now in this case all that I require is that the chapel of ease should be placed on the same footing as the church on which it depends. St. Paul's is consecrated ; the chapel which is intended, as is asserted, to receive the overflowings of St. Paul's, and which is within a few yards of its walls, ought, in my opinion, to be consecrated too. Nothing can befall the chapel in consequence of consecration which would not also befall St. Paul's.

The same clergy would officiate in both buildings, there would be doubtless in both the same style of divine service.

But you urge that it would be unwise to put another building under the power of Parliament, and you support yourself with the extract of Mr. Keble.

Your mind is so possessed with gloomy forebodings that you distrust the good Providence which hitherto has averted the evils you anticipate; I am more hopeful, and so are all those who, to your surprise, still cause the churches they have built to be consecrated, and still enter into Holy Orders. It is clear, then, that these suspicions are not generally entertained, whatever examples may occur here or there to the contrary, and it is well for the Church that they are not. Because if all felt as you do, the consequence would indeed be most serious. No one would enter into Holy Orders, no church hereafter be consecrated. The terrors of impending disasters would paralyse us, and would go far to hasten and help on the evils which you dread.

I must say it is unreasonable to represent me as withholding the privileges of public worship from 1,000 people, when I offer to consecrate the chapel on the easiest conditions.

Mr. Wagner expects that concessions should be made to his own feelings or apprehensions. But he forgets that some concessions on his part may also be expected.

You appeal to the case of St. Bartholomew's. When I licensed that building I had every reason to suppose that it would be offered for consecration when it was freed from debt, and could obtain a legal and definite district. In this calculation I have been disappointed, and such disappointments do not engender confidence.

Let me say further, and I wish to say it without offence, that if you and those who think with you suspect and mistrust State interference, there is reason for alarm on the other side. Mr. Wagner does not conceal that circumstances may compel him to make his submission to Rome. One of his curates has gone over to Rome, after writing a book which foreshadowed his change of creed. The arguments brought forward in that book exceedingly resemble those used by Mr. Wagner himself. Roman doctrine, and even modern Roman decrees, do not either repel or alarm him. I cannot regard his future course but with the greatest uneasiness. But he cannot say that I have ever shown any 'animus' against him, or treated him with unfairness or unkindness. Now if you could have seen your way to counsel compliance instead of resistance you might have done the Church in Brighton a lasting service. I fear that the part you have taken will only confirm Mr. Wagner in his resolution, and with all possible respect for your character, I cannot depart from mine.

Faithfully yours.

Reply to an Unreasonable Complainant

The Palace, Chichester: November 5, 1877.

My dear Mrs. ——,—I called to-day in the hope of seeing you and sparing myself a letter.

At the time when Ridley pulled down altars and all belonging to them at the end of the reign of Edward VI. there may have been reasons to fear that things which had been abused to superstition might continue to exercise a bad influence. But when the Reformation was fairly established, there was no need for such precautions, and then the shelf which is called by the grand name of Super-Altar, in Elizabeth's time and since, has been lawful. Indeed it is hard to see what offence can be taken at a few flowers put in a vase, or two candlesticks with candles not lighted except in case of need. For I suppose it is not seemly that the Holy Table should be in the darkest and most dismal part of the church, when all save that eastern end is bright with light.

If the parishioners meet after being properly summoned, what they decide must be held to be the voice of the parish. I really cannot see why the churchwardens, who represent the laity, should be supposed to be indifferent to the general mind of the parishioners, and in this particular case I believe they are respectable gentlemen and loyal Churchmen.

Now one word about your pastor. His income from his living is 33*l.* a year—less than is given to a cook. For this salary, or a little more, he devotes talents of no common order, time valuable to him, his whole heart and powers, to the service of his Master in this parish. I do really think it very ungrateful to carp at any little matters which may not quite please you or others. Still more unjustifiable is it to leave the parish church and go elsewhere, and of such desertion I think you are incapable. I want no rash changes—I defend nothing outside the order or law of our Church—but I think a minister keeping within both, and labouring for the good of his people, ought to meet with fair construction of his motives and conduct at their hands.

Sincerely yours.

CHAPTER IV

Addresses at Diocesan Conferences—Confederation of Church Schools —Appointment of Diocesan Missioner—Liturgical Questions— Fasting Communion—Correspondence, 1878–1884.

In the course of the difficult and anxious period which has been sketched in the foregoing chapter, the Bishop had won the respect and confidence of the diocese. He had held the balance between conflicting parties with firmness, tact, and strict fairness ; he had infused new life into all the existing diocesan institutions, and had resuscitated some which had been nearly or altogether defunct. His ability consisted rather in sharpening and directing the use of instruments already existing and originated by others than in devising new ones himself. Every fresh project submitted to him was most carefully examined and criticised ; he grasped all the details of any scheme with wonderful quickness, and was acute in detecting the weak points. Until he had thoroughly satisfied himself that it was sound and practicable, and likely to do real good, he would not commit himself to it ; but once satisfied on these points, he would give it all the support in his power, grudging neither time nor pains to assist the executive body by his counsel and sympathy, and commending it to the diocese by his written and spoken utterances on every possible occasion.

One institution which engaged his warmest sympathy and support was the Mothers' Guild, formed with the view of helping mothers by means of a few plain and simple rules, together with the benefits of mutual prayer and counsel, to understand and discharge their responsibilities to their children in training their characters and guiding their conduct.

He composed the prayers for the use of this Guild and carefully examined all the rules ; and after the scheme was launched he commended it to the clergy of the diocese in his charge delivered in 1890, and in a circular letter issued in the following year.

One letter out of many to the Hon. Mrs. Campion, who was one of the most active originators of the Guild, will suffice to show the minute care which he bestowed upon every detail of its working.

Palace, Chichester : April 14, 1886.

My dear Mrs. Campion,—I much approve of your service. In a very few instances I suggest an alternative word, chiefly from fear that the word in your text may not be generally understood. Titus ii. to verse 7 would supply a useful alternative lesson ; the advice to keep at home is invaluable. I suppose it is not intended to go through the whole service always, but to select such parts as may be suitable. I dare say the 127th Psalm occurred to you. It is very applicable in its whole strain to such meetings as you have.

Perhaps you know that the word 'guild' in some quarters provokes suspicion. I know of no better word, and it certainly ought not to be suspected. Let me thank you for this as well as your other labours on behalf of those who greatly need guidance, counsel, and, above all, sympathy.

The following letter refers to a Training Home for workhouse girls which the same lady was instituting at Hurst:

The proposal has my hearty approval and best wishes for its success. No class of girls can have a stronger claim on the G.F.S., for none are more friendless and none more helpless. They require, as all who know their case must allow, a special education to fit them for domestic service, the only occupation usually open to them. A workhouse school does not teach them habits of activity, industry, and self-reliance, and the atmosphere of a workhouse, however well conducted, is not favourable to vigour and independence of character. I look upon the (Training Home) as a means of weaning these young girls from workhouse associations and all pauperising influences, encouraging them in the desire and the purpose to earn an honest livelihood and enabling them to begin life hopefully and happily.

The letters to Mr. Wakeford, the Diocesan Missioner, which are appended to this chapter, evince the same solicitude concerning all the details of his work.

In the selection of subjects for discussion at the diocesan conferences he always advocated those which directly affected the religious life of the diocese, in preference to larger and especially to controversial questions which might lead to heated debate without any useful practical result.   He urged that the discussions should not be of an academical type, or made the occasion for oratorical display or for airing theories ; but that they should be such as would stimulate interest in diocesan work and wants : devising new plans, calling attention to defects in existing agencies, and suggesting means for their improvement and extension.   In these respects he considered a diocesan conference of greater value than a Church Congress.   ' I am far,' he said, ' from underrating the importance of those periodical meetings, but they are open to the objection that they begin in talk, continue in talk, and end in talk.   They decide nothing, they show no tangible result.   A diocesan conference, with far more moderate pretensions, has a real and definite field of action as well as of discussion.'

Amongst the subjects debated in the conferences during his episcopate were the promotion of habits of temperance and thrift, parochial councils, parochial missions, Sunday schools, children's services, Church finance, parochial libraries, friendly societies, the boarding out of pauper children, a society for the promotion of religious study, a scheme for the confederation of Church schools.

Committees were appointed to inquire into these subjects, and their reports formed the basis of discussions, which led in many instances to lasting practical results. Of course, a demand for the consideration of larger subjects, such as the constitution of ecclesiastical courts, or patronage, or what are commonly called 'burning questions,' could not always be resisted, but the Bishop only tolerated them as concessions to the temper of the times. ' I have no love,' he said, 'for what, in the language of the day, are called " burning questions." The smell of such fires, the fierceness of such flames, is hateful to men of peace and charity, and to all those who " study to be quiet and to do their own business." '

Nevertheless he admitted that good might arise from the occasional discussion of such subjects in a full and open assembly where arguments could be heard on both sides, and persons who were wont to read only such newspapers and pamphlets as supported their own opinions might discover that there was more to be said by their opponents than they had been willing to believe.

His opening addresses to the conferences, in which he touched upon the several questions about to be discussed, were remarkable for their practical wisdom, and for the concise, vigorous, scholarly English in which his opinions were expressed ; but he intervened in the debates as little as possible, and refrained from obtruding his own views upon the assembly.

' I do not think,' he said, ' that it is my office (as president) to sum up each debate after the manner of a judge. If I had the ability to compress into a reasonable space the arguments of opposing speakers and to declare my own opinion as to their cogency, I should shrink from such an exercise of authority. This conference—composed, as it is, of thoughtful and well-instructed men—ought to be allowed to form its own conclusions. Neither is your president in the position of a moderator in academical disputations. There the office of the presiding dignitary is to declare on which side lies the truth. Nor is this assembly to be likened to a synod, in which we are told the Bishop simply promulged what was to be accepted. It is the duty of your president to lay before you in the simplest and shortest way the work prepared for you, in which you are invited to share. In this respect, to compare little things with great, his address at a diocesan conference is a sort of Queen's speech, but with this difference, that one head and one mind only is concerned in its concoction, and this may probably have some advantage as regards both brevity and clearness. The president is, according to English usage, the chairman of the assembly. It is his duty to see that the rules of debate be observed, that order be maintained, and in any contested question (of order) to give to the best of his power an impartial decision.'

And for assistance in the discharge of this duty, as well as for other reasons, he regarded the presence of members of Parliament as a very great advantage.

'Their familiarity,' he said in his address at the seventh conference, 'with the rules which have hitherto been observed by the greatest representative assembly in the world, their habits of business, and that fairness and largeness of mind which results from treating of great affairs and hearing the ablest exposition of opposite ideas, not to mention the sense of their responsibility as rulers, gives them great weight in our councils. So far from importing the disturbing element of politics into our midst, they have often, by their impartiality and moderation, smoothed difficulties and suggested means of agreement. On the other hand, I think it is good that they should have some experience of a diocesan conference. They will be convinced by observation that the representatives of the diocesan clergy and laity, differing as much in their rank and position as in their opinions, can discuss questions of great interest with perfect freedom of speech, yet without passion or asperity. They will also be satisfied that the difference of feeling which is said to separate the clergy from the laity either has no existence or has been grossly exaggerated.

'Provision has been made by our constitution that in any case of serious divergency of opinion the two orders should vote separately, if such separate voting should be demanded ; but in our six sessions there has been no instance, I believe, of such a demand. Nor have I observed that in any debate the clergy have been ranged conspicuously on one side, and the laity on the other, even when such a separation seemed probable.'

Great alarm was excited in 1885, when a general election was impending, by the discovery that 400 candidates were pledged to vote, if elected, for the disestablishment of the Church, and that the Society for the Liberation of Religion from State Control was actively engaged in disseminating its doctrines.

In his address to the diocesan conference of that year, the Bishop, then eighty-three years of age, sounded a note of earnest warning in language of uncommon force and fire, pointing out the imminence of the danger from the determination and unscrupulousness of the enemy, and describing in glowing terms the disastrous consequences which would ensue to the nation should the attack be successful.

' Disestablishment,' he said, ' and disendowment are now familiar words. They have indeed been long heard, but, like the muttering of distant thunder, their sound conveyed no sense of danger. Now the storm is hovering over us and marching onwards. The scheme promulgated by the Liberationist Society is circulated by thousands. It is well devised to unite all enemies of the Church as by law established in the work of its overthrow. The Secularist is to be gratified by the State, as a State, repudiating religious obligations. The Socialist sees his opportunity in the confiscation of Church property and the admission thereby of a principle and precedent ready for wider application. The Liberationists used to give out that their object was purely religious, to free the Church of England from State control, from the corrupting influence of endowments which cramped her efficiency, and thus enable her to do her Master's work as His Spirit might lead. This mask, however, is now dropped. Calmly, indeed, and with no violence of language, but with thorough and relentless consistency, the plan of spoliation is unfolded and the consequences discovered. There is an assured tone of victory. *Væ victis* is printed in every clause. We are counted as '' sheep appointed to be slain." " How are the mighty fallen ! " is the song of triumph to be sung by those who have won the battle and divide the spoil. Depend upon it, these people are terribly in earnest. They know their purpose, and are ready to pursue it to the bitter end. Nor are they scrupulous as to means. It was said of old : " Great is truth and will prevail." The modern view seems to be that the opposite course must command success. Witness the flood of falsehoods in speech and print as to the income and payment of the clergy, their duties, their lives, their work, the origin of the Church of Christ in this land, and its connexion with the civil government. . . . If the Church of England had failed to fulfil its mission, if the poor, its special charge, had been neglected, if its clergy were sunk in sloth and luxury, if the laity had been selfish and unsympathising, if the Church had been without faith or charity, then it would have deserved the contumely now thrown upon it and the punishment with which it is threatened. Sixty years ago or earlier there would have been a better plea for disestablishment and disendowment. But now the Church of England is manifesting a zeal for her Master's work such as scarcely any period of her existence has shown. I say no more, for I do not wish to exaggerate.

'This diocese affords probably a very fair specimen of the results that would ensue from disestablishment and disendowment. It contains some 366 parishes ; of these 307 may be set down as agricultural, the rest are urban. You, the representatives of the several deaneries, know well the rural parishes. In how many, do you think, a resident pastor could be maintained if the

possessions of the Church were confiscated ?   Judge
for yourselves and make a calculation, which I
decline as too melancholy a task.   But this I can
predict, that full many a flock would be left without
a shepherd, full many, misled by the delusive
promises of demagogues, would rue too late the
dying out of the very springs of long-enjoyed charities, the cessation of kindly intercourse, of fatherly
help, and of the regular ministrations of religion.'

The Bishop's warning words were not thrown
away.   The machinery of the Church Defence Association, which had been somewhat at a standstill in
the diocese, was set in vigorous motion, and many
of the clergy did good service in explaining in popular lectures, which were largely attended, the true
history of the Church of England—especially of its
origin, establishment, and endowments, about which
great ignorance and misconception prevailed, partly
from want of teaching and study, partly from the
misrepresentations and lies which were diligently
disseminated by the Liberation Society and other
kindred agencies.

The Bishop returned to the subject in his Visitation Charge delivered in 1887.   The immediate
danger had then passed by.   The mind of Parliament had been too much occupied with the difficulties of the Irish land question to turn its attention to
the Church.

' But,' said the Bishop, ' the respite which has
been allowed may come to an end.   Our adversaries
are many, aggressive, and, I fear, unscrupulous.
The pamphlets and papers circulated by them in

thousands are but the light skirmishers ; the heavier troops of agitators with their speeches and their meetings follow.   Now these men should be met, and met in public.   The contradiction of error should be immediate and as open as the attack.   Truth is great and will prevail, but it must assert itself. . . . The clergy are the natural instructors of the people, who have a right to be guarded against plausible misrepresentation and to be enabled to form just and true opinions upon a question which so nearly concerns themselves.   The question is not political but religious, however it may have been abused to political ends, and it might be well if from time to time, as our services may give opportunity, the pulpit were to bring the authority of God's Word to bear more directly upon the history, constitution, and the spiritual use and office of a visible Church.'

Once more, in the charge which the Bishop wrote in 1895 but did not live to deliver, he refers to the recent defeat of the measure for the disestablishment of the Church in Wales in terms of mingled thanksgiving and warning.   Although he had nearly completed his ninety-third year when he wrote the charge, it betrays no diminution of vigour, either in thought or expression.

'One subject which last year overshadowed all others is no longer before us.   The national verdict has been pronounced upon it.   A change in public feeling and action which is marvellous in our eyes has sent the Welsh Church Bill to the limbo of failures, there to keep company with other measures of like political character.   I say political character, for no charity can make us believe that the attack on the Church in Wales sprang from simply religious motives. The demagogues who have the ear and the confidence of Welsh Dissent stirred up their zeal, I doubt not in many instances a real though mistaken zeal, against the Church which stood peaceably among them, of which their ancestors have all been members, with a view to ulterior schemes dearer to them than any question of doctrine or discipline. The Church, thank God, has now a respite. Let us not deceive ourselves. It is not a permanent deliverance. The spirit of our adversaries is not changed by defeat; nay, it may be expected to show even more irritation. But a season is allowed to the Church in Wales, and not to the Church in Wales alone (for the whole Church of England is bound up inseparably with those four Welsh dioceses), to strengthen its weak places, and to win by faithful work for Christ the confidence and affection of the people. The Welsh Bill has had an effect which its promoters probably did not anticipate. It sounded out a note of alarm and warning which Church people could not but hear. It convinced them that the extreme measures of spoliation were no longer mere theories or distant dangers, but near and threatening, and embodied in practical legislation. Church defence has become a watchword with us. Truths either not known, or half known, or forgotten, have been brought into light by lectures, able tracts, and public meetings, as well in villages as in towns throughout England. Men have learned on what foundations rests the Church of which they are members. They have learned why it claims the title of Catholic and Apostolic, why and how at the Reformation it was cleared from errors and abuses and delivered from the dominion of the Pope of Rome, what is the authority of its spiritual rulers, what the origin of endowments. Ignorance on all these and many kindred subjects prevailed because the people had never been taught. They were not unwilling to learn, but no one felt it his duty to instruct them, so that on these points no less than on points of doctrine the mass of the people were uncatechised. What wonder that they should be indifferent or fall an easy prey to every false statement? The results of the late election have been ascribed by observers able and cautious, and by no means prejudiced in favour of such a theory, to the increased influence of the Church of England. This is an unexpected encouragement; only let us not be lulled into a false security. Our adversaries never sleep. Let us take a lesson from their activity, and see that we hold fast the ground that we have won.'

There was indeed no duty upon which the Bishop insisted more constantly and strenuously in the latter years of his life than that of sound teaching in regard to the principles, the constitution, and the history of the Church; for he perceived that the future safety of the Church largely depended upon it. In 1891 he strongly advocated the claims of a society which had been recently established in the diocese to promote systematic study of the Bible, Church history, and the Book of Common Prayer.

'We can never,' he said, 'open a newspaper without observing that the interest in religious questions increases every day, especially those that concern the Church of England; but it is equally true that in the treatment of those questions there is often displayed a prodigious amount of ignorance, and statements entirely unsupported by historical fact find ready acceptance amongst the unlearned. A sound knowledge of Church history is essential to the right treatment of such questions, and to the formation of religious opinion in regard to them. It is not creditable that members of our communion should be so ill instructed as they often are in the principles of the Church of England. It is this ignorance, or very imperfect knowledge, which a regular course of reading under the direction and supervision of well-qualified instructors is calculated to remedy. There must be many in the great towns of East Sussex who have leisure for such reading, and this plan of religious study not only offers the opportunity, but supplies the method and system without which reading is apt to be vague, desultory, and unprofitable.'

He recommended, also, that the public press should be employed more largely for the diffusion of sound information on Church subjects.

'The newspaper,' he said,[1] 'whatever its complexion, is read in every cottage. We must meet the requirements of an active and inquiring age and be able to show that our Church can satisfy them. From my own experience I should say that the periodical press is by no means unfavourably disposed towards the Church of England. I am bound to acknowledge much consideration and courtesy shown to me by the press, and I am inclined to think that the editors would be always prepared to

---

[1] Address at Diocesan Conference, 1893.

report, with impartiality, any account of Church matters which might be submitted to them. We do not presume to ask that we should have any preference over accounts of Roman Catholic proceedings or of Nonconformist proceedings. We want no exclusive privileges, and we only expect that whatever the Church may do should be impartially reported in the great vehicles of communication.'

The deep importance which he attached to regular and systematic instruction in the elementary Church schools, and the earnestness with which he repeatedly urged this duty upon the clergy, have been already mentioned. Unless this duty was faithfully performed, the preservation of the voluntary schools was, in his opinion, of comparatively little value; but, in order that this distinctive teaching might be possible, he was of course most anxious that they should be preserved. And for this purpose he earnestly advocated the scheme for a confederation of Church schools in the diocese, which was established, largely through the energy of Canon Sanderson, in 1892. He welcomed it, not only as a means of saving Church schools from extinction, but as a salutary check to the evils of parochial isolation, in which he discerned with alarm the seeds of much weakness and danger.

'If Churchmen,' he said, 'will not combine to rescue distressed schools, what will they do when other and even graver interests are threatened? This is a good opportunity, if it is no more, to learn and to practise a habit of concert and co-

operation, so that we may be able to defend ourselves in contests still more vital.'[2]

And in his circular letter to the clergy on the
subject he urged them to 'recommend the plan as
an instrument of moral and spiritual good, binding
together managers and teachers, clergy and laity,
in town and country, in a steadfast purpose to
maintain the religious teaching of the children of
the Church, and to stand shoulder to shoulder, so
that the strong may help the weak, the richer assist
the poorer, and that the world may see that we are
not concerned for mere local and separate interests,
but for the benefit of the young flock of Christ in
the whole of the country.'

Side by side with the work of maintaining and
strengthening sound religious education, the Bishop
was not less anxious to provide means for deepen-
ing the spiritual life and elevating the moral standard of the people.   And experience convinced him
that the services of a Diocesan Missioner would be
a valuable help in this direction if the right man
could be found for the post.

The fiftieth year of the Diocesan Association
was to be celebrated in 1888, and to be marked, if
possible, by some new undertaking.   In the Diocesan Conference of 1887, the Bishop accordingly
recommended the appointment of a Diocesan
Missioner.

'I should be the last,' he said, 'to depreciate
the quiet and regular work of the parochial

<hr>

[2] Address at Diocesan Conference in 1892.

minister. None surely is more necessary, none more blessed. But I believe full many of the most faithful of God's servants would gladly receive the occasional help of a missioner, who might, by the grace of God and the power of the Spirit, breathe new life into the parish, comfort the sinful, awake the indifferent, and strengthen the faithful.'

At the Conference of 1888 the Bishop announced that with his license the Rev. John Wakeford, long known and valued as a missioner in the diocese of Exeter, would undertake a mission in certain rural parishes which were prepared to receive him in the autumn ; and he expressed a hope that Mr. Wakeford would in the end be permanently attached to the diocese. There was much division of opinion in the Conference as to the expediency of definitely appointing a missioner, and as to the conditions of the appointment if it was made. The Bishop, however, clenched the matter by asserting, at the conclusion of the debate, that he claimed the right to appoint whom he pleased, and that he should exercise it in favour of Mr. Wakeford. He had seen him and heard him, had formed the highest possible opinion of his fitness for the office, and he meant to have him.

At the next Conference, in 1889, he was able to announce that Mr. Wakeford had held missions in twenty-one parishes, and had revisited fifteen of them, and that in all of them the hope had been expressed that the people might see his face and hear his voice again. It was the particular wish of the

Bishop that the visits of the missioner should be paid to the rural parishes which abound in Sussex. He was sure that those who knew most of the state of rural feeling and moral conduct in rural districts would not be led away by dreams of Arcadian innocence and rural simplicity; yet he considered the people to be for the most part orderly, patient, and industrious. They deserved all the help and care that the Church of England could give them, and if a mission could help in recalling to the fold those who had strayed from it, and planting in the hearts of the people principles of godliness, temperance, soberness, and chastity, he trusted that every pastor, nay every Christian, would rejoice and give thanks; for such a work was not of man but of God.

But, however effective the labours of a missioner might be, the Bishop knew that the real hold of the Church upon the people depended upon the regular ministrations of the parochial clergy. In most of his later charges he insisted with increasing earnestness on the supreme importance of parochial visiting. He discerned in the social conditions of the age the urgent need of strict attention to this duty. The possession of the franchise had given the working people a new sense of independence and importance; and the old respect for rank and station, as such, had declined. Much of the literature current and popular among them was directed against authority in Church and State, and was replete with misrepresentations.

The only way to counteract the evil influence of these new conditions was for the clergy to prove that they were the real friends of their people by all manner of kindly intercourse. For the lack of this no system, however well devised, could possibly compensate ; and he urged the duty of pastoral visiting on all candidates for ordination all the more earnestly because he feared, from the evidence that was brought to him from time to time, that the duty was one in which there was a growing tendency, especially among the younger clergy, to be rather remiss. Some were inclined to delegate it too much to the district visitor, a very poor substitute for the pastor, who was entrusted with a divine commission to tend his flock ; others seemed to expect that their parishioners would resort to them for spiritual instruction of their own accord. But it was vain to hope for such docility ; the people must be sought out in their houses, and the voice that was familiar to them there would be heard with gladness in the church.

He viewed also with alarm and indignation the neglect by some of the clergy of the duty, which he had so often urged, of giving regular religious instruction in their day schools. Such neglect exposed them to the taunt that they, who had clamoured for the right to teach as inherent in their office, made little or no use of it when it was given. He censured also the too prevalent neglect to give religious instruction to the pupil-teachers—a duty the importance of which could hardly be overrated, inasmuch as they were the teachers of the future. Yet it appeared from authentic returns made to the two Archbishops that in 1888 only 41 per cent. of the pupil-teachers entering training colleges from all England had received religious instruction, and in 1889 only 36 per cent.

In regard to all liturgical questions the Bishop, with advancing years, took his stand more and more resolutely upon the lines marked out in the Book of Common Prayer, and refused to give his sanction to any practice or form of service which he thought could not be clearly reconciled with its letter or spirit. He expressed his disapproval of evening communions because the practice was one of modern invention, which found no countenance in the rubrics of our Communion service, still less in the customs of the Church Catholic. Although defended on grounds of convenience and even of necessity, he was persuaded that the end desired might be better secured by early morning celebrations. Experience proved that the working people, used as they were to early hours, would gladly take advantage of such opportunities.[3]

He was also opposed on similar grounds to the increasing practice of attendance at Holy Communion without communicating. It was modern, and, though not expressly forbidden by any rubric, appeared to him to be at variance with the whole scope and intention of the English Communion office. He spoke his mind very plainly on the sub-

---

[3] Charge, 1890, p. 14.

ject in the Diocesan Conference of 1894, the last which he ever attended, at the close of a debate upon Worship, in which one of the speakers had advocated the practice. He pointed out that some of the greatest English liturgical authorities— Philip Freeman, Scudamore, and Maskel (who afterwards seceded to Rome)—had declared that it was not the practice of the Primitive Church, and he quoted the following words from John Keble:

'I have a strong feeling against the foreign custom of encouraging all sorts of persons to assist at the Holy Eucharist without communicating. It seems to me open to two grave objections. It cannot be without danger of profaneness in very many, and consequent dishonour to the Holy Sacrament, and it has brought in or encouraged, or both (at least so I greatly suspect), a notion of a quasi-sacramental virtue in such attendance which I take to be a great part of the error stigmatised in our 31st Article.'

The Bishop indeed was willing to allow that it might be profitable for persons who were preparing for Holy Communion to attend a celebration without communicating, and occasionally even for habitual communicants who for some special reason might not be disposed to communicate; but these cases should be the exception, not the rule.

'If,' he said, 'the belief should be encouraged that the mere presence of worshippers is enough, and that a sacramental blessing may flow vicariously from such attendance, then it is but a short step to the solitary mass—that abuse which contradicts the very idea of communion, and which was abolished for good reasons by the reformers of our Church.'

In like manner the Bishop would not accord his sanction to daily celebrations unless he was satisfied that there would always be some security for the minimum number of worshippers required by the Prayer Book not only being present, but also actually communicating; and he disliked the multiplication of small chapels and side altars in the cathedral or large parish churches, because he thought they increased the risk of this requirement being neglected.

He also viewed with strong disfavour the teaching which insisted on fasting before communicating as an essential and indispensable condition. The rigorous imposition of this rule seemed to him to be dictated by a material conception of the Sacrament, not warranted by the Prayer Book, and the result in too many instances was that the greater duty was sacrificed to the less, the plain divine command to communicate being disregarded if compliance with the human rule was difficult or impossible. On this subject he placed a high value upon the opinion of Dr. Pusey as expressed in the following letter :

Christ Church, Oxford : March 15, 1879.

My dear Perry,—I have been in the habit of saying :

i. That there can be no intrinsic irreverence in non-fasting Communion, since (*a*) our Lord instituted it after supper ; (*b*) the Communion is given to the sick, although not necessarily *in extremis*.

ii. There is no positive law of the Church upon the subject.

At one time *it was supposed* that there was, and Bishop Forbes (whose authorities were often out of the common path, but accurate) told me that in consequence dispensation used to be given to the kings of France and Spain to receive Communion non-fasting, because it was thought edifying to their subjects to see them communicate.

Provincial Councils and the Council of Constance have forbidden non-fasting Communion, but no Council to which we owe obedience.

On the other hand, there is a universal custom, reaching back to the second century, of communicating before receiving any other food.

iii. That the division of the twenty-four hours so that day shall begin at midnight is of course perfectly arbitrary. The Roman Communion has, of course, perfect right to lay down what rules it thinks proper for its communicants ; but the eastern division of the day, whereby it should begin at sunset, and morning at sunrise, is much more natural. We retain it still in our 'midday,' 'midnight,' 'fortnight,' 'se'nnight.' It is, then, perfectly arbitrary to date the beginning of the fast from 12 P.M. We are not bound to it, not being under Roman rule. This might meet the case of taking food, e.g. milk, at night before 6 A.M.

iv. Though on account of the abuses of evening Communion and their increase one would be very sorry to infringe this rule, yet the case of the midnight Communion on Christmas night shows that the mere fact of having taken food is not in itself a hindrance to communicating. For if Christmas day fell on a Monday (as it did a few years ago), then the Roman Communion also allows a person to have full meals all through the Sunday. I have heard two different accounts : (*a*) that persons have to abstain from 6 P.M. on the Sunday, which if the dinner has been (as it may be) a full meal is no abstinence at all, or (*b*) that they are under no limitations. But anyhow there is no difference in principle between a person communicating at the midnight Communion after all the meals of Sunday (the midnight being merely a conventional distinction) and taking what is necessary to sustain strength, to keep up attention, and so to communicate devoutly, at a sufficient distance of time. All Roman Catholics hold that the Bishop of Rome could dispense with the rule of communicating fasting ; they cannot, then, hold it to be a divine law.

v. The command to communicate is divine. The rule of non-communicating after food is human. If, then, they notably clash, the divine command supersedes the human.

This is decisive in the case of A., in which you say the priest told her that if she could not go fasting ' she ought not to go at all, even if she did not communicate for years.' But in the Church in which God has placed her it is a command to communicate three times a year : everywhere the Easter Communion is a law of the Church, one who did not communicate *then* would be *ipso facto* excommunicate. She, then, according to her adviser, is to break the law of God and of the Church, and to excommunicate herself.

I wish these rigorists who sew new cloth upon old garments would think a little of what is meant by mortal sin ; of course all know (though they may not bring it home to themselves) that mortal sin expels the grace of God and slays the soul in that single act.   But non-fasting Communion, according to them also, is only 'mortal sin,' as breaking a commandment of the Church.   I wonder whether they think that they commit a mortal sin and are out of the grace of God if they neglect on any occasion to say the morning and evening service.

And if she, A., did not know that it was anything wrong, her director made it mortal sin to her by telling her so, for to break commandments of the Church in ignorance is not sin at all.

I see that the conductor of the retreat to which B. went also said that 'God would not allow a soul to be harmed if it broke the command to communicate for years and years.'   Our ladies would do well to abstain from going to retreats if the clergy are to entangle them.   I wonder whether they think as energetically against people speaking evil of authorities and of their neighbours.   Church topics used to be full of it ; but God said 'Speak not evil one of another.'   This would be a very onesided God.   Yours affectionately,

E. B. PUSEY.

CORRESPONDENCE, 1878–1882

*Letter to a Clergyman who was on the eve of
seceding to the Church of Rome*

The Palace, Chichester : March 1, 1878.

My dear ——,—I need not say that the announcement contained in your letter of February 27 has filled me with disappointment and trouble.   I always hoped that now in the eighth or ninth year of your ministry you were stablished and settled yourself, and would serve as a steadying power to the younger clergy around you.   That expectation has been rudely broken.

You cannot say that you have not enjoyed full liberty of teaching, or that you were unable to use such ritual as you deemed to edification.   You had an attached people hanging on your lips and prepared to follow you as their spiritual leader.   But doubts arise in your mind, and I fear you have given them too favourable a hearing.   You look to the difficulties of your position in the Church of your baptism, whatever they may be ; you resolve to face the far greater difficulties of the desperate step you have perhaps by this time taken.

For such expressions of kindness as you have written to me I thank you, and I can assure you that I had always a real respect for your labours among the people of your district.   This makes your defection all the more grievous to me ; your renunciation of your orders, even of your baptism, your reception into a communion which I am bound to believe is greatly in error, both in the things which it admits and which it rejects.

You seek for peace of mind, and to obtain it you make a great sacrifice.   This must be confessed, for I do not doubt your heart yearns towards your old flock, and you cannot but think of what they will suffer on your account.

But I cannot believe that you have taken the real way of peace, or that you will be allowed to find it among your new friends.   This much I am bound to say, not in anger, but in deep and real sorrow.

Believe me faithfully yours.

To a Clergyman on Ritual

The Palace, Chichester: April 1, 1878.

My dear Mr. ———,—In your printed letter of March 22 you write: ' If my Bishop called upon me to surrender either practice, I should immediately obey.'

This declaration is in accordance with the principles which, as a minister of the Church of England, you have uniformly professed.

I was therefore justified in expecting that when I requested you to desist from lighting the candles on the altar when light is not needed, and from mixing water with the sacramental wine, you would at once, to use your own words, have ' obeyed.'

But instead of such acquiescence you argue the case on two grounds.

(i.) That the practices which I desire to be reformed are in use in other churches and chapels in the diocese, and (ii.) that the judgment prohibiting them is in your opinion bad in law. I decline to enter on the second of these grounds of objection, because I do not admit your right to draw me into discussions of that nature. But as to the first. You must remember that I have to look only to the officiating minister, and that I have nothing to do with the absent proprietors. The license, indeed, was in the name of Dr. M., but it is revocable at the Bishop's pleasure and constitutes no freehold right. So far from your compliance with my request provoking opposition on the part of the congregation, I am persuaded that an alteration in the direction of obedience to the laws would be welcomed by the great majority, and as it would

be perfectly consistent with your position in the
Church hitherto you would be able to explain your
course of action with much advantage.

For a declared Ritualist such a retractation
might be difficult, but for you, who have always
stopped short of Ritualism, it would be easy.

Believe me faithfully yours.

To the same

The Palace, Chichester : April 5, 1878.

My dear ——,—I must adhere to my request
that candles be not lighted on the Holy Table
except when light is required, and that the wine
administered to communicants be wine and not
wine and water.

In themselves these things are indifferent, but
indifferent things fall within the determination of
the law of the Church, and that law as respects the
two points above mentioned has been interpreted
by the highest existing authority. I do not myself
presume to ignore or contravene this interpretation,
and, with all respect for your legal training, I hardly
think it becoming in you to contest the decision of
the Court of Final Appeal on the ground that you
understand the law better than the judges of that
court.

You complain that a measure of repression is
meted out to you that is not applied to others who,
you intimate, transgress the law far more perti-
naciously and ostentatiously. But you overlook the
difference between those transgressors of the law
and yourself. They may commit irregularities, but
they do not proclaim and justify their disobedience
in the public papers, nor claim their Bishop as

willing to sanction or at least to connive at them. But you represent me as not disapproving of practices to which, as being forbidden by law, objection was made, and this representation you make in a local journal in a letter signed with your name within this diocese.

Now you had no authority to make any such statement. As a matter of fact, I do disapprove of these illegal practices, and by your own act I am compelled to show my disapproval. My contradiction must be as public as your assertion. It was open to me to contradict your statement in the same manner as that in which it was put forth. But I abstained from this course, and took one which I believed was calculated to spare your feelings, and, I may add, my own. May I be allowed to suggest to you that a clergyman is not seen to advantage as a writer in a local paper? Nothing is more welcome to editors than to draw the clergy down into that arena, for a large part of the readers of newspapers like nothing better than to be bystanders in a religious controversy.

But if a clergyman be compelled to come forward in the columns of the newspapers, he ought to be very careful not to forget the sacredness and dignity of his calling, and should not suffer any provocation to goad him into retaliation. I see that in your letter to the 'News' there are passages, allusions, and expressions in a tone such as I should not have expected from you.

As to the danger which you apprehend that Dr. M. may dismiss you on the ground of your conforming to the law, I wish you to remember that he holds his license simply at pleasure, and that I should undoubtedly withdraw it if he should presume to constrain his *locum tenens* in his iron licensed building.

I am sorry that our correspondence should have been upon points of difference rather than as heretofore upon the far more numerous points in which we are well agreed, and am

Very truly yours.

The schismatical body against which the following letter is a warning had its origin in America in 1873, when eight clergymen formally severed their connexion with the Episcopal Church in the United States under the leadership of Dr. Cummins, the Assistant Bishop of Kentucky.   Having designated themselves 'the Reformed Episcopal Church,' their first act was to elect a certain Dr. Cheney as a second Bishop, who was consecrated on December 14 by Dr. Cummins.   The so-called Bishop Gregg referred to in Bishop Durnford's letter had been Vicar of East Harbourne, in the diocese of Lichfield.   After an absence of some duration from his family, he returned with the announcement that he had been made a Bishop, and the only probable explanation of the mystery is that he had been to America, and had obtained consecration at the hands of Dr. Cummins.   Another Bishop appeared in the diocese of Bath and Wells, and there may have been others elsewhere.   They and their followers styled their self-constituted body 'the Reformed Church of England.'   A few extracts from one of the leaflets which they circulated will suffice to show the nature and design of their society.

'The Reformed Church of England is intended to meet the needs of persons who, owing to the Ritualism and Romanism in their Church, do not know what to do. They do not like to go to church to countenance what they disapprove, and they do not wish to go to chapel and abandon the liturgy which they love.

'The Reformed Church of England does not believe in baptismal regeneration, nor in the real presence in the Lord's Supper, nor in the power of anyone except God to forgive sins, and it uses a revised Book of Common Prayer which has only been altered in those matters which are contrary to Evangelical and Protestant principles.'

To the Members of the Church of England in Littlehampton

My dear Brethren,—A notice having been put forth that on Thursday next 'St. Saviour's Reformed Episcopal Church will be opened by the Right Reverend Bishop Gregg,' it is my duty to remind you that the Church in England as by law established is the Reformed Episcopal Church in this realm, and that no other body of Christians has any right to that title. From the time that your forefathers were converted to the faith of Jesus Christ, the Church of the South Saxons has continued within this county and diocese to the present day. The succession of Bishops, first of Selsey and then of Chichester, has never been broken.

The Church of England, in which Sussex was

comprehended, reformed itself more than three centuries ago. It then rejected the usurped authority of the Pope of Rome and the false doctrines and superstitious practices with which Rome had overlaid the true faith. But it remained, and is still the original Church of the nation ; Reformed because it has cast off Roman errors, Episcopal because it adheres to the apostolic form of Church Government. The Reformation of the Church was effected in a solemn and legal manner, and ratified by the clergy in their Convocation and by the Laity in Parliament.

But the so-called ' R. E. C.,' now for the first time appearing among you, is the creation of certain individuals who, of their mere will and motion, have set it up in plain opposition to the ancient and lawful Church of this nation. It is simply a self-constituted body, and if it stood on the same ground as the Nonconformist bodies in England I should not have thought it necessary to interfere. But there is a great difference between the Nonconformist bodies in England and this ' R. E. C.' The Nonconformist bodies, with the single exception of the Roman Catholics, reject the authority of Bishops, and therefore are so distinctly separated from the Established Church that none can mistake the one for the other. But inasmuch as the self-styled ' R. E. C.' professes to adhere to the government of the Church by Bishops, there is danger that members of the Church of England may be misled, and may join this new Church, being ignorant that by so doing they separate themselves from the communion of the Church of England.

It is also announced that the Bishop of the

'R. E. C.' will shortly hold a confirmation in Littlehampton.

I am therefore constrained solemnly to warn you that any Bishop officiating in this diocese without my sanction is an intruder. Whether really a Bishop or not (and there are grave doubts whether the Bishops of this 'R. E. C.' have been lawfully consecrated), he commits by this intruding an open act of schism, in direct violation of the laws of God and His Church, and I do hereby warn you that if any members of the Church of England shall, after this notice, seek confirmation at the hands of such a Bishop they will be partakers of his transgression, and that no blessing can be expected to follow such ministrations.

I address these words of serious caution to you because, however unworthy of so great a charge, I am, by God's permission, the Chief Pastor of this diocese, and I earnestly and affectionately commend them to your consideration, being now as always

Your faithful Friend and Bishop,

(Signed)   R. CICESTR.

Palace, Chichester : Easter, 1878.

The orthodox Bishops in America were delighted with this letter. The schismatical body has disappeared from Sussex, but still exists in some other parts of England.

To the Rev. Canon Ashwell (Principal of the Theological College)

The Palace, Chichester : May 23, 1878.

My dear Canon Ashwell,—Circumstances have prevented me from having a conversation with you on the subject of the Guild of the Holy Rood, and perhaps it is better that the remarks which I have to make should be stated in writing.

I have to thank you for your explanation of the ' Book,' for the book itself, and your offer that if there be anything in it, as generally in the Guild, which seemed to me objectionable, my objection should be attended to even if I should require the abolition of the Association. I should be sorry to suppress a society which, in your opinion, has done, and is calculated to do, much good. The rules and regulations appear to me, in the greater part, un-exceptionable, and tending to edification. But I ought not to have been left without any knowledge of such an Association within the college of which I am visitor. In point of fact, my first information concerning it was derived from a Manchester paper, and I could hardly believe that it was correct. But it appears that Mr. —— originated it, and it was since carried on wholly without my sanction.

Yet the Bishop of the diocese, the official visitor of the college, is of course compromised by a Guild of the sort existing within the college. It would be no defence for me to say I knew nothing of it ; no defence, because nobody would believe me, and would charge me with culpable want of atten-tion to the concerns and interests of the institution. I am sure you will see the force of this argument, and it is sufficient to have thus mentioned it. In another sheet I specify some objections, and some alterations which I must request may be made if the Guild is to continue.

I have forborne all captious objections to words and phrases, though I may entertain dislike for some here and there in the prayers, and have confined my remarks to points which I deem essential. I confess to a certain fear that the use of Romish and mediæval words may have a tendency to draw men insensibly into the. Roman toils. We have suffered so much from these perversions that any approximation to Rome is suspected, and not without reason.

Believe me sincerely yours.

Notes on the Guild of the Holy Rood

The word 'rood' in popular acceptance, though not in strict significance, is taken to mean ' crucifix.' The roodloft was the place in which the figure of our Blessed Lord on the Cross was displayed, usually with the Virgin and St. John at the side. In order to avert suspicion I should suggest that another word be substituted—e.g. Chichester College Guild. Pages 4, 9.

The meeting is ordered to be held on Holy Cross Day—i.e., I conclude, the day of the Invention of the Cross. This is one of the black-letter saints' days which are not ordered by our Church to be kept holy or observed, but are retained, it is supposed for convenience, in the Calendar. The Invention of the Cross is a legend, moreover.

The choice of this day may give just cause of offence. The qualification, as you term it at the head of the ' Rules of Life,' is in truth no qualification at all, because it would apply to the most positive laws, human or divine. A man can only keep them to the best of his ability. So with these rules.

I object to Rule 2.

If it means that the Holy Communion must be

received every Sunday and Holy Day, and always fasting, then it is supposed that every member must be so prepared as to desire to communicate. I think a contrary state of mind and conscience occasionally quite conceivable, and if this should be the case the rule would be a snare.

If to be present means to be present without receiving, I object to such a rule being laid down. But I object most of all to the requirement that the Holy Communion should always be received fasting.   No such rule is to be found in our Church.

A distinction unknown to our Church is hereby raised—those who receive fasting and those who communicate after partaking of necessary food. The celebrant, if he does his office at midday, suppose after morning service and Sunday school, and other duties which fall on an English clergyman, will be faint for want of food.

Early Communions will not be found in all the churches in which the students of the college will be placed, and therefore they will be exposed to the danger attending the long morning fast when prayers are to be said and sermons preached, and the Communion administered.

The Roman Catholics who profess to observe the rule (I mean the clergy) are drawn by it into inconsistent practices ; eating very late the night before—taking snuff or smoking, which they hold to be permissible, though to eat a fragment be a fault, in their eyes a sin.

This is, in my eyes, superstition, and I believe it to be based on a gross and material view of the Sacrament.

I am aware that the word 'compline' is found

in some Anglican books of devotion, but I do not like it, and should be glad if another name were substituted for the Evening Service of Prayer.

To a Clergyman on Ritual

The Palace, Chichester : Nov. 8, 1878.

My dear ——,—Your frank explanation has put me in full possession of information on all the points in question, and I thank you for it.

Now I shall deal with you as one who, however unworthy, is in authority, and is your Father in God ; I shall communicate to you my wishes and resolves, and I trust that in the loyal spirit which has marked all your interviews with me you will not be reluctant to conform to them.

From circumstances peculiarly affecting this diocese it is quite impossible for me to sanction the use of the chasuble—of whatever material—of the mixed chalice, or of candles lighted when there is no need of light. I therefore earnestly exhort you to leave off these usages, and to content yourself with the surplice, unmixed wine, and unlighted candles. I am aware that you found these usages when you came to the church, and did not introduce them. Perhaps in the days of your predecessors matters were not as, alas! they are now. There had not been these defections to Rome which alarm all thoughtful minds, nor that studied approximation to Romish teaching, language, and ritual which has, in my opinion, prepared for that defection. The real danger of such ceremonial had not been observed.

I may point out to you that your teaching is not

interfered with by this request, nor can I think that the dignity of the Sacrament of the Lord's Supper is involved in the wearing of a special garment or in the use of particular ceremonies. These are in their nature indifferent.

However, it is not argument I intend to employ, for that has usually little influence, but rather that power of fatherly direction to which at your ordination and your institution you engaged with willing zeal to listen.

I put my request to you on the ground of being your Bishop. Perhaps you may also be disposed to consider the enormous difficulties which encompass a Bishop who wishes to act fairly and kindly, and you might feel it a duty to relieve your spiritual head as much as possible from this crushing burden of care.

May I say one word as to the effect of your conforming to my admonition upon your people?

You might think, perhaps plead, that by such obedience on your part the faithful would be alienated, the other party would not be conciliated.

Now, when you came you found vestments, &c., in full use, and for some years this had been so. Was the spiritual life of the parish what might be desired?

Has it not by God's blessing been quickened since? Yet certainly not by these outward things, which existed before, but by your zeal, love, prudence—all under God. These gifts, I trust, shall abide and increase. And I am persuaded that congregations are attracted, held, advanced, by the preaching of the Gospel and by the personal devotion of the minister.

The proof is that Low Churchmen, no less than High, can thus attract and thus hold.

I see no advantage in an interview, unless, after you have read this letter, you desire one. We shall, I hope, meet on Monday 18, but it is right to say—not at all as a threat, but as a determination which I cannot change—that my coming to you depends wholly on your answer to this appeal.

Believe me very truly yours.

Answer to the above

November 9, 1878.

My Lord Bishop,—With the deepest feelings of respect I received your letter this morning. I thank your lordship for so fully entering into the subject (which I am thankful to feel you do not recognise as 'a trifle'), and for your courtesy in not mentioning the 'legality' of the three points, but admonishing me in your office as Father in God.

These two points have had with me the greatest weight, and my duty to your lordship as my Bishop leaves me only two courses before me—*obedience* or *resignation*. The latter course I should have felt it my duty to take if your lordship had simply admonished me to obey courts of law which I could never acknowledge. I have ever felt that the three points of ritual which you forbid are strictly ordered or permitted in the Church of England, and that their prohibition by secular courts was a fearful encroachment by the State upon the liberties of the Church. I do not say that I should have myself introduced vestments, but, finding them in use, I have felt it my duty to retain them. I have suffered a good deal already by my desertion of the Society of the Holy Cross at your lordship's request, and my motives have been misjudged as cowardly by friends who have had themselves to suffer in silence the stigmas placed upon them. By obeying your lordship in this instance I shall have to suffer still more, probably throughout my life; but *I submit*, owing to your kindness to me, and your admonition being given with a purely spiritual authority.

Although I feel that the abolition of altar lights and vestments will make no difference in the parish with any of the aggrieved (for to these points of ritual they have never objected), and although I feel a great wrench (as I am sure your lordship knows well) in giving up so much which adds solemnity to the celebration of the Blessed Sacrament, and although I have the interests of the Catholic Church in England so much at heart that I place them far above local success in a human point of view, I feel that upon your lordship rests the responsibility of my obedience.

As to the mixed chalice I would fain make an appeal. I have used it constantly ever since my ordination to the priesthood, and should now feel deeply thankful if your admonition were simply against a *ceremonial* mixture of wine and water.

Your lordship will permit me to say a few words as to your remark on the secessions to Rome, amongst whom I number many of my friends; and I am able, therefore, to speak with some knowledge. From the time of the lamentable secessions of Newman, Manning, and Wilberforce there were none of *importance* till the unhappy Public Worship Regulation Bill was passed.

Till that Act is abolished nothing will stop manifold secessions. The clergy and laity are not joining the Roman communion, as a rule, from disbelief in the validity of Anglican orders, but from the feeling that the Archbishops, and too many of the Bishops, have handed over their spiritual authority to the State. If this Bill were abolished, as well as the newly invented Court of Lord Penzance, the *two* Houses of Convocation might frame whatever rubrics they willed, and I could promise there would be an almost unanimous obedience on the part of the clergy and an end of the present difficulties in the Church. These rubrics could be afterwards passed through Parliament. There would be no objection to this. 'Church and State' are still believed in by far the largest number of members of the Catholic school of thought. The objection is, and ever will be, to the State governing the Church and the Bishops resigning their authority. Your Lordship will pardon my writing this. By obeying you, and obeying you at once, you will see that I am writing from no feeling of opposition, but from my love to the Anglican communion, and from a feeling that, though I am only a humble priest in your diocese, I am representing the views of a vast number of devout clergy and laity in each diocese of the English Church.

I am very grateful to your lordship for your kind promise of visiting me on Monday week, and asking you to pardon the length of this letter,

I have the honour to remain

Your Lordship's obedient Servant.

The Right Rev. the Lord Bishop of Chichester.

*From a Clergyman who was intending to lecture in
a Chapel of Lady Huntingdon's Connexion*

December 6, 1878.

My Lord,—I am in receipt of your lordship's letter concerning my proposed lecture in Lady Huntingdon's church in North Street.

I will not willingly do anything contrary to the law of the Church of which I am a minister. But I confess to your lordship that I cannot, without ascertaining the distinct law upon the subject, yield what I believe to be the *clear right* of every British subject—clergyman or other—to deliver a lecture on any topic whatsoever in any place of which the lawful owner may permit him to do so.

A most important principle is involved in this. If, therefore, my lord, there be any *law* which shall forbid my delivering a lecture in Lady Huntingdon's church, and your lordship will inform me of it, *I will at once obey.* But if not, still let me assure your lordship that I will not take any part in the conduct of a 'service' in that or any other Nonconformist chapel, although I confess frankly to your lordship that this is a matter of *mere submission*—not of heart. If I deliver the lecture it shall be *simply so*, with a word of extempore prayer for a blessing, and a hymn of praise. I will not enter the pulpit nor put on a gown. . . .

Answer to the above

December 7, 1878.

Rev. and dear Sir,—You lay it down as a principle 'that it is the clear right of every British subject, clergyman or other, to deliver a lecture on any topic whatever in any place of which the lawful owner may permit him to do so.'

If this principle be accepted, a clergyman of the Church of England may lecture in a Socinian, Mormonist, or Socialist chapel, if only he can obtain leave from the owner. And he may lecture on any subject—for instance, against the doctrines which he has solemnly undertaken to preach, or the Prayer Book to which he has engaged to conform, or against the connexion of the Church with the State as by law established. No one doubts that a layman may, if he please, lecture to this effect. But a clergyman of the Church of England is in quite a different position. He is by the law clothed with certain privileges, and he has contracted corresponding obligations. By virtue of his ordination and the license or institution he has received from the Bishop, he can officiate in churches and chapels under the Established Church, which no British subject may do without such qualification.

On the other hand, the clergyman parts with a certain portion of his liberty as a British subject. He must conform to the law of the Church, to its courts and constitution which regulate its discipline. Indeed he, when he is licensed or instituted, signs a declaration of assent to the Thirty-nine Articles of Religion and to the Book of Common Prayer, and he swears that he will pay due obedience to the Bishop—in all things just, legal, and canonical.

He may not in his preaching contradict the doctrines of the Church to which he has declared his assent.

Thus both in matters of order and of teaching

he is bound by obligations peculiar to his status as an ordained clergyman in an Episcopal Church.

I hope, on consideration, you will see the force of this argument, and will believe on my assurance that the course you propose to adopt—viz. to lecture in a Nonconformist chapel, whether in a gown or no, whether from the pulpit or not—is contrary to the law of the Church.

If, unhappily, against this warning you should persevere, I shall be compelled, much against my will, to do what is necessary to vindicate the order of the Church and my own authority as Bishop.

I do not dispute that your chapel may be your own property. I do not inquire into the value of it. Dr. Winslow, your predecessor, officiated in it by order of my license, and you are in precisely the same position. It is not a 'church' nor, strictly speaking, even a 'chapel,' but simply a building licensed for divine service. And let me remind you that without the Bishop's license you could not as a clergyman of the Church officiate in it, and that such license is by the terms of it revocable.

One word I must say as to the scandal which would be caused by your lecturing in the chapel belonging to Lady Huntingdon's Connexion. You may not be aware of the feeling among those who are not of your party, as you profess yourself an exceedingly Low Churchman, and say your congregation agree with you ; but it is the fact that grave offence is already given to many by the appearance of the 'placard,' as I am aware by communications received from Brighton, and the offence will be far more extreme if you adhere to your purpose as expressed.

I have no wish, as you must have seen, to fetter your rightful liberty, but I cannot allow license. . . .

R

Answer to foregoing

Hove : December 9, 1878.

My Lord,—I bow by necessity beneath the pressure which your lordship sees fit to impose. The lecture will therefore *not* be given.

I remain, my Lord,

Your Lordship's obedient Servant,

J. G. G.

To the Right Rev. the Lord Bishop of Chichester.

To the Rev. A. Wagner

The Palace, Chichester : February 8, 1879.

My dear Mr. Wagner,—In the passage of my late charge, to which you take exception, I had in view those priests of our Church who have re-nounced their own communion, and with it their Orders and their baptism. I feel for your disap-pointment, for these clergymen were your curates, and on your nomination were licensed by me.

It is a great misfortune, and you doubtless, of all men, have suffered most by it (and it was far from my desire to add to your troubles on that score), that such unstable spirits seem to be attracted to St. Bartholomew's, and that you have been so little able to ensure their steadfastness. Whether after they had left their posts and had gone over to Rome some open protest might not have been made in the church, some paper printed or circulated among the congregation of St. Bartholomew's dis-owning their act, and showing the danger of it, and warning the people not to be misled—this was for you to decide. As you know, I desired that such a protest should have been made, and I do not think the notice taken of their colleagues' defection by Mr. —— and Mr. —— sufficient. Therefore, when an opportunity offered I could not but express my grief and indignation at the conduct of men who have been false to you and their Church.

If you are satisfied, as you seem to be, that up to the very moment of their forsaking our communion they took care to guard their flock against Romish doctrine, and never recommended or insinuated what might facilitate perversions to Rome, I must leave to you all the comfort such a persuasion can give. When Messrs. —— and —— passed over to the Romish obedience, a considerable number of persons, variously estimated, passed over with them. Is it to be believed that these men and women blindly followed them from mere personal attachment? Or is it not evident that they had been prepared for such a desperate step, and had been subjected to teaching, private and public, which made them ready to go whither their spiritual guides led the way?

I entirely refuse your challenge to produce this man or that woman who was thus disposed to distrust the Church of England and to look favourably on the Church of Rome. The facts speak, and that is enough.

No one acquainted with the arts of the Roman Propaganda will think my description of them overstrained. They can be no secret to you. Many a distressed parent, many a distracted family, can witness to these arts and to the entire accuracy of my representations.

Believe me, my dear Mr. Wagner,
                    Very truly yours.

To a Clergyman who objected to School Children bowing at the name of Jesus

The Palace, Chichester : December 2, 1879.

My dear Sir,—It is certain that in the 18th canon the Church of England sanctions and enjoins the practice of bowing the head at the holy name of Jesus, and in the canon the reasons are given why such respect should be shown by all persons in time of divine service.   Children are taught in school what they ought to do in church, and I cannot understand how, whether in school or in church, such reverence can be construed into Popery. By forbidding and discontinuing due and proper reverence you give a handle to the Papists who go abroad in your parish to charge you with a contempt for and neglect of sacred usages.

The texts which you so magisterially assert to have nothing to do with the outward gesture may, notwithstanding, embrace that special sort of reverence, and that mark of inward devotion, to our Lord and Saviour.

It may be safer not to pronounce with such confidence on a doubtful passage, lest haply you should be found to fight against Christ.   The belief that Jesus Christ is the very and eternal Son of God, of one substance with the Father, is now rudely shaken in many quarters, and I think those who love Him in sincerity will be careful to do nothing which may detract from the honour due unto Him as God of Gods—our Redeemer.

Believe me

Truly yours.

*To a Lady with reference to a Friend who contem-
plated joining the East Grinstead Sisterhood*

8 St. James's Place, London, S.W. : May 10.

Dear Madam,—The point upon which I requested the Sisterhood of East Grinstead to yield
was this: the reservation of the consecrated elements
after the act of Communion.

The elements are now reserved not in the
chapel, but in a room adjoining, as I am informed.
This practice is in my judgment unnecessary—
likely to lead to false and superstitious opinions and
practices, and forbidden by our Church expressly.

It is unnecessary, because the sisters communicate
daily, and the Holy Sacrament ought to be administered to any of them at a very short warning. It
is likely to lead to superstitious opinions and practices, because it seems to countenance a material
presence of our Blessed Lord, independent of the
act of Communion, in the elements themselves. It
is forbidden by our Church, as you may see by
the rubric at the end of the Communion Service,
beginning : 'and if any of the bread and wine
remain unconsecrated'—so expressly forbidden that
no evasion is possible. The community of East
Grinstead professing to be attached to the Church
of England, and as such desirous of my sanction
and presence among them, I showed them that this
custom of 'reservation' was contrary to the order
of the Church, and asked them to discontinue it.

They positively refused so to do, and I on my
part most reluctantly found myself unable to give
them that full countenance which I should have
desired to give to a body whose good works are so

conspicuous and whose purpose and life are, I doubt not, holy.

But they met my advances with firm though civil resistance, and left me as Bishop really no choice.

I suppose the young lady in whom you are interested has well and carefully considered all the rules to which, even as a novice, she will be expected to conform.

The printed rules are in my opinion far less ascetic and severe than the *written* rules.

It is well she should see and reflect on the whole code, written and unwritten, before she puts her hand to the plough.

This I say not in the way of discouragement, but of caution, and you will not understand me in the least to depreciate the merits of these devoted women or their services, for it is impossible not to recognise both. But I do repeat that so many things in their rules and in their words—e.g. the name of the *convent*—studiously used, show an approximation to Rome which is hardly safe, and which provokes needless opposition and suspicion.

I am faithfully yours.

Reply to a request to appoint a Day of Humiliation and Intercession on account of the Sin of Intemperance

The Palace, Chichester : January 12, 1880.

Rev. and dear Sir,—My answer to your letter of December 24 has been delayed in the hope that the subject to which it refers might be considered at some meeting of Bishops of both provinces. But as no such opportunity has been afforded, I now

reply simply as an individual Bishop. On the part
of the Church of England Temperance Society you
request the Bishops to appoint a day of humiliation
and intercession on account of the sin of intemperance by which the Church of Christ is suffering
loss, and you suggest the coming Ash Wednesday
as a suitable day for such united prayer.

This is a request with which I am unable to
comply. I am far from denying the evils, social,
moral, and spiritual, caused by intemperance. Every
Christian must deplore them as they exist in
our midst, as we see and know and feel them.
I also believe firmly in the efficacy of united prayer.
But special calls to general humiliation ought, in
my opinion, to be reserved for special emergencies.
Unless the people are prepared to welcome such
calls from their chief pastor, unless a chord is struck
to which hearts will gladly answer, no good effect
can be expected. The opportuneness of the invitation is sure to be questioned, and the observance
of the day will be wanting in fervour and reality,
and even in agreement. Now, is there any proof
that at this time drunkenness is on the increase?
The evidence taken by the Committee of the House
of Lords and the report founded thereon rather
point to an abatement of drunkenness. The last
returns of the excise led to the same conclusion.
It would, indeed, be most lamentable and most
discouraging if the vast organisation of Temperance
Associations among which your society holds no
mean place, and the many plans for the promotion
of temperance among the working classes, not to
speak of legislation directed to the same end, and
of the spread of education, had failed to diminish

what has been called our 'national sin.' Publicly and privately intemperance has been attacked on all sides, and, so far as my observation goes, not without the success which all friends of religion, morality, and domestic comfort desire and long for. The best cause loses by being overstated. It is obvious to object to your request on the ground that the sin of intemperance should not be singled out as the special subject for general humiliation when other sins, certainly as ruinous to body and soul, and perhaps more widely prevailing, are passed by as if they were of no account. Much may be done, much indeed is doing, by Christian charity, both in the way of active pastoral help and of earnest and habitual intercession. But those efforts are directed, and ought to be directed, not against intemperance alone, but other sins also.

As the work of grace is deepened in the hearts of our people, while they purge themselves of all filthiness of the flesh and spirit, they will not neglect to pray for the deliverance of all whom Satan holds captive.

I am, rev. and dear Sir,
Faithfully yours.

To a Secretary of the Church of England Temperance Society

Chichester : February 21, 1880.

My dear Sir,—I have no doubt that a great career of usefulness is open to the Church of England Temperance Society, if it carries on its work upon the principles upon which it was founded. These I understand to be principles of temperance, as distinguished from total abstinence. I am ready to allow the absolute necessity of total abstinence in some cases, and to permit it whenever it may be desired ; but it is, in my opinion, an undue narrowing of a temperance platform to confine it to those only who declare that they purpose to abstain from all use of intoxicating drinks.

Let us rather endeavour, in a liberal and, as I believe, Christian spirit, to comprehend all those who desire with God's help to be temperate in the use of all His creatures.

I am glad to find that you are prepared to advocate fully and faithfully the true principles of the society. By so doing you will enlist many supporters and avoid a cause of offence which has, I fear, alienated many minds from an excellent and necessary work, in which I heartily wish you success, and am

Very truly yours.

To the Rev. Howard Hopley

The Palace, Chichester : June 7, 1880.

My dear Mr. Hopley,—Only yesterday I heard of the fatal termination of your dear wife's long illness ; but when I was at Eastbourne last week the ill tidings which reached me caused me great anxiety. If the general grief of a whole neighbourhood, and indeed of all who knew her, can be any comfort, that at least you enjoy ; not a thought of her but must be sweet and pleasant, not a remembrance which is not full of love and beauty. I shall not forget the quiet grace with which she filled her place, and the little kind attentions which made an impression on me, as on all who came within her circle.

Alas! such an excellent wife cannot be replaced, and truly your house is left unto you desolate. But of this I am sure, that you will think of her as only parted from you by a very thin veil—for 'two worlds are ours'—and that you will strive to be as good and pure and pious as she was, so that in God's good time you may be reunited. I hope your little folk are well, and with sincere regard and compassion I am

Your faithful Friend.

From Rev. E. Heath

34 Buckingham Street, Brighton : July 23, 1880.

My Lord,—May I ask your lordship kindly to direct me how to act under the following circumstances ?

I am *constantly* having children brought to St. Mary Magdalen's, Bread Street, for holy baptism.

(*a*) Without godparents, or possibility of procuring such.

(*b*) With godparents who do not understand in the least what they are doing, and *cannot even be made to repeat the answers after me.*

(*c*) With notorious drunkards and evil livers as godparents ; or, more frequently, such as never even attend any place of worship.

Am I to refuse to baptise in all or any of these cases ? or am I to do the best I can under the circumstances, and baptise without godparents, as Bishop Selwyn once directed under very similar circumstances ?

I ought here to add that most of the people who come in the ways I have named live outside the district (sometimes a long way off), and that many of the children are illegitimate. If I do not baptise them, they will probably never trouble about the matter again.

The immediate cause of my writing is a woman who came with a child last night ; she informed me that she could not get sponsors, and said she would answer for the child herself.

When I put the first question, and told her the answer, she replied, 'Am I to renounce the child ?' It afterwards turned out that she never goes to church, and knows nothing about religion ; she lives at some distance.

Amongst the replies I frequently receive, even when prompting the answers myself, are—'All right,' 'Go on,' 'That will do,' 'Anything you like,' &c. I have been told that they have never before been asked any questions.

I feel very loth to refuse to baptise these little children ; still, if I am to baptise them I must omit the questions to godparents, or prompt answers which they neither understand or believe—in fact, baptise them on the strength of promises which I know to be lies.

I have not felt comfortable in either omitting, without authority, such an important part of the service as the questions to sponsors, nor have I felt that I ought to *insist* upon the mockery of persons being present as godparents who are quite unfit to be such ; this has made me now apply to your lordship for direction.

I am your Lordship's obedient Servant,

E. HEATH.

Answer to the foregoing

The Palace, Chichester.

Dear Mr. Heath,—The account of the state of ignorance and neglect in your district is very grievous and, I fear, by no means peculiar to that part of Brighton.

Of course, whenever it is possible the sacrament of baptism ought not to lack its accessories prescribed in our service for infants, and indeed for adults.

But there is a necessity above all rubrics, and that is that children should be baptised.

In such cases it must be held that it is the collective Church which receives and answers for them, even though the regular sponsion should fail.

I cannot advise that the rubric should be neglected, neither would you desire to neglect it, when it can be observed; but when there is a real impediment to infant baptism by reason of lack of sponsors, then rather than suffer the sacrament to fail I think in your particular case you might simply baptise—of course using all such parts of the service as are not connected with the interrogatories and answers. And I think the final address might be used, with some variation so as to make it applicable.

For surely those who bring infants to be baptised ought to be reminded what their duties to those children are.

Frequently, generally, they are parents.
Believe me very truly yours.

*From the Rev. C. A. Durrant on the Burial of a
Suicide*

Petworth : January 7, 1881.

My Lord,—I had occasion to take a funeral
yesterday of a parishioner who had drowned himself.
The inquest was held at Wisboro' Green, and I
did not hear what verdict was given; but the
coroner's certificate for burial was given me as I
met the funeral at the gate.

I read the whole service as usual, but whether
I was right in doing so I should be obliged if your
lordship would give me your opinion.

Yours faithfully,

CHAS. A. DURRANT.

Answer to the foregoing

The Palace, Chichester : January 10, 1886.

My dear Mr. Durrant,—If the verdict of the
jury had been *felo de se*, I suppose the coroner
would not have given an order for burial; but in
the absence of any knowledge as to the verdict, I
need not enter on that subject.   In a general way,
when parties dying by their own act are acquitted of
suicide on the ground of insanity, it is safest to take
the verdict for your guidance.   For the jury are
serious, they hear evidence, and they give their
deliberate sentence.

Of course it is possible cases may occur in
which the verdict of the jury is directly contrary to
your own knowledge.

Then I do not see what course remains to the

clergyman but to act according to his conscience and to take the consequences.

The new Burial Act does provide an alternative form of burial on the request of the relatives. It would be well for you to look at the 13th of the Act.

Until a general form should be agreed upon, or one put out for this diocese, I should be content that the form sanctioned by the Lower House of Convocation should be used on such occasions.

Believe me very truly yours.

To the Bishop of Truro, Dr. Benson, on the Primacy

The Palace, Chichester : Christmas Day, 1882.

My dear Bishop,—The air has long been full of ecclesiastical rumours, but I have forborne writing to you because, depending entirely upon the newspapers, I could find no confirmation of the report that you were to succeed to the late Archbishop. But as there seems a general persuasion that you have consented to obey the high call, I could not bear to be later than others in assuring you how gladly I should see you in the place of our late beloved chief. I am confident that we should rally loyally around the one whom the Queen or her advisers should nominate, whoever he might be; but I believe that there is no one who would be welcomed with more general satisfaction than yourself. Before the Archbishop's death I divined that the choice would fall upon you, and my wish was father to my presentiment.

No doubt it will be a sore wrench to you to leave your diocese. You have known it, as it were, from its beginning, and have moulded it under God to your own mould. Every year binds clergy and laity closer to you, and it is grievous to sever such bonds of love and mutual esteem. But, I will not say the *greatest* of our primates, for that word is misplaced in such a matter, but those who most live in the memory of the Church, learned the art of ruling in lesser and inferior dioceses. I believe, therefore, that this consideration will not prevail with you.

I am most sincerely yours.

Answer from the Bishop of Truro

Truro : New Year's Eve, 1882.

My very dear Bishop of Chichester,—About 700 letters are being answered by devoted scribes, but I have dug yours out and must answer it with my own hand, though this has kept it longer than I designed.

I looked anxiously for your letter—I wanted to know whether you thought I had done *right* to listen to what *seemed* the notes of a call. I think the Queen's goodness, coming so separately from the Prime Minister's strong word, has made me feel that it must be right. But *quis crederet ? Ora, ora, orate.*

My only happiness is this, that when I see one after another such seniors all, like the senators whom Brennus saw, worthy in the highest degree of that work, and severally held back by years or by health, their younger brother may feel sure that as long as he is loyal to them they will guide him, and if he were to fail they would still guide the ship. Your goodness to me, so spontaneous, dear Bishop, and so constant, has made me feel at Lollards Tower like a son of your house, and as such I pray you always to tell me plainly of any fault or danger I run into. These will be full·many.   May God, by the wise heads and mighty hearts that I look up to, check mischief at every turn!   There are surely wondrous things opening out before us from Him, *qui facit mirabilia magna Solus.*   May we follow Him!

Your most sincere and affectionate

E. W. TRURON.

Most earnest wishes and kindest regards for you all in the fast breaking year 1883.

CHAPTER V

Death of Mrs. Durnford—Loss of Friends—Unabated Activity—Drafts
Encyclical Letter for Lambeth Conference—Made Honorary Fellow
of Magdalen—Celebration of Ninetieth Birthday—Speech in Convocation on Fasting Communion—Speech at Chichester on
Voluntary Schools—Correspondence.

THE first and greatest cloud of sorrow that ever
cast a shadow on the Bishop's life was the death of
his wife, which occurred on October 16, 1884. He
himself had truly described her in one of his farewell
addresses to his parishioners at Middleton as 'a
woman, if ever there was one, without the slightest
pretence, and with the most genuine desire to
benefit her neighbours, and to live on terms of peace,
amity, and love with all, high and low.' In Chichester she devoted herself as far and as long as her
health and strength permitted to charitable work ;
and residents in the city and visitors to the Palace
after her death keenly missed and mourned the
gentle and tender influence of her loving, humble
Christian spirit. After a little season of retirement
the Bishop, with the fortitude and conscientious
sense of duty for which he was always distinguished,
strengthened by a spirit of Christian faith and resignation, resumed his ordinary work ; but the entries
in his diary on successive anniversaries of his loss

show how deep and ineffaceable the blow was. Year after year recurs the prayer: 'Lux perpetua luceat ei, neque ejus unquam obliviscar'; and if he was at home it was his custom to take flowers to place upon her grave in the peaceful little country churchyard at Westhampnett.

The Bishop also lost many of his most intimate and valued friends in the course of his episcopate, especially during the last decade of it; many of them much younger, others but little older, than himself.

The premature and violent death of Bishop Wilberforce in 1873 was a great shock and real grief to Bishop Durnford, for he had, as junior Bishop in the House of Lords, seen much of him in London; and Lavington, the country home of Bishop Wilberforce, was only twelve miles from Chichester. Bishop Durnford relied much on his experience, and derived much valuable help from his counsel on some of the anxious and difficult questions which he had to face at the outset of his episcopate: he admired the wonderful versatility of his powers, and enjoyed talking with him about natural history and the culture of trees, subjects in which the two Bishops were equally interested and almost equally learned. Bishop Wilberforce would occasionally give his brother prelate a mount and take him for a ride over the Downs which he loved so well. Bishop Durnford, indeed, did not profess any skill in riding, and used to say that in his youth his father had told him that according to all the rules of the equestrian art he ought to fall off, although as a matter of fact he never did.

Two years after the death of Bishop Wilberforce the Bishop of Chichester lost another and a nearer neighbour through the death of the Dean. Dr. Hook had given him and his family a very hearty welcome on their first arrival : the Bishop could appreciate the value of his celebrated work at Leeds and admire his robust and generous character as well as his sound learning ; for, like the Dean, he had thought out his convictions and opinions for himself, before the rise of the Oxford movement, arriving at them by a careful study of the Bible and the Book of Common Prayer, and the history of the Church, together with the writings of the greater English theologians.

Dean Hook was succeeded by Mr. Burgon. With such a vehement and positive temperament as his, occasional disputes and differences were inevitable, but the general relations between the palace and the deanery continued to be of the most cordial character. The Bishop was amused by the Dean's quaint and original humour, admired his untiring industry in theological studies, and respected his intrepid defence of what he believed to be truth. Dean Burgon died in 1888, and in the same year the Bishop had to mourn the loss of his two Archdeacons. John Russell Walker, Archdeacon of Chichester, had been his assistant curate at Middleton, and the Bishop loved him like a son. He was made Canon Residentiary by the Bishop in 1872, and Archdeacon

in 1877.   He had in that office endeared himself to
all sorts and conditions of men in the diocese by his
unselfish labours, his loving sympathy, and his practical wisdom.   The remarkable intellectual gifts of
Dr. Hannah, Archdeacon of Lewes, and his successful work as Vicar of Brighton, have been already
mentioned.[1]   In the year following the deaths of the
two Archdeacons, Dr. Crosse, Vicar of Holy Trinity,
Hastings, was called to his rest.   The Bishop had
made him a Canon Residentiary and Precentor in
1882.   He was a thoughtful and striking preacher
and an effective speaker, remarkable for clearness
of mind and soundness of judgment, which may
have been partly due to his training in early life
as a barrister.

As the years rolled on, and the Bishop, who had
survived so many men younger than himself, carried
on his work with little or no diminution of vigour,
he became an object not only of increasing
affection and respect, but also of public curiosity and
admiration.   Moreover, with advancing age, although
his critical faculties remained as keen as ever, there
seemed to be an increasing gentleness of manner
and of fatherly kindness and sympathy which
endeared him more and more to his clergy.   In his
Visitation Charges delivered after he had passed the
limit of fourscore years there was generally some
reference to his great age.   He would express his
thankfulness to God for the signal goodness and
mercy which had followed him all the days of his

[1] See above, pp. 147–149.

life, he would exhort his hearers to pray that the God who in His mercy had carried His servant unto hoar hairs would bless the remainder of his days. He would address them as one who could not expect to meet them again. In 1887 especially, his concluding words had all the solemnity of a parting exhortation. He referred to the ancient tradition that the Apostle St. John, when age and weakness disabled him from preaching, was wont to enter the congregation and repeat the precept of his Master, 'Little children, love one another.' With like words of love and peace the Bishop desired to take leave of his clergy.

'I may not speak,' he said, 'of divers forms and elements of discord which multiply continually outside the bounds of our Church. "Without are fightings." These may be permitted for our chastisement and for our trial ; they are far beyond our control. But our more serious danger lies in our own unhappy divisions : "Within are fears." If all Christians are exhorted to be of one mind, to love as brethren, to be at peace among themselves, how much more do those lessons which we preach apply to ourselves ! How much closer ought to be the bonds which unite the clergy to each other ! How true should be their sympathy with their brethren, how real their charity, how large their tolerance ! For there is a region of things indifferent ; opinions and practices within which the Church of England, careful as she is to secure substantial agreement in fundamentals, allows her clergy and her members a wise liberty. Let this liberty be acknowledged and respected by you. It is not only the sense of a

common danger nor of common interests that
should bind us one to another: these are but inferior
motives.   Our unity should be the unity of the
Spirit, unity cemented by love, breathed into our
hearts from above, and living in thought, in word,
and deed.   No jealousies, no party feeling, no evil
surmisings, should enter in and trouble our concord.
We have one Master, the Lord Jesus Christ; we
have one work, to serve Him by edifying the
Church, which is His body; we pray in the same
words, we preach the same Gospel, we proclaim the
same creeds, we minister at the same Holy Table.
Never forget so to speak and so to live that all men
may see and know that you are brethren indeed.
   ' " My little children, love one another." '

Such exhortations, plain and simple as they
were, uttered with affectionate earnestness from
such aged lips, appealed to the hearers with the
force of an apostolic message.

Three years later, in 1890, being then eighty-
eight, he used expressions which many persons
understood as a distinct announcement of his
intention to resign.   'At my last visitation I
said that another such meeting could hardly be
expected: still more forcibly is it now borne on my
mind than before; this diocese, which for twenty
years has known me as its head, will be entrusted to
another and a younger Bishop.'   These words,
however, were merely an anticipation of his removal
by death.   With the high standard of episcopal
duty at which he had always aimed there can be no
doubt he would have resigned his office had he felt

unequal to discharge its functions.   But he was not
as yet conscious of any such inability as would
demand his resignation.

'I am well aware,' he said, 'that the inroads of
old age upon the faculties of mind and body, not
unperceived by me, may be felt yet more by the
diocese.   Though I am not conscious of feebleness,
yet my administration may be weakened by the
coldness and hesitation of senility.[2]   I need more
and more all the support that can be given by your
united help in every good work : by your confidence
in my honest purpose and endeavour to be your
servant for Christ's sake, without fear or favour, so
long as I may be permitted to hold my office : above
all by your prayers and intercession on my behalf
that grace and strength may be granted to me in
proportion to my increasing need.'

And the touching words which follow indicate
the reason which perhaps weighed most strongly in
determining him against resignation.

'My successor may have greater gifts than ever
fell to my lot, and may make better use of them,
for my shortcomings are not hidden from me ; but
he cannot know the people of Sussex as my experience has taught me to know them, he cannot have
a truer love for his beautiful flock in these fair
pastures.'

[2] These expressions were very probably suggested to his mind by
the passage in Virgil, *Æn.* v. 395 :

        'Gelidus tardante senecta
    Sanguis hebet,'

or the description of the old man in Horace, *A. P.* 171 :

      'res omnes timide gelideque ministrat
    Dilator.'

The Lambeth conference of Bishops met in 1888, and the confidence of the Archbishop in Bishop Durnford's clearness of intellect and skill in literary composition was shown by his entrusting to him, in conjunction with the Bishops of Durham (Dr. Lightfoot) and Chester (Dr. Stubbs), the task of framing the draft of the encyclical letter which was to be issued by the Bishops, embodying the principal conclusions of their debates upon the various questions that had been discussed. This difficult and responsible task had to be accomplished in two days, and the Bishop's diary for July 25 records how he rose at six in the morning to set about it.

From the Archbishop of Canterbury

Lambeth Palace, S.E. : July 20, 1888.

My dear Bishop of Chichester,—I have a great favour to petition you for. I beg you, with the Bishops of Durham and Chester, to be so kind to me as to draft the encyclic letter. It would be delightful if it could be born in Lollards Tower like the first Prince of Wales in Carnarvon. A more perfect committee than the three prelates would constitute cannot be devised or imagined.

The principal part of the raw material would be the concrete propositions which the chairmen are— as settled this afternoon—to send in. On these you would exercise a divine, plastic, and plasmatic art, and give it a living head and an elastic cauda.

The two Bishops whom you left behind consent, and hope heartily for your 'collaboration.'

I would, of course, be on the committee if you wished it for any necessary uses.

The letter should be ready to read in the main on Thursday, and be complete on Friday. The conference will, of course, not debate its language.

Sincerely ever yours,

EDW. CANTUAR.

In the same year he was much gratified by being elected an honorary fellow of his old college, Magdalen. The 'festivities' mentioned in one of the following letters are an allusion to the dinner which he afterwards attended, when he delighted and astonished the company by the vigour and brilliancy of the speech in which he responded to the toast of his health. It was a specially interesting occasion, being the 200th anniversary of the restoration of the President and Fellows who were arbitrarily ejected by King James II.

Cadenabbia : September 26, 1888.

My dear President,—Your very kind letter, with its full explanations,[3] caught me here to-day. I now quite understand the whole plan, and if it be agreeable to Mrs. Warren and yourself I will come to you on the 25th (the great day), as you propose, and stay over the 26th, *quod felix faustumque sit.*

I hope the St. Luke's summer will hold on for a week, and that your groves will still be in leaf.

---

[3] The President had written to him in March asking his consent to be proposed for election, but the election could not actually take place before October. The Bishop, not knowing this, had asked for an explanation of the delay.

It is indeed glad news that such recruits as you speak of should offer themselves for the ministry of the Church. Old South said, ' God has no need of man's knowledge, but still less of man's ignorance,' and we suffer now from the ill-instructed and ill-equipped soldiers who come forward to do battle for the Lord.

I look forward very much to this visit, which I trust I may be allowed to pay to my old college.

Little did I think in the days of the ancient Routh that I should ever be a guest in that house which I used to visit with such awe, though never without pleasure.

Sincerely yours.

Chichester : October 1888.

My dear President,—Although in your kindness you excuse me from answering your letter of the 9th, I must express to you, and through you to the college, my thanks for my election, and also my hope to present myself at the lodge on the 29th in time for the festivities. I have often visited the lodge in the days of the old Patriarch,[4] and well remember his venerable face and figure.

There was also in those days a female occupant, but, I suspect, very unlike Mrs. Warren.

Believe me, with many thanks,

Sincerely yours.

The following letter was written just after his visit :

The Palace, Chichester : November 2, 1888.

My dear President,—My visit to Oxford is full of pleasant memories, and I am glad to have a

---

[4] Dr. Routh.

cause, or rather opportunity, of repeating what I said in public of the great and welcome honour which the college has conferred on me. As for Mrs. Warren and yourself, I cannot sufficiently thank you both, not only for your hospitality, but your care to make my stay with you pleasant by bringing around your table so many young and old whom I should desire to meet and to know.

Oxford, as it is, is so different from the Oxford of my time that it was to me in the highest degree interesting, and even instructive, to find myself in this altered society, and to make acquaintance with such good samples of its members. I cannot despair of the future career of the university or our college —observe I speak as a Fellow—while there is such a body of seniors and such a succession of youth.

Sincerely yours.

Magdalen College is patron of some livings in the diocese of Chichester, and business in connection with these livings led to much friendly correspondence between the Bishop and the president. The Bishop greatly enjoyed his society, and in conversation and correspondence with him would freely indulge in those classical allusions and quotations which only a scholar could appreciate or understand. The following letter, written when he was in his eighty-ninth year, shows him as actively engaged as ever in diocesan work, and looking forward to attending the 'gaudy' at Magdalen in the summer.

April 12, 1891.

My dear President,—I need not say that it was a great disappointment to us not to catch you on your way to Eastbourne, but at this season, and indeed almost in all, I live like a spider 'along the line,' and cannot count on being at home for many days together.

Now for your very kind invitation.

Audiit, et voti partem concedere Phœbus
Mente dedit, partem volucres dispersit in auras.[5]

I can come, and will come, D.V., to the gaudy. The other dates, I regret to say, for an earlier visit are impossible. . . .

On June 24 of this same year 1891, the Bishop preached at Eton College on the occasion of the consecration of the lower chapel. The sermon, entitled 'The Royal Saint and his School,' was a concise and vigorous sketch of the character of the royal founder, of the circumstances under which the school was founded, and of the vicissitudes through which, in the course of 450 years, it had been wonderfully preserved. A copy of the sermon was presented to her Majesty the Queen, who remarked after it had been read to her that 'it was excellent in itself, but that as the production of a man who had nearly completed his eighty-ninth year it was astonishing.'

A gratifying proof of the general and increasing

---

[5] Verg., *Æn.* xi. 793. The Bishop has, by a slight lapse of memory, transposed the words *partem* and *Phœbus*, and substituted *concedere* for *succedere*.

esteem and affection for the Bishop had recently been given by the request that he would sit for his portrait to some eminent artist.   Mr. Ouless, R.A., was selected by the committee, the cost of the picture, 600*l*., being easily met by subscriptions from all parts of the diocese.   The Bishop is represented life-size, sitting in his robes, and the picture, if not a perfect likeness, is certainly a beautiful work of art, worthy of the distinguished painter.   It was presented on behalf of the subscribers in 1890 by his Grace the Duke of Richmond, who made a singularly happy speech on the occasion.

On November 3, 1892, the Bishop completed the ninetieth year of his age.   Gifts (especially of flowers), letters and telegrams of congratulation, including one from her Majesty the Queen, poured into the Palace all day long.   After Choral Communion in the cathedral he was presented in the south transept with the following address, which had been signed by the Dean and all the members of the Chapter, residentiary and non-residentiary.

Reverendo in Christo Patri ac Domino, Domino Ricardo, permissione divina Cicestrensi Episcopo, diem natalem nonagesimum agenti, nos Decanus et Capitulum Ecclesiæ Cathedralis Cicestrensis Salutem.

Hoc die Pater Reverende nobis præcipuo in honore habendo pia te volumus observantia adire, cum pro nobis ipsis tum pro tota hac diocesi cui tu tot annos feliciter præfuisti, gratias Deo agentes Qui te huic Episcopatui præposuit, præpositum ' usque ad senectam ' servavit, simul precati ut Idem te nobis et Ecclesiæ conservet Deus, firmâ qua nunc utaris valetudine, viribus ingenii sicut hodie integris.

Tu Reverende in Christo Pater hanc nostram erga te voluntatem et studium ut pro tua benignitate benigne excipias obsecramus.

The first part of the Bishop's reply was in Latin, of which, unfortunately, no notes have been preserved, as the reporters were naturally unable to follow it, and none of the clergy present expected a Latin speech. The latter part of the reply was in English, the Bishop observing that he could express the warmth of his feelings more freely in the mother tongue, which he did with an affectionate earnestness that none who heard him can forget.

He also received an address from the Mayor and Corporation of Chichester, and one from all the members of the Diocesan Conference, in which they thanked God 'that an episcopate so marked by singular wisdom, judgment, and sympathy should have been happily prolonged, and be numbered among the most famous of the ancient see.'

The President of Magdalen had sent him the following sonnet in the same year, on April 3, which is marked in our calendar as the day of ' Richard, Bishop of Chichester : ' [6]

> Richard of Chichester, so ran the style
>   Of him who now six centuries away,
>   Ruling Cicestria's ' realm ' [7] with gentle sway,
> Sent light and peace out o'er our troubled isle,

[6] Richard of Wych—Bishop 1245-1253. He was much revered for his saintly character and life, and was formally canonised by Pope Urban in 1262.

[7] Regnum was the Roman name of the place afterwards called Chichester.

His very name the record[8] of his smile
　　And of his sweetness and his charm, they say :
　　So ran the style, and so it runs to-day,
Though the saint sleep beneath the hallowed pile ;[9]

For still a Richard fills Cicestria's throne,
　　Whose ninetieth year mellows and not impairs
The ruler wise, learn'd scholar, faithful priest,
Courtly and kind and dear to all his own,
　　Friends who shall yet, if God so grant their prayers,
Send him more greetings on his namesake Feast.

The Bishop acknowledged the sonnet in the following letter :

The Palace, Chichester : Easter Tuesday, 1892.

My dear President,—If a δίκη ἀχαριστίας lay in English as it used to lie in Athenian courts, full surely I should be arraigned and condemned. I have no good excuse for such ungrateful delay in acknowledging and thanking you for your pretty and welcome present, unless continued absence from home and many worries—some real, some of my own making—can plead for me in a favourable court such as yours is certain to be.

Richard of Chichester was really a very holy man, and though one may decline to accept the legends of his miracles his canonisation was well deserved. In mediæval days his shrine was much visited, and a source of wealth to a church which greatly needed such assistance, for it was always

---

[8] Dicit quidem Petrus Ravennas quod ipsa sæpe sanctorum nomina meritum indicant, testantur insignia : Ricardus igitur etymologice potest dici quasi *Ridens*, *Carus*, et *Dulcis* . . . ut metrice merito de ipso dicatur :

Nominis in primo *ri*des, *du*lcescis in imo ;
Si medium quæris, *car*us amicus eris.

'Life of St. Richard of Chichester' (*Acta Sanctorum*, April, i. 285).

[9] St. Richard is buried in Chichester Cathedral.

a poor corporation. I only wish that the present
'Richard' could be in a remote degree what
Richard de la Wych was.

.   .   .   .   .

The Bishop lost a most devoted friend this year
by the death of Elizabeth Radcliffe, who had been
in his service more than fifty years. A native of
North Lancashire, very shrewd, very warm-hearted,
deeply attached to the Bishop and all his family, she
was quite a part of their life. She died from the
effects of influenza caught after nursing a fellow-
servant through a severe attack of the same malady.

In February 1893 the Bishop took part in a
debate in Convocation on the subject of Fasting
Communion. Further experience had confirmed
him in the opinion that this practice was carried by
some of the clergy to a very pernicious extreme,
being taught by them as an imperative duty, any
deviation from which, except in cases of necessity,
amounted to positive sin.

The consciences of such persons, he said,
ought no doubt to be respected in any document
that might be issued by Convocation on the subject. But, on the other hand, they ought to consider the consciences of persons who had been
tried by the teaching that non-fasting Communion
involved an act of sin. It was a very grievous
thing to add to the list of sins ; it was really serious
to bind another sin on the conscience of Christians,
and teachers of whatever kind ought to be very
well advised before they spoke in that direction.

Instances had occurred within his own knowledge of the evil of insisting too rigorously on this practice. A very devout woman, suffering from grievous sickness, after long years of pain and weakness, found it impossible to go as early as she had been wont to go to her parish church. She consulted her spiritual director on the subject, but she got no mercy or comfort from him ; she turned to another, but with no better result. At last, on the advice of a friend, she applied to the Bishop, who gave her such counsel as enabled her to come to the later celebration (after breaking her fast) with a quiet mind and conscience, and receive the benefits which she had so long enjoyed and deeply valued. Another case was that of a nurse whose patient desired to communicate, and for medical reasons the hour fixed for the service was late. 'Now this good woman, instead of doing her duty by day, as she ought to have done, lay in bed neglecting her proper work, in order that she might partake of the Holy Communion with the sick man fasting. She was clearly ignorant of proportion in duty.'

This speech elicited the following letter from Sir George Prevost, then Rector of Stinchcombe, Gloucestershire, one of the original Oxford Tractarians, who, like his friend Keble and other holy and distinguished men of that school, had happily and humbly spent all his clerical life in the care of a quiet country parish.

Stinchcombe, Dursley : Sunday, February 19, 1893.

My dear Lord,—I am anxious to tell you how much comfort your speech in Convocation has given me. I am not very much younger than yourself,

T

being half through my eighty-ninth year. And now for full fourteen years I have been unable to receive the Holy Communion fasting. In 1878, towards the end of the year, I suffered very much from distressing and alarming attacks of giddiness, and was ordered by my doctors always to take some food before I rose out of bed. These attacks came on at various times, but especially as soon as I got out of bed, when I knelt down to say my prayers. My earliest prayers are now therefore generally said in bed. My comfort has been that those to whom I looked for advice uniformly deprecated pressing the strict and positive rule of fasting Communion. I may mention both John Keble and his brother Thomas.[1]

By following the doctor's advice I have been able to go on ministering to my little parish (I preached this very day), though I do find myself obliged to do rather less than I used to do a year or two ago.

I have no doubt that what you and the other Bishops say will be a great comfort to many tender and devout souls, who, having more sensitive consciences, need the comfort more than I do.

This is written simply as the expression of my feeling and gratitude and sympathy. I do not look for an answer, and would only ask you for one prayer put up, one blessing invoked for me, and I feel sure that I shall have this without your telling me.

Believe me, my dear Lord Bishop,
Yours faithfully and in all reverence,
GEORGE PREVOST.

---

[1] Rector of Bisley, Gloucestershire.

In the latter part of this year some serious difficulties in connexion with elementary education in
the city of Chichester were brought to a crisis.
The British, or Lancastrian schools as they are
called, which had been established in the years
1811 and 1812, were in debt to the extent of about
600*l*., and the committee had announced that unless
the deficiency was met and some provision made
for increasing the annual income of the schools they
must be closed. Opinion was much divided as to
the best way of meeting the difficulty; some persons
were for a voluntary rate, others for making a
special effort to pay off the debt and to obtain
increased subscriptions, others for a School Board,
which indeed was almost inevitable if the schools
were closed. In response to a largely signed
requisition, the Mayor called a public meeting of
ratepayers to discuss the question. The situation
which had to be faced was clearly and ably described
by one of the Town Councillors, Mr. Prior. The
Bishop followed him in a long speech of remarkable
force and spirit.

He began by reminding the citizens that in
no city in England had the celebration of the
Queen's Jubilee in 1887 been more entirely satisfactory than in Chichester, mainly owing to the
wisdom of the Mayor, the same who was now presiding over their meeting that evening. As one way of
celebrating the Jubilee they had resolved to expend
1,100*l*. in putting their elementary schools on a
sound, solid, and permanent foundation. By that

resolution the citizens of Chichester had become an example to all who loved peace and ensued it. So far as he knew, all the years he had been in the city peace had been greatly promoted by the existence of the Lancastrian system of education, side by side with the Church schools. They had not heard of any animosities; he was sure there had been no violent competition between the two. The only object in view seemed to be the education of the young in principles which were believed to be sound and good, and tended to make them good men and women to take part in the battle and struggle of life hereafter. Was it their wish that peace should continue? If it was, would it not be absolute wisdom to secure it by preserving the system by which it had been promoted? They all dreaded a School Board, and they dreaded it for good reasons. The cost of the School Board was very great and could not be foreseen, but this was not the most serious reason for dreading it. He dreaded it because of the periodical elections. He dreaded it because it introduced a new and quite unknown element of strife in the community, because of the political animosities, because of the germs of religious disputes and hatred that it was sure to bring in. They all thought that their schools should be made as efficient as possible. He considered that the voluntary schools, as far as the quality of the education went, in no sense fell behind the Board Schools. He would not have education stunted because they preferred voluntary schools, but there was no reason why it should be. The Education Department would not allow any slackness. The screw was constantly being put on, and with increased force;

there was no fear that the managers of voluntary schools would be allowed to fall short of their duties. He considered it an advantage that those citizens who did not agree with the doctrines and discipline of the Church of England should have an opportunity of having their children educated after their own conscientious faith. He therefore desired to see the Lancastrian schools so well supported that there should not be these periodical agonies, this constant deficiency; that the managers should have a happy margin, if managers ever had such a thing, and that the schools should go on with success. How was this to be accomplished? He himself had not been averse, like some of his friends, to a voluntary rate, but if they shrank from that, let all parties in the city, Churchmen and Nonconformists, be asked once more to face the danger, and strengthen now and constantly the resources of the Lancastrian schools. It was not a difficult task; the sum asked for was not very considerable. Much larger sums were raised for less worthy objects, and this object was not only good, but it avoided an evil; and if people would not open their pockets, depend upon it they would have their pockets opened for them; first for building, then for establishment, then for maintenance and all other expenses, then for election—every election costing a large sum to the city, every election sure to provoke a contest, and the persons who provoked it riding off in security, because they did not provide a farthing of the expense. A small sum then voluntarily given would save them from a large sum painfully extorted from them.

The Bishop's speech, of which only a very con-

densed summary has here been given, was received
with enthusiastic applause, and at the conclusion of it
a resolution was proposed that a committee should be
formed to canvass the city for subscriptions with a
view to extinguish the debt on the Lancastrian
schools, and to place them permanently, by means
of annual subscriptions, in a safe financial position.
An amendment in favour of a School Board was
moved by the minister of the Congregationalists,
but received very little support, and the resolution
was carried with only two dissentients. It was
generally felt and acknowledged that this result was
largely due to the speech of the Bishop, replete as
it was with shrewd practical wisdom and humour ;
and, whether they agreed with him or not, none
could fail to be impressed with such a vigorous and
spirited utterance from a man who had just completed his ninety-first year.

And it must be borne in mind that a speech of
this kind was no extraordinary effort such as an old
man can make now and then if he nurses up his
strength for it and takes a good rest after it. It
was merely an item in that round of activities which
the Bishop was constantly carrying on in all parts
of the diocese with indefatigable vigour and zeal.

CORRESPONDENCE, 1885–1894

To the Duke of Cleveland

The Palace, Chichester : August 14, 1885.

My dear Lord Duke,—I feel bound to offer my thanks to your Grace for your letter published in the ' Times.' . . . The consistent tenour of your political life and your long experience in affairs cannot fail to add weight to the wise and well-timed warning which you have addressed to the Liberal electors of England.

The distinction between the position of the Irish Protestant Church and the Established Church of England is most sound and true, but has not been sufficiently observed. Your Grace does well to remind your readers of that distinction. It is no doubt most unfortunate that the opportunity of endowing the Roman Catholic clergy was let slip, for that measure has commended itself to the judgment of our greatest statesmen without exception. In a private conversation Mr. Gladstone confessed to me that such was the case, but added 'that it was now impossible.' That, however, only means that it was prevented or made impossible by the opposition of certain parties whose religion is mainly one of antipathies. The same parties, with the addition of an infidel section, are now clamouring for the disestablishment and disendowment of the Church of England. It is a fair question to ask what they would put in its place. I do not find that they are prepared with any plan for filling up the breach which disestablishment and disendowment of the very thorough nature which they advocate must infallibly make in our religious and social system.

They shut their eyes to the consequences which must, as your Grace so well points out, follow in most of our villages and many of our towns, and to which no thinking man can look without unfeigned alarm.

Begging your Grace's pardon for thus addressing you, I am very faithfully yours,

R. CICESTR.

The letter to which the following is a reply has not been found, but its purport may easily be gathered from the Bishop's letter.

The Palace, Chichester : October 8, 1885.

Dear Sir,—The Bishops and clergy of the Church of England do not receive a farthing from the State.

If they were paid by the State—that is, out of the taxes—the sums for such payments would be voted by Parliament, just as the sums required for the army and navy are voted annually. But you will never find any vote for the payment of the Bishops and clergy.

Their incomes arise from endowments, some very ancient, some of modern times.

The State—that is, the civil power, the law of the land, and what is known as the Constitution—recognises the Church of England as the National Church, allows it certain privileges, and secures to it the enjoyment of the aforesaid endowments.

But no Act of Parliament has ever ' established ' the Church, although many have acknowledged its existence from the earliest days until now.

In fact, the Church is as old as the State, and both, from the very beginning of English history, have been linked together.

I should advise you, if you wish for fuller information, to address yourself to your own clergyman.

Believe me faithfully yours.

On Non-communicating Attendance and Observance of Black-letter Days

The Palace, Chichester : December 4, 1885.

My dear Sir,—Your letter, though not answered, has never been out of my mind.

I do disapprove of 'non-communicating attendance' as a regular practice, whether in parishes or in such institutions as St. Michael's. I say, as a practice for all; because it is conceivable that in certain cases the chaplain may see fit to permit, or even suggest it—for example, for those confirmed, between their confirmation and their first Communion. But that those who have communicated should attend a second time, or that young girls unconfirmed should be gazers at a sacrament which they are not allowed to partake of, is in my opinion not to edification.

It is, I should have thought, for the chaplain to order the course of divine service, and therefore to object, if he thinks necessary, to choral Communion.

But this question stands on different ground. If the celebration is to be choral—and doubtless our Church does contemplate choral celebrations—then there must be singers young and old, as in cathedrals the choir, men and boys, remain, though the former do not necessarily communicate and the latter cannot.

The objection against the observance of black-letter days is quite just. Where no Epistle or Gospel is provided, then the day is not to be celebrated. The maintainers of such days may be reminded that in the first Prayer Book of Edward VI. the observance of all such days was abolished (with the exception, I think, of St. Mary Magdalen).

I cannot find that you have been licensed. This would seem necessary, as a recognition of your relation to the Bishop and as a sanction of your own spiritual position.

My secretary has been so much engaged in election business that I have been unable to consult him on this subject, as it affects St. Michael's.

Very truly yours.

To the President of Magdalen—Recollections of the College

The Palace, Chichester : March 2, 1886.

My dear Mr. President,—Let me thank you very sincerely for your kind letter, the Memoirs [2] of your predecessor [3] and Mr. Hopkins,[4] and your address to the undergraduate members of the college.

The late President was the last survivor of my contemporaries, and I always felt as long as he lived that I had still one friend left where once I had so many.

[2] 'In Memoriam Rev. Frederic Bulley, D.D., President of Magdalen College, Oxford, and Rev. Thomas Henry Toovey Hopkins, M.A., Fellow of Magdalen College, Oxford.' Reprinted from the *Oxford Magazine* for October 21, 1885.

[3] Dr. Bulley, President, 1855–1885.

[4] Rev. T. H. T. Hopkins, Fellow and Estates Bursar.

Occasionally we corresponded, sometimes when I was anxious to recommend a boy for the post of chorister, sometimes on other and more serious matters, but there was always a prompt and kind answer and a recognition of the happy and pleasant relations that subsisted between us in years long gone by.   I think his character is well drawn in Latin by the Vice-Chancellor;[5] in English, better than the Latin, by yourself.   His real goodness and simplicity and strong sense of duty enabled him to keep a steady course in very difficult times.

I often wondered how he would bear himself in the changed constitution of the University and his own college, but he seems to have met these circumstances with great wisdom and no small measure of success.

He was, as I apprehend, content not 'tentare majora,' but he was 'præsentibus æquus.'   One may really say of him 'He has not left a wiser or better behind.'

Mr. Hopkins I never knew—but I understand him well by your description—and I can feel what a useful element such a manly Christian gentleman must have been in your society.   He must have had many of the qualities and gifts which made my late dear friend Bishop Selwyn a power at Eton and Cambridge, in New Zealand and Melanesia.

But I have read with even deeper interest your address to your pupils.   (I could not but say within myself, Oh that we had had such counsel from our tutors!)   The tutorial system in my day was a mere skeleton, dry bones, sapless and lifeless.   I speak of course of Magdalen—for elsewhere I think it was

---

[5] Professor Jowett.

somewhat better.   There was no real care for us, no confidence, and so we were left to go our own way, often a very bad way, never unkindly treated, but never treated as real friends, younger brothers greatly needing tender, loving discipline.

It is also a great advantage that there is now opportunity and assistance for minds of various bents to pursue the course of study to which natural taste inclines.   There always were many who had no love for classics—and perhaps as little for Aristotle—and so finding themselves hopelessly distanced by their companions in the only race open to them, they fell into utter idleness, or contented themselves with just enough of classical knowledge as might enable them to go respectably through the schools.

Yet some of these were not dull men, and might have applied themselves with success to some of the studies which are now cultivated in Oxford.   No doubt this variety was always in the view and purpose of the great founders of our colleges, the very fairest of which I shall ever hold our own S. M. Magdalen to be.

To this day I remember freshly the impression which the beautiful quadrangle made on me when I was, to my great surprise, elected Demy ; the groves and walks in their summer glory, and the very fragrance of the mignonette which then blossomed on all the walks.   'Tis truly a noble foundation, and has, I do believe, a grand future before it, as it has had no unworthy past.

I do remember it in my prayers, though I fear not so regularly as I might, and with it I shall couple your name as you are pleased to desire.

May the Lord grant you to sit as long, as

happily, and as usefully in your seat as your two predecessors !

Your letter invited what has proved to be a long reply. I enclose a cheque towards the ' Barge.' Have you thought of applying to Lord Winmarleigh, Winmarleigh, Garstang ? He is collaterally descended from your founder, was a Gentleman Commoner of Magd., and has a very warm attachment to his old college.

Believe me, dear Mr. President,
Very truly yours.

To a Clergyman who omitted the ' Gloria ' in the Holy Communion Office

The Palace, Chichester : Feb. 26, 1887.

Dear Sir,—A complaint has reached me from a lady who regularly attends the services at Christ Church that during Lent you omit the ' Gloria in Excelsis ' in the Communion Office. There is no warrant for such omission, and I hope it will be sufficient to point out to you that it cannot be made without transgressing the Order of the Church which you are bound, and I doubt not you are desirous, to respect.

If the omission is not made and the lady has been mistaken, you will correct me.

Apart, however, from the principle that the officiating minister may not add or take away from the form prescribed at his own caprice, I think the omission of so grand and solemn a part of the service quite indefensible, and if you should have taken such a liberty I must strongly censure it.

The service does not cease to be Eucharistic because it is celebrated in a penitential season.

Believe me truly yours.

To the same, on Prayers for the Dead

The Palace, Chichester : Feb. 26, 1887.

The pressure of much business has not allowed me to examine with the care I should have wished to devote to it the sermon herewith returned. But I have found in it certain statements which appear to me, to say the least, so questionable that they ought not to have been propounded with authority from the pulpit to a congregation of members of the Church of England.

In the first place the text is chosen from an Apocryphal book ; now I refer you to the sixth Article, in which you will read the Church 'doth not apply the Apocryphal books to establish any doctrine.'

The purpose of your sermon is to exhort your hearers to pray for the dead. But even if this text could serve that purpose it has no authority as of inspiration, not being taken from the canonical Scriptures. No chance expression in the Homilies can invalidate the plain statement of the sixth Article. But even supposing that this text was of divine authority, it has nothing to do with prayers for the dead. Elijah prayed that the dead child should be restored to life, and his prayer was heard ; so was the prayer of Elisha in like circumstances. But these signal miracles are nothing to your purpose. You allege 1 Tim. ii. 1, and the prayer commonly called the Prayer for the Church Militant, founded on St. Paul's direction ; but it is expressly said to be a prayer for the 'whole Church militant here on earth,' so that the Church not of the earth is in terms excluded. I am quite aware that the Church of England does not prohibit prayer for the dead, but she has nowhere enjoined it, and, looking at the great abuse of a doctrine true in itself, it should not be laid before a congregation without great caution, for you know full well how the Romanists have employed it.

I object very much to your naked statement, page 4 : 'He can purify them with fire, or leave them impure,' and your speculation about 'souls capable of change and of voluntary actions,' and that this is 'spiritual evidence.'

No dogma can be established upon texts of Scripture which are dark, doubtful, or allegorical, or enigmatical—and such are the texts that you must have in your mind.

It seems to me that your teaching leads directly to a Purgatory.

It was, therefore, of the greatest moment that you should prove, not from dark and dubious texts, but by plain words or invincible experience, that there is a Purgatory—which would be hard to do.

Secondly, that you should warn your hearers against the cruel teaching of the Romish doctors even as to souls departed this life in Jesus Christ. I do not doubt you have studied the teaching of the Church of Rome on this point, and you had an opportunity of showing your congregation how painful and distressing it is, and to what super-stitions it has led and is leading those who accept it.

So far as I have learned, in the earlier and purer Church prayer for the dead was directed to this end—that by the mercy of God in Christ their blessedness might be increased, and that His light might shine perpetually upon them to their endless comfort. Pious Christians, out of their love to those dear to them on earth, will not forget them in their abode of peace. But such pious practice, founded on such charitable and holy remembrance, is a very different thing from general prayer for the dead, which, as I beg you once more to remember, finds no countenance (as public prayer) in the Church of England.

I hope you will take what I have written in good part, for my whole desire is to keep you from excesses of statement not capable of proof, and which are, in my opinion, thus unguarded, likely to lead your hearers to accept, to their infinite loss and danger, the Romish view of the soul after death.

To the Rev. J. Wakeford (Diocesan Missioner)

October 9, 1888.

I am much concerned to find that you have been in uncertainty as to my feeling, wishes, and resolution towards you and your work. From the moment of our interview at Lancing and that pleasant walk, I have never hesitated in my purpose, if possible to obtain your help in the rural missions of this diocese. My absence from home and the delay inseparable from a roundabout correspondence with Bishop Earle may have obscured this purpose in your view, though to me it has always been distinct and clear.[6] So I hope you will come to your work rejoicing, and I am sure you will be welcomed. As soon as you appear, or before, I shall forward the authority, and may God bless and guide you now as heretofore.

[6] See above, page 214.

To the same

November 20, 1888.

Your report of the Sussex peasantry is such as I expected. They have scarce any sense of humour, and this defect betokens a character of some heaviness—enemies would say dulness ; but they are true and honest, thoughtful and shrewd, and, like their native clay, impressions once received abide in their minds and hearts. They will not say much, but I believe they will trust one whom they respect, and follow when well led. All I hear confirms me in my opinion that a very good beginning has been made by your teaching and preaching, God helping by His grace.

To the same

December 4, 1888.

So far as I know the rural population, they are, when disposed to dissent, given to a kind of solidified satisfaction in themselves, without corresponding evidence of obedience or progress in their hearts and lives : when not dissenters, or inclined to dissent, then dull and indifferent.

But any good parish priest must know more on these points than I can pretend to do. At confirmations they look strangely unmoved and stolid, but rarely are outwardly inattentive.

On the 'Angelus' and ' Confessionals'

The Palace, Chichester : Dec. 7, 1889.

My dear ——,—I was sorry to observe some marks of soreness in your reply to my letter about the 'Angelus' and the 'Confessionals.' What I

U

wished you to see was the unwisdom, to say the least, of adopting terms borrowed from mediæval Roman usage, such as the 'Angelus,' which was introduced into France in the fifteenth century, and the latter part of it.   I cannot say how much earlier into Italy.   But the name and the use and time of the service are distinctly Roman, and thus offence is given and opportunity of imputations not deserved. For your object was laudable—to remind your people of the mystery of the Incarnation.   The Roman ceremony looked first to the Blessed Virgin herself, and was a sign and a means of the undue honour, amounting in the ignorant mind to worship, which is paid to her.

While guarding jealously the great doctrine of the Incarnation—and jealously, too, the proper respect to be shown to the mother of our Lord—we have need to be very careful lest the honour due to the Son alone, the λατρεία, should be directed to the Saviour's mother.

On this point I wished to caution you, and I do not think I exceeded my duty in doing so, acknowledging as I did your faithfulness and zeal.

Now a word as to the confessionals, for such they are.   I never heard of them from Archdeacon Hannah, one way or another.   But if they are within the rails of the altar they are in a wrong place—not the place for penitents.

The hearing of confession cannot be too open. Why should not the confessing party kneel at the rails—the priest hearing confession within the rails —before or at the side, so that there should be nothing secret, in the sense that both are *seen* but not heard ?

Believe me sincerely yours.

A Case of Conscience

The Palace, Chichester: March 15, 1890.

My dear ——,—You ask my opinion, and I have taken time to consider my answer—perhaps you will think a long time.

I could not advise you to write anything to the lady in question—least of all through the medium of her maid.

So far as I remember the story, it was that of a husband, of good repute in the world, carrying on an adulterous intercourse with the governess—at any rate, the husband is unfaithful. You know this from the wife, who has in some way discovered the sad fact.

I seem also to remember that you had some intercourse with the husband and put his sin before him, but of this I am not clear.

Now, if the lady communicates her trouble to you *sub sigillo*, you are forced to give her such ghostly counsel as may seem right to you ; but I think this must be given orally, and it would be best for you, however inconvenient, to repair to Scotland for that purpose, or to await her coming to this country. There is nothing on which the English mind is more jealously suspicious than confession.

If it were known that a spiritual person inter-fered in matters affecting conjugal relations *marito inscio*, it could not fail to discredit the spiritual counsellor, and to raise a storm never to be allayed. All the opposition of the country would be roused.

In Roman Catholic houses the confessor is a recognised condition. But not so with us nor does our Church contemplate the habitual intrusion of such a one into homes. I say habitual, for the purpose of direction.; the feeling is what a heathen so well expressed,   ' Scire volunt secreta domus atque inde timeri.' That is the cause of alarm—not, I think, unfounded.

You will gather that I cannot advise your writing unless the husband knows you write.

Sincerely yours.

To the Rev. J. Wakeford (Diocesan Missioner)

The Palace, Chichester : June 7, 1890.

My dear Wakeford,— . . . Last year you took a run into Brittany. I do hope you will do something of the sort again, either in England or on the opposite coast or in the Channel Isles, or, in short, where you please. I think Sanderson will back me up and supply what is needed, for people can't travel now as Oliver Goldsmith did, supporting himself by his flute and his logic.

The sisterhood question is never out of my mind, and I sometimes think of Horace's character of the old man—' res omnes gelide timideque ministrat ' ; the hesitation is not as to principle, but as to the wisdom of starting (so to speak) such an experiment without some consent from other Bishops, my brethren. I might be sorely blamed if I dared to move alone.

I hope you keep well and strong.

Sincerely yours.

To the Rev. H. Hopley

The Palace, Chichester : July 26, 1890.

My dear Hopley,—The lychnis arrived quite fresh, is planted, and rears its scarlet crest nobly.

Many thanks to you for remembering my wish to possess what I so well remember as an ornament of my paternal garden for years.

Sincerely yours.

[The Bishop noticed a lychnis in my garden, and remarked that he loved the flower from memories of his home garden when a boy ; so I had a root sent to him to Chichester.—H. H.]

From Dr. Harold Browne, Bishop of Winchester

Farnham Castle, Surrey : October 13, 1890.

My dear Brother,—I must thank you from my heart for what you say of my intended retirement. The wrench and the sorrow are very great to me, but I know it is inevitable. I have loved my work very much, and I would gladly carry it on to the end if I had your vigour of body and mind ; but some fresh attacks of a paralytic nature have rendered me very useless. I have loved, too, our gatherings and my brother Bishops, and you may be sure I shall very specially miss your genial and fraternal society. If we are not to meet often, or perhaps ever, again here, I trust we shall meet in a more blessed and abiding home hereafter.

Ever your affectionate Brother,

G. Harold Winton.

The Lord Bishop of Chichester.

To a Clergyman who wished to set up a Private Altar

The Palace, Chichester : October 27, 1890.

My dear ——,—I am sorry to inform you that I cannot break ecclesiastical order in your favour.   If you and your wife, being both in ill-health and incapable of attending the church of the parish, desire that Holy Communion shall be administered to both (for your family does not enter into the question, as it is not said that they or any of them are sick), you must send notice to the Vicar of the parish, and make your request to him.

I do not apprehend that your condition is such that you cannot repair to the church, which cannot be far distant, and in the case of your wife the Vicar may render you the required service as the Prayer Book provides.

It is in the highest degree objectionable, in my view, that, on the ground of alleged convenience, private altars should be set up in parishes by clergy happening to be sojourning therein, and I know not to what irregularities such a practice may lead.

Very truly yours.

The three following letters have reference to a complaint that a clergyman had advocated the Salvation Army from his pulpit.

The Palace, Chichester : November 22, 1890.

Dear Sir,—I have been absent from home and much engaged this whole week, and have consequently not been able to attend to your letter without date.

I have now asked the Rev. Mr. —— to send me some explanation of his action on Sunday last.

But may I observe that I have no right to limit the liberty of a clergyman in his pulpit, if he does not transgress the laws of the Church nor preach erroneous doctrine?

And I am afraid that if parishioners were to make dissatisfaction with their pastor's arguments or propositions a reason for leaving the Church, there would be a great unsettledness, and many more Dissenters than now there are.

When I have heard Mr. ——'s explanations I will again write, and am

Faithfully yours.

The Palace, Chichester : November 22, 1890.

Dear Mr. ——,—A parishioner (as he represents himself) has written to me complaining that on Sunday last you advocated the scheme of General Booth from the pulpit, and announced that there would be collections made in the church on behalf of the same.

Mr. ——, not sympathising as you do with the scheme, feels aggrieved that it should be put forth with your authority and support, and advocated in your sermon.

Now I do not presume to limit your liberty of teaching, nor do I give any opinion as to the merit of General Booth's proposals. But perhaps you may think it worth consideration that a clergyman ought to endeavour to be the pastor of all his people, and therefore that it is his duty in religion, in politics, and in that mixed region which embraces both, to avoid, as much as he can, topics that may give offence. This is all that I urge.

It is certainly not your wish to alienate Mr. —— and those who think with him, for they probably are worthy people, and have the interest of your parish at heart; and possibly a word of explanation might be serviceable in allaying Mr. ——'s alarm and that of his friends, at what he represents as an open adhesion, not only to General Booth's great plan, but to his action generally as a religious and partisan leader.

I write, of course, only on such information as Mr. —— has afforded, and which may need correction and addition from you.

Believe me

Truly yours.

The Palace, Chichester: November 26, 1890.

My dear Mr. ——,—I am obliged to you for your explanation on the subject of your introducing General Booth's scheme to your congregation, and suggesting offerings towards it.   The scheme is itself not political, or rather not party, but it is devised and pushed forward by a man who is at the head of a very decided religious movement; whose army—so they are called—is entirely under his control, and is taught implicit obedience to his orders in matters spiritual.   At first he professed to advocate no particular line of doctrine, only to reform and convert; so that they who had no religion might be led to believe in the truths of the Gospel, and they who professed to be Churchmen or Dissenters might be made more faithful members of their respective bodies.

But of later years Mr. Booth comes forward as the head of a new sect, most certainly having no good will to the Church of England, and probably little more to the dissenting societies.

His agents are entirely employed in drawing away men, women, and children from our Communion.

Such is my view of the facts. I had much sympathy with Mr. Booth in his beginning, because I thought that as a firm believer in Holy Writ he combated the Atheist and the Socialist. All Socialists are not Atheists—God forbid—but all Atheists are assuredly Socialists.

I think, therefore, that ministers of the Church, if they think fit to advocate Mr. Booth's social projects, should be careful to separate themselves from his methods of religious teaching, and in some points from that teaching itself.

It seems to me that if the sums of money poured into Mr. Booth's coffers had been given to some of the plans which have been for years working, and greatly need help—e.g., in London, whence Mr. Booth expects to draw the main body of his recruits—the result would have been more certain and satisfactory.

The Bishop of Bedford, an experienced man, does not hesitate to declare that the Salvation Army has done next to nothing in the East of London.

The object of a pastor is, as I said before, not to offend but to reconcile his people. You and Colonel —— have strong opinions ; no one desires you to give them up. Mr. —— and I presume others have opinions equally strong. Let them abound in their opinions. But the Church is not the place for ventilating either. I hope discordant politicians may equally be true members of a true Church. That is, I hope, your case ; and according to it will be your position.

Very truly yours.

To the Members of the Mothers' Guild in the Diocese of Chichester

The Palace, Chichester : January 23, 1891.

My dear Friends,—I cannot permit the first report of the Mothers' Guild, now established in this diocese, to go forth without a few words of hearty commendation and earnest good wishes.

The purpose of the Mothers' Guild is to unite mothers in a religious society, so that they may help and support one another in the great duty which is bound upon them—namely, to bring up their children virtuously and godly. This is a mother's duty, and it is a mother's work, for none but mothers can fulfil it.

It is a great mistake to think that education begins at school. Education of a child begins at home—begins almost with the cradle. Home is the first and best school, and mothers the natural teachers. God, who gives them children, gives them the charge to train them for Him. And He gives them the tender, loving influence which none but mothers have.

My dear friends, the Mothers' Guild is for the encouragement of mothers to do this work for God.

Be sure of this, that the Lord will be with you and help you. Dutiful children are among the greatest of blessings ; undutiful children are the source of troubles ; and it is by neglect of timely

care, by suffering children to grow up without controlling their ill tempers or their ill habits, by letting
them have their own way, that mothers have to
mourn, too late, the waywardness and disobedience,
even the vice and wickedness, of their offspring.

The rules of the Guild are few and simple.
The counsels are such as may be followed, and, if
followed, will tend to your own happiness and the
happiness of those who are as dear to you as your
own lives.

The Guild is firmly and widely established in
Sussex. I see no reason why every parish should
not have a Mothers' Guild, and why all mothers
who are really anxious that their children should
be brought up in the knowledge and obedience of
God's Holy Word should not thus be banded
together in a union of love and prayer.

Your faithful Bishop and Friend.

*On the Lincoln Judgment. To the Reverend the
Clergy of the Diocese of Chichester*

The Palace, Chichester : January 31, 1891.

Reverend and dear Brethren,—The Archdeacons and Rural Deans assembled in our annual
meeting have unanimously represented to me that
the clergy generally desire an expression of my
opinion as to the authority which the judgment pronounced by the Archbishop of Canterbury, in the
case of the Bishop of Lincoln, ought to command
in this diocese.

Such a request is more than an invitation : it
is a call to me to speak plainly, as I ought to
speak.

No one can contend that bishops are exempt from obedience to the Law Ecclesiastical, or that they are not subject to correction and penalties for the breach thereof. Doubts, indeed, may be entertained as to the proper constitution of a court for the trial of a bishop, but the question of jurisdiction has been practically settled, and to this I need not advert. The Archbishop of Canterbury has delivered his judgment, to which the Bishop of Lincoln has loyally submitted.

I, for my part, am prepared to accept it in the same spirit, and I give my episcopal and canonical sanction to the judgment, so far as the same may be required in order to give it force in the diocese of Chichester.

But beyond this formal communication to the clergy, with the purpose of commending the judgment to general acceptance, I will state certain grounds upon which it appears to me to claim and to deserve respect and obedience.

The judgment has been delivered in a spiritual case by a court confessedly spiritual. The Archbishop of Canterbury, Primate of all England and Metropolitan, heard the cause, with five grave and learned bishops, his assessors. The Judge, the highest person in the Anglican hierarchy in place and dignity, combining in himself all the just powers and traditions belonging to his ancient see, after long pleadings and arguments on either side, pronounced the sentence. The assessors, with one exception, and that on one point only, assented to his conclusions.

Objections based on the constitution of other courts in which lay judges preside and decide, cannot attach to the court of the Archbishop, which is simply and wholly spiritual.

The judgment is independent, and stands on its own merits. The Archbishop, indeed, professes his respect for the decision of the eminent persons before whom, in their several courts, similar questions have been tried and determined; but he does not follow with servile fidelity the precedents they have set. He claims the right to examine each point for himself, and to draw his own conclusions from such evidence, whether old or new, as he has been able to obtain. Patient research, careful balancing of testimony, strict impartiality, judicial calmness, are the characteristics of this remarkable judgment. By general consent the judgment is admitted to be a great judgment, and the Archbishop to have proved himself a great Judge.

It is also a ground of satisfaction that the Archbishop gave out that the court had not to 'consider expediency, but legality.' This is an important *dictum*, because there is a suspicion widely prevalent that some former decisions were influenced by that motive of expediency which in this instance the Judge disclaims.

Further, the Archbishop laid down that the position of the celebrant at the Lord's Table is, in itself, a thing indifferent, and possessing no doctrinal significance. No doubt such significance may be attached to it on both sides; those who suspect and oppose the eastward position arguing that it has a sacrificial character, and sets forth the doctrine of a material sacrifice and of the continually repeated immolation of our Lord's body: those who adopt it contending that it does indeed involve the doctrine of a sacrifice, but of a Eucharistic sacrifice, spiritual and commemorative, such as our Church, in accordance with the greatest teachers of primitive antiquity, sanctions. The Archbishop holds that there is no such doctrinal significance in the position of the celebrant, inasmuch as such significance cannot be proved, and men who maintained the highest doctrine in regard to that Holy Sacrament (for example, Archbishop Laud and the non-jurors) stood at the north end of the Holy Table during the whole of the Communion Service. And so the judgment, while permitting the eastward position, provided the manual acts prescribed by the Rubric are so done as to be seen by the congregation, allows that the position of the celebrant at the north end of the Table is a good liturgical use. In the opinion of the Judge, in which I concur, it is not allowable to attach an arbitrary significance to any liturgical use. The piety and imagination of devout persons have always been disposed to discover and dwell upon inward meanings in outward ceremonies. But such inward meaning cannot be simply assumed ; it must be proved either by Holy Scripture, or the testimony of councils, or by the teaching of the Church Universal, accepted and ratified by the formularies of our own branch of the Church. No such decisive authority can be alleged in favour of the doctrinal significance of the celebrant's position.

The principle thus stated, if cordially admitted and acted upon, will be of material force and value. It may induce faithful members of the Church of England to look with less distrust upon usages pronounced by the highest authority not to be illegal, and to possess no doctrinal significance. Thus unfounded suspicions may be dispelled, and Christian concord and unity promoted.

My Reverend Brethren,—You will not fail to observe the distinction, drawn in the judgment, between such practices as are enjoined, and such as are permitted.

Where the Archbishop, the spiritual Judge, has given a plain direction, there duty and conscience require cheerful obedience. But where certain practices are declared to be lawful, but are not enforced, much is left to your wisdom and charitable discretion, enabled and directed by the Holy Spirit, to do all with considerate and tender care for the good of the people committed to your charge. You will not interpret the judgment as though it encouraged the introduction of ritual uses without instruction and preparation, or the pressing such upon ill-informed or unwilling congregations. You will bear in mind for your guidance the great principle involved in the Apostle's words : 'All things are lawful for me, but all things are not expedient : all things are lawful for me, but all things edify not.'

Commending you to the grace and guidance of Almighty God,

I remain
Your faithful Friend and Brother
in the Lord Jesus Christ,

R. Cicestr.

To the Rev. J. Wakeford (Diocesan Missioner) [7]

The Palace, Chichester : February 14, 1891.

My dear Wakeford,—Your letter and card have reproached me for weeks. Something has always interfered to prevent my considering the card properly. The number distributed is amazing, and testifies to your unwearied toil. We may hope that the teaching you give is fixed and perpetuated by the card.

The only point I would wish you to consider is No. III. 'Christ our King.' The text you print is incorrectly given.

It is found in 1 Tim. vi. 15. But this text seems to me hardly proper to your purpose, which is to set forth the kingly office of Christ. It points rather to Christ as included in the Divine Essence—one with the Father and the Holy Ghost—for it could not be said of Christ that no man hath seen Him! Thus the text is hardly suitable for your purpose, which is to set forth Christ in His Person as King, 'Son of David.' Perhaps Rev. xix. 13–16 or Rev. xvii. 14 would be more appropriate. Pearson, when discoursing of our Lord as King, does not quote 1 Tim. vi. 15, which is rather conclusive against such application. I searched other books, but found nothing to justify your quotation. Of course you have searched out texts inferring our Lord's sovereignty, but in a card you cannot use such texts. All must be plain, short, and open to simple people.

[7] The references in this letter are to 'Mission Memorial Cards'; one which was already in circulation, and another which was being prepared. The letter is introduced to illustrate the minute care and pains bestowed by the Bishop upon details of this kind.

The following letter has reference to disturbances in Eastbourne, caused by the persistent attempts of members of the Salvation Army to parade the streets in opposition to the wishes of the people.

July 2, 1891.

Dear Sir,—I have read the extracts from Mr. Bathurst's and Mr. Hunter's sermons, enclosed in the letter in which you request me to reprove these clergymen for their remarks on the proceedings of the Salvation Army in Eastbourne. Permit me to say that I see nothing in the tone or language of these remarks that calls for censure on my part.

The Salvationists have put themselves in the wrong by resisting and defying the law which every Christian is bound to obey. I need not remind you of the counsel of St. Peter, ' Submit, &c.'

Messrs. Hunter and Bathurst admitted the good intentions of the Salvationists, but could not but reprehend their obstinate refusal to submit to lawful authority. It is this resistance which has been the cause of disorder in your usually peaceable town, and which has let loose passions which, but for such provocation, would not have been roused to those acts of violence of which you complain.

I cannot think it right to parade the streets with noisy instruments on the Lord's Day, when the musicians or their leaders have been warned that such music on that day is offensive to the greater part of the inhabitants.

The Salvationists, as professing Christians, ought to respect the feelings of their neighbours, although they may think them mistaken. There is no ground whatever, so far as I can see, for attri-

x

buting Mr. Hunter's observations to a feeling of jealousy at the success of the Salvationists in his parish. Imputation of motives is not warranted by the law of Christ, and I hope you will regret having made such an imputation.

If you have any influence with the Salvationists, you might exercise it usefully in persuading them, while they are zealous in their religious calling, not to forget their duty as citizens.

I am faithfully yours.

P.S.—Your letter is perfectly proper and respectful.

To the Vice-President, Magdalen College

The Palace, Chichester : August 12, 1891.

My dear Vice-President,—A haunch of venison from your woods has been most kindly sent to me by the President. I know he is abroad, but where I do not know.

It is probable you may be communicating with him, and, if so, might I request you to convey to him my thanks for his present, doubly acceptable as coming from your Park?

I believe the animal is long-lived, but I can scarcely flatter myself that he is one of those whom I used to feed out of my bedroom window with the remnants of breakfast rolls.

Believe me very truly yours.

On his Eighty-ninth Birthday

The Palace, Chichester : November 4, 1891.

My dear Mrs. Boothby,—I think your most useful lamp will greatly aid my spectacles when they come, but they delay terribly. However, I could not have read a line, for I have been busy all day answering congratulations, &c., and acknowledging gifts, of flowers especially.

A neighbour, moreover, has sent me a grand sapphire ring, engraved with the arms of the see, so that hereafter I shall display the emblem like so many of my brethren, only I think they are content with amethyst.

.   .   .   .

Sincerely yours.

To a Diocesan Missioner

Lollards Tower : November 11, 1891.

. . . . You seem to have scruples respecting your being entertained in comfortable quarters, and you suggest that a cottage of some labouring man would be a fitter abode for you—and that it would be better to share his fare. I think that is the sort of feeling you express, but as I have *per incuriam* left your letter at home, I write from memory. Now when our Lord sent out His apostles and the seventy, He bade them accept the hospitality offered them and stay in the house they entered, not necessarily a poor house ; nor did St. Paul find hospitality in cottages—rather with opulent women, and people well to do. I do not see that the merits of these servants of Christ were lessened by their accepting the hospitality of disciples who were in easy circumstances. But I see a great advantage in such a course. Do not the upper classes need help in religious matters, knowledge, and enlightenment, as much as the poor? And by living among them you would have opportunities of influencing them which would be totally lost if you determined only to sojourn in the cottages. There is the middle class also, perhaps the most difficult.

I think you have a message to all classes—to the high as to the low—and I am sure both need to hear it. Why favour one at the expense of the other? I know socialistic and democratic theories have little charm for you, but if you took the course to which your over-sensitive conscience leads you, Socialism and Democracy would claim you for their own.

Non-Communicating Attendance

Brighton : January 7, 1892.

My Lord,—When I was licensed to this curacy your lordship's kindness in giving me advice respecting one or two points on which I asked for counsel emboldens me to ask a similar favour again.

We have here a daily celebration of Holy Communion, but the communicants thereat very frequently fall below three in number. Indeed, since some attend this service without communicating, even the presence of three in church does not necessarily involve their reception of the Holy Communion.

Under these circumstances, though Mr. —— feels no difficulty in celebrating Holy Communion, when officiating by myself I hardly feel justified in proceeding with the service, certainly in cases where three persons are not even present possibly to communicate.

The benefit of your lordship's advice and direction on this subject would be gratefully received by me.

I am, my Lord,
Your obedient servant,

——.

Answer to the foregoing

The Palace, Chichester: January 11, 1892.

My dear Mr. ——,—I can only answer your question as the Church answers it in the third rubric at the end of the Communion Service. The words are peremptory: 'There shall be no Communion.'

If there are more than three or four persons in the church, and you have reason to think that all of them or the greater part do not purpose to communicate—so that, for instance, only one or two would be left to communicate with you—it might be well to send some officer of the church before the service begins to ascertain their intention.

Strictly speaking, they are all bound to give you notice, so they cannot complain of this inquiry.

I greatly disapprove of neglect of this rubric, because it was aimed at the abuse of solitary Masses, now a great scandal in the Church of Rome, which abuse I fear is not unknown in our own Church, although so clearly guarded against.

Believe me
Very truly yours.

A Visit to Scotland

Pitlochry : September 10, 1892.

My dear Mr. Boothby,—We had a very pleasant week at Edinburgh—weather fair always, sometimes fine, but the place was crowded with travellers and trippers beyond conception. But this may give you an idea ; our rooms, which we had ordered beforehand, were on the fifth floor, but happily there was a lift. We did not forget to visit Hawthornden and Rosslyn, but the day was dull, and that curious gorge requires sun. The paths had not recovered themselves from the constant rain, and after emerging safely from the rocky path, I slid down on the muddiest of paths—without damage except to my garments. We could not *make* Melville, but I saw enough of the country to believe that it is very pleasantly situated.

Another day we spent at Linlithgow, a grand palace quite in ruins—that is, roofless and broken floors, but otherwise in tolerable preservation.

The Board of Works keeps it from ruin, and it is worth preservation. Those old Scots kings must have kept great state. Holyrood is a very poor place compared with Linlithgow or Stirling. The Primroses called and we returned their visit, and luckily found Miss Primrose at home—this we owe to you—and I was glad to make the acquain·tance of so very pleasant a person. They asked us to luncheon, but on the day on which we left Edinburgh.

This puts me in mind of Dalmeny and the Forth Bridge. Can anything be more stupendously ugly ? It must be a hideous object from Dalmeny. But it is a wonder of strength and audacity. We went on a little steamer around and under it, and saw the principle of construction very well. But one thinks the towers could have been designed so as to secure the necessary strength without the insufferable ugliness of form and outline. Edinburgh is happy in possessing quarries of incomparable stone within easy reach. The buildings of every kind— I mean public buildings—astonished me.

The English Cathedral, as they call it, is a very fine building, and on Sunday night was absolutely crowded, not only by the upper ranks, but by people of all conditions. The service was excellently performed—that is not the right word, but you will mend it.

Pray remember me and my daughter very kindly to Mrs. Boothby.

Sincerely yours.

On his Nineteth Birthday

D. B. Friend & Co.,

77 Western Road, Brighton : November 2, 1892.

My Lord,—Although I am _only_ a bookseller—and worse still, as some think, a Dissenter—I feel constrained to ask your lordship to accept my sincere congratulations on your having attained your ninetieth birthday, and to express the hope that for years to come you may be spared to preside over this diocese ; your firm yet moderate, mild yet authoritative, rule and action have tended greatly to preserve us from much that was dishonouring both to God and man in the past.

I have been staying in a parish not far from Chichester with the Congregational Minister of the place, the clergyman of which is on friendly terms with both my host and myself. While there I read aloud with much pleasure your lordship's wise and timely utterances at the opening of the diocesan conference, and, with scarcely an exception, my friend and I heartily endorsed and were thankful for what you then said. It has been the same whenever I have had the privilege of hearing you speak or preach, notably at the Church Congress years ago, and more recently at the opening of my friend Mr. Peacey's church at Hove.

As the shadows of evening gather round you in these latter days, may the horizon be full of the glorious rays of the Sun of Righteousness, not as setting, but only assuring you of an abundant entrance into 'the perfect day,' with its rest and reward.

Believe me, my Lord,
Yours very respectfully,
D. BURCHELL FRIEND.

To the Right Rev. the Lord Bishop of Chichester.

Answer to the above

The Palace, Chichester : November 18, 1892.

Dear Mr. Friend,—The date of your letter now lying before me reproaches me, and, when I read it again, I felt that you had just cause to complain that so kind a congratulation and so many good wishes should remain without acknowledgment.

The fact is, that I have been altogether unable, even with the use of all diligence, to overtake the letters which the kindness of friends poured upon me, and so many, and among them yours, have remained too long unanswered.

I am very grateful for your good opinion, and only wish that I more deserved it.

It was a happy chance which took your friend the Congregational minister and yourself into the Town Hall on the occasion of our annual Confer‑ ence. Whatever else you may have observed, you will have seen that clergy and laity sat together in perfect harmony, and on terms of perfect equality. And indeed I think that during the two days the

latter filled the chief parts in the debates.   Of course
I could not expect you to agree with all that I and
others then said, but I am sure you heard nothing
that savoured of religious acrimony, or that could
hurt the feelings of any Nonconformist.

Believe me, dear Mr. Friend,

Very truly yours.

*On his Ninetieth Birthday.   To the
Right Reverend the Lord Bishop of Chichester*

St. Alban's Rectory, Sussex, Wisconsin,
United States of America : November 24, 1892.

My Lord,—Permit me on behalf of an old
gentleman, a parishioner of mine, who has to-day
celebrated his ninetieth birthday, to tender you his
kindly congratulations upon the completion of your
own ninetieth year, of which notice has come to us
through our Church papers.

You will note the appropriateness of this greeting
from one so far away from you, and who is unknown
to you, when I have put you in possession of the
facts in the case.

Mr. William Weaver was born at Peasemarsh,
in the eastern part of your diocese, and was confirmed by one of your predecessors, who was then
so infirm by reason of age that he was compelled to sit during nearly the entire confirmation service.   Afterwards this lad was carefully
taught every Sunday with three of his brothers and
some other lads by a certain Lady Maskell.   Her
teaching had the effect of making staunch Churchmen
of this William Weaver and his brother James, who
afterwards came to this State in the year 1837 and

helped to form the English settlement, which they named Sussex in honour of the old home in England. In 1841 these two brothers heard of the band of missionaries, Breck, Hobart, and Adams (who afterwards founded Washotah College, fourteen miles distant from Sussex), and set out to find them, and obtained their services from time to time. Mr. James Weaver (now dead) read lay service when no minister was to be had, and the houses of the two brothers have from that time on been resting-places for all ministers who have been to the parish.

October 2, 1842, the saintly Bishop Kemper, first Missionary Bishop of the Church in the United States, with Rev. Messrs. Breck, Hobart, and Adams, held a service in James Weaver's barn, and there organised this parish, naming it St. Alban's. William Weaver is the only one living of the vestry elected that day. October 2 and 3 of this year we celebrated the semi-centennial of the organisation, and twenty persons of the original congregation were present.

St. Alban's parish and church are noted, by the few who are so fortunate as to find them, as a ' little bit of Old England.' It is also worthy of note that the quiet efforts of Lady Maskell resulted in building so firm a churchmanship in these boys as has resulted in the founding of a strong parish in what fifty years ago were ' the wilds ' of North America.

You will thus see, my lord, that the greeting comes from one who was formerly a resident of your diocese, and is indebted to the teaching there received ; one who has, too, a kindly remembrance of the Church in Old England, and wishes to testify to this remembrance by this his message of love to you, though unknown to you.

May I be permitted to add my own congratulations to his, for I too am a son of old Sussex, born in the see town of Chichester, and retain a love for the old home where, at the Litten School, I received as a boy eleven years old a certificate of good conduct and satisfactory progress signed by the Bishop of Chichester.

Praying God's blessing upon your lordship,

I remain yours in Christ,

LUKE PAUL HOLMES,

Rector of St. Alban's.

To the President of Magdalen

Brighton : December 6, 1892.

My dear President,—' Non obtusa adeo gestamus pectora ' as not to acknowledge your clever version of those charming hendecasyllables.[8] And

---

[8] Martial, *Epig.* v. 20.

Pereunt et imputantur

Dear Martial, if with you I could
Taste days of gladness free from care,
Arrange my moments as I would,
Leisure, and life worth living, share,
On halls and houses of the great,
Dull glories of heraldic state,
Crabbed cases in the dismal court,
On these, on these we would not wait :
But walk and talk, and book and sport,
The cool alcove, the shady tree,
The bath, the Maiden Fount, should be
Business and haunt for you and me.
    To day, alas ! nor you nor I
    Can be ourselves : the bright hours meant
    To be so good, they pass and fly—
    Still scored against us ' had and spent.'
Ah ! is not this the moral, say,
He who *might* live must not delay ?

I owe you a double debt, for—though I am ashamed to confess it—I did not know the original.

The terseness of the verse in which 'Virgo' figures [9] makes it very difficult of translation ; indeed, I should have been sore puzzled if Grævius had not come to my help.   That water still retains its excellence and pre-eminence, for I believe it supplies the Fontana di Trevi.

The modern Roman's ideal of well-being is summed up in three gifts : Aria di Campo Marzo, Acqua di Trevi, and Pan del Governo ; so 'Virgo' is not out of date.

Only one line seems to me capable of improvement : ' Crabbed cases in the dismal court.'

Might you not put, as is so usual with Milton and others in that metre, ' Crabbed cases in the court '—a sort of catalectic because of the beginning of the verse ?

I can only think of one instance, in the Veni Creator, ' Praise to Thy Eternal Merit,' but there are plenty in the ' Allegro ' and ' Penseroso.'

I hear much good of Daubeny—Hill is delighted with his successor because he takes so kindly to the garden.   Perhaps he has a little of the Professor of Botany in him.

Believe me sincerely yours.

To the Rev. J. Wakeford (on Fasting Communion)

1892.

Mrs. ——'s is a sad case.   I fear it is typical. These ' Rigorists,' as Pusey called them,[1] are harder than the nether millstone.   I cannot dispense with a law of the Church which I do not believe to exist. The Pope dispenses with all laws, human and divine, but we dare not.

---

[9] ' Campus, porticus, umbra, Virgo, thermæ.'   [1] See above, page 221.

One can grant a dispensation from a custom, but that does not seem to go high enough. I have written pretty fully to Mrs. ——, much pitying her hard case, and I hope—perhaps against hope—that my letter may have some effect.

This rigour leads directly, as you say, to infrequent communions, and to non-communicating attendance. It is therefore all dangerous : but one sign of many that ' the heady setting forth of extremities' is prevalent among our clergy of a certain type.

To the President of Magdalen

Lollards Tower : March 16, 1893.

My dear President,—If you had asked me to do some greater thing at your instance, I could not have refused, but now you ask a very little thing, and that I can give with the most ready mind.

It is an excellent sign, when so much is dark and threatening, that schools and colleges now combine to care for people less happily circumstanced. No one thought of such charitable works in my day, now they are general. So write me as one of the Magdalen band who are trying to do something for dark, dreary, dingy London. And though I cannot be a benefactor in any real way so far as money goes, for my diocese calls more loudly for such help than even Magdalen College, yet I send a poor gift just to show my good will and interest.

My daughter and I thank Mrs. Warren and yourself for proposing an Oxford visit—I fear it cannot be compassed. My old coadjutor, Bishop Tufnell, is detained in Malta by the illness of his son, and I have to work double tides. Then there is that Welsh Church Act—a visitation this summer. τίς ἱκανός; . . . . .

John Sarum has had influenza in this tower, and after a week's sickness appeared to-day in the House of Lords. I came up *multa gemens* at the Archbishop's call to sit and back his Bill, which went through smoothly.

Sincerely yours.

To the Rev. J. Wakeford

The Palace, Chichester : June 3, 1893.

My dear Wakeford,—I wish to send you and your future wife some remembrance, and not knowing, as you must know, what would be really useful, I think a convertible gift is the most reasonable and acceptable form of a wedding present ; not the most romantic, but when you are entering on the realities of wedded life romance must be in good measure dispelled.

My gift expresses only in a very small degree my sense of your services to this diocese and myself during your sojourn in it. Your loss is not yet realised as it will be, but I hope some gratitude may survive in the clergy and laity who have benefited by your self-denying labours for our great Master.

You may be assured that the 7th of June will not be forgotten by me, and I hope you on your part will not forget our close relations, and will from time to time correspond with me.

Sincerely yours.

'Felices ter et amplius,
　　Quos irrupta tenet copula, nec malis
　Divulsus querimoniis
　　Suprema citius solvet amor die.' [2]

[2] Hor. *Od.* I. xiii. 17-20.

To the same

October 27, 1893

My dear Wakeford,—You may have heard of the *Requiem* service for the dead on the *Victoria* a month after the calamity. *I* must think it was in the nature of a scenic attraction. I forbad the repetition of such Popish affairs, but —— came to plead that on All Souls Day, and whenever else it was desired by special request, sanction should be given that prayers were asked 'with intention' at the celebration for persons specified by name, some lately, some perhaps long since, deceased. I cannot see that our Church does sanction prayers and oblations—'Pro viventibus et defunctis'; on the contrary, that provision, existing in Edward VI.'s Prayer Book, was not continued in 1552 nor reinstated in 1661, and the prayer is now for 'Christ's Church *militant here on earth.*'

Prayers for the dead may not be forbidden in private use, but are nowhere sanctioned for public use in the congregation, and so I stuck to my prohibition, despite the assurance that such prohibition would inflict unknown pain upon many pious souls—long used to this sort of 'diptych' use—and notwithstanding an assurance that all the faithful were well and constantly instructed as to the tenets of the primitive Church touching 'Purgatory.'

This sort of people are ever hovering about the intermediate state and making up all sorts of theories (?) to explain a subject on which the Holy Spirit has left very little and very obscure teaching, and which later doctors have rather confused than elucidated. In fact, the Ritualist lays down rather what ought to be, and must be according to his notion of God's dealing with departed souls, than what the γράφη teaches.

I am really alarmed at their approximations, often servile imitations of Rome, which place men and women on a grassy slope down which they slide hopelessly towards the precipice beneath.

Sincerely yours.

Mr. Metcalfe, the Vicar of Hellingly, found on arriving in his parish that no Church Catechism was taught in the schools according to the trust deed, and there was considerable opposition on the part of the Baptists to his attempts to introduce it. He conferred with the Bishop on the subject, who suggested and drew up the following letter to the managers from the three trustees.

The Bishop's letter to Mr. Metcalfe of Dec. 22 is the reply to one from him informing him that the religious teaching was now being carried on in accordance with the trust deed, and that matters were settling down peaceably, although the Nonconformist ministers had not availed themselves of the privilege accorded to them.

To the Managers of the Hellingly National School

The trustees of the Hellingly School having had before them the minutes of a meeting of managers held in the school on November 20, 1893, which show that a resolution was passed respecting the religious teaching in the school, think it to be their duty to remind the managers that in conjunction with the trustees they are appointed for the purpose of carrying out the provisions of the trust deed, which enjoins 'that the school shall be conducted on the principles of the Incorporated National Society for Promoting the Education of the Poor in the Principles of the Established Church, all due regard being paid to the Conscience Clause.'

Such being the case, the trustees cannot admit any right on the part of the managers to prescribe any form of teaching other than that which is contained in the trust deed; and they would further remind the managers that if they desire to have the use of the said school premises continued to them they can only do so by carrying on the school in future in strict conformity with the conditions of the said trust deed.

The trustees desire that the religious teaching of the children of parents who are members of the Church of England shall be in entire accordance with Holy Scripture, the doctrines and services of the Book of Common Prayer, and the full use of the Church Catechism, to be given by the clergyman and the teaching staff of the school. And further, the trustees desire to recommend that on two mornings in each week, to be selected by the managers, the children of parents who are Nonconformists, and who may desire it, shall assemble at the same hour as the other children, but in another room, when instruction may be given by an authorised Nonconformist minister known to and approved by the managers of the school.

R. CICESTR.
ROBERT SUTTON, Archdeacon of Lewes.
A. METCALFE, Vicar of Hellingly.

Chichester: December 6, 1893.

To the Rev. A. Metcalfe

December 22, 1893

No Christmas news could have been more acceptable—and, I may say, more unexpected—than that contained in your letter of the 20th.

The evident fairness of the proposal, I suppose, commended assent and disarmed sectarian opposition. Like yourself, I am doubtful whether the Nonconformists will be able to agree on an exponent of their own views, but they will have the opportunity, and will not be able to complain that they are ignored or suppressed.

I do trust the plan will work so as to satisfy all reasonable people, much more all truly religious ones.

On Father Ignatius

December 4, 1893.

My dear ——,—I wonder you should propose Lyne. He goes about in the dress of a Benedictine monk, to which he has no more right than to the dress of an English admiral; and though I dare say he is a good Protestant, he shows the external badge of a strange communion. Everyone finds an open door at Brighton, and perhaps Mr. Lyne may have had some access to some church there, but quite without my knowledge. . . . I like less and less all approximation to Rome and Romish dress and ritual.

Sincerely yours.

On Marriage with a Deceased Wife's Sister

The Palace, Chichester : January 15, 1894.

My dear Prebendary,—The law of the land prohibits the marriage of a man with his deceased wife's sister, and the issue of such a marriage is declared to be illegitimate.

The law of God forbids a woman to marry the brother of her deceased husband, and by parity of reasoning forbids the husband to marry the sister of his deceased wife.

The Table of Inhibited Degrees, to which I refer you, includes (No. 17) marriage with a deceased wife's sister.

Therefore the person of whom you write cannot have been married by a minister of the Church of England, or with the service appointed for holy matrimony, unless the facts of the case have not been stated.

Where and how the alleged marriage has been solemnised is uncertain, but neither the law of the land nor the law of the Church can have permitted its solemnisation in the form and under the conditions prescribed.

For notice is given in the opening address of the minister to the parties presenting themselves to be married in these words : ' Be you well assured that so many as are coupled together otherwise than God's Word doth allow, are not joined together by God, neither is their matrimony lawful.'

You gave notice before the marriage to the man that such a marriage as he intended to contract was not lawful, and of that warning he took no heed.

It is a painful duty to refuse the Holy Sacrament of the Lord's Supper to a parishioner ; but in this case you have no choice.

This man and this woman have openly broken

the law of the Church, and are living together in what the Church declares to be a marriage not sanctioned by God nor lawful.

I give this opinion, as you request it, and can give no other under the circumstances.

Believe me sincerely yours.

To the President of Magdalen

Palace, Chichester : January 22, 1894.

My dear President,—Two such good vicars as Tindall and Steward[3] have rarely been appointed in succession to any parish, and both were taken away, we may not say *ante diem*, but after a very brief career of bright promise. The college has twice made an admirable choice, and I trust may be guided and enabled again to send the right man.

The grief at Mr. Steward's death was very deep and general, and I am told the attendance at his funeral unexampled and the outward demonstration of sorrow on the part of his parishioners very striking. I claim the privilege of age and do not attend funerals. You may remember Juvenal's touching lines :[4]

> Hæc data pœna diu viventibus, ut renovata
> Semper clade domus multis in luctibus atque
> Perpetuo mærore et nigra in veste senescat.

I have observed that full many owe their death to such ceremonies.

Sincerely yours.

---

[3] Successive Vicars of New Shoreham.

[4] *Sat.* x. 243. The Bishop has substituted 'atque' for 'inque' at the end of the second line, and has inserted 'in' between 'nigra' and 'veste.' Little variations like these from the original show how entirely he quoted from memory

On Sunday Golf-playing

The Palace, Chichester : June 25, 1894.

My dear Mr. ——,—A notice has been sent to me, or rather a sort of placard, of the Birling Gap Golf Club. The prominent feature in it, and that which alone can justify my drawing your attention to it, is the ostentatious manner in which Sunday golf-playing is advertised. Little is said about other days, but special inducements are held out for Sunday golf.

I infer from the connexion of this placard with your 'Manor Office' that you are more or less concerned in the Golf Club, and if this be so, I desire to represent to you the desecration of the Sunday which this notice involves.

People are invited, even tempted, to break what I am sure you hold sacred—the rest and the holiness of our Sunday.

Attendants must be provided for the players, and this is promised, so that the country folk also who dwell near will be drawn in, and in many cases boys who ought to be in the Church or in the Sunday School.

Some reverence for the Christian Sabbath still remains among the agricultural population of Sussex, and if this feeling be weakened a great blow to religion is given, and no one can foretell what ill consequences may follow.

The upper classes, who have the least excuse, set the bad example, and the classes below them are but too likely to follow.

I do hope that you, as a religious man, responsible not only for what you do but for what you countenance and allow to be done, will, if it be in your power, protest against and prohibit this Sunday sport.

If you cannot do this entirely, you may, perhaps, limit the hours of play, and prevent the putting forth of placards so aggressive and so offensive as that which, undated, has reached me.

In any case I trust you will excuse this representation on my part, and believe me

Very truly yours.

CHAPTER VI

Theological Position—Literary Taste—Favourite Authors—Ordination Charges—Examination of Candidates—Pastoral Sympathies— Love of the Country—Knowledge of Botany—Of Architecture— The Palace Garden—Love of Animals—The Cat—Walking Powers —Reminiscences—Mr. A. Benson—The President of Magdalen.

THE Bishop's theological position will have become evident to the reader from the whole tone of his correspondence and the general character of his administration. He was a High Churchman who had formed his opinions before the 'Oxford' or 'Tractarian movement,' as it came to be termed, had begun. He belonged to the old school of High Churchmen who derived their principles from a careful study of the Bible and Book of Common Prayer, together with the early fathers and the best divines of the reformed Church of England: Hooker, Andrewes, Bramhall, Laud, Pearson, Cosin, Bull, Waterland, Wilson, Butler, and William Law, the Nonjuror. Even in the dreariest and most torpid periods of the life of the English Church there had not been wanting a succession of good representatives of this school. Some of them, both lay and clerical, eminent for learning, piety, and activity in good works, were contemporary with the earlier portion of the Bishop's life. Such were Bishops Van Mildert, Lloyd, and Jebb, Mr. Alexander Knox (a friend of Bishop Jebb), William Stevens, the Treasurer of Queen Anne's Bounty, Joshua Watson and his friend Henry Handley Norris, the principal founders of the National Society ; and Dr. Hook, who was only five years his senior.   The Bishop habitually used the Greek prayers of Bishop Andrewes,[1] and the liturgical works of Bishop Cosin.   He was specially well read in Hooker and Pearson, Barrow, Bull, and Butler, and was wont to speak of Law's Letters to Hoadly

[1] On a slip of paper, dated 1881, in the Bishop's copy of Andrewes's *Devotions*, the following list is made of subjects for special intercession :

Ἐντεύξεις.

ὑπὲρ τῆς γυναικός.	ὑπὲρ τῶν συγγένων.
τῶν υἱῶν.	τῶν οἰκείων.
τῆς θυγάτερος.	τῶν φίλων.

τῶν ἀδελφῶν.
τῶν ἀδελφίδων.
τῆς ἐκκλησίας.
τῆς ἐκκλησίας καθολικῆς τῆς ἐν ἡμῖν.
τῶν ἐν τέλει.
ἐπισκόπων.
τοῦ κληροῦ.
πρεσβυτέρων ⎱ ἐν τῇ διοικήσει ταύτῃ, τῆς σπουδῆς,
διακόνων ⎰ εὐσεβείας, σοφίας αὐτῶν.
τοῦ λαοῦ, τῆς σπουδῆς καὶ τῆς ἑνώσεως αὐτοῦ.
τῆς εἰρήνης.
τοῦ ἐν Κικεστρίᾳ φροντιστηρίου θεολογικοῦ.
σχολῶν ἐν ἀγρῷ . . .
Otter's.
Woodard's (3).
C.D.A. (*i.e.* Chichester Diocesan Association).
Eton.
Bishopsford.
ὑπὲρ καιρῶν καρποφόρων.
τῆς εὐκρασίας τοῦ ἀέρος.
τῆς ὑγιείας.

The other side of the leaf is thus inscribed :

Δόξα Σοὶ Κύριε ὑπὲρ τῶν πολλῶν Σοῦ εἰς ἐμὲ ἀναξιώτατον τῶν δούλων Σοῦ εὐεργετημάτων.

as the most perfect defence and statement of the Anglican position that had ever been written. He had much sympathy with the Nonjurors and was in the habit of saying that their ejection was the most serious damage and loss that the Church had ever sustained.

In the theological and ritual questions which came from time to time before him, requiring some expression of opinion or some action on his part, he took infinite pains to arrive at sound conclusions by a careful investigation of patristic authorities and other ancient evidence. In these inquiries he frequently availed himself of the services of a finished scholar with whom he was on terms of intimate friendship and whose learning and ability he highly valued—the Rev. Cowley Powles, who resided in Chichester, and whom he had made a Prebendary of the cathedral and one of his examining chaplains. Amongst the subjects thus investigated were Purgatory, the Sacrifice of the Mass, Prayers for the Dead, Fasting Communion, Confirmation not a Sacrament.

'The task,' writes Mr. Powles, 'was sometimes rather laborious, for the inquiries were to be as exhaustive as possible, but the labour was abundantly repaid. In the discussions which followed my investigations, the Bishop's criticisms were of peculiar interest. His keen insight into meanings about which I had been doubtful, his patience in considering difficulties, and his scrupulously fair estimate of the value of the evidence in each case, made our conversations on the several subjects morally as well as intellectually valuable. . . . The more I think of these conversations the more impressed I am, not merely with a sense of his ability, of which everyone who knew him at all must have been aware, but of his benevolence. I used often to wish that some of the clergy who resisted his authority could have seen for themselves with what freedom from irritation he entered on points of controversy brought before him, with what ungrudging pains and tireless patience he sifted and tested them, and how calm and unprejudiced was the judgment with which he decided them.'

The following notes on divorce and remarriage, copied from a manuscript in the Bishop's own hand, show with what diligence he himself was wont to collect materials for forming a judgment upon a difficult and critical question.

' Tholuck on the Sermon on the Mount v. 31, 32. Only on the presumption that the spiritual life is planted and propagated by parents in their children is the communication of the bodily life a benefit.

'Mark x. 11, 12 ; Luke xvi 18 ; Eph. v. 31 to be completed and interpreted by Matt. xix. So 1 Cor. vii. 10, 11, 12. πορνεία, adultery, on either side breaks the bond ; ὁ πόρνος ἔφθασεν ἑαυτὸν διαστήσας (Theophylact); pauciora exponi debent per plura—so with sin against the Holy Ghost. παρεκτὸς λόγου πορνείας. πορνεία includes μοιχεία, λόγος= reason, cause : Ursache.

' *Opinions of Fathers.*—1. As to the grounds of a legal divorce.

' 2. Whether the innocent party is forbidden to marry again ; whether death alone dissolves the marriage tie.

' Origen and Augustine class idolatry as a $\mu o \iota \chi \epsilon i a$, the latter also covetousness, because it is "idolatry"; generally, the Fathers agree that adultery is the only ground of divorce. Clemens Alex., Hilarius (?), Chrysostom (on Matt. xix.), Isidore of Pelusium, L. v. Ep. 129.

' 2. *Remarriage of innocent party.*—Ambrosiaster on 1 Cor. vii. 15; Epiphanius, "Hæreses," 59, 4; "Apost. Constit." lxi. e. 15; Basilius, Ep. 199; Canon 21; Theodoret, "de Cur. Græc. Aff." L.ix.[2] This is the use of the Greek Church (Hermas; Tertullian against remarriage).

Roman law under the Emperors lax, allowing divers grounds of divorce. Roman Church; Council of Trent, Session 24, 17. See Chemnitz, P. II. Can. 7. Marriage indissoluble.

The Council of Trent (see Sarpi); Sota set himself to reply *in divers manners* (?) to the argument from Scripture, and at last betook himself to *tradition*, but the tradition of the Greek Church was a paralysing force.

Luther and Beza admit three causes of divorce: (1) want of virility; (2) adultery; (3) *malicious desertion.*

Bucer and Melanchthon more indulgent as to divorce, but urged the execution of the adulterer without mercy.

Question how far the blessing of the Church can be given to a second marriage of the guilty party.

This [3] must be firmly established, that the Church cannot wholly ignore such a transgression (*Bruch*)

---

[2] The reference must, I think, be to *Græcarum affectionum curatio.*

[3] The whole of the following passage in the text must be understood as representing the opinions not of the Bishop, but of Bucer and Melanchthon.

of the commandment of Christ : that the Church should impress upon the heart of the guilty party, and in the case of a second marriage contracted contrary to Christ's commandment, let it be understood by the manner in which she blesses such a marriage, that she cannot acknowledge it as purely Christian, therefore cannot give it her full blessing. Circumstances in each case must be considered, p.234. No instance can be alleged where our Lord or St. Paul uses the words πορνεία and μοιχεία in any sense but as indicating the act of adultery.'

Although the Bishop attached very high value to the writings of some of the Fathers and of the theologians of the sixteenth and seventeenth centuries, he by no means neglected the Biblical and liturgical scholarship of modern times ; and the entries in his diary show that the works of Dr. Lightfoot, Dr. Salmon, Archdeacon Freeman ('On the Principles of Divine Worship'), Dr. Westcott, and some German commentators were frequently in his hands. Of that school which arrogates to itself the title of 'the higher criticism' he had very considerable distrust. He brought a very critical and acute mind to bear upon the theories advanced, and he was of opinion that many of the conclusions arrived at, and proclaimed with the utmost confidence, were based on very precarious or incomplete evidence, and very faulty reasoning. There was an assumption, also, of superiority on the part of many writers of this school which seemed to him inconsistent with the reserve, caution, and modesty that became the true scholar and the wise man.

In his charges to candidates for ordination he insisted on the great importance of the study of those great divines of the English Church from whose writings he himself had derived so much profit.

' I am thoroughly convinced,' he said, 'that such theologians as Hooker, Andrewes, Pearson, Barrow, Jackson, Sanderson, are our best guides even in these days. You may think their methods antiquated, their arguments unsuited to the needs of these times. It is not so. There is a continually recurring cycle of false teaching, and the very errors prevalent then are prevalent now. Their arguments and learning are especially sound against the teaching of Rome.'

Alike in literature, in sermons, or in speeches he abhorred obscurity, slovenliness, or slipshod grammar, clumsy or uncouth phrases, florid rhetoric, affectation, or overstrained sentiment ; and, above all, vulgarity and pretence.

In all his own utterances, whether written or spoken, he aimed at expressing with the greatest possible clearness and precision the meaning which he intended to convey ; and in dealing with any controversial matter he preferred rather to understate his view of the case than run the least risk of saying, or seeming to say, more than he really thought or felt. His pure scholarly English may be partly attributed to great familiarity in early life with Addison's 'Spectator' and admiration of his style. His criticisms on character were often cast in an epigrammatic form, with a touch of delicate satire, keen, but never ill-natured.   In fiction his favourite authors were Sir Walter Scott, Miss Austen, Mrs. Gaskell, and (in the earlier works) George Eliot. He loved the poetry of Scott and Wordsworth, and many of the older lyrics collected in Palgrave's 'Golden Treasury.'   In sacred poetry he was especially fond of the works of Manzoni and Henry Vaughan ; and he never failed to read Keble's 'Christian Year' every Sunday or to have it read to him.   He was not an enthusiastic admirer of Tennyson, and Browning he could not read at all. His love for Dante was intense, and probably no man living had a more profound knowledge of the 'Divina Commedia.'   Often might he be found absorbed in it late at night after others had gone to bed, and a little Italian edition of it was his invariable companion in travelling, together with Goethe's 'Hermann and Dorothea.'

In current literature he read a good deal of biography, and anything relating to the Oxford movement especially interested him ; more particularly the account of it by the late Dean Church, together with his Life and Letters, and the correspondence of Newman.   Of periodical journals his reading was limited for the most part to the 'Times,' the 'Spectator' (of which he had a high opinion), reviews in the 'Guardian' of such books as interested him, occasional articles in the 'Quarterly' or 'Church Quarterly,' and selections from some of the missionary magazines.

The Bishop wrote a fresh charge for almost every ordination, although of course the same topics were often rehandled. None of his utterances exhibit more strikingly the inner nature and character of the man, his deep personal piety, his extensive learning, his knowledge of human nature, his sound practical wisdom, his affectionate sympathy and fatherly kindness.

'Preach Christ,' he says, 'rather than Christianity. The people of our day are too apt to speak of Christianity rather than of Christ; of doctrines taught by Him, depending on Him, derived from Him, I grant, but not of Christ Himself. A Christian means one who believes in Christ, belongs to Christ, confesses Christ, lives to Him and in Him, and hopes for salvation and eternal life through Him as the source of all life; but Christianity is a cold word, and it is an unspeakable loss if such a word shall be substituted for Himself. The human heart and affection must cling to a person, and to a person who can sympathise with its wants, its moods, its perplexities, its weaknesses, and such a Person is our Lord Jesus Christ.

'Why do I thus press the reality of Christ's nature and Person and the necessity of our thus receiving Him in our hearts as the Gospel presents Him? Chiefly because it is our office to bring men to Christ, and this can never be done with effect unless we have learned Christ ourselves, and have a full and clear vision of His adorable reality. Remember that whatever your flocks may be—whether they consist of the educated or uneducated, the rich or the poor, simple or learned — one manner of teaching suits them all.   The loftiest understandings bow to the obedience of faith, they need as much as their less gifted brethren the Saviour of sinners. . . . Consider such texts as "Put ye on the Lord Jesus Christ," "Christ Who is our Life," "To me to live is Christ"—texts which so abound that time would fail me if I were to quote them.   They all point to the Person of Christ : to our dependence on Him, our union with Him, and a devout spirit will be careful not to resolve them into mere figures, not to weaken and dilute them by interpretations which belong more to reason than to faith.   It is a very wholesome exercise to read a gospel or an epistle through with this special view in your mind, that, as St. Paul says, Christ may dwell in your heart by faith.'

And the Bishop then proceeds to show how exhortations to every kind of Christian duty could be enforced by reference to some special feature in the person or work of Jesus Christ.

In these addresses to candidates he constantly enlarged on the study of the Bible as a primary and paramount duty for a parish priest : 'bonus textuarius est bonus theologus.'   'If,' as South remarked, 'God had no need of man's learning, He had still less need of man's ignorance'; all available helps to the study of the Bible, both ancient and modern, were to be used, but the best interpreter of the Bible was the Bible itself.   And next in importance to the study of the Bible was the study of the Book of Common Prayer.   'The more we reflect on its language, the more we compare it with the rock whence it was hewn—the Holy Scriptures—the more we shall recognise its transcendent power and beauty.' He strongly recommended clear and simple explanations of the Prayer Book, such as George Herbert was accustomed to give to his people at Bemerton, which would enable the most unlearned flock to understand and love it. And in like manner he advocated the careful explanation of theological terms, attributing to the misunderstanding of these terms much of the prevalent unbelief in some of the doctrines of the Church. He mentions Regeneration and the Real Presence as instances of such doctrines. Of the latter he says :

' I cannot doubt that such Presence is asserted in our Catechism, in our Communion Service throughout, and in our Articles. Further, it has been sanctioned by our greatest divines, and by none more clearly than by the martyr Ridley in his last trial. Why, then, should this doctrine be so much neglected? Evidently because in the popular mind it is confounded with the doctrine of Transubstantiation—that is, with the mediæval corruption of the truth, first set forth as an article of faith by Rome in the thirteenth century, and ever since riveted on the minds of Roman Catholics. No wonder that the enemy of truth should divert men's minds from the truth by the substitution of an error which resembles it. But the truth is not less the truth because it has been disguised and deformed, nor is safety to be found by giving it up, but rather by showing its true beauty and nature and so recommending it to the acceptance of the faithful.'

It was in speaking of pastoral work that the depth of the Bishop's sympathy and real love of souls, and his high sense of the nobleness and awful responsibility of the ministerial calling, were most clearly manifested.   In a letter to a friend he thanks God for one of his clergy recently deceased, who for many years had 'faithfully and lovingly discharged the sublime duties of a parish priest.' The blessedness of the country pastor's lot was a theme on which he frequently enlarged in his Visitation Charges ; more especially as he observed with great regret an increasing reluctance on the part of the younger clergy to take work in country parishes, and too many instances among the older country clergy of indolence and neglect of duty.

'Yet how happy,' he said, 'those pastors should be who can know their own flock by name, the circumstances, the tempers, the moral and spiritual condition of each person, who can lift the latch of every house within their charge, and approach all as more than a common friend, as their spiritual counsellor, bearing our Lord's own message!   How favoured are they in comparison with the clergy settled among the masses of our towns ; who, so far from being acquainted with their flock, can scarce be known even by sight and name!   Surely one may say of such 'O fortunatos nimium sua si bona norint!' tilling a manageable portion of our Lord's vineyard, much removed from the vices, and corruption, and artificial condition of the towns.   Yet it is precisely in such spots that instances of neglect are com monly found.   I speak as unto wise men.   Take heed to yourselves.   If your lot is cast in the country village, never think it beneath you (God forbid) ; never disdain to teach the humblest and most ignorant ; never weary of what may seem dull or forbidding tasks. You may often be grieved by instances of coarse profligacy, hardened contempt of the means of grace, dull insensibility to God's promises and threats ; but there are great compensations. If pastoral visits are profitable to the people, they are equally profitable to the minister. In many a cottage there are lessons for him if he will learn them. What examples of patience under trials, of contentment under pain and poverty, of clear abiding trust in God's Fatherly goodness, of resignation to His will—what a loving dependence on the one personal Saviour may be found in the families of the poor !'

He quotes more than once the lines from the 'Christian Year' beginning :

> How sweet with Thee to lift the latch,
> Where faith has kept her midnight watch, &c.,[4]

and Chaucer's touching description of the Good Parson in the Prologue to his 'Canterbury Tales,' especially the lines :

> Wyd was his parrishe and houses fer asonder,
> But he ne lafte nat, for reyn ne thonder,
> In sicknes, nor in meschief, to visyte
> The ferreste in his parrisshe, much and lyte,
> Upon his feet, and in his hand a staf.
> This noble ensample to his sheep he gaf,
> That first he wroghte, and afterward he taught ;
> Out of the Gospel he the wordes caughte.
>
> .   .   .   .
>
> He wayted after no pompe ne reverence,
> But Cristes lore, and His apostles twelve
> He taught, and first he followed it himselve.

[4] On the 'Visitation and Communion of the Sick.'

The Bishop's old flock at Middleton could testify how closely his life there corresponded to this picture of a faithful pastor drawn by the father of English poetry.

In dealing with the subject of preaching he laid great stress on the necessity of a deep sense of responsibility, of careful study, reflection, and prayer.

'You appear as the Ambassadors of Christ. The people sit at your feet listening to a message which, if it is to be of any weight, must be felt to be not of man but of God. It is, then, of the highest moment that nothing should be said which has not been well considered, which is not thoroughly supported by Scripture, which has not a practical bearing upon the Christian life and heart. And the preacher, if he is earnest, will be careful to give his people the results of his own experience. What he has known and felt that will he tell; for he can tell it, and so tell it that others will feel with him, and the power of sympathy, the strongest of all powers, will pass from his heart into theirs. No sermon can be dry and uninteresting which is real. . . . Is it fair to our people to give them shallow undigested effusions? Would a lawyer, would a statesman venture on such an experiment? Is that a fulfilment of our engagement to " take heed unto the doctrine"? I trow not. Yet there is a great tendency to preach without book, as though there were some charm in words so delivered. But I feel bound to tell you that the gift of eloquence, like the gift of poetry, is one of the very rarest; and more than that, the greatest speakers confess that their speeches are not only prepared most diligently, but that large parts of them are written and re-written with anxious care. Fluency is not eloquence. It is a simple gift of words, often with little force and small meaning. Fluency, I grant, is abundantly common. I can testify to the utter inanity of such sermons and to the trial to which they subject the listeners. Bacon truly said " Reading makes the full man, speaking makes the ready man, writing the exact man." Of these qualities the first and the last are far the most important for those who have to teach divine truth. I advise you all to begin by writing your sermons, and that not negligently. Much knowledge, hard practice, and much natural talent are required to justify any young divine in preaching without book.'

In common with most men who belonged to the old school of High Churchmanship, and not a few of the leaders in the Oxford movement, he had no liking for elaborate ritual. It seemed to him un-English, and inconsistent with that sober standard in teaching and practice which was the peculiar mark of our reformed Church ; and further, he thought that in many instances an inordinate amount of time and thought was bestowed both by the clergy and their congregations on petty details of church ornament and ceremonial, to the neglect of weightier duties. Nevertheless, he always carefully considered all the arguments that could be urged in favour of any practice that to him might seem trifling and insignificant, and he was tolerant of the largest amount of ritual that was not in his judgment irreconcilable with the true teaching and position of the reformed Church. With regard to the use of Eucharistic Vestments he was accustomed to say that it was not inconsistent with anything that he had taught from the beginning of his ministry, and that he thought it was the intention of the reformers to retain a special vestment for the celebration of Holy Communion, although he believed the vestment intended was the cope and not the chasuble. In October 1892 some of his Brighton friends offered to present him with a mitre, and he accepted the offer; but afterwards wrote to say that he had reconsidered the matter, and should prefer to pass the short remainder of his days without an ornament which he had never been accustomed to wear.

What did most seriously vex and irritate him was the pertinacity with which a few extreme men would cling to points of ritual which he considered positively objectionable and had required them to abandon. He himself related an interview with an incumbent of this kind: 'Do you mean to say,' I asked him, 'that you allow all this nonsense to take the place of your proper parochial work? I desire you as your Diocesan to discontinue it immediately.'

'What did he say?' inquired the Bishop's auditor. 'Say! He hadn't a word to say. But I know the man; he'll go on just the same.'

He spoke frequently and emphatically in his ordination charges on the duty of obedience to the Bishop, remarking in one of them that there never was an age in which such resolute independence was manifested, and such hard things were said against spiritual rulers. 'Men love their own opinions, and are a rule to themselves. This tends to insubordination and distrust. The Romanist profits by this undutiful and unsatisfied temper to draw men into a Church where all freedom of thought must be surrendered: the unbeliever and the half-believer look on and scoff and rejoice.' If a promise made at ordination reverently to obey the Ordinary, follow his godly admonitions, and submit to his godly judgment were to be construed, 'I will submit to the judgment if I believe it to be godly, and will follow his admonitions if I believe them to be godly, but not otherwise,' the promise was nugatory. The judgment rested not with the superior, but with the inferior. The priest or deacon erected himself into a tribunal. The whole order of government was inverted. Conscience was often pleaded as an excuse for disobedience. Conscience, of course, should be obeyed, if the Bishop commanded anything plainly against the command of God, but cases were very rare in which he had to touch questions on which God had plainly spoken, and if he should have to touch them it was almost inconceivable that he should speak in contradiction to God's utterance. If it was maintained that his admonition was not godly, that was to make the individual conscience an absolute judge of the question, and conscience might be wrongly informed or even perverted—as in the case of St. Paul when he countenanced the stoning of St. Stephen. If the point at issue was not essential, the reason for reverent submission was all the stronger. Surely there was a blessing in being directed in such matters by one who had authority to direct, who without any unusual stretch of charity might be supposed to take a calm, fair, dispassionate view of each case as it came before him, and might be credited with having a deeper insight into the tendency of things which he reproved or forbad, and more solid grounds for such things as he recommended, than the private individual could possess. He might censure or prohibit usages long disused in our Church but retained in the Church of Rome, and evincing in those who adopted them an inclination to draw perilously near to that corrupt communion; or he might see shortcomings in a different direction, daily service withheld when it was desired by the people, saints' days studiously passed by, a neglect of directions concerning the administration of both sacraments, and generally a shrinking from adherence to the rules, orders, and customs of the Church. There were defects as well as excesses, and correction was needed for both.

The Bishop always personally examined every candidate for ordination in Greek Testament and the Catechism. The examination was always searching, and to shy, nervous, or ignorant men rather formidable. No vagueness or looseness in translation was allowed to pass without comment and correction. On one occasion a candidate who had been summoned to the Bishop's study found him on his knees on the hearthrug, groping for a hot cinder which had fallen out of the fire. 'Take the book,' said the Bishop, mentioning the passage he was to construe, 'and begin. I shall hear you.'

The young man made a good start, but presently he came to a sentence about which he felt doubtful. The Bishop seemed absorbed in his search for the cinder, so the candidate murmured some sort of construe, and hoped for the best; but the Bishop looked up sharply from the floor with ' Eh! what's that?   Repeat that more distinctly, if you please.' In truth the scenes in the study at these *vivâ-voce* examinations were often a curious mixture of the comic and pathetic.   On one occasion a candidate was rather deaf; and the Bishop, who of course did not like ordaining a man with any bodily infirmity, was anxious to ascertain the extent of his deafness.   After the candidate had construed some Greek sentences, the Bishop put a question to him which he was unable to answer.   The Bishop thought he did not hear, so he repeated it in a louder tone : still the poor man was dumb ; yet a third time was the question put, even more loudly than before : still no response.   ' Why,' said the Bishop, turning to a chaplain, ' the poor fellow is as deaf as a stone!' Explanations then followed, with questions which the terrified candidate was able to answer, and kindly conversation, which put him at his ease. Such was frequently the termination of these personal interviews.   In an examination the Bishop's natural characteristics as an exact scholar and critic were in the first instance most conspicuous, but when, passing from the direct subject of examination, he inquired about the candidate's home and past life, and talked about his future work, all the fatherly kindness and sympathy of the Bishop's nature was drawn out, and many a young man who had entered the study in fear and trembling, and had felt ready to sink into the earth under the harrow of the examination, left the room consoled and encouraged, with the assurance that in the Bishop he would ever find a friend who would stand by him in difficulty or trouble.

There were, indeed, none in whom the Bishop took a more tender and compassionate interest than young deacons in their first curacies, and as far as he could he insisted that they should not be over-burdened with work, and should receive help and direction from the incumbents whom they assisted. ' It has been to me,' he says in one of his charges to candidates, ' a real grief that too often the deacon has been left to learn his strange work alone, and to grope his solitary way through his difficulties, or that he is at once charged with such heavy duties that he has no leisure for study. . . . If any of you should find this to be your case, or if for any cause you are not comfortable in your calling, I invite you to come to me, and I promise that I will do my best to remedy your grievance.'   And in another charge, ' Do not hesitate to speak to me about your doubts and difficulties.   I cannot engage to relieve you from all, for that is in no man's power ; but counsel, assistance, sympathy, these at least shall not be wanting.'

The following Latin prayer is a specimen of several which occur in his pocket-book on the days appointed for ordinations :

Domine Deus custodi me in *die isto*.[5] Da mihi gratiam, da Spiritum Sanctum ut officium mihi *commendatum*[5] toto corde, totis viribus, implere possim. *Et omnibus qui*[5] ordinandi sunt, concede ut donum Spiritus Sancti puro corde recipiant, ut tanto beneficio roborati tibi serviant, populum tuum verbo tuo et doctrina fideliter pascant, per Jesum Christum Dominum nostrum.

Deo gratias.

He himself had all the interests and sympathies of a true pastor, and he was wont to employ some of his scanty intervals of leisure when he was at Chichester in visiting a few chronic invalids or the aged poor in the workhouse. One of his visits to the latter was paid on the afternoon of his ninetieth birthday, when he took presents of tobacco for the old men and of tea for the old women. There was no character which more entirely commanded his respect and won his heart than that of the quiet, unpretending, contented, and diligent country clergyman, the true father of his flock, constantly going in and out amongst them not only as their parish priest, but as their neighbour and friend, sharing in all their interests and pleasures, sympathising with them and advising them in all their difficultes and troubles.

Certainly there was no kind of life which seemed to him more truly blessed than that of the pastor, but more especially of the country pastor, and, above all, in such a beautiful part of England as his own southern diocese. He knew the characteristics

---

[5] The words are difficult to decipher in the manuscript, but I think these are correct readings.

of every portion of it, and all had their interest and charm for him.   He delighted in walking over the smooth and breezy downs, collecting specimens of the various fungi that grew there, of which he had a rare knowledge, and enjoying the lovely views over the Weald to the north, the region covered in ancient times by the forest of Anderida, or over the rich fertile belt to the south, studded with villages and homesteads, and bounded by the sparkling sea, rising out of which might be seen on clear days the long wavy line of the Isle of Wight.   He was thoroughly familiar with all the wild flowers and ferns with which the lanes and woods and copses teemed, and all the trees that abounded in the stately parks of Goodwood, Arundel and Petworth, Cowdray and Up Park.

He could advise people as to the various kinds of flowers, plants, trees, and shrubs that were best suited to the soil of the particular district in which they lived.   At the diocesan conference of 1892, when he was ninety years of age, in summing up a debate upon thrift he made an admirable spontaneous address upon the management of cottage gardens, mentioning the most profitable kinds of fruit to cultivate in them, at the same time making the suggestion that the County Councils might facilitate the transport of fruit from districts where it was plentiful to others in which it was scarce.

He observed everything wherever he went, and the results of his observations were stored up in a most retentive memory.   Diligent as his Archdeacons, 'the eyes of the Bishop,' were, he took care to use his own eyes as well, and was thus in a great measure his own Archdeacon, minutely investigating the condition of churches, parsonages, and school buildings, besides studying with the greatest care all the answers to the articles of inquiry which he issued before his triennial visitations.

He was familiar with the architectural features of every church in the diocese, and took a lively interest in all the historical associations of such places as Pevensey and Battle, Lewes, Selsey, and Chichester. It may be truly said that no Bishop of Chichester ever walked so much about his diocese, and knew every corner of it so intimately from personal inspection. 'I am a walking Bishop,' he once said, 'not a talking Bishop.' No one, indeed, could be a more interesting talker than he was, but the remark is a true illustration of one chief characteristic—the concentration of his energies in the most devoted yet unostentatious way upon the administration of his diocese. 'I do not think,' he said, 'that I have a mission to the Church at large, but to the Church in this particular diocese;' and certainly he had no ambition to figure outside it as an orator or preacher, although he never shrank from any call to public duty that could not be avoided.

No doubt the variety of his tastes, but more especially his intense love of the country and of all that makes country life enjoyable, was one secret of his excellent health prolonged to extreme old age.

Constant touch with nature seemed ever to renew his youth, assisting him to throw off the effects of many of the worries and vexations that are inseparable from a Bishop's life. It was wonderful how quickly a few turns round the garden, with his daughter or some congenial friend, where everything that his eye lighted on had its own peculiar interest, would soothe the irritation or clear away the cloud of depression caused by some unsatisfactory meeting, some distressing interview, or some painful correspondence. His garden, indeed, was an inexhaustible source of delight. In his Lancashire home, of course, he had been able to cultivate only the hardier kinds of roses and such other flowers as could resist the malign influence of a smoky atmosphere and a damp chilly climate, but in the more genial air of Sussex his horticultural tastes could be fully gratified. The Palace garden at Chichester is partly bounded by the old city wall, and from the top of the turf terrace which skirts the wall there are charming views of the cathedral towers and spire. The garden itself abounds in a variety of trees and shrubs planted by successive Bishops, more especially by Bishop Carr; and Bishop Durnford made some additions to the inheritance. Nothing gave him greater pleasure than to take his guests a tour of the garden, and talk to them about the flowers and trees which he so thoroughly understood and loved : the large Mespilus, the Catalpa, the flowering Ash, the Majorca box, the red and yellow Chesnuts, the Japanese privet, the standard fig trees,

The Bishop in his Garden.

From a drawing by Miss Rose Barton, in the possession of Walter Durnford, Esq)

the Mandevillia (which he had planted in a sheltered corner and matted up every winter), the Judas tree, the Pomegranate Choysia, and many more. He had a nursery for young trees, out of which he made presents to friends, together with bags of yellow chesnuts for planting in their gardens. He was skilled in the arts of budding and pruning, although for these and other operations of practical gardening he had, as Bishop, of course very little leisure; but a familiar sight on summer mornings to occupants of the Palace, up to the last year of his life, was the Bishop sallying forth before breakfast, generally bareheaded, with a basin of soapy water to bestow on some favourite rose, or a watering-pot to pour upon his favourite lilac lobelia. On warm summer evenings he would sit on the grass terrace in view of the cathedral until nine, when the great bell tolled the day of the month; and then he would pace awhile under the great sycamores at the end of the broad walk that runs westward from the house, and well pleased was he if he caught a glimpse of the white owl flitting noiselessly across the lawn, or heard the hum of the great stag beetle.

Everything on God's earth had an interest for him—birds, beasts, and insects, as well as flowers, plants, and trees. It might be truly said of him as of the learned king of old: ' He spake of trees, from the cedar tree that is in Lebanon even unto the hyssop that springeth out of the wall; he spake also of beasts and of fowls, and of creeping things and of fishes.' Mr. Sutton, the present Archdeacon of Lewes, remembers taking the Bishop for a country drive soon after his appointment to the see, and being startled by his suddenly jumping out of the carriage to pursue a butterfly. And when the diocesan missioner, Mr. Wakeford, was a guest at the Palace, the Bishop was not only anxious to know everything about the moral and spiritual condition of the places that he had just visited, but also everything remarkable that he might have noticed in the gardens of the houses where he had stayed ; and any stories that he had picked up illustrative of natural history were carefully noted—the herons that had deserted their waters and gone into Kent because some carpenters had been working near their haunts, the owl that was stolen by a workman from Washington Tower and had been brought back from Whitechapel, the great pike that lorded it over other fish in Balcombe pond. He loved to watch the wood pigeons which built in the high trees in his garden and occasionally paced the gravel path outside his study window, and he always noticed the first appearance and chirp or ' chink,' as it has been aptly called, of the ' chiff-chaff' in spring.

The garden abounded with white-throats, water wagtails, and flycatchers, and occasionally a yaffle or green woodpecker made its appearance there. The Bishop was fond of all animals, but especially of his domestic pets, the pug dog Gyp, the fleet Welsh pony which he drove for twenty-three years and used to feed with sugar, but above all his cat, and more particularly one named Dare, a black

The Bishop & his Cat. 1894.

Persian which had been consigned to his care by its former mistress when she married and went to live in France. This beautiful creature used always to be perched on a wicker table by the Bishop's side at meals, and was fed by him with brown bread, asparagus stalks, and other dainties, such as it loved. A chair in the study was specially appropriated to it. On one occasion when a candidate for ordination was being examined by the Bishop in Greek Testament, Archdeacon Walker came in and was about to take possession of the sacred seat, but the rash intruder was smartly checked by the Bishop. 'Don't sit there, Walker; don't you see that's the cat's chair?' The beloved cat, however, after the instinct of its kind, was a 'terrible fowler,' and preyed upon the young family of one of the Bishop's favourite birds, the missel thrush, which he admired for its stately and delicate walk ('like Agag,' as he used to say), and for its cleverness in teaching its young how to feed. In 1887 the Bishop contrived a plan to foil the designs of Master Dare upon the infant thrushes. He cased the stem of the tree in which the bird had built its nest for about three feet from the ground with Butcher's Broom, setting the bristles downwards. The device was successful, to the great satisfaction of the Bishop, and the thrush reared her brood in safety. When he was on a visit to Cadenabbia on Lake Como in 1894, being then ninety-two years of age, he observed a large bird of the falcon tribe seize a snake and carry it off to the hillside, where it devoured it.   The Bishop watched the transaction through a glass, exclaiming, as the bird gradually drew down the snake, ' He swallowed him up like macaroni.'   Some of his letters, abounding with allusions to matters of natural history or of agricultural or horticultural interest, read like extracts from the correspondence of Gilbert White of Selborne, whose book, as the Bishop used to say, when once read is your friend for life.   ' The white butterfly produces the caterpillar which eats cabbages and cauliflower plants.   The gooseberry and currant pest is a spotted moth.   This year a great many gardens show only bare poles, and the oak trees in Hants and in parts here are devastated.'[6]

' Your list of plants is wonderful ; I suppose the land is limestone.   I did *not* know the meaning of the herb Paris.   It grows in Hants, where, as well as in Switzerland, I have gathered it ; also in Lancashire and the northern limestone woods.   Star of Bethlehem grows near Eton, on the Thames.   Narcissus bifrons grows in Catsfield.[7] . . .   " O terque quaterque beatus "—the shepherd that found so gigantic a morel![8]   I am bound to say, after due experimental proof, that the fungus was not quite so " sapid " as some smaller congeners sent to me from our southern hills, but he was abundantly good and approved of by connoisseurs.   This heavenly rain (the Bishop's letter is dated April 18,

[6] In a letter to the late Rev. Carey Borrer, Treasurer of the Cathedral and Rector of Hurstpierpoint.

[7] To the same.

[8] A Selborne shepherd who had brought it to the Rev. Prebendary Gordon, Rector of Harting, who had sent it to the Bishop.

1894) has, I trust, set all your birds free and your grass a-growing, and made your hedges vocal. I have not heard the nightingale, but she has been heard here and at Clapham, near Worthing ; nor can I see a swallow. I shall try to-day to go in search of the St. George's mushroom ; it ought to be now seen, and is worth seeking and eating.'

The following letter is from the Rev. Prebendary Gordon, of Harting, to the Bishop:

October 18, 1890.

My dear Lord,— . . . You quite accurately describe the ordinary sheldrake (*Tadorna vulpanser*) which I have seen at Newton on the rabbit burrows of the old sea boundary, now half a mile inland, marking the site of Newton Church, which originally stood, like Shoreham and Pevensey Castle, on the brink of the sea. The Welsh called them the 'St. George's Channel ducks,' quite truly referring them to Ireland. But my bird is a much rarer 'ruddy sheldrake' (*Tadorna casarca* or *rutila*), which loves the warmest countries in Europe, and is rarely seen north of the Carpathians. Mr. Pratt said that he had never seen one in the flesh before.

A bunch or two of swallows still with us daily, but both swallows and swifts went from us earlier last year. All hail for your white-throat, which lingers longer than usual, a fine testimonial to the mercy of your cat !

The Bishop went over to Brighton on purpose to see this new unique Sussex specimen of the ruddy sheldrake at Pratt's, a well-known bird-stuffer, where he was delighted with the innocence of a little girl who came in with an empty cage to buy, as she thought, a living bird, so lifelike were the stuffed specimens in the window.

The Bishop's annual tours abroad afforded the fullest scope for all his manifold interests and tastes, and the brief notes made in his pocket-book on these journeys as to details of architecture, the varieties of flowers seen in his walks, or of the fish displayed for sale in the markets, or the condition of the peasants' houses and gardens, betoken no diminution in his powers of observation down to the last days of his life. The Archdeacon of Chichester, Mr. Mount (a cousin of the Bishop, but beloved by him as a son), accompanied him on many of these foreign tours, and bears testimony to the astonishing range of his knowledge manifested at such times, the unfailing alertness of his mind, and the quickness of his eye. In passing through a railway cutting he would call attention to the various strata, and name the fossils that would probably be found in that district; in a picture gallery he would single out the most typical examples of the several schools of painting, and indicate and criticise their characteristics; in a walk or a drive any peculiarities in methods of gardening or farming were carefully noted. In Italy especially he would illustrate by quotations from the Latin poets the identity of many existing modes and implements of agriculture with those of ancient times. His enjoyment of travelling abroad was, of course, greatly enhanced by his wonderful linguistic powers. He spoke French, German, and Italian, specially the two

latter, with the greatest fluency, and with a per-
fection of accent and pronunciation that astonished
natives. Nor had he any difficulty in understanding
the rougher speech of the working people, with its
local peculiarities. Nothing gave him greater
pleasure than to converse with the boatmen on the
Italian lakes about the different kinds of fish which
they caught, or with the peasants in their gardens
and fields about the nature of the soil and the
cultivation of their crops, their methods of dressing
and pruning their vines and propagating their olives.

And what he had once seen and heard he never
forgot. On my return from a tour in Sicily in 1893
he talked to me a great deal about it, and displayed
such an accurate knowledge of the country that I
said I presumed he must have seen it. 'Yes,' he
replied, ' I was there about seventy years ago ' ; but
his recollection of everything seemed to be as vivid
and fresh as if he had visited the island only the
year before.

His feats in extreme old age on these foreign
tours in walking and mountain climbing were really
prodigious. In 1885, when he had nearly completed
his eighty-third year, he ascended the Schmidten-
höhe from Zell am Tyrol, walking nearly the whole
of the way, the ascent and descent occupying about
eight hours ; and in the same year he went up the
Tra-i-Sassi from Cortina d'Ampezzo on a day when
the heat was tropical, and he was the first of the
party to find edelweiss on the summit. In 1886 he
ascended the Pic d'Arzinol from Evolena, little short

of 10,000 feet, and reached the top before any of his companions, the guide exclaiming with exultation, 'Ah! Monsignor, you are the first man of your age who has ever accomplished this.'

In 1888, September 21, when he was staying at Cadenabbia, on Lake Como, he started with his daughter at 9 A.M., crossing the lake to Nesso, whence they walked up to Pian de Tivano and down to Asso. It was late in the afternoon and getting dusk when they arrived at that place, and they had still to make their way to Bellagio, a distance of seventeen kilometres. An open carriage was obtained at the inn, and the landlady lent the Bishop some wraps to protect him from the evening chill. When they arrived at Bellagio about nine o'clock the last steamer for Cadenabbia had gone, and so they crossed the lake in an open boat, reaching Cadenabbia about ten o'clock, much to the relief of their friends.

In 1890, September 13, he records in his pocket-book 'a hot and tiring walk of six hours from Alagna to Alp Pila to get a view of Monte Rosa,' and in 1891, under the date October 8, being at Monte Generoso, 'Went to Bella Vista at sunrise to see Monte Rosa. In afternoon took road along ridge to San Pietro. Saw Chiasso and Como, three and a half hours' walking.'

One principal cause, no doubt, of the Bishop retaining both his physical and mental powers unimpaired to such an advanced age was that, although always actively exercised, they had never been overstrained.   Competition was not carried to excess in his youth, either in study or in recreation.   That passionate ambition for distinction in athletic sports which is so characteristic of the present age, and which must be considered a symptom of decadence rather than of progress, did not exist in the Bishop's Eton and Oxford days.   Young men were all the stronger for not being so frequently subjected to the strain of competitive examinations, or of making frantic efforts to ' break records.'

Of course, like all Eton boys, the Bishop had learned to swim, and he, with George Selwyn, the future Bishop of New Zealand, was one of a hardy band who used to bathe in the river every day all through the winter.[9]   One of his exploits in swimming as a young man would probably in these days have been chronicled with much exultation, but no one ever heard of it until he related it incidentally in extreme old age to Archdeacon Mount.   They were standing on the bridge which spans the broad and rushing Rhine at Cologne when the Bishop remarked, ' I once swam across the river at Bonn, and hard work it was.'   On the Archdeacon inquiring what had induced him to attempt such a feat, he replied that he had been challenged by a young German to a race ; he did not like to refuse, and happily succeeded in beating his antagonist.

His temperate and hardy habits no doubt helped very much to preserve his health and prolong his life.   He rarely indulged in the luxury of a fire in

[9] See above, p. 65.

his bedroom, and never swathed himself in those numerous overcoats, and coils of comforters about the throat and chest, which render the wearer more sensitive to chills.

I have a vivid recollection of a meeting of the Great Chapter at Chichester in the bitter winter of 1894–5. We sat for three hours and a half debating some vexatious questions in connexion with the proposed restoration of the cathedral; and the stove of the Vicar's Hall, where the meeting was held, refused to draw by reason of the north-east gale. Although the discussion was sometimes warm, the atmosphere was intensely cold. The nonagenarian Bishop, however, serenely presided over the shivering assembly, summing up the results of a tangled debate, and delivering his own opinion in one of the clearest, wisest, and most good-humoured speeches that I ever heard him make.

It was only natural that one who loved above all things reality and simplicity should have been fond of young children, and that they should have been equally devoted to him. When they came to the Palace he delighted in taking them about the garden, or to feed the cows with cabbage leaves, or the pigs with apples which they threw down from the old city wall bounding the kitchen garden, and then watched them rolling down the sloping roofs of the pigstyes below. Many are the instances recorded of the affection of very young children for him, more especially little girls; there was one who always wrote to him on his birthday, another with whose poetical efforts he was exceedingly diverted, another, aged three, who, being about to leave her home for London, said, 'I'll take 'oo with me.' After the Bishop's death, the Vicar of Brighton's youngest child, about four years old, informed her mother that she was going to be very good, because 'I want to go to the good place where the Bishop is, and that he shall take mine hand as he used to do.' The Children's Hospital at Brighton was an institution in which he took special interest. He never failed to attend the annual meeting, and used to visit the wards in company with his friend Mr. Boothby and amuse and cheer the children with his pleasant and kindly talk.

As children grew older, whether boys or girls, their liking for the Bishop was generally mixed with a considerable amount of awe. This was mainly because he assumed a somewhat stiffer manner towards them, and was wont to put questions to them to test their intelligence and draw out their knowledge, which made them feel as if they were under examination. Such was the experience of Mr. Arthur Benson, son of the late Archbishop, and now a master at Eton.

'I first saw the Bishop,' he writes, 'in 1877. When my father was appointed Bishop of Truro, the Archbishop (Tait) offered him rooms in Lollards Tower (at Lambeth Palace), which was given up to three or four Bishops as a London residence. It was a little collegiate establishment, each Bishop having a sitting room with a couple of bedrooms attached,

and with a common dining room and library. The
Bishop of Chichester was by seniority a kind of
informal president of the establishment. I used to
think him very formidable. He would rap out short
questions to me about Eton, with his eyes cast down
on his plate, and require categorical answers. Then
he would raise his eyes sharply, wrinkling up his
forehead, and I generally felt that my answers
were unsatisfactory to him. Nevertheless, he was
extremely kind, and would take the trouble to show
me books, and point out the interesting features of
the place.'

But when the intermediate age was passed and
the school boy and girl had developed into the
young man and the young lady, the Bishop's manner
changed, and they could not fail to be charmed with
the free and genial way in which he would converse
with them on all manner of subjects, almost as if
they were contemporaries and knew as much as
himself. Thus, to quote Mr. Benson again :

' After I had become a Master at Eton I went two
or three times to stay at the Palace. I don't know
if he was different in reality, but I certainly thought
that he was more tolerant and good-humoured. He
always took the greatest trouble to entertain me,
and I used to feel flattered at the way in which
he would ask questions about books and people,
particularly connected with Eton, and seem to
give weight to my answers.'

Mr. Benson accompanied him to the great Naval
Review at Portsmouth in 1887, and supplies the
following interesting account of the excursion :

'We had places on a great white troop-ship, assigned to the use of the House of Lords. He was in high spirits. We started early; it was a cold blustering day, with spurts of vindictive rain. Everything had been prepared for a fine summer day; there was an elaborate cold luncheon: the whole thing took an immense time, and though the actual procession was very inspiring, we were glad, most of us, to sit huddled behind bulwarks and in sheltered corners, anywhere out of the wind. The Bishop was indefatigable; he was received with great honour by the officers, and made friends with them at once, asked questions, and saw over the whole ship from top to bottom. The day was a very long one, and we were glad when it was over. When we were ready to depart the Bishop could not be found. At last he made his appearance, clambering up a small iron ladder from the lower regions, having gone to inspect the stoke hole.'

Reference has been made above to the little group of Bishops who occupied rooms in that part of Lambeth Palace which goes by the name of Lollards Tower. Bishop Selwyn of Lichfield and his brother William Selwyn (Lady Margaret Professor of Divinity at Cambridge) had been granted the use of the tower by Archbishop Tait, and they let two rooms in it to Bishop Durnford, who was their intimate friend. On the death of Bishop Selwyn in 1876, the Tower was granted to Bishop Durnford, who assigned rooms there from time to time to various Bishops, including Dr. Benson of Truro, Dr. Lightfoot of Durham, and his successor

Dr. Westcott, Dr. Stubbs of Oxford, and Dr. Wordsworth of Salisbury. They attended the services in the Archbishop's chapel and had a common dining hall, so that they formed, as Mr. Benson has said, a kind of collegiate establishment with the Bishop of Chichester as their president. It was indeed a delightful gathering of learned and cultivated men ; affording opportunities not only for grave conference about the affairs of the Church and nation, but for conversation, often witty and brilliant, on literature and other lighter topics. It was in such intercourse that the Bishops learned to appreciate at their full value the wonderfully rich and varied powers of their brother of Chichester.

The resolution passed in Convocation after Bishop Durnford's death spoke of 'his extraordinary diligence and activity in spite of his great age, his vigorous judgment, his readiness in debate, his high principles of action.' Bishop Stubbs, in seconding the resolution, said :

'Looking at it all round, I have always regarded him as one of the most remarkably gifted men that I ever knew—perhaps the most. In every function, in every department, in every relation, without any faltering or falling back, or being weakened by age or weariness, he was always ready, always judicious, always fully informed, always full of sympathy. . . . He was a brilliant scholar, and I do not know whether there was any subject upon which he could not on the spur of the moment have given you a Latin, a Greek, or an Italian quotation. Your Grace knows well from the part that he took in the Conference at Lambeth in 1888 how valuable we all found his advice. . . . But perhaps the most remarkable point was the intense devotion of all his gifts and faculties to his diocesan work, in which he never flagged and never showed any defect of judgment. To the very last day of his life, and I believe to the very last moment, he was thinking about, and working for, those connected with him in his work.'

And in a private letter to the writer of these pages Bishop Stubbs says, ' He was, I almost think, the most wonderfully complete person I ever knew, and the same to the last.'

Equally emphatic is the testimony of Archbishop Benson in the following entry in his diary for October 14, 1895.

' *October* 14.—Received by telegram the sad news of the Bishop of Chichester's death. Ever since 1877 he has been the kindest, tenderest, most judicious of friends. He was born in 1802, the same year as my father, and my father has been dead more than fifty-four years. He could walk several miles without fatigue—a year or two ago *twelve* miles. He *tripped* along, and it is not long since I could scarcely overtake him on the pavement. He made at the last Convocation and the bishops' meeting before it, the brightest, clearest, most sensible, and beautifully expressed speeches. Canon Philpotts used to say, " he knew everything," and that his reputation was as a boy at Eton the reputation of the best of scholars, the most instructed in all interesting things, and the readiest. He was an excellent botanist. His knowledge of trees, their ways and habitats, was amazing. Of all the people I have known who visited him at Chichester, everyone has told me of the delight of a walk with him round his garden. He spoke French, Italian, and German with a *verve* and a native *sound* which I have never heard equalled. I am told he spoke Spanish equally well,[1] and that everywhere he had the wonderful gift of catching the *patois* of the peasants in a short time and talking easily with them. His quotations of Horace and Virgil and Greek poetry were most rapid and ready. He surpassed the Bishop of Hereford, and we shall have, alas! to reckon him as almost the last of the quoters. Dante he quoted almost more often, and with the greatest appreciation of both sound and sense. The last time I saw him was in my chapel. He was the picture of devotion and simplicity. His white hair, his eyes without glasses fixed on something before him, the reverent bend of his shoulders, his clasped hands as he sat unconscious of eyes, his bright, fresh, clear complexion, made him a perfect picture. He was of a generous spirit. He was a true Churchman without fads, an evangelical spirit with a true ecclesiastic's love of peaceful order. I had a letter from him last week full of pain at a Brighton man's reservation of the Blessed Sacrament with rough defiance of his Bishop, and a setting of " canon law " above rubric as settling the question! I was to see him on Thursday and bring him with me here to see how we could deal with this man and not go to the courts.'

---

[1] This statement must be accepted with reservation. He could read Spanish, and would no doubt have quickly learned to speak it had there been opportunities for practice.

The following interesting reminiscences have been kindly contributed by the President of Magdalen :

'With regard to my own impressions of Bishop Durnford, I was going to begin by saying I never knew him as a young man, but I at once correct myself.   It is true that he was hard upon his eighty-sixth birthday when I first saw him. But he neither looked nor seemed old.   I once said to him, " You must remember President Routh as comparatively a young man." " Routh was never a young man," said the Bishop.   I would invert the saying.   Bishop Durnford was never an old man, unless indeed he may have been so in youth or middle age.   He was certainly not old when I first made his acquaintance. It was on October 25, 1888.   My college was celebrating the bicentenary of the most famous event in its history, the restoration of President Hough and his fellows after their expulsion in 1688 by James II. The Bishop of Winchester (Dr. Harold Browne) was with us in the capacity of Visitor.   Bishop Durnford came as an Honorary Fellow, the college having just elected him to that position.   I went myself to meet the visitor, and arranged for a carriage to meet the Bishop of Chichester.   But he could not be found.   Soon after he turned up, having walked from the station and visited I know not how many old haunts on the way.   From that moment to the end of his visit he was untiring, every moment active and delightful.

'In the evening there was a dinner in Hall. After dinner there were a number of speeches. Several were, I think, good, some were certainly long. We had sat down at seven.   Bishop Durnford was not called on until very late, about eleven o'clock. He made the speech of the evening, full of gaiety, grace, and spirit.   He spoke of the revival and extension of the Founder's ideas in these latter days, more especially of the development of his prælectorships in the new professorships, and ended up by saying playfully that he intended to come to us frequently and show himself as good a fellow as anyone there.

' He stayed two days.   On the second day he gave away the prizes at the College School, making again a very happy and pretty speech.

' I find in my official notebook the following entry : " October 27, 1888.   At 4 P.M. the President saw the Bishop off, his visit, alas ! coming to an end."

' He had charmed everybody by his delightful manners and wonderful vivacity and variety.   He seems equally at home in ancient and modern languages, and equally retentive and accurate about persons, places, and things.

' He quoted Homer with readiness and fluency, more than once ; discussed a passage in Bentley's " Phileleutherus Lipsiensis," conversed with Mr. Hogarth[2] about the topography of Cyprus as if he had been there in person, and with Mr. and Mrs. Chapman with the same wonderful fulness of information about the people and places of Lancashire.

' The Bishop came and stayed with us again on several occasions.   In particular he came to the College Gaudy in 1891, and again made a very neat and happy speech, proposing the health of Lord Selborne, who had just been made High Steward

---

[2] Fellow of the college ; author of *Devia Cypria : the Wandering Scholar in the Levant*, &c.

of the University, and quoting *à propos* of him from Dryden's " Absalom and Achitophel " :

> In Israel's courts ne'er sat an Abbethdin
> With more discerning eyes or hands more clean.

' My wife and I also had the pleasure of staying with him at Chichester, and making in his company many delightful excursions in the neighbourhood, to Cowdray and Goodwood, Bosham, Kingley Bottom, and elsewhere.

' My impression was always the same.

' I never saw, and never expect to see again, a specimen of the human race like him.   I saw in him what extreme old age under the happiest circumstances might be, as beautiful and as attractive in a different way as youth or childhood, what a fine winter day is to a fine day in summer or spring, so that a man may have a positive charm and grace at ninety.   We talk of wonderful old men, but he was more, far more, than most wonderful old men.   Mr. Gladstone's powers, especially his force and strength in extreme old age, were spoken of as wonderful, and so indeed they were.   But Mr. Gladstone's sight was far from good, and Mr. Gladstone was distinctly deaf at eighty-five.   The Bishop's senses—sight, hearing, perception—at ninety seemed to me practically perfect ; certainly as good as those of most men of fifty.   He had a slight slowness in reply, something like that of a child.   At first I thought that even he was a little deaf.   The answer, when it came, showed that he was nothing of the sort, that he had only been taking time to deliver judgment, to say exactly what he wanted, and to say it as he wanted.

' Both his manner and his manners were delightful and engaging.   He had a playfulness of gesture, voice, and smile which was quite irresistible, a sharpness and crispness in conversation which, mixed with his kindliness and courtesy, seemed to me exactly to realise the scriptural ideal: "let your speech be always with grace, seasoned with salt, that ye may know how to answer each one."

'If he was not old, neither was he old-fashioned. He had indeed one or two old-fashioned pronunciations, which sat very well on a man of ninety, and interested me not a little. Such were "quirister" for chorister, an ancient pronunciation still preserved at Winchester, and which is known, of course, to students of literature, but like many other pronunciations has been killed by the spread of spelling; and "Rooshians" and "Prooshians," pronunciations also more historically correct than those now in vogue. But he was as quick and keen and as much up-to-date in everything in which being up-to-date was an advantage as men thirty or forty years his juniors.

'On the last occasion when he stayed with me we had a small party to dinner—Lord Selborne, Mr. Daniel of Worcester College, and one or two others. The conversation turned on Mr. Gladstone's verse translation of Horace which had just appeared. "Why should he or anyone attempt the impossible?" said Lord Selborne. I did not know at the time that Lord Selborne had himself tried his hand at the same task. In particular we discussed the famous passage about the coming of spring:

> Nam seu mobilibus veris inhorruit
> Adventus foliis, seu virides rubum
> Dimovere lacertæ,
>
> Hor. "Od." i. 23.

with Bentley's bold emendations.

'Both Bishop and ex-Chancellor showed themselves equally at home in the minutiæ of scholarship and the truths of nature.

'As a complement to this, I may give another recollection. My wife and I were staying with the Bishop at Chichester.   In the afternoon he drove us himself in a carriage drawn by an odd, pulling, bolting little nag, which he seemed thoroughly to understand, to Kingley Bottom to see the old yew-trees.

'Coming back he steered this somewhat head-strong and eccentric steed with the greatest nerve and skill through the narrow old-world streets of Chichester, crowded with the miscellaneous vehicles of the Goodwood mob.   Arrived at home, he sat awhile at tea in the garden patting his favourite cat and talking with unabated vigour, then suddenly jumped up, fetched two cans of soapsuds, and began to water and weed his flower-beds, sitting crouched down for the purpose, and remaining in this position for more than an hour without apparently any fatigue, when he broke off and said he must go in to write letters till dinner.   At dinner there was a consider-able party, whom he entertained with the most charming grace and readiness.   When the ladies withdrew, he at once attacked one of his guests who had been up at Goodwood, and asked him about the performance of certain horses, when it soon appeared that the Bishop, who had not been there, knew as much about the races as the guest who had. He had been, I fancy, to the stables for a few minutes and picked up all the news from his coachman.

'Yet another memory of a very different sort that dwells in my mind is that of the Bishop as he appeared in his private chapel at the simple prayers which were held there every morning, and in particular his own brief exposition of the second lesson for the day—brief, masterly, scholarly, yet so simply put as to come home to the most unlearned.

'With this memory goes another, my meeting him at his own well-beloved Eton, when by what I cannot but consider a fortunate chance it fell to him to unveil the monument of Bishop William of Waynflete, the first headmaster and second provost of Eton, and founder of Magdalen. He performed the ceremony with happy grace, notwithstanding that the canvas covering refused to fall when he pulled the string, and that the string broke, and a man and a ladder had to complete the process. In college he made a charming little pronouncement on the foundation days of Eton, touching off with terse but delicate language the character of Henry VI. and of Waynflete. I always wish I had kept notes of the speech, which seemed to me a model of its kind.

'Most vividly of all, perhaps, do I remember the impressiveness with which he gave the Benediction at the special service in the school chapel.

'My last meeting with him was at the funeral of the Bishop of Winchester, Dr. Thorold. After the service—a stately and beautiful ceremony, but by reason of the numbers attending necessarily not short—and after he had disrobed, I met him and walked with him to the Deanery. Escorted by his old and dear friend the Dean, formerly one of his chaplains, he went all over the beautiful garden and interesting outbuildings, climbing, I remember, up some ladder steps into a mediæval loft to see an old timber roof, which filled him with pleasure, and on which he delivered one of his delightful, instructive, yet absolutely unpedantic, little disquisitions. In the drawing-room I left him, full of sympathy and friendship, full of interest in what he had seen, full of vitality, full of anticipation of his autumn holiday, in Italy and Switzerland, from which he never returned. I never saw him again, but I shall never forget him—his beautiful and inspiring personality—or cease to cherish his memory ; not if I should live to be as old as he was then.'

CHAPTER VII

Last Days—Visit to Winchester—Journey to Italy—Death at Basle—
Memorials.

THE intense cold of the winter of 1894–5 had no
visible effect upon the Bishop's health and strength.
He went hither and thither through it all as usual
about his diocese, and to London for Convocation.
In starting for a round of confirmations at the
beginning of March he grazed his leg badly by
slipping on the step of his carriage, but he went on
with his work for three days, at the end of which
the wound was so painful that he was persuaded
to consult a doctor in Brighton, who immediately
ordered him to bed, where he remained for a
fortnight in the house of his friends, Mr. and Mrs.
Boothby. In no very long time the wound was
healed, to the astonishment of the doctors, and
the Bishop was going about his duties as before.
While he himself seemed to be impervious to the
effects of weather, he was constantly exhorting
friends who were advanced in age, although younger
than himself, to be cautious. ' Pray respect your
years,' he wrote on February 19, 1895, to Canon
Borrer, the Rector of Hurst, ' and remember that
you are not so able to withstand cold and subtle air

as you were *validus juventâ*'; and again in a letter
to the same on May 9: 'I am sorry you have been
caught by that treacherous blast. I was in the
East at Sedlescombe after the grand meeting at
Brighton—for which God be thanked—and I really
thought there must be snow. The sound of cuckoo
and nightingale sounded as a mockery. But now all
is genial, and I hope you feel the good effect.'

The 'grand meeting at Brighton' here referred
to was held to protest against the measure recently
proposed to Parliament for the disestablishment of
the Church in Wales. The entry in his diary on
the following day records that he paid a 'surprise
visit to the school at Sedlescombe : very orderly and
good.'

In addition to all his active work up and down
the diocese there was, of course, the constant
correspondence to be carried on which is one of the
heaviest burdens of the Bishop's office, especially on
his return home. Most of Bishop Durnford's letters
were written with his own hand, and in the year
1895, the last of his life, he notes in his diary having
written as many as fifteen in one morning. His
handwriting when he wrote slowly and took special
pains was of a good scholarly type, but, partly from
the pressure on his time, partly perhaps from defect
of eyesight, it became extremely illegible, although
the deterioration was not particularly marked in the
last few years of his life. An exceptionally legible
letter to his old friend, Bishop Claughton, drew
forth the following humorous reply :

My dear Cicestr.,—You cannot think what a pleasure it was to me to see your well-known handwriting again; but before I say anything about myself, I have a question to ask you touching this same 'manual act' of yours. Did you take extraordinary pains in consideration of my infirmity and *probable* blindness, or is your handwriting really improved? For the first time for many years I have read a letter of yours from end to end without a single stumble. I think you must have been condescending to my weakness, like the clergy who come to see me and evidently suppose that as I am retiring I must be *deaf*.

The last time that I saw the Bishop was at Winchester on July 29, 1895, just ten weeks before he died. He came to attend the funeral of Bishop Thorold. He travelled from Chichester in the morning, arriving at Winchester about noon. It was the first time that he had visited the Deanery, and with his usual keen interest and thoroughness he inspected every part of the beautiful old house and garden. The service in the cathedral and at the grave was necessarily long, but after it was ended he went all round the Deanery garden (an extensive one) again, with his friend the President of Magdalen, and ascended to the loft over the stables to see the beautiful fourteenth-century timber roof; that building having been part of the hall in which, in monastic times, the pilgrims who visited the shrine of St. Swithun were lodged. After tea, and of course much talk, he set out about five o'clock on his return journey of two hours to Chichester, not having shown the slightest symptom of fatigue.

Nevertheless the end was approaching. For

some years past it had been observed that he did not like to talk much by anticipation about his autumn tour on the Continent.   And in this year there were some indications of reluctance to make the venture.   To a friend who wished him a pleasant visit to the Italian lakes he replied, 'Wish me rather a safe return;' and in a letter to Canon Borrer on September 4, two days before he started, he writes (the cautions to his aged yet junior friend being very characteristic), ' I am told you are going to exchange your north view for the sunny aspect of your son's house.   This is wise; but do not presume, and be careful.   We leave England, D.V., on Friday.   For my own part I had as lief stay in this bonny garden, now at its best, but I must vacate the house for the annual lustration. . . . Mind my counsel.

On Sunday, September 1, the Bishop celebrated Holy Communion in the cathedral at eight, as was his custom when in residence.   It was the last Sunday he was ever to spend in Chichester or in England.

On the 5th he wrote the following letters to the Rev. Canon Cooper, Vicar of Cuckfield, and to his parishioners with reference to a mission about to be held there.   They were the last letters written from Chichester about diocesan affairs, and on the same day on his way to London he performed his last public ministration by officiating at the marriage of Miss Scrase-Dickins near Horsham.

The Palace, Chichester : September 5, 1895.

My dear Cooper,—I have had no time to write as I could have desired, but such as I can I send. To-morrow, D.V., we cross the Channel for a stay of some weeks.

I need not add that I pray your mission may be abundantly blessed. I do not know personally either of the missioners, but take them cheerfully on trust. Sherard, it seems, belongs to St. Albans.

Believe me sincerely yours.

My dear Friends,—Your Vicar has asked me to commend the coming mission in your parish to your hearts and to your prayers.

In my opinion this has been already done in your Vicar's letter, which is in your possession. I can add nothing to that full and touching address. It reminds you of the purpose of such a mission ; of the necessary preparation for it ; of your duty to do all that is in your power for the promotion of its objects, which are simply to enlarge the kingdom of Christ among you, and to build up His Church in righteousness and true holiness.

Remember that a mission comes but seldom. It is a great opportunity rich in blessing to those who embrace it with earnest desire to be brought nearer to God through the intercession of His Son Jesus Christ : to cleanse themselves by His grace from all filthiness of the flesh and spirit, to live in the fear of God and to do His holy will. Remember that the missioner has a message to all : to them that stand, that they may be established, strengthened, and settled ; to them that have strayed from the fold, that they may be brought back to Christ the true Shepherd ; to them that are wavering, that they may be fixed in the faith; to them that are ignorant, that they may be taught the way of life and happiness. The missioner, I say, has a message to all of you : not of his own, but as the ambassador of Christ the Great Shepherd of the sheep.

'I write as to wise men : judge ye what I say.' Let me repeat my words. The opportunity is great. To many of you it will never return. Your happiness in this life and in that which is to come may depend on the choice that you now make, on the spirit in which you receive into your hearts the seed that the missioner is coming to sow.

The Vicar speaks to you from experience of the good that missions have wrought by God's blessing under his own eye.

I can add my testimony to the same effect. But to make the mission fruitful two conditions are needed :

1. To give earnest heed to the things that you hear from the missioner, lest you let them slip.

2. When the mission is past to stir up your good affections by devout use of the means of grace always open to you : watching and praying that you may not enter into temptation nor fall back into the sins that you have repented of and forsaken, holding firm the ground that you have won. I pray that a special blessing may be vouchsafed to the missioners and to all who are over you in the Lord and admonish you, being always

Your faithful Friend and Bishop,
R. Cicestr.

Chichester : September 5, 1895.

On the 6th he and his daughter left London, and reached Rheims the same evening. The heat was intense, and the Bishop describes the journey to Lucerne on the following day as 'a most fatiguing one for heat, dust, and smoke.' Sunday the 8th was spent at Lucerne, and the next day they proceeded to Lugano—'a truly torrid journey' is the Bishop's entry in his diary. On the following day he felt so unwell that a doctor was consulted, and for several days he suffered considerably from internal pains, together with a sense of great weakness and languor caused partly by the excessive heat. Nevertheless he gradually got better, and took occasional walks and drives, besides beginning to write his address for the diocesan conference, which was to take place soon after his return to England. On the 21st he removed from Lugano to Cadenabbia, the place in which he loved to sojourn above all others in Italy, partly on account of its lovely situation on the Lake of Como and partly because he had friends among the English residents there whose society he enjoyed and who always gave him a hearty welcome. On this occasion he stayed a week with Mr. Long in his beautiful villa, and here he recovered in some measure his usual strength, and was able to cross to Bellagio to see his friends Mr. and Mrs. Pechell. She was in a dying condition, and his pastoral ministrations to her, and the comfort and sympathy which he afforded to her husband, were greatly valued by them both. On the 28th he moved into the Hotel Belle Ile, where he was well known, and was always provided with comfortable quarters, in which he felt quite at home. Before leaving his friend Mr. Long's villa he wrote the following lines in his album :

> Villula quam liquidis circumdat Larius undis
>   Non est in lato pulcrior ulla lacu.
> Quam lætus montes et littora nota reviso,
>   Candidaque in summis oppida fixa jugis.
> Hic mihi grata quies ; hic fessus membra repono,
>   Meque fovet dulci Longus amicitia.

September 21 to 28, 1895.

Mr. Long has placed a brass in the ' Church of the Ascension ' at Cadenabbia to the Bishop's memory, bearing the following inscription :

> Hic sæpe Deum veneratus est
> Ricardus Durnford, S.T.P., Eps. Cicestrensis,
> Vir sapientia insignis, litterarum cultor assiduus,
> Amicus unice dilectus.   Basileæ
> Ob. xivmo die Oct. A. S. MDCCCXCV. anno æt. xciido.

The Bishop remained at Cadenabbia till October 12. He had recovered his usual health, had been able to enjoy some excursions on and around the lake with his friends, and had finished writing his address for the impending diocesan conference.

This address, never delivered, was printed and circulated in the diocese after his death. It certainly betrays no signs of failing power. The thoughts are as clear, and are expressed in language as vigorous, scholarly, and concise as ever.

The conference was to have been held at Worthing, and the address began with a reference to the terrible outbreak of typhoid fever which had occurred in that town a few years before.

'We remember with what kindness we were received in 1889 by the town and people of Worthing. Since that time Worthing has endured the severest visitation that any town in Sussex has suffered within living memory, but that visitation brought into strong light the Christian courage and charity of those who were untouched by the plague. All honour to them! They did not flee from the infected town. They stood firmly to their posts; ministering to the many sick in their homes and in the hospitals, sparing neither their money nor their labour, going about on their errand of mercy with their lives in their hands.'

A vigorous and spirited passage on the rejection of the Bill for the Disestablishment of the Church in Wales has been already quoted (pp. 208–210). In the latter part of his address he commented in a tone of severity quite unusual with him upon the teaching and practice of the most extreme section of ritualistic clergy. He had no doubt gradually come to regard that party with increasing distrust and dislike; but the exceptional severity of his language at this time may have been provoked by the defiant attitude recently adopted by one of his clergy on the subject of 'Reservation.' He had intended on his return to England to consult the Archbishop as to the best course to be followed, for the line of action taken by the clergyman in question was, he thought, such as no Bishop could or ought to tolerate.

On Saturday, October 12, the Bishop and Miss Durnford started on their return journey, arriving at

Lucerne the same evening.   On the following morning, Sunday, the Bishop attended the celebration of Holy Communion at 7.45 in the church near the Schweizerhof, and also Mattins at a later hour.   In the afternoon he went by steamer to Alpnach and back, without landing, just for the pleasure of the view at Stanzstadt, with its old tower standing out conspicuous against a fine background of mountains.

On his return to the hotel at Lucerne he looked out some papers which he intended to read on his journey to England in preparation for the diocesan conference.   About 7 P.M. he and his daughter proceeded by train to Basle, a journey of two hours. A colonial judge, Mr. Justice Lawrence, of Capetown, was in the same carriage, and wrote the following interesting account of his impressions of the Bishop a few days afterwards in the 'Times.'

' Having been probably the last Englishman to enjoy the privilege of any personal intercourse with the venerable Bishop of Chichester, it has occurred to me that you may consider a few lines of reminiscence likely to prove of sufficient interest to some among the many friends and admirers of the late prelate to justify insertion in your columns.   On Sunday last I was travelling from Como to Paris. The Bishop, accompanied by Miss Durnford, joined the train at Lucerne, and we travelled together as far as Basle, where he was to break his journey for the night.   It proved to be the last stage of all.   I did not at first recognise the Bishop, who was in travelling costume, and whom I had not seen for many years. Some casual reference to the diocese of Chichester led me to make a remark, "What a wonderful old man the Bishop is!" Miss Durnford then explained that I was addressing the Bishop. In the conversation which ensued, and which continued without interruption and without any sign of fatigue on his Lordship's part for the next two hours, I was most deeply impressed by the extraordinary energy, the keenness of the senses, the accurate memory ranging from classical quotations to historical anecdotes, and the complete conversance with current topics in politics, literature, and archæology of the most miscellaneous description, displayed by one who explained to me that Mr. Gladstone at Eton had been too much his junior for him to recollect having made his personal acquaintance till a later period, and who favoured me with some interesting reminiscences of Dr. Routh, who was President of Magdalen when Mr. Durnford became a member of that distinguished society. I cannot help feeling how exceptional was my fortune in being thus brought into momentary but intimate contact with such a link with the past, though there was nothing in the Bishop's appearance or bearing calculated to produce any apprehension that the connection was indeed so fragile. On alighting at Basle, the Bishop was kind enough to ask for my card and to invite me with characteristic courtesy to come and see him at Chichester should an opportunity occur. The last subject which we discussed was that of the grave depression in the incomes of the beneficed clergy, which he observed was a source of much anxiety to him, and caused serious difficulty in the exercise of his patronage. He cordially concurred in a suggestion which I ventured to make that Parliament might well afford some measure of relief by remedying the present inequitable system of assessment of clerical incomes to the Poor Law and similar local burdens. The personality of the Bishop appeared to me to present a combination of quiet dignity and genial courtesy, unique in one who was nearly a contemporary with the closing century. With your permission, "his saltem accumulem donis." '

After supper at Basle, the Bishop read the Psalms and Lessons for Evensong, and went to bed about eleven. When his servant called him about seven o'clock, he said he had not slept well owing to internal pain, and that he should lie a little longer in bed. His daughter summoned a doctor about eight o'clock, who administered some medicine to relieve the pain, and did not seem to have any anxiety as to his condition ; but he gradually fell into a deep slumber from which he could not be roused, and half an hour after noon he peacefully and painlessly fell asleep in Christ.

'Deo gratias pro itinere feliciter peracto.'[1] Such is the last entry in his diary written at Lucerne on the day before his decease. To us who survive him it reads like a thanksgiving for the happy accomplishment of his long life-journey in this world, and his peaceful translation to a better.

The prayer which he must so often have uttered

---

[1] 'Thanks be to God for a journey happily accomplished.'

in using the devotions of Bishop Andrewes was entirely fulfilled in him.

> We beseech of Thee
>   for the close of our life,
> that Thou wouldest direct it in peace,
>   Christian, acceptable,
>   Sinless, shameless,
> and, if it please Thee, *painless*,
>   Lord, O Lord,
> gathering us together
>   under the feet of Thine Elect,
> When Thou wilt and as Thou wilt,
>   Only without shame and sins.

Thus tranquilly ended the earthly life of this aged servant of God: a singularly complete life, whether we have regard to length of years, or to work accomplished, or to the character of the man himself, so thoroughly equipped with intellectual gifts and moral graces, and all these so evenly balanced. As a scholar, a pastor, a prelate, he was equally excellent; in his love of the country and all its charms and interests, in his simple hardy habits, his straightforwardness, his dislike of anything in speech or in action that was over-strained, intemperate, or unreal, he was a noble specimen of the very best type of the English gentleman.

On October 19 his body, followed by more than 300 clergy, was borne into the cathedral at Chichester, where the first part of the service was performed, and then it was conveyed to the village churchyard at Westhampnett, and laid to rest by the side of his wife, and hard by the grave of his predecessor Bishop Gilbert, and of Archdeacon Walker.

References to him in churches, not only in the diocese, but outside it, were of course numerous. The most remarkable testimony, however, to the respect in which he was held by people of another creed was a special memorial service held by a congregation of Jews, of which the following is a report.

'The congregation worshipping at Beth Hamedrash, London, mainly consisting of Russo-Polish Jews, have held a service in memory of the late Bishop of Chichester. The ark, containing the scrolls of the law, was draped in black, and black candles were burned during the ceremony, whilst the name and titles of the deceased Bishop were written in white characters on a black ground and placed in front of the ark. Mr. Cohen, the English Secretary, read two letters from the late Bishop, written in acknowledgment of their good wishes at the opening of the new year. In the later letter the Bishop said : " If the Church of which I am an unworthy minister did not feel an affection for the people of God, it would be false to the teaching— inspired teaching, we believe—of its greatest Teacher." Mr. Cohen added: " Faithful, even as we are, to his own religion, Dr. Durnford was no fanatic. He was one of the wisest, as well as the oldest, of the able band of liberal-minded Bishops and noble Englishmen whose letters of sympathy you have received for now some seven years. Whilst leaders of the stamp of the late Bishops of Chichester, Winchester, and Nottingham, and gentlemen like the late Sir Andrew Clarke, M.D. (who was ever our firm friend), are to be found among the foremost representatives of the Church of England, we may rest assured that there will be no persecution here for us, such as exists in other lands."

'Subsequently, Mr. M. Schwartz, the Reader, recited the prayers used in the Jewish faith on occasions of this description, making special mention of the name of the deceased prelate. After this an address was delivered by the Rev. Isaac Hirshenson, a learned Rabbi of Jerusalem, who is studying at present in the Beth Hamedrash. He based an eloquent sermon upon the text : " A good name is better than precious ointment," in the course of which he spoke feelingly upon the letters, life, and character of the one who was gone.'

A beautiful recumbent effigy of the Bishop, in alabaster, under a rich stone canopy, has been erected in Chichester Cathedral on the south side of the nave. It was unveiled by the Duke of Richmond, and dedicated, with a special service, on May 23, 1898.

A brass has been placed to his memory in the chapel of Eton College, bearing the following inscription, composed by his son, Mr. Walter Durnford, one of the assistant masters

RICARDUS DURNFORD, S.T.P.

EPISCOPUS CICESTRENSIS
HUJUS COLLEGII OLIM SCHOLARIS
COLLEGII S. MARIÆ MAGDALENÆ
APUD OXONIENSES SOCIUS
VIR PIUS MITIS SAPIENS LITTERIS
NON MEDIOCRITER IMBUTUS
PRESBYTER GREGEM SIBI COMMISSUM PER
XXXV ANNOS INNOCENTIA SUA PAVIT
EPISCOPATU PER XXV ANNOS ITA FUNCTUS EST
UT CARITATEM OBSERVANTIAM REVERENTIAM OMNIUM
CONCILIARET AD EXTREMAM PROVECTUS ÆTATEM
INTEGRO INGENIO VIX IMMINUTO
CORPORIS VIGORE IN CHRISTO OBDORMIVIT
QUARTO DECIMO DIE OCTOBRIS A. S. MDCCCXCV. NATUS ANNOS XCII.
HOC PATRIS CARISSIMI MONUMENTUM
P. C. FILIUS NATU MINOR.
'BEATUS HOMO QUEM TU ERUDIERIS
DOMINE ET DE LEGE TUA DOCUERIS EUM.'

INDEX

www.ingramcontent.com/pod-product-compliance
Lightning Source LLC
Chambersburg PA
CBHW020237110726